3/01

The Dedalus Book
of
Spanish Fantasy

The Dedalus Book
of
Spanish Fantasy

Edited and translated by
Margaret Jull Costa and Annella McDermott

Dedalus

Funded by
THE
ARTS
COUNCIL
OF ENGLAND

Dedalus would like to thank the Eastern Arts Board for its support of the Dedalus publishing programme.

The editors made every effort to contact the rights holders of the stories by Wenceslao Fernández Flórez, Alberto Insúa and Alonso Zamora Vicente, without success, and would like to hear from them.

Published in the UK by Dedalus Ltd, Langford Lodge, St Judith's Lane, Sawtry, PE17 5XE

ISBN 1 873982 18 6

Distributed in the United States by Subterranean Company, P.O. Box 160, 265 South Fifth Street, Monroe, Oregon 97456

Distributed in Australia and New Zealand by Peribo Pty Ltd, 58 Beaumont Road, Mount Kuring-gai, NSW 2080

Distributed in Canada by Marginal Distribution, Unit 102, 277 George Street North, Peterborough, Ontario, KJ9 3G9

Typeset by RefineCatch Limited, Bungay, Suffolk
Printed in Finland by WSOY

THE EDITORS

Margaret Jull Costa has translated many novels and short stories by Portuguese, Spanish and Latin American writers, amongst them Bernardo Atxaga, Mário de Sá-Carneiro, Ramón del Valle-Inclán, Carmen Martín Gaite and Luisa Valenzuela. She was joint-winner of the Portuguese Translation Prize in 1992 for her translation of *The Book of Disquiet* by Fernando Pessoa and, with Javier Marías, she won the 1997 International IMPAC Dublin Literary Award for *A Heart So White*.

Annella McDermott is a lecturer in the Department of Hispanic, Portuguese and Latin American Studies at the University of Bristol. Previous translations include a biography of Simón Bolívar and *The World of Mestre Tamoda* by the Angolan novelist Uanhenga Xitu.

ACKNOWLEDGEMENTS

The editors would like to thank the following for their generous help and advice on various aspects of the anthology: Bernardo Axtaga, Steve Howell, Javier Marías, Antonio Martín, Pilar O'Prey, Ben Sherriff and Palmira Sullivan.

Contents

Introduction

For this anthology, we based our choice of stories (including four extracts from longer works) on a broad definition of fantasy, as being any fiction depicting events which depart from what is possible or plausible in reality. We were looking too for that *frisson* one gets from the best literary fantasy, be it of fear, surprise, shock or pleasure. Such stories offer the reader new perspectives on reality by defamiliarising the familiar.

As well as major contemporary writers, such as Bernardo Atxaga, Juan Benet, Juan Goytisolo and Javier Marías (all of whom are available in English translation), and classics, such as Gustavo Adolfo Bécquer, Emilia Pardo Bazán and Ramón del Valle-Inclán (either patchily translated or with translations long out of print), we have included writers who, though widely read in Spain, are entirely unknown to an English-reading public. We also discovered some excellent writers, whose books were much read in Spain in the 1920s and 1930s, but whose names are now little known even there, for example, Noel Clarasó, Wenceslao Fernández Flórez and Alberto Insúa. Inevitably, there are omissions – because of personal taste and the inevitable limitations of any anthology – but in the case of two fine Galician writers of fantasy, Álvaro Cunqueiro and Xosé Luís Méndez Ferrín, it is because a number of their stories are, gratifyingly, already available in English translation.

Both Cunqueiro and Ferrín (like Dieste and Fole in this anthology) write in Galician, one of Spain's four official languages. Other stories included here were originally written in Basque (Bernardo Atxaga), Catalan (Pere Calders, Pere Gimferrer, Quim Monzó, Joan Perucho and Mercè Rodoreda), and the remainder in Castilian. Galicia is a region particularly rich in fantasy, a land of storytelling and superstition (see Valle-Inclán's atmospheric tale 'My sister Antonia'). Writers like Dieste and Fole were keen collectors of oral folk tales and drew on this fertile source in their own writing.

Folk tales, fairy tales and ghost stories have, of course, been around for centuries and, in Spain, in the late medieval period, and in the sixteenth and seventeenth centuries, these provided the literary bedrock of the innumerable works of literature dealing with miraculous and supernatural events. However, one would hesitate to use the term 'fantasy' to describe such works, because then both author and reader inhabited a world of religious belief in which the supernatural and the miraculous were considered part of reality. Spanish fantasy really came into its own in the mid-nineteenth-century Romantic period and continued to flourish up to the 1930s, under the influence of such movements as Symbolism, Expressionism and Surrealism, all of which posed a challenge to rationalism and realism. However, while there were a few notable examples of fantasy literature in the early post-Civil War period down to the late 1950s, it was common for writers, particularly those opposed to the Franco regime, to feel that realism was the more appropriate mode to deal with the situation in Spain at the time. It is only since the 1960s and, in particular, since Franco's death in 1975, that Spanish writers have felt confident that fantasy would not be dismissed as mere escapism. This reacceptance of fantasy as a valid literary genre might be taken as a healthy sign of Spain's reintegration into the European mainstream.

Other writers, of course, used and still use fantasy as a way of approaching reality from a metaphorical or symbolic angle. Amongst the stories here, Pilar Díaz-Mas' tale of a wingless child in a world of bird-people becomes a reflection both on disability and on the ambiguous nature of motherhood; Juan Goytisolo's cobbler, on the other hand, sprouts wings in order to win back his wife, and the story can be read as a meditation on the human cost of emigration; in his highly original story, Alfonso Sastre probes another of the key Spanish experiences of this century, political exile; and Julio Llamazares summons up the haunted landscape of one of the many deserted villages in an economically threatened rural Spain. Fantasy can also provide the reader with a 'Martian' view of social and religious rituals, literally Martian in the case of Eduardo Mendoza's 'No News from Gurb' and, more obliquely, in Quim Monzó's 'Family Life'.

Themes in this anthology include doppelgangers, people returning from the dead or being buried alive, the transmigration of souls, people metamorphosing into other creatures, inanimate objects becoming invested with human powers or emotions, and fiction shading into reality. All these themes touch on deep-seated fears and concerns – our fear of death and what, if anything, lies beyond it, what it is that makes us human, and the nature of time. Fantasy provides writer and reader with a way of approaching these issues, for example, Pardo Bazán's 'woman who came back to life' is greeted by her loved ones not with joy but with horror; in Javier Marías' darkly comic 'Gualta', the protagonist entirely loses his sense of identity when confronted by a man identical to himself; the anonymous narrator of Alonso Zamora Vicente's 'A Poor Man' slips in and out of his body and into another's as if souls were fitted with a revolving door.

There is a fascination, too, with the narrow line that divides us from our animal selves. People become transformed into other creatures for all kinds of reasons: in order to escape the cruelty of their fellow man (Bernardo Atxaga's 'An Exposition of Canon Lizardi's Letter' and José Ángel Valente's 'The Condemned Man'); as part of a compact with the Devil (Valle-Inclán's 'My Sister Antonia'); for possibly satirical motives (Sender's 'Cervantes' Chickens'); and, in Monzó's story 'Gregor', in a reversal of Kafka's *Metamorphosis*.

Fantasy can also convey that deeply buried sense one has of an animistic universe, in which houses harbour grudges and wreak a terrible revenge (Enrique Vila-Matas), where statues rise up to defend their long dead spouses (Gustavo Adolfo Bécquer) and where glass table tops become home to disembodied faces (Pere Gimferrer). As is only fitting, literary fantasy also deals with our relationship with fiction itself and

13

the power of the imagination to alter reality, eerily blurring fact with fiction (José María Merino's 'The Lost Traveller' and Juan José Millás' 'The One Where She Tells Him a Story'). Part of the enjoyment of reading literary fantasy often comes from recognition of familiar themes and of writers' ingenious variations on those themes. In selecting stories that we ourselves enjoyed, we hope also to have given some idea of the variety of themes and styles in Spanish literary fantasy over the last two hundred years.

An Exposition of Canon Lizardi's Letter

BERNARDO ATXAGA

The letter in question covers eleven sheets of quarto paper, parts of which have been rendered illegible by the many years it lay forgotten in a damp cellar, for it was never sent. The first sheet, the one in direct contact with the floor, is in a particularly parlous state and so badly stained that one can scarcely make out the canon's opening words at all. The rest, with the exception of one or two lines on the upper part of each sheet, is in an excellent state of preservation.

Although undated, we can deduce that the letter was written in 1903 since, in the closing words that immediately precede the signature, the author states that he has been in Obaba for three years and, at least according to the cleric who now holds the post, everything seems to indicate that Canon Lizardi took over the rectorship of the place around the turn of the century.

He was clearly a cultivated man, judging by the elegant, baroque calligraphy and the periphrastic style laden with similes and citations he uses to broach the delicate matter that first caused him to take up his pen. The most likely hypothesis is that he was a Jesuit who, having left his order, opted for ordinary parish work.

As regards the addressee, he was doubtless an old friend or acquaintance, even though, as mentioned earlier, the poor condition of the first page does not permit us to ascertain that person's name and circumstances. Nonetheless, we feel justified in assuming that he was a person of considerable ecclesiastical authority, capable of acting as guide or even teacher in the very difficult situation prevailing in Obaba at the time, if one is to believe the events described in the letter. One should not forget either that Lizardi is writing to him in a spirit of confession and his tone throughout is that of a frightened man in need of the somewhat sad consolation of a superior.

On the first page, according to the little that one can read at the bottom, Lizardi writes of the 'grief' paralysing him at that moment and describes himself as feeling 'unfitted to the test'. Those few scant words allow us to place in context the story that the canon unfolds over the subsequent ten pages and prevent us being misled by the circuitous, circumlocutory style. Let us look now at the form the text referred to at the very start of the letter might have taken. This is what Lizardi writes on the second page, which I transcribe word for word.

. . . but first, dear friend, allow me to speak briefly of the stars, for it is in astronomy books that one finds the best descriptions of this daily wandering, this mysterious process of living which no metaphor can adequately encompass. According to the followers of Laplace, our universe was born out of the destruction of a vast ball or nucleus drifting through space, drifting alone, moreover, with only the Creator for company, the Creator who made everything and is in the origin of all things; and out of that destruction, they say, came stars, planets and asteroids, all fragments of that one lump of matter, all expelled from their first home and doomed ever after to distance and separation.

Those, like myself, who are sufficiently advanced in years to be able to discern that dark frontier of which Solinus speaks, feel cast down by the description science so coldly sets before us. For, looking back, we cannot see the world that once enwrapped us like a cloak about a newborn babe. That world is no longer with us and because of that we are bereft of all the beloved people who helped us take our first steps. At least I am. My mother died fifteen years ago and two years ago the sister who shared my house with me died too. And of my only brother, who left to travel overseas whilst still only an adolescent, I know nothing. And you, dear friend, you yourself are far away; at a time when I need you so, you too are far away.

This paragraph is followed by a few barely legible lines which, as far as I can make out, refer to the psalm in which the Hebrews in exile from Zion bemoan their fate. Then, on the third page, the canon concludes his long introduction and embarks on the central theme of his letter:

. . . for you know as well as I, that life pounds us with the relentlessness and force of the ocean wave upon the rocks. But I am straying from my subject and I can imagine you growing impatient and asking yourself what is it exactly that troubles me, what lies behind all these complaints and preambles of mine. For I well remember how restless and passionate you were and how you hated procrastination. But remember too my weakness for rhetoric and forgive me: I will now explain the events that have led to my writing this letter. I hope with all my heart that you will listen to what I have to say with an open mind and ponder as you do so the lament in Ecclesiastes: '*Vae soli!*' Yes, the fate of a man alone is a most bitter one, even more so if that man, like the last mosquitoes of summer, can barely stagger to his feet and can only totter through what little remains of his life. But enough of my ills; I will turn my attention to the events I promised to recount to you.

Nine months ago last January, an eleven-year-old boy disappeared into the Obaba woods, for ever, as we now know. At first, no one was much concerned by his absence, since Javier − that was the boy's name, that of our most beloved martyr − had been in the habit of running away from home and remaining in the woods for days on end. In that sense he was special and his escapes bore no resemblance to the tantrums that, at some point in their lives, drive all boys to run away from home; like that time you and I, in protest at an unjust punishment at school, escaped the watchful eyes

17

of our parents and spent the night out in the open, hidden in a maize field ... but, as I said, this was not the case with Javier.

I should at this point explain that Javier was of unknown parentage or, to use the mocking phrase so often used here to describe him, 'born on the wrong side of the blanket'. For that reason he lived at the inn in Obaba, where he was fed and clothed in exchange for the silver coins furnished to the innkeepers – *vox populi dixit* – by his true progenitors.

It is not my intention in this letter to clear up the mystery of the poor boy's continual flights, but I am sure Javier's behaviour was ruled by the same instinct that drives a dying dog to flee its masters and head for the snowy mountain slopes. It is there, sharing as he does the same origins as the wolves, that he will find his real brothers, his true family. In just the same way, I believe, Javier went off to the woods in search of the love his guardians failed to give him at home, and I have some reason to think that it was then, when he was walking alone amongst the trees and the ferns, that he felt happiest.

Hardly anyone noticed Javier's absences, hardly anyone sighed or suffered over them, not even the people who looked after him. With the cruelty one tends to find amongst the ill-read, they washed their hands of him saying that 'he would come back when he was good and hungry'. In fact, only I and one other person bothered to search for him, that other person being Matías, an old man who, having been born outside of Obaba, also lived at the inn.

The last time Javier disappeared was different, though, for so fierce was my insistence that they look for him, a whole gang of men got together to form a search party. But, as I said before, nine months have now passed and poor Javier has still not reappeared. There is, therefore, no hope now of him returning.

Consider, dear friend, the tender hearts of children

and the innocence in which, being beloved of God, they always act. For that is how our children are in Obaba and it gives one joy to see them always together, always running around, indeed, running around the church itself, for they are convinced that if they run round it eleven times in succession the gargoyle on the tower will burst into song. And when they see that, despite all their efforts, it still refuses to sing, they do not lose hope but attribute the failure to an error in their counting or to the speed with which they ran, and they persevere in their enterprise.

Javier, however, never joined in, neither then nor at any other time. He lived alongside them, but apart. The reasons for his avoidance of them lay perhaps in his character, too serious and silent for his age. Perhaps too it was his fear of their mockery, for a purple stain covered half his face, considerably disfiguring him. Whatever the reason, the conclusion . . .

The third page ends there. Unfortunately the top of the following page, page four, is badly affected by mould and none of my efforts to clean it up have met with much success. I have only been able to salvage a couple of lines.

Reading them, one has the impression that Canon Lizardi has once more abandoned the story and returned to the sad reflections of the beginning of the letter. At least so I deduce from the presence there of a word like 'santateresa', the local word for the praying mantis, an insect which, according to the nature guide I consulted, is unique in the natural world for the way in which it torments its victims. The author of the guide comments: 'It devours them slowly, taking care not to let them die at once, as if its real hunger were for torture not for food.'

Was Lizardi comparing the behaviour of that insect with the way life had treated the boy? For my part, I believe he was. But let us leave these lucubrations and look at what Lizardi did in fact write in the legible part of that fourth page.

19

. . . do not think, dear friend, that I ever abandoned or neglected him. I visited him often, always with a kind word on my lips. All in vain.

I was still caught up in these thoughts when, at the beginning of February, one month after Javier had run away, a pure white boar appeared in the main street of Obaba. To the great amazement of those watching, it did not withdraw before the presence of people, but trotted in front of them with such calm and gentleness that it seemed more like an angelic being than a wild beast. It stopped in the square and stayed there for a while, quite still, watching a group of children playing with what remained of the previous night's fall of snow.

The upper part of the fifth page is also damaged but not as badly as the page I have just transcribed. The dampness only affects the first three lines. It goes on:

. . . but you know what our people are like. They feel no love for animals, not even for the smallest which, being too weak to defend themselves, deserve their care and attention. In respect of this, I recall an incident that occurred shortly after my arrival in Obaba. A brilliantly coloured bird alighted on the church tower and I was looking up at it and rejoicing to think that it was our Father Himself who, in His infinite kindness, had sent me that most beautiful of His creatures as a sign of welcome, when, lo and behold, three men arrived with rifles on their shoulders . . . they had shot the poor bird down before I had a chance to stop them. Such is the coldness of our people's hearts, which in no way resemble that of our good St Francis.

They reacted in just the same way towards the white boar. They began shooting at it from windows, the braver amongst them from the square itself, and the racket they made so startled me that I came running out of the church where I happened to be at the time. They only managed to wound the animal, however, and in the midst of loud squeals, it fled back to the woods.

Since it was a white boar, and therefore most unusual, the hunters were in a state of high excitement; they could already imagine it as a trophy. But that was not to be, at least not that day. They returned empty-handed and, faint with exhaustion, they all ended up at the inn, drinking and laughing and with great hopes for the next day. And it was then, on that first day of the hunt, that Matías confronted them with these grim words: 'What you're doing is wrong. He came here with no intention of harming anyone yet you greet him with bullets. You'd be well advised to consider the consequences of your actions.'

As you will recall from the beginning of the letter, Matías was the old man who loved the boy best and was so grieved by his disappearance that many feared he might lose his mind. And there in the inn, hearing those words and what he went on to say, no one doubted that this was exactly what had happened. For in his view, the white boar was none other than our lost boy, none other than Javier, who, because of the sad life he had led as a human being, had changed his very nature. It seems he argued his case as follows:

'Didn't you see the way he stopped in the square to watch the boys playing in the snow? Isn't that just what Javier used to do? And, again just like Javier, didn't the boar have a purple stain around its snout.'

Those who were present say that the old man's speech was followed by a heated discussion, with some hunters denying that the boar had any such stain and others passionately affirming that it had. Now tell me, dear friend, can you imagine anything more foolish? What kind of a person is it who raises not the slightest objection to the idea of the boy's metamorphosis and believes, therefore, that it was indeed Javier hiding beneath the boar's rough coat, and yet grows irate and argumentative over the incidental detail of a birthmark?

21

But, as you well know, superstition still lingers in places like Obaba and just as the stars continue to shine long after they are dead, the old beliefs . . .

The first ten lines of the sixth page are completely illegible and we can learn nothing of what happened in the days following the boar's first appearance. We can, on the other hand, find out what took place later, since the latter part of page six and the whole of page seven are perfectly conserved.

. . . but one night the boar returned to Obaba and, gliding through the shadows, made its way to a solitary house situated some five hundred yards from the square. Once outside the house, it began to beat and gnaw at the door, emitting such furious grunts that the people who had been sleeping inside were dumbstruck and unable to call for help, so great was the terror that gripped them.

I should not say that the animal acted with criminal intent for I know it is wrong to attribute to animals faculties that are proper only to men. And yet I am sorely tempted to do so. How else can you explain its determination to enter the house? How else explain the damage it caused to the livestock when it saw that it could not break down the door? . . . for I should tell you that, before disappearing back into the woods, the boar killed a horse and an ox kept by the inhabitants in a nearby outhouse. But I am not proud and I know that only our Father can know the true reasons behind such behaviour.

After what had happened, the hunters' anger was roused and many who until then had remained calm decided to throw in their lot with the hunting parties that had already been established. And, as ever, old Matías was the one dissenting voice. He went out into the streets and pleaded with those setting off for the woods:

'Leave the boar in peace! You'll only enrage him by doing this! Javier will recognise you!'

22

The hunters responded with violence, forgetting it was an old man they were dealing with, an old man speaking to them, moreover, out of his delirium. Then they continued on their way. But you should not judge their rudeness and their intemperance too harshly. For, as I explained, they were quite beside themselves with terror. They feared the boar would continue to attack their livestock, livestock which is on the whole of the poorest quality, so poor it barely provides enough to feed and clothe them. But Matías had his reasons too:

'Javier has nothing against you! He only attacks those who did him harm before!'

Unfortunately for everyone concerned, what the old man said was not pure madness. For the family the boar had attacked was the least Christian in Obaba, its members having for generations been much given to cruelty, a propensity they gave full rein to during the recent war. Often, when they got drunk at the inn, they had made Javier the butt of their cruelty, mocking and even beating him, for evil always vents itself on the weak. But was there a connection between the two facts? Should I entirely disregard what the old man said? These were the questions I asked myself, the questions that tormented me.

Mothers in Obaba tell their children a story in which a daughter asks her wicked father if he believes he will ever die. The father tells her that this is most unlikely because, as he explains: 'I have a brother who is a lion and lives in the mountains and inside that lion is a hare and inside that hare is a dove. That dove has an egg. If someone finds that egg and breaks it on my forehead, then and only then will I die.' However, the person listening to the story knows that the little servant of the house will discover the connection between all those things and that the father, who is in fact a demon, will die. But I lacked the little servant's ingenuity and was unable to answer my own questions. Perhaps I was slow; perhaps the thread that led from the boar to Javier was more difficult to find than that linking the father's life to the dove's egg.

However, subsequently, things happened so quickly that there was little time for reflection. For on the third day of the hunt, the boar pursued and wounded a straggler from one of the hunting parties.

The letter continues on the eighth page of which the top half is well preserved, the sheet having been placed the other way up from the preceding pages. Of the lower part, however, about eight lines remain illegible.

The man's companions considered that the white boar had again acted with prudence and discernment, waiting amongst the leaves and watching the party until one of them, the man whom he later wounded, was alone and defenceless. Old Matías summed up the thoughts of all of them:

'It would be best if from now on you cover your faces. Especially those of you who did Javier wrong. It's clear he wants vengeance.'

It was on one such day that I suddenly realised that spring was upon us and that the fields were fragrant and full of the lovely flowers the Creator provides us with. But for me and for the other inhabitants of Obaba that whole garden of flowers bloomed in vain; no flower could perform its true function there, no flower could serve as a balm to our spirits. The pinks and lilies in the woods bloomed alone and died alone because no one, not the children or the women or even the most hardened of the men, dared go near them; the same fate awaited the mountain gentians, the thickets of rhododendrons, the roses and the irises. The white boar was sole master of the land on which they grew. One of the broadsheets published in your own town put it well: 'A wild animal is terrorising the small village of Obaba.' And do you know how many nights it came down to visit us only to . . .

The eighth page stops here. Fortunately the next two pages are perfectly legible. In this final part of the letter, Canon Lizardi's handwriting becomes very small.

. . . what Matías had foretold came to pass with the exactitude of a prophecy. Night after night, without cease, with the resolve of one who has drawn up a plan and does not hesitate to carry it out, the white boar continued to attack the houses of those who were members of the hunting parties. Then, when panic had filled every heart, the old man came to see me at the rectory. The moment he came in, he said: 'I've come to ask you a question and the sooner I have your answer the better. I want to know if I can kill the white boar?'

His words filled me with fear and not just because of the brusque manner in which he spoke. For, since in his eyes there was no difference between the boy he had known and the boar currently plundering our valley, what the old man really wanted was for me to give my blessing to a crime. I must confess that I myself had my doubts on the matter. I was wrong, you will say; a simple priest has no right to doubt what has been proven by so many theologians and other wise men. But I am just an ordinary man, a small tree that has always grown in the utmost darkness, and that animal, which in its actions seemed to exhibit both understanding and free will, had me in its power.

For all those reasons, I wanted to avoid a direct answer. I said:

'There's no point even trying, Matías. You're an old man. You'll never catch an animal like that, one that has made fools of our best hunters.'

'It will be easy for me,' he replied, raising his voice and not without a certain arrogance, 'because I know Javier's habits.' Then he added: 'Anyway that's my affair. What I want to know is whether or not I can kill the boar. You have a duty to answer me.'

'But is it necessary? Why kill an animal which, sooner or later, will leave Obaba? Provided that . . .'

'Of course it's necessary!' he broke in almost shouting now. 'Have you no pity for him? Don't you feel sorry for Javier?'

'Matías, I wouldn't want to . . .'

But again he would not let me finish. He sat up in his chair and, after scrabbling in the bag he had with him, placed a filthy handkerchief on my table. Do you know what it contained? No, how could you? It was the bloody foot of a boar. It was a ghastly sight and I stepped back, horrified.

'Javier is in terrible pain,' the old man began.

I remained silent, unable to utter a word.

'The people of Obaba are cowards,' he continued after a pause. 'They don't want to meet him face to face and so they resort to snares and traps and poison. What do they care if he dies a slow and painful death? No good hunter would do that.'

'It's only natural that they should be afraid, Matías. You're wrong to despise them for that.'

But I wasn't convinced by what I said and it was an effort to get the words out. The old man was not listening anyway; he seemed to be in mid-soliloquy.

'When a boar falls into a snare, it frees itself by gnawing off the trapped limb. That is the law it lives by.'

He spoke hesitantly, breathing hard.

'Don't you think Javier's learned fast?' he asked, looking into my eyes. The smile he gave me was that of a father proud of his son's achievements. I nodded and thought to myself how utterly justified his feelings were and that on the last day, God our Father would not have the least hesitation in bestowing on him the paternity he claimed. Yes, Matías was Javier's true father; not the one who abandoned him at birth, nor the other one who, having taken him in, treated him only with contempt.

'Can I kill him?' the old man asked me. He had grown sombre again. As you know, dear friend, pity is an extreme form of love, the form that touches us most deeply and most strongly impels us towards goodness. And there was no doubt that Matías was speaking to me in the name of pity. He could not bear the boy's suffering to continue. It must be ended as soon as possible.

'Yes, you can,' I said. 'Killing the boar would not be a sin.'

Well done, you will say. However, bearing in mind what happened afterwards . . .

The tenth page stops at that point. The first four lines are missing on the next and last page; the rest, including the signature, is perfectly preserved.

. . . on the outskirts of Obaba, not far from this house, there is a thickly wooded gully in the form of an inverted pyramid, and at one end there is a cave that seems to penetrate deep into the earth. That was where Matías sensed the white boar was hiding. Why, you will ask, on what did he base such a supposition, a supposition that later – I will tell you now – was to prove correct? Because he knew that was what Javier used to do when he ran away from the inn. He would hide there in the cave, poor boy, with only the salamanders for company.

But, as I said, I only knew all this when it was too late. Had I known before, I would not have given my consent to Matías. No, you can't go into that cave, I would have told him. No hunter would wait for a boar in a place like that. It's too dangerous. You'll be committing a grave sin by going there and placing your own life in mortal danger.

But God chose not to enlighten me. I made a mistake when confronted by a question whose rights or wrongs I could not hope to fathom and, later, there was no time to remedy the situation. The events I will now recount happened all in a rush, the way boulders, once their support has gone, hurtle headlong down hillsides. In fact, it was all over in a matter of hours.

When Matías left, I went into the church and it was there that I heard what, at the time and to my great astonishment, sounded like an explosion. At first I could not establish the origin of such a loud noise, so unusual in Obaba. It was certainly not from a rifle, I thought.

'Unless the shot were fired in a cave!' I exclaimed. I knew at once that I was right. With God's help, I had guessed what had happened.

Matías was already dead when I reached the gully. He was lying face down at the entrance to the cave itself, his rifle still in his hand. A few yards away, further inside the cave, lay the white boar, panting and losing blood from a wound in its neck.

Then, amidst the panting, I thought I heard a voice. I listened more carefully and what do you think I heard? The word that any boy would have cried out at such a moment: 'Mother!' Before my very eyes, the boar lay there groaning and whimpering and saying over and over: 'Mother, mother' . . . pure illusion, you will say, the imaginings of a weary, overwrought man; and that is what I tell myself when I remember all I have read in science books or when I recall what faith requires us to believe. Nevertheless, I cannot forget what I saw and heard in that cave. Because then, dear God, I had to pick up a stone and finish him off. I could not leave him there to bleed to death, to suffer; I had to act as honourably as the old man would have done.

I can go no further and I will end here. I am, as you see, a broken man. You would be doing me the greatest favour by coming here to visit me! I have spent three years in Obaba. Is that not enough solitude for any man?

With that question – and the signature that follows it – both letter and exposition end. I would not, however, wish to conclude my work without reference to a fact which, after several conversations with the present inhabitants of Obaba, seems to me significant. It concerns the matter of Lizardi's paternity. Many of those who spoke to me state that Javier was, without a doubt, his son, a belief which, in my view, a second reading of the document certainly tends to substantiate. That fact would also explain why the letter never left the rectory where it was written. A canon like Lizardi would never dare send a confession from which, in the end, he had omitted the one essential detail.

Bernardo Atxaga is the pseudonym of José Irazu Garmendia (Asteasu, Euzkadi, 1951). He is the best known of contemporary Basque writers and has done an enormous amount to promote the Basque language and its literature in post-Franco Spain. He has written short stories and novels for children and adults, as well as poetry and songs. Two of his novels: *Gizona bere bakardadean* (1994) and *Zeru horiek* (1996) (*The Lone Man* and *The Lone Woman*, tr. Margaret Jull Costa, Harvill, 1996 and 1999) deal with the social and political situation in the Basque country. This story is taken from *Obabakoak* (1989; *Obabakoak*, tr. Margaret Jull Costa, Hutchinson, 1992), a collection of twenty-six stories, some independent, some interconnecting. In Spain it won the National Prize for Literature and the Critics' Prize and has, to date, been translated into twenty-one other languages. Other works include *Bi anai* (1995), *Behi Euskaldun Baten Memoriak* (1992) and *Lista de locos y otros alfabetos* (1998).

The Raincoat

MAX AUB

To my fiancée, who told me the story

This was in the days when people still celebrated Carnival. In other words, many years ago. Not that it matters, you won't believe what I am about to tell you anyway. His name was Arturo, Arturo Gómez Landeiro. He was not bad-looking really; the only thing that obstructed his path through life was his large nose. It wasn't exactly huge, but it was a bit larger than normal. Because of it he toyed with the idea of becoming a sailor. But his mother wouldn't let him. The surprising thing is that the story I'm about to relate should have happened to him. I've often wondered why, but never managed to find an answer. It seems that extraordinary things can happen to anyone; what matters is how you react to the surprise. If Arturo Gómez had been an exceptional man I wouldn't be writing this; he would have undertaken to recount the story himself, or he would have investigated further. But he took fright, so I have to be the one to tell it, because I can never keep anything to myself.

The whole thing began on the 28th February 19 . . . That day – or that night, rather – Arturo was twenty-three years, four months and a few days old. I mustn't forget to say that his father was dead, and his mother sat up every night, waiting for Arturo to come home, go to his room and get into bed, before going off to sleep herself; this had the effect of making Arturo a very shy young man, indeed his friends thought him a bit of sissy, and only rarely expected his company when they went out for a night on the town. He read little, first of all, because, according to his widowed mother, it 'ruins your eyesight', and because his late father's excessive fondness for books, to the detriment of his other duties, had caused her a lot of problems.

31

He had been a typical Galician, a bit of a joker, rather evasive by nature, given to making statements whose meaning he didn't explain, to strange whims and sudden bouts of happiness for no apparent reason. Some Sundays he would stay in bed all day smoking his pipe, or sometimes – and this was much worse – he would disappear for ten days or a couple of weeks, then rejoin his respectable Christian household without a word of plausible explanation. Doña Clotilde had been careful to shield her son from these bizarre influences. The late Don Arturo seemed to pay no heed to her. One fine day he died, peacefully, without saying goodbye to his family, which his good wife considered the final insult, not to mention the fright she got when she woke up next to the corpse.

So, it was the last day of February and it was Carnival Sunday, for time presses on. Arturo – the son – went into the dance hall in his dark suit and slowly and carefully began to look round him. He was looking for Rafael, Luis or Leopoldo. He couldn't see any of them. That annoyed him. He had arrived a quarter of an hour late, quite deliberately, to show that he didn't think much of the place, and to make an impression, however slight. Now it turned out he was the first to arrive. He couldn't think how to behave; he didn't know any of the girls there. Rafael was supposed to be introducing him, and the dance was in a remote part of the town, which he barely knew. He leaned against the wall and prepared to wait. Naturally, at that very moment, he saw her.

She was alone, standing in a doorway almost directly opposite him. They were separated by the whirling dancers. She looked lost; she was staring as though trying to remember something, peering hard at everything, as if to accustom herself to the place. Her gaze travelled round the room and fell on him, but her pupils pressed on, like a fishing trawl, sweeping everything up. Arturo was shy, and that drove him to act, after taking a bet with himself. The first thing was to swim across the centre of the room, filled with dancing couples. The young man gathered together a sufficient stock of 'excuse mes', 'sorrys' 'beg your pardons', and plunged in; he made the crossing without difficulty, by simply turning sideways, holding his tummy in and gliding – audaciously, he felt – through the crowd. Besides, they were playing a polka, which always helps. He formally requested a dance. The girl, who was looking the other way, turned slowly towards him and wordlessly placed her hand on his shoulder. They were dancing.

Her eyes had an amazing effect on Arturo. They were clear, of an absolutely incredible blue, celestial, fathomless, pure water. That is to say, they were the colour of air, extraordinarily limpid, pale as the sky, endless. Her body appeared weightless. Then she smiled. And Arturo, in a state of bliss, noticed that he too could not help smiling.

Everything was whirling round. Round and round. And not only because it was a waltz. He felt himself fixed, attached, nailed to his companion's clear gaze. All he wanted was for this to last for ever. He was smiling like an idiot. The girl seemed happy. She danced divinely. Arturo let himself be swept along. He realised, from afar, that he had never danced so well, and he congratulated himself. It lasted an eternity. He felt no tiredness. His feet came together, drew apart, whirled round and round, in perfect time. The girl was the lightest, fleetest dancer who had ever existed. He was unaware of when it all ended. But clearly a time did come when they found themselves sitting side by side on two seats, chatting. There was hardly anyone left in the room. The lanterns and paper chains, the streamers frivolously decorating the roof, seemed tired. Strips of paper hung this way and that, all unfurled. Coloured confetti spotted the floor, making it like the sky in reverse, tired, motionless, possibly dead. The musicians from the sorry band were drinking beer.

As the girl refused to tell him her surname or her address – her first name was Susana – Arturo decided to stick to her side, come what may. Having made this decision, he felt better. They stayed till everyone else had gone. Suddenly the hall was deserted, looking larger than it really was, the chairs all higgledy-piggledy, the flickering light making the dirty white walls recede, casting all kinds of blurred shadows on them.

In the end the young man could not resist the impulse to pronounce the 'Shall we go?' which had been struggling to emerge from his lips for some time. Susana gazed at him expressionlessly and moved slowly towards the door. Arturo fetched his raincoat and they went out into the street. It was pouring, she had nothing to cover herself with. Her little white dress looked very sad in the darkness. They stood there for a moment. Susana had still not revealed where she lived.

'Are you walking home?'

'Yes.'

'You'll get soaked.'

'I'll wait for a bit.'

Arturo adopted his most resolute air, thrusting his chin forward:

'Me too.'

'No, don't.'

'Yes, I'm going to.'

Arturo was wracking his brains, anxious to say something deep and meaningful, but he couldn't think of anything at all. He felt empty, as though he had been turned inside out. Not a word came into his head, his throat was dry, his mind a blank. Empty. After a long pause, he stammered:

'Can I see you again?'

Susana looked at him in amazement, as though he had suggested something utterly insane. Arturo did not insist. The rain was still falling and showed no sign of abating. Puddles had formed, and the one sound uniting the couple was woven out of the drops of water.

'Which direction are you going in?'

As though forgetting her earlier refusals, Susana pointed vaguely to the right, towards the upper part of town.

'Shall we wait a bit longer?' the young man asked.

She shook her head.

'I can't.'

'Is there somebody expecting you?'

'Yes, always.'

Her tone was so meek and resigned that Arturo felt suddenly clothed in valour, as though he knew, all at once, that

Susana needed his help. His limited imagination produced, in an instant, a huge, cruel guardian, a great fat aunt, with a moustache and hands like pliers, given to dealing out dreadful pinches, instigator of unimaginable acts of penitence. If he had had to fight with someone at that moment, she would have found none braver. A carriage passed. Arturo hailed it with an imperious gesture. He had never in his life taken one on his own initiative. The only time he could recall was when his mother had been taken ill five years earlier, and he had had to fetch the doctor. In his attempt to sound nonchalant, his voice came out too high.

'Put this on.' (He placed his raincoat round the girl's shoulders.) 'Get in.'

Susana did not reject the offer.

'Where to?'

She looked more lost than ever, yet she whispered an address and the coachman set off. Arturo was beside himself with joy and fear. No doubt about it, he was a grown-up. What would his mother say if she could see him now? His mother who was at that moment waiting for him. He shrugged. Inside he was trembling. With extreme caution, very slowly, he took the girl's hand. It was cold, terribly, horribly cold.

'Are you feeling chilly?'

'No.'

Arturo did not dare slip his arm round the girl's shoulder, as he would have liked, and felt it was his duty, to do.

'Your hands are freezing.'

'They always are.'

If only he dared hug her, kiss her! He knew he could never do it. He had to do it. He summoned up all his courage, lifted his arm and was about to let it fall softly on Susana's farthest shoulder when, by the passing light of a street lamp, he saw that she was looking at him, her eyes transparent with fear. In the face of this appeal, Arturo gave up, happy to do so; he was content with very little, what had happened would suffice for several days. Suddenly, Susana spoke to the coachman in her sweet, deep voice:

35

'Please stop.'

'We're not there yet, miss.'

'It doesn't matter.'

'Is this where you live?' asked Arturo.

'No. A few houses further up, but I don't want to be seen. Or heard . . .'

She got out quickly. It was still raining. She wrapped herself in the raincoat as though it now belonged to her.

'I'll meet you here, tomorrow at six.'

'No.'

'Yes, tomorrow.'

She disappeared without answering. Arturo got out and just managed to catch a glimpse of her going into a doorway. He congratulated himself on having behaved like a man. No doubt about it. He was pleased with the authoritative tone of his last words to her, which he was sure would do the trick. She would keep the appointment. Moreover, hadn't she taken his raincoat as a token?

It was his first truly happy night. He revelled in thoughts of his prize, you might even say conquest. He had done it all on his own, with no help from anyone, he had won her by his own efforts. She would be his girlfriend. A real girlfriend. His first girlfriend. This was all new to him.

By half past five on the following day he was pacing the uneven paving stones of the street. The house was old, small, just one storey he was pleased to see, for he had worried at times that there might be several families living there. The skies had not cleared, thick clouds were racing, and there was a cruel little breeze. 'She'll give me back my raincoat,' he thought involuntarily. (The previous night his mother could easily have thought he had hung it up on his way in, but this evening he had to go home for dinner and would have to explain the absence of the coat.)

Six o'clock rang out from St Águeda's. He was still pacing up and down, though with no hint of impatience. It began to rain. He took shelter in a doorway opposite the house of his beloved. Half past six. The wind and the rain gathered force. He turned up the collar of his jacket. Raindrops pattered gently on the shining cobbles of the deserted street. Seven o'clock sounded, then, a long time later, half-past. Night had fallen ages ago. He heard eight o'clock strike. Then he had an idea: Why not call at the house on the pretext of recovering his raincoat? What could be more natural, after all?

No sooner said than done. As fast as his legs would carry him, he crossed the road and entered the doorway. The entrance was dark. He knocked on the first door, which he took to be the main door of the flat. Soft footsteps could be heard, then the door was opened a few inches. A nice old lady appeared.

'What can I do for you?'

'Well, you see, the thing is . . .'

'Do come in.'

Arturo went in, a little surprised by his own audacity, ready to withdraw into his shyness.

'Do sit down. I must apologise. I wasn't expecting any visitors. So few people come. I hardly see anyone.

It was the same tone of voice, the same nose, the same oval-shaped face. This must be her mother or her grandmother.

'Is Susana home?'

The old lady stood speechless, astonished, dumbstruck.

'She's not here?'

The old lady asked in a trembling whisper:

'Who is it you want to see?'

Arturo spoke less confidently.

'Susana. Doesn't she live here?'

The old lady was looking at him fearfully. Already uneasy, Arturo felt unease creep monstrously up his spine. He tried to justify himself.

'I lent her my raincoat last night. I thought I saw her coming into this house . . . She's a young girl of about eighteen. With blue eyes, pale blue eyes.'

There could be no doubt about it, the old lady was frightened. She stood up and backed away, staring at Arturo in bewilderment. He got to his feet, uncertain how to react. Evidently the distrust was mutual. The old lady bumped into the wall and stretched her arm out towards a console table.

With his eyes, the young man instinctively followed the movement of her arm, which was simply seeking support. Beside the place where her trembling hand stopped, the blue veins clearly visible against the transparent skin flecked with ochre – suggesting that rust is not only the sign of ageing metal but of old age in general – he saw an embossed silver frame and in it a photograph of Susana, smiling.

The old lady was sidling now towards a door which gave onto a corridor, she was inching along the wall, not realising that her shoulder was pressing against an oval engraving in an ebony frame which swung to one side and finally fell to the floor. What with the noise and her previous fright, the old lady subsided, almost fainting, into a faded red chair. Arturo went forward to offer her some assistance. He was confused, more surprised than anything else. Even so, he did wonder: 'Has anything happened to my raincoat?' The old lady watched him approach with terror; she seemed about to call out, but could only manage a tremulous sigh.

'What's wrong? Can I do anything for you?'

Arturo turned his head slightly towards the photograph, the old lady followed the direction of his gaze.

'Is that her?'

'Yes.'

'That's my niece, Susana.' She paused, then in a much lower tone, she added: 'She died five years ago.'

Arturo felt the hairs on the back of his neck rise. Not because he believed what the old lady had just said, but because he assumed she was mad, and there was no other sign of life in the house. Only the sound of the rain.

'You don't believe me?'

'Yes, I do, but I could have sworn . . .'

They looked at each other with stricken expressions.

'We met at a dance.'

The sentence struck the old lady full in the face. The fine wrinkles on her skin trembled.

'Her father never allowed her to go dancing. He's in South America. May God forgive him . . . ! You don't believe me?'

'Yes, I do.'

Suddenly, the little old lady's tone of voice calmed Arturo. 'She's probably not dangerous,' he thought to himself, 'the main thing is to humour her.'

'If you like we can go to the graveyard and I'll show you her grave.'

'Of course.'

'I'll get my cloak. I'll just be a moment . . .'

Arturo was left alone. Gripped by fear, he tiptoed towards the door. But caution made him slow. He had not quite reached the door when the old lady came back.

They went out. The rain had stopped, it was a clear night with clouds scudding across the sky. As they walked up the hill to the place where the cemetery lay, their feet grew heavy with mud. The wind had died down, and the coolness of the earth refreshed everything. In vain they called for the gate-keeper. Evidently he had gone out or fallen fast asleep. Arturo insisted they should turn back. Her word was good enough for him. (It must be very late. His mother would be expecting him.) They were just about to leave when the old lady made one last attempt and discovered that the gate was only closed, not locked. As might be expected, the hinges creaked, making them stop in their tracks, just in case, they didn't know why. They went in. There was no moon, but the light of the stars was growing bright enough for them to make out the paths and the cypress trees. Puddles glistened. Frogs. They advanced without difficulty till they came to a long wall, in which the recesses for the coffins seemed blacker against the night.

'Have you got a match?'

Arturo patted his pocket, brought out his lighter and produced a flickering light, which seemed immense in the darkness and enabled him to read on a glass-covered plaque:

Here lies the body of Susana Cerralbo y Muñoz.
Died aged eighteen years.
28 February 1897

Between the marble plaque and the glass, in a frame just like the one in the sitting-room, was a portrait of Susana smiling.

Arturo slowly lowered the hand holding the lighter, which fell to the ground. Mechanically, he followed it with his eyes and when they reached the earth they discovered there, dry and neatly folded, his raincoat. He picked it up. He stared at the old lady, his mouth open in astonishment. In the distance a light was approaching. It was the gravedigger.

'What do you want? Don't you know you're not supposed to wander around here at this time of night?'

On the other side of the wall, a youngster passed singing a song:

'I'll be glad when you're dead, you rascal you . . .'

Arturo took to his heels. Afterwards, as usual, the years passed. ('Silence runs with mute steps,' as Lope de Vega put it.)

The young man, who soon ceased to be one, became very friendly with the old lady. In her house, while the evenings limped away into night, they talked interminably of Susana. He died not long ago, a bachelor, a virgin and poor. He was laid to rest beside the girl, though no one could explain this vehemently expressed wish. The old woman disappeared. I have no idea what happened to her; the house was knocked down.

The raincoat went from owner to owner without ever wearing out. It was one of those garments that get passed on to sons or younger brothers, not because the owner has had a lucky win, or grown too fast, but because nobody really likes it. It travelled far: the Rastro market in Madrid, the Encantes in Barcelona, the Flea Market in Paris, a second-hand clothes shop in London. I've just spotted it, altered to fit a child, in the Lagunilla Market in Mexico City, because clothes get smaller rather than bigger as they grow older.

It was bought by a sad-faced man for a little girl, pale and drawn, who clung to his hand.

'It suits you!'

The girl seemed happy. Now, don't go jumping to conclusions: her name was Lupe.

© Helena Aub
Translated by Annella McDermott

Max Aub (Paris, 1903–1972) was the son of a French mother and a German father. The family moved to Spain in 1914 and later took Spanish citizenship. In 1939, following the Spanish Civil War, Aub crossed to France, spending three years in a French concentration camp, before leaving for Mexico, where he spent the rest of his life. There he published three novels on the Spanish Civil War: *Campo cerrado* (1943; *Field of Honour*, tr. G. Martin, Verso, 1989), *Campo de sangre* (1945) and *Campo abierto* (1951), as well as a large number of short stories and novels on other themes. Aub is best known as a writer of fiction, though he also wrote plays and essays. He made several incursions into the world of fantasy, notably in the book of short stories, *Ciertos cuentos* (1955), from which this story is taken.

The Kiss

(A legend from Toledo)

GUSTAVO ADOLFO BÉCQUER

I

When, at the beginning of this century, a part of the French army seized the historic town of Toledo, its leaders, mindful of the dangers they risked if billeted separately in Spanish towns, began by adapting Toledo's largest and finest buildings to serve as their barracks.

Having occupied the Alcázar, the magnificent fortress palace of Charles V, they next took over the Tribunal, or *Casa de Consejos*, and when that was full, they began to invade the seclusion of monasteries and convents, till finally they turned even churches into stables. Such was the state of affairs in the town where the events I am about to relate took place, when, one night, very late, there arrived as many as one hundred dragoons, tall, broad and arrogant (as our grandmothers still recall with bated breath), wrapped in their dark uniform capes and filling the narrow, deserted streets that run from the Puerta del Sol to the Plaza de Zocodóver with the clanking of their weapons and the loud ringing of their horses' hooves, which struck sparks from the cobbles.

They were under the command of a youngish officer who rode about thirty paces in front of his men, speaking in low tones to another man, also a soldier, to judge from his clothing.

The latter, who was walking ahead of his companion with a lantern, appeared to be his guide through that labyrinth of dark, narrow, winding streets.

'Truly,' said the rider to his companion, 'if the lodgings being prepared for us are such as you describe, it would perhaps almost be better to set up camp in the countryside, or in the middle of a square.'

'What can I do, Captain,' replied the guide, who was, in fact, a billeting officer. 'You couldn't squeeze another blade of grass into the Alcázar, far less a soldier. And as for San Juan de los Reyes, there are monks' cells with fifteen hussars sleeping in them. The monastery where I'm taking you wasn't a bad place, but three or four days ago, one of those special squadrons that are everywhere in the province suddenly appeared, and we should be grateful that we managed to pile them into the cloisters and leave the church free.'

'Very well,' said the officer after a short silence, as though resigning himself to the strange lodgings offered him by fate. 'At least if it rains, as seems likely from the look of those clouds, we shall have a roof over our heads, which is something.'

The conversation ended at this point, and the horsemen, preceded by the guide, continued in silence till they arrived at a small square on one side of which could be discerned the dark silhouette of the monastery, with its Moorish tower, its belfry and steeples, its pointed dome and the dark, uneven ridges of its roof.

'Here is your lodging', exclaimed the billeting sergeant to the officer, who, having ordered his troops to halt, dismounted, took the lantern from the hands of the guide and advanced in the direction indicated.

As the monastery church had been stripped of its furnishings, the soldiers occupying the rest of the building had taken the view that the doors were now of little use; and gradually, one board at a time, they had ripped them out to serve as firewood.

Our young officer thus had no need to force locks or slide back bolts in order to enter the church.

By the light of the lantern, whose flickering beam wavered among the dark shadows of the naves and cast on the wall the monstrously enlarged shadow of the billeting sergeant who went before him, he examined every corner of the church, inspecting all the deserted chapels one after the other, then finally, having satisfied himself as to the nature of the place, he ordered his troops to dismount and organised them as best he could, men and horses all together.

As we have said, the church had been dismantled: from the tall cornices of the altar there still fluttered the tattered remnants of the veil with which the monks had covered it before abandoning the church; all along the naves there were altarpieces leaning against the wall, with the images removed from their niches; in the choir, a beam of light revealed the strange shapes of the larchwood pews; amongst the paving stones, which were cracked and broken in several places, one could still see broad tombstones engraved with seals, coats of arms and long Gothic inscriptions, and in the distance, in the depths of the silent chapel and along the transept, stone statues could be glimpsed in the darkness, like motionless ghosts, some lying full length, others kneeling on the marble of their tombs, seemingly the only inhabitants of the ruined building.

Anyone less exhausted than the officer of dragoons, who had covered fourteen leagues that day, or less accustomed to observing these acts of sacrilege as if they were the most natural thing in the world, might have been kept wide awake by his imagination that night in the dark, imposing church, where the blaspheming of the soldiers, loudly cursing their improvised lodgings; the metallic ring of their spurs on the tombstones on the floor; the sound of the horses, neighing impatiently, tossing their heads and clanking the chains with which they were tethered to the pillars, created a strange and fearful cacophony that filled the whole of the building and set off a muffled echo in the lofty vaults.

But our hero, though young, was already so familiar with the vicissitudes of military life that no sooner had he settled his men than he called for a sack of fodder to be placed at the bottom of the chancel steps and then, wrapping himself as best he could in his cloak, he lay down and, within five minutes, was snoring away as peacefully as King Joseph himself in his palace in Madrid.

Using their saddles as pillows, the soldiers followed his example and gradually the murmur of voices died away.

Half an hour later, all that could be heard were the stifled moans of the wind whistling through the broken glass of the arched windows, the confused fluttering of the night birds who had made their nests in the stone canopies over the statues lining the walls and the steady pacing of the sentry, wrapped in the ample folds of his cloak, and marching up and down in the portico of the church.

II

At the time of these events, which are as true as they are extraordinary, and still indeed today, for those with no appreciation of the artistic treasures contained within its walls, Toledo was no more than an ancient, tumbledown, dilapidated town, devoid of interest.

Needless to say, the officers of the French army, who were by no means men of an artistic or archaeological disposition, to judge from the acts of vandalism for which, sadly, the occupation is eternally remembered, were monumentally bored in that ancient seat of kings.

In that state of mind, the idlers eagerly welcomed even the most insignificant event which might break the quiet monotony of those everlasting and indistinguishable days. Thus, a promotion to the next grade for one of their companions, the news of some strategic move by one of the special squadrons, the departure of a courier or the arrival of any new troops in the city became a rich source of gossip and the object of much comment, till some other incident came along to take its place, giving rise, in turn, to new complaints, criticisms and suppositions.

The officers, as was their custom, gathered next day to take the air and chat in the Plaza de Zocodóver, and, inevitably, there was but one topic of conversation: the arrival of the dragoons whose commander we left in the previous chapter sound asleep, resting from his tiring journey.

The conversation had been circling around this point for an hour or so, and already different explanations were being offered for the non-appearance of the new arrival, who was known to one of the company from their time together at the military academy, and who had been invited to come to the gathering, when, finally, our gallant captain was seen at the end of one of the streets leading into the square. He had cast aside his cloak and was resplendent in a metal helmet with white plume, indigo jacket with red facings and a magnificent broadsword in a sheath of steel, which clanged in time to his martial stride and the clean, sharp ring of his golden spurs.

As soon as his comrade spotted the captain, he ran forward to meet him, as did nearly all those present at the gathering, whose curiosity and interest had been aroused by tales of his strange and unusual character.

After the usual greetings, exclamations, handshakes and questions which characterise these meetings, after long and detailed discussion of the news that was doing the rounds in Madrid, the varying fortunes of war, and dead or absent friends, after touching on this and that, the conversation came round eventually to the unavoidable topics, namely, the tribulations of army life, the lack of amusements in the city and the discomfort of their lodgings.

At this point, one of those present, who seemingly had news of the young officer's reluctance to lodge his men in the abandoned church, asked him in a bantering tone:

'Speaking of lodgings, what sort of night did you have in the place they gave you?'

'Not too good, yet not too bad', replied the officer. 'For though I did not get much sleep, the reason for my insomnia made it all worth while. To lie awake beside a beautiful woman is not the worst of fates.'

'A woman!' responded his questioner, expressing his surprise at the new arrival's good fortune. 'You certainly wasted no time!'

'Perhaps it's some long-standing mistress from Madrid who has followed him to Toledo to comfort him in his exile,' someone suggested.

'Not at all,' the Captain replied. 'Nothing could be further from the truth. I give you my word that she was not known to me, and that I never thought to find such a beautiful landlady

47

in such uncomfortable lodgings. This was what one might call a real adventure.'

'Tell us about it! Tell us about it,' chorused the officers surrounding the Captain.

And, since he seemed prepared to do so, they all listened attentively while he began the story as follows:

'I was sleeping last night as a man sleeps who has ridden thirteen leagues, when I suddenly sat up, resting on one elbow, roused from this profound slumber by a horrible din, a noise so great that it left my ears ringing for about a minute, as though a hornet were buzzing round my head. As you will have guessed, the cause of my alarm was the first stroke of that infernal great bell, a sort of bronze choirmaster, which the canons of Toledo have hung in their cathedral with the laudable aim of harassing to death anyone in need of repose. As the last of the strange and horrible sounds died away, I was about to lie down and try to get back to sleep, cursing under my breath both bell and bell-ringer, when a most extraordinary sight caught my eye and captured my imagination. In the pale moonlight filtering into the church through the narrow mullioned windows of the main chapel, I saw a woman kneeling by the altar.'

The officers exchanged glances in which surprise mingled with incredulity. The captain, paying no heed to the effect his story was having, continued in this vein:

'You cannot imagine anything to rival that fantastical nocturnal vision, whose blurred outline could be discerned in the darkness of the chapel, like those pale, luminous Virgins depicted in stained glass windows that you will have glimpsed in the depths of cathedrals. Her oval face bearing faint traces of spiritual suffering, her harmonious features filled with a sweet, melancholy tenderness, her intense pallor, the pure lines of her slender figure, her serene and noble air, her floating white gown, all these reminded me of the women I had dreamed of as an adolescent. Chaste, celestial images, illusory objects of some vague, adolescent love! I believed myself prey to an hallucination, and though I did not take my eyes off her for a moment, I hardly dared to breathe, fearing that the

48

slightest disturbance might break the spell. She was completely still. Seeing her so transparent and luminous, the thought occurred to me that she was no earthly creature, but a spirit who, momentarily taking on human shape, had come down on a moonbeam, leaving in the air behind her a bluish trail that fell from the mullioned windows onto the opposite wall, piercing the darkness of that mysterious, gloomy place.'

'But,' cried his former fellow-cadet, interrupting him, 'how did that woman come to be there? Did you not speak to her? Did she not explain her presence in that place?'

'I could not bring myself to speak to her, for I was sure she would not answer me, nor see me, nor hear me.'

'Was she deaf?'

'Was she blind?'

'Was she dumb?' cried two or three of his listeners at the same time.

'She was all of those things at once,' the captain finally explained, after a moment's pause, 'because she was . . . made of marble.'

On hearing this amazing end to such a strange adventure, the whole company roared with laughter, while one them said to the storyteller, who alone remained silent and serious:

'So that's it! I have more than a thousand women of that kind, a veritable harem, in San Juan de los Reyes. A harem which, from now on, I place at your disposal, since it seems you are as happy with a woman of stone as with one of flesh and blood.'

'No, thank you,' said the captain, paying no heed to the laughter of his companions. 'I am sure they are not like mine. Mine is a true Castilian lady, who by a miracle of sculpture seems not to be buried in her grave, but to be still alive, kneeling motionless on the stone that covers her, hands joined in a supplicant gesture, deep in an ecstasy of mystical love.'

'From the way you speak, you will soon have us convinced that the myth of Pygmalion was true.'

'For my part, I confess I always thought it nonsense; but since last night I have begun to understand that Greek sculptor's passion.'

49

'In view of the very particular nature of your new mistress, I imagine you will have no objection to introducing us to her. I for one cannot wait to see this wonder. But . . . what the devil is wrong with you? You seem almost reluctant to perform these introductions. Aha, don't tell me we're making you jealous already?'

'Jealous', the captain hastened to reply, 'jealous . . . No, not of men . . . Yet judge, nevertheless, the extent of my madness. Near the statue of this woman is a warrior, also made of marble, solemn and seemingly alive, like her . . . Her husband, no doubt . . . Well, now, I shall confess all, though you may laugh at my foolishness . . . Had I not feared to be taken for a madman, I believe I should by now have smashed him into a thousand pieces.'

An even louder burst of laughter from his fellow officers greeted this droll revelation by the eccentric lover of the stone statue.

'That's it,' said some, 'we must see her.'

'Absolutely!' said others. 'We must find out if your beloved merits such intense passion,' exclaimed others.

'When can we meet up to have a drink in the church where you're lodging?' demanded the rest.

'Whenever you like. This very night, if you wish,' the young captain responded, recovering his usual good humour, which had vanished for a moment with that flash of jealousy. 'By the way, in my baggage I have brought no fewer than a dozen bottles of champagne, real champagne, the remains of a gift to our general, to whom, as you know, I am distantly related.'

'Bravo, bravo!' chorused the officers, adding various joyful comments.

'Here's to good French wine!'

'We'll sing a song by Ronsard!'

'And talk about women, especially our host's mistress!'

'Till tonight, then!'

'Till tonight!'

III

The tranquil inhabitants of Toledo had long since locked and barred the heavy doors of their ancient houses, the great bell of the cathedral was announcing the curfew hour, and, from the heights of the Alcázar, now a barracks, the bugles were sounding lights out as ten or twelve officers, who had been slowly gathering in the Plaza de Zocodóver, set off along the road leading from that square to the monastery in which the captain was lodged, inspired more by the hope of draining a few bottles of champagne than by any desire to see the marvellous statue.

Night had closed in, dark and menacing. The sky was covered with leaden clouds. The wind hummed, imprisoned in the narrow, winding streets, making the dying light from the torches flicker in their niches, and the weather vanes on the towers creak as they spun round.

No sooner had the officers caught sight of the square where their new friend's lodgings were to be found, than the man himself, who had been waiting impatiently, stepped forward to greet them and, after exchanging a few words in low tones, they all went together into the church, where a feeble light struggled fitfully against the deep, dark shadows.

'Upon my word,' said one of the guests, gazing around him, 'the place could hardly be less suited to a party.'

'Quite true,' said another. 'You brought us here to show us your mistress, but we can hardly see our own hand in front of our faces.'

'And it's so cold you would think we were in Siberia,' remarked a third, wrapping his cloak tightly around him.

'Patience, gentlemen, please,' their host said. 'Everything will be taken care of. You, boy,' he called to one of his attendants, 'fetch us some wood and light a nice fire in the main chapel.'

The boy, in obedience to this order, took an axe to the choirstalls and once he had obtained a large pile of firewood,

51

which he gradually piled up by the presbytery steps, he seized the torch and set to work making a bonfire of those richly-carved fragments; amongst the scattered debris could be seen, here, part of a twisted column, there, the portrait of a holy abbot, the trunk of a woman or the monstrous head of a griffin.

A few minutes later, the whole church was filled with sudden light, signalling to the officers that the festivities were about to begin.

The captain, who was doing the honours with quite as much ceremony as he would have in his own home, addressed his guests:

'Whenever you wish, the buffet is served.'

His companions, affecting the utmost gravity, replied to his invitation with a comical bow and made their way to the main chapel, preceded by the hero of the feast, who, on reaching the stairs, paused for an instant and, gesturing towards the place where the tomb stood, said with the most refined elegance:

'I have the pleasure of introducing the lady who occupies all my thoughts. I think you will agree that I have not exaggerated her beauty.'

The officers turned their gaze towards the spot their friend was indicating, and an involuntary gasp of amazement arose from every man.

In the depths of a burial arch faced with black marble, kneeling at a prie-dieu, with her hands joined and her face turned towards the altar, they saw indeed the image of a woman so beautiful that no sculptor could ever produce her rival, nor could desire itself have painted a fantasy of greater loveliness.

'It's true, she's an angel,' murmured one.

'What a pity she's made of marble,' added another.

'Truly, though it is only an illusion, to be close to such a woman is reason enough not to close your eyes all night.'

'And you don't know who she is?' some of those contemplating the statue asked the captain, who was smiling in pleasure at his triumph.

'Recalling a little of the Latin I knew as a youth, I have managed finally to decipher the inscription on the tomb,' the latter replied, 'and from what I gather, it is the tomb of a Castilian nobleman, a famous warrior who fought against the French in Italy with the *Gran Capitán,* Gonzalo Fernández de Córdoba. His name I have forgotten, but his wife, whom you see here, is named Doña Elvira de Castañeda, and by my faith, if the copy resembles the original she must have been the most beautiful woman of her century.'

After this brief explanation, the guests, who had not lost sight of the principal object of the gathering, proceeded to uncork some of the bottles and, as they sat around the fire, the wine began to circulate.

As the libations grew more frequent and the fumes from the sparkling champagne began to go to their heads, the excitement, noise and jubilation grew amongst the young men, some of whom began to throw the empty bottles at the granite monks standing before the pillars, while others sang drunken, indecent songs, and yet others guffawed or applauded or quarrelled amongst themselves, uttering oaths and blasphemies.

The captain drank in silence, with an air of desperation, and his eyes never left the statue of Doña Elvira.

Through the veil that inebriation had drawn over his eyes, he seemed to see the marble statue, in the red light from the bonfire, transformed into a real woman; he seemed to see her lips move as though in prayer, to see her breast stir as though she sighed, her hands clench, and finally her cheeks blush, as though she were shocked by that sacrilegious and offensive spectacle.

The officers, noticing their companion's silence, shook him out of his trance and, giving him a goblet, they chorused:

'Come on, propose a toast, you are the only one who has not done so all night!'

The young man took the goblet and, standing up, he raised it on high and defiantly addressed the statue of the warrior kneeling by Doña Elvira:

'I propose a toast to the Emperor and his feats of arms, which have enabled us to march to the heart of Castile, to court the wife of one of the victors of Cerignola, on his very tomb.'

The soldiers greeted the toast with a round of applause and the captain staggered a few steps towards the grave.

'No,' he said, still addressing the statue and wearing the stupid smile common to drunkards, 'don't think I hold a grudge because I see you as a rival. On the contrary, I admire you as a long-suffering husband, an example of broadmindedness and tolerance, and I wish to be generous in turn. Since you were a soldier, you must surely have been a drinker . . . Never let it be said that I let you die of thirst watching us empty twenty bottles . . . Have a drink!'

So saying, he lifted the goblet to his lips and, after wetting them with the liquor it contained, he threw the rest over the statue's face, roaring with laughter when he saw the wine spilling onto the tomb as it trickled down the stone beard of the motionless warrior.

'Have a care, Captain!' cried one of his companions in a bantering tone. 'Don't forget that these jokes with people of stone tend to be paid dear. Remember what happened to the hussars of the Fifth in the monastery at Poblet . . . They say the warriors in the cloisters one night laid hold of their granite swords and set about the soldiers who were amusing themselves drawing charcoal moustaches on them.'

The young men greeted this sally with loud guffaws, but the captain, paying no heed to the laughter, doggedly pursued the notion:

'Do you think I would have offered him wine if I hadn't thought he would at least swallow the drops that fell into his mouth? Certainly not! I don't believe, as you do, that these statues are pieces of marble, as lifeless now as the day they were wrested from the quarry. Unquestionably, the artist, who is almost a god, breathes some vitality into his work, not enough for it to move and walk, yet enough to instil a strange, incomprehensible form of life, not one I can explain, yet I feel it, especially when I have drunk a little.'

'Magnificent!' said his companions. 'Have some more to drink and carry on.'

The officer drank and, fixing his gaze on Doña Elvira, he continued with growing exaltation:

'Look at her! Look at her! Can't you see the changing reds in her delicate, transparent flesh? Doesn't it appear as though, below that smooth, bluish alabaster skin, there glides a rose-coloured fluid of light? What more life could you want? What more reality?'

'A great deal more' said one of his listeners. 'We would like her to be made of flesh and blood.'

'Flesh and blood! Misery and decay!' said the captain. 'During an orgy, I have felt my lips and my head burning. I have felt the fire that runs through the veins like boiling lava from a volcano, whose misty vapours confuse and disorder the brain and make us see strange visions. Then, the kisses of those tangible women seared me like a red-hot iron, and I thrust them aside in distaste, in disgust, even in horror, for then, as now, I needed a touch of sea-breeze for my fevered brow, to drink ice and kiss snow . . . snow tinged with faint light, snow coloured by a golden ray of sun . . . A beautiful, cold, white woman, like this stone woman who seems to incite me with her fantastic beauty, who seems to stir with the flickering of the torchlight and provoke me by half-opening her lips and offering me a token of love . . . Yes! A kiss . . . only your kiss can quell the ardour that consumes me . . .'

'Captain!' some of his companions exclaimed, seeing him advance towards the statue as though half-mad, with wandering gaze and stumbling gait. 'What madness is this? Stop joking and leave the dead in peace!'

The young man did not even hear his friends' words and, staggering, he managed to approach the tomb and draw near to the statue; but as he held out his arms, a cry of horror rang through the church. With blood gushing from his eyes, nose and mouth he had fallen flat on the floor at the base of the statue, his face disfigured.

The soldiers, struck dumb with terror, dared not move a muscle to help him.

55

At the very moment that their companion tried to place his fevered lips on those of Doña Elvira, they had seen the motionless warrior raise his hand and knock him down with one massive blow from his stone gauntlet.

Translated by Annella McDermott

Gustavo Adolfo Bécquer (Seville, 1836–Madrid, 1870) is Spain's best-known Romantic poet, author of the *Rimas*, poems on the themes of love, solitude and the nature of poetry, which were published after his death. Bécquer also wrote prose, letters, essays and legends, of which this story is an example. (A translation by R. M. Fedorchek is available as *Legends and Letters*, Bucknell University Press, 1996).

Fables 9, 10 and 10a

JUAN BENET

9

A servant arrived at midday, in a state of profound anxiety, at the home of his master, a rich merchant, and recounted what had happened to him in the following words:

'Master, this morning when I went to the market to buy cloth for a new garment, I met Death, and she asked after you. She also inquired if you were usually at home in the afternoons, as she intended shortly to pay you a visit. I wonder, Master, if it would not be better to leave everything and flee this house, so that she will not find us here if she chances to call.'

The merchant thought hard.

'Did she look you in the face, did you see her eyes?' he asked, without losing his habitual composure.

'No, Master. Her face was covered with a linen cloth, rather an old one, as it happens.'

'And did she also have a handkerchief over her mouth?'

'Yes, Master. It was a cheap and rather dirty handkerchief, as it happens.'

'Then there can be no doubt, it was she,' said the merchant and, after reflecting for a few moments, he added: 'Listen, we are not going to do what you suggest; tomorrow you are to return to the cloth market and visit the same shops and if you should chance to meet her in the same or a similar place, try to greet her and get her to speak to you. And if she does speak and asks after me in the same or a similar manner, you are to tell her that I am always at home in the hour before nightfall and that it will be a pleasure to receive her and offer the hospitality appropriate to a great lady.'

The servant did as he was bidden and, the following day at midday, he was back in the home of his master, in a state of uncontrollable agitation.

'Master, again I met Death in the cloth market and I gave her your message, which she heard, so far as I was able to observe, with great satisfaction. She confessed that she is usually received with such reluctance that she can never visit any person more than once and, since your invitation is so unusual, she intends to respond to it as soon as the opportunity arises. And she hopes to repay your kindness by demonstrating that there is a great deal of myth in what people say about her. Would it not be better to flee from here and avoid this demonstration?'

'You see?' said the merchant, with visible satisfaction. 'We have frightened her off. I can assure you it will be a long time before she comes here, if indeed she ever comes at all. It is this lady's boast that she never makes the first move, that everyone – voluntarily or involuntarily – summons and solicits her. Moreover, what she enjoys above all are surprises and what she loathes above all are prearranged appointments. I am sure you know the ancient story of the encounter she had with a man who was endeavouring to flee from an appointment she had never made. Well, I have no hesitation in affirming that, because we have invited her, she will not come to this house, unless one of us loses his composure and surrenders to one of her cunning stratagems.'

That afternoon, Death – in a sincerely friendly and relaxed mood – called at the merchant's home, aiming to take advantage of a few hours' leisure to show her appreciation of him and enjoy his company and conversation. But when the servant opened the door he could not suppress his fear at seeing her on the threshold, her face covered with an ancient linen cloth and her mouth protected by a dirty handkerchief, and believing that it was a plot between his master and the lady to destroy him, he rushed, incandescent with rage, to his master's office, where his master was resting, and, without even announcing the visitor, stabbed him to death and escaped by another door.

58

Death, surprised by the silence that reigned in the house, and the negligence of the merchant, who had not even invited her in, made her own way to the merchant's office and, seeing his lifeless body lying in a pool of blood, she could not suppress a gesture of astonishment, soon replaced by a habitual sigh of resignation:

'Oh, well, the usual story. Better luck next time.'

A famous general of antiquity, known to all the armies of the civilised world for the systematic care with which he planned even the smallest military operation, was entrusted by his king with a very important campaign in which he must defeat and disarm his country's historical enemy and win a period of peace lasting at least several generations.

The general asked the monarch for time to rearm his troops and, more especially, to plan the campaign down to the last detail, persuading him that the longer the time spent on developing a plan of operations, the shorter and less bloody would be the war. The king gave him a year, by the end of which time the army was perfectly prepared and equipped. Then the ruler sent for the general and asked him if he was prepared to begin the campaign. However, the general answered that he was not, for he had only had time to elaborate half of his plans, requesting therefore an extension of one year to complete them.

At the end of that second year, the king sent once again for his general who, in response to his sovereign's enquiries, again apologised, assuring him that as there remained only a few more details to be resolved, he would be ready in just six months and could begin the campaign which, after such careful preparations, would be short-lived.

When this third period was over, the king again summoned his general and urged him to begin the campaign immediately, for not only were the troops becoming demoralised, the soldiers' wages were beginning to exhaust the treasury. The general thus decided to begin the campaign, though there was one detail – just one – still to be resolved. In any case, it was a minor detail – the capture of a distant fortress, where an exhausted enemy would take refuge after being beaten on every occasion – and the general took the liberty of concealing from his officers the fact that he had not resolved it, hastening to open hostilities and confident that he would contrive a solution in the course of the short war.

The campaign proceeded with such admirable conformity to the general's plans that, in the end, it proved even shorter than anticipated. In battle after battle his forces were victorious, and the enemy, subjugated by his implacable advance, were reduced to a few heterogeneous companies, deprived almost entirely of weapons and leaders, and fled to take refuge in that isolated fortress, a long way from the border. So rapid was their flight that the general had time only to pursue them, but none to stop and think about how to conquer that last redoubt.

When his army set up camp before the fortress, the general summoned his captains and harangued them in the following manner:

'Gentlemen, we are approaching the end of this war. You have obeyed my orders implicitly and followed my plans down to the last detail, and here you see the result: observe our enemies, reduced to a hundredth part of what they were, confined to a miserable fortress, unable to offer a dignified resistance to the force of our arms. Miserable wretches, all that awaits them is destruction. Go ahead, then, and consummate it. This is the reward for your fortitude, your valour and your skill in battle. Do not ask how it is to be achieved. I do not wish to know; that is your decision. I wish to avert my gaze from this bloody conclusion, and, moreover, I fear I underestimated the effort I would be forced to make and feel the need for a rest, a long rest. So tomorrow when I rise – and I shall rise late – I wish to see our flag flying from yonder tower. That is all, gentlemen. Good night to you. I do not believe it any part of my soldier's duty to wish you luck, for you have no need of it. Yet good luck all the same, gentlemen. And good night.'

Such was the general's ascendancy over his men that none of his captains felt a need for his orders; his last word was accepted as such and they prepared without hesitation to place, at dawn, their country's flag on the tower in question.

At this point, the fable divides into two versions which in

the end will become one; the most widely-known version records the words of the general when he emerged from his tent at noon the following day, refreshed by sleep. Seeing his country's flag fluttering from the tower against a bright blue sky, he exclaimed:

'It could not have been otherwise.'

The second version, more private and mysterious, also records the words of the general when he emerged from his tent at noon the following day, after a fitful night, to be confronted by the remnants of his defeated army lying at the foot of the walls, and the enemy flag fluttering from the tower against a bright blue sky.

He murmured to himself:

'It could not have been otherwise.'

© Herederos de Juan Benet
Translated by Annella McDermott

The Catalyst

JUAN BENET

After a week without sun, September had once more opened
its sampler of colours and tints, and the weather, from on high,
had made a selection for that fleeting season which is the
prelude to autumn. The rains of the preceding week had
managed to obliterate all traces of summer, closing down the
refreshment stalls, carrying off the remains of picnics and
emptying the beach and its surroundings – the promontory
and the road left hanging in the pause of that sudden solitude,
like a schoolyard after the bell has gone, abruptly deprived of
the children's cries that give it its identity, the sea restored to
its eternal progress to nowhere, the constant commotion with
which it had attempted to stamp itself on the present now
stilled.

'This is one of the few privileges left to us.'

They strolled along the entire length of the road, arm in
arm, stopping at the places from which they had absented
themselves during the summer invasion, like people taking an
inventory of a property they had let out for the season. And
though not a day passed without their celebrating the benefits
of the calm that was restored to them every year at the end of
September, in their heart of hearts there persisted an overwhelming sense of being locked away and abandoned, with
the more or less simultaneous departure of the crowds that
had caused so much inconvenience.

One holiday-maker lingered, a middle-aged man who
walked his dog and whom initially they had welcomed as
company until the end of the Indian summer; but due to his
melancholy appearance, he would become instead the perfect
illustration of a bleakness for which they could find no other
consolation than gratitude – expressed over and over again,
without enthusiasm, but with the confidence that maturity

brings, with the prudent certainty of people who, for the sake of their mental balance and composure, need to attribute to free and voluntary choice the acceptance of a solution for which there is no alternative – for an isolation forced upon them for reasons of health and finance.

Every afternoon they went out for a walk, towards the promontory and the river if the sky was clear, beyond the beach and towards the village if it looked like rain; every day they had to communicate to each other the little changes they noticed (always in respect of their neighbours or surroundings) and the small surprises that their life, though sedentary and monotonous, still provided. Because for them nothing could change, and there was no possible room for novelty, since they had been telling each other for years that they would grow old together.

Although they lived in the village (they were the only people with book-learning, as the locals put it, to live there all the year round), they had no contacts beyond those necessary to their subsistence, except for a smallholder and his wife who occasionally came to have tea at their home. All they received from town were newspapers, magazines and letters from the bank, and they had never been known, in all the time they had been there, to leave the village for a single day, despite the inconvenience caused by the summer visitors. They were not unsociable, they could not be said to live any differently from the better-off locals, and they were extremely careful never to express, even in private, any nostalgia for the city, nor voice the usual grumbles about the lack of comfort or amusement in the environment in which they had chosen to live, apparently for the rest of their lives.

They appeared to have measured and weighed up everything with extreme care, to have taken into consideration their age, their frailties, their income and tastes, and chosen that isolation in order to eke out – without extravagance, or waste, with no gesture of impatience, no costly indulgence in enthusiasm – financial resources that must last exactly until the day of their death; that was why they had to deprive themselves of any unnecessary luxuries, avoid even the most innocent temptation; they could not afford to feel curious about outsiders or visitors, they could not allow themselves any feelings of envy, promptly stifled, nor any gesture of surprise over the appearance of the unknown which would allow the irruption on to the stage, set for the last act of the play, of those hidden elements and agents that every age keeps concealed in order to provide itself from time to time with the possibility of a plot. Yet every day they must have hoped for something unusual, though they did not confess it even to each other. Because the refusal to accept novelty, the submission to routine and discipline in order to abort any sign of a chimerical and unfounded hope, these – more than the village with its two brief months of animation, to which one might add the preparations for the summer and the last few faltering stragglers – constituted the essence of their withdrawal from the world.

They decided to go as far as the level crossing, a rather longer walk than usual. When they first came across him, they must have thought that the situation of the man with the dog was not unlike their own. 'Look, they've cut down the trees that were there. Remember?' or 'Heaven alone knows what they'll put up here, maybe even a block of flats', or 'The baker's wife told me they're closing down the bakery and opening up a shop selling souvenirs and knickknacks and sun cream,' such was the repertoire of banal phrases with which, day by day, they followed the course of a series of changes which did not affect them and which afforded such a contrast with the monastic austerity of their existence, where having to discard a shirt or a duster posed a threat to the harsh vow of endurance which they had firmly and staunchly undertaken, in order to survive.

The rain and the disappearance of the summer visitors provided everything else that they needed on that occasion; in other words, they again blessed the day they had moved there and gave thanks for the beauty of nature, returning in all her splendour to reign over the place, after two months of humiliating slavery to the demands of summer.

'Just smell the air: wonderful. All it takes is a few drops of rain, and look at the difference it makes.'

A prayer of thanks with renewed faith and such sincere conviction that they scarcely noticed their second encounter with the dog and the summer straggler, a man dressed in half-mourning, whom they had overtaken earlier going in the same direction, and who must, therefore, have followed the same route as themselves, but covering the ground more quickly and following a parallel path.

They stopped to listen to the song of some starlings, which, perched on a line of leafy plane trees, were also preparing to move on. They stood gazing at the sea from the road as it bends round the promontory, huge, intermittent waves that broke at their feet with a bow expressing reverence and submission to all those who, like themselves, had managed to rise above everyday considerations and accept sacrifices at the end of their lives, concerned only with what does not change. They had seldom walked so far on an afternoon; it was one of those days brimming over with trust and confidence, so necessary for the coming six months of cold. They had often commented on how those walks strengthened their spirit.

'We'll walk as far as the inn. It still doesn't get dark till late, there's plenty of time. It's a splendid day.'

The inn was almost a kilometre away. Lately, they had only gone that far, to sit in the shade drinking a beer or a lemonade, when someone from the village gave them a lift in their car.

They had walked down the slope of the promontory and started along the road at the end of which the inn could be found, round a bend hidden amongst a grove of trees, when she suddenly stopped, to listen to something which she had heard indistinctly. 'What was that?' she asked, looking up at the sky? 'Didn't you hear something? Didn't you feel something odd?'

It was like an ordinary flash of lightning which, unaccompanied by thunder, and glimpsed only out of the corner of the eye, requires confirmation to dispel the uneasy feeling aroused by something seen but not heard. 'I'm not sure . . . there, or perhaps over there. Didn't you see anything?'

'There must be a storm in the distance. The weather is unsettled. Maybe we should turn back.'

'Let's go as far as the inn.'

They walked on, with frequent glances at the sky, exchanging those reassuring phrases that optimists always hope will reach the elements and persuade them to restrain their stormy impulses.

They reached the bend while there was still a couple of hours' light left. Impatient to catch sight of their goal, he kept craning his neck, or stepping out into the middle of the road, to calm the anxiety that had seized his steps. And again she stopped suddenly, with her feet together and her mouth open, staring straight ahead.

'What's wrong?'

He shook her arm, grasped her hand and squeezed it tightly, an inert hand, through which he could feel flowing into his own body all the force of her apprehension, a hand reduced almost to nothing, then, with the countryside steeped in the sudden silence that is the prelude to the storm, when you sense that even invisible beings are crouching down to shelter, then, in another very different place, but, again, behind him, he felt – he did not see – the flash of lightning, the simultaneous, contradictory rupture of sea and sky which, after the mirage, took on a graver, more deceptive look, like a child trying to hide with his body some damage he has caused, both sea and sky suddenly made old and worn by a film of dissolute rust.

He had turned round to look at the walker with his dog – now incredibly far away, considering he had just crossed their path, at the moment of crisis – when she emerged from her trance.

'What about the inn? Where is the inn?' she asked.

It was that insistent question that completed his sense of disorientation. He walked forward a few steps, leaving her alone on the road, he climbed up a little mound to look around in all directions and came back more confused than ever.

'I think we passed it.'

'It's round that bend.'

'I don't know what we were thinking of. Anyway, let's go back.'

But she looked at him very oddly; her face was expressionless, but incredulity had invaded her whole body to such an extent that he could not suppress a gesture of annoyance.

'Let's go,' he said to her, trying to turn her in the opposite direction to the one they had been following. But she stood there rigid, staring straight ahead.

'It's no good,' she replied.

'What do you mean, it's no good? Come on, it's getting late. It's time we went back.'

'It's no good,' she repeated.

'What on earth do you mean, it's no good?'

'I mean it's different. Everything is different. Look how different it all is. Give me your hand. Look.'

He obeyed, and the lightning flashed again, perhaps as a direct consequence of the electric charge he had felt when he touched her hand. It was true that everything had changed; after the dazzle produced by the lightning, everything around him, though there was not the slightest perceptible alteration, was unrecognisable, just as a photograph of a familiar landscape, printed the wrong way round, is hard to recognise because there is no actual deception.

They took a few light, faltering steps in the direction they had been following earlier; then he stammered incoherently:

'The inn . . . further on, a bit further on.'

'Exactly, a bit further on.'

They stood rooted to the spot, hand in hand and staring open-mouthed up the road, not moving a muscle or giving the faintest reaction when the man walking his dog crossed their path once more, paying no heed to the unusual sight they presented.

Nor did the dog cast a glance in their direction, but tore on, straining at the leash.

As for them . . . the last vestiges of their senses did not allow them to notice that, as well as the dog, the man used a stick, held out in front in him, almost motionless, above his stiff, rapid steps, he did not look to left or right and his eyes were hidden behind dark glasses.

Translated by Annella McDermott

Juan Benet (Madrid, 1927–1993) was unusual in combining the profession of engineer with the practice of literature. Benet wrote a large number of novels, short stories and essays. His style is generally considered difficult, but he is widely admired, particularly by other writers, and is felt to have opened up new possibilities for the Spanish novel. *Volverás a Región* (1967; *Return to Región*, Columbia University Press, 1987) was the novel that first brought him to prominence. *Meditación* (1969; *Meditation*, tr. Gregory Rabassa, Persea Books, 1982) won Spain's Biblioteca Breve prize. 'The Catalyst' is from the book of short stories, *Cinco narraciones y dos fábulas* (1972) and is an example of Benet's characteristically demanding style. The limpid and economical 'Fables 9, 10 and 10a' are from *Trece fábulas y media* (1981).

The Desert

PERE CALDERS

At the end of a pleasant June, Enric Espol turned up with his right hand bandaged, revealing a clenched fist beneath the gauze. His very presence, full of unfamiliar facets, created a sense of foreboding, but no one could imagine the full impact of the blow that had felled him.

His face, which had never before provoked the slightest interest, now bore the air of melancholy victory so characteristic of modern wars.

The day on which his life experienced this change had dawned entirely unannounced. He awoke in his customary foul mood and then walked about his flat, from the bathroom to the dining room and from the dining room to the kitchen, to see if walking would help him wake up. He felt a pain in his right side and a slight breathlessness, two conditions that he had never before experienced jointly and which increased so rapidly that his sense of alarm jerked him into full consciousness. Dragging his feet and leaning on the furniture he found in his path, he returned to the bedroom and sat down next to the bed, prepared to die.

Fear covered his entire body. Slowly, health was clambering up the tree of his nervous system intending to escape out of his mouth, but, just in time, Espol rebelled. At the moment of death, he seized hold of something and closed his hand tight around it, trapping life inside. The pain stopped and his breathing returned to normal. In a gesture of relief, Espol drew his left hand across his forehead, because his right hand now had a new mission to fulfill.

Prudence warned him not to ponder too many different possibilities. He was sure, right from the start, that there was only one solution: on no account to unclench his fist. In the

71

palm of his hand, wriggling gently like a little fish or like a drop of mercury, lay Espol's life.

In order to avoid endangering his life by a single moment of inattention, he decided to bandage up his hand, and then, feeling slightly calmer, he drew up a provisional plan of action. He would go and see the manager of the company where he worked, he would ask the advice of his family doctor and of his friends, and he would gradually try to explain the facts to the people closest to him.

That was when the new Espol appeared. He would walk along the street, staring into space, his face transfigured (for it was stamped with a quite understandable look of stupefaction). And although they had grown accustomed to strange sights, people seemed to sense that his bandage was in some way different and they would often turn round to sneak a furtive glance.

Today, halfway through the morning, the manager is listening to the story with growing interest. When Espol tells him that he will have to leave his job because, being right-handed, he will no longer be able to wield a pen, he replies:

'Let's not rush things. Sometimes, these things go as quickly as they come . . .'

'This is permanent,' says Espol. 'The day I unclench my fist to pick up my pen, my life will escape.'

'We could move you to the department dealing with the preparation and setting up of subcontracts.'

'No.'

'And how will you make a life for yourself?'

'I have it here,' he says, showing him his right fist. 'This is the first time I've actually been able to locate it and I must find a way of making use of it.'

An hour later, his family doctor, coolly attentive, is listening to the story. He is tired, weary of all the tales his patients tell him; he merely nods, occasionally asking questions and more questions: 'Do you cough during the night?' 'Have you ever had diphtheria?' and other equally mysterious things. In the end, he says that it's obviously some kind of allergic reaction; he prescribes a special diet and 500 units of penicillin. As the consultation is about to end, he mentions a Swiss school for the partially disabled where they can teach you to write with your left hand in about six months.

Back in the street, Espol feels the charm of his newly acquired importance. He goes to his girlfriend's house and tells her everything. At first, she experiences a rush of maternal solicitude; she insists on applying hot compresses to the clenched fist and, when Espol refuses to let her, she declares the bandage horrible and says that she will knit him a mitten for his fist. The idea appeals to her and, forgetting about him, she phones her mother:

'Listen, Enric's life was just about to escape, but he caught it in his hand. Now he has to keep his hand closed all the time so that it doesn't escape once and for all.'

'I see.'

'And I was thinking that perhaps we could knit him a kind of bag, in a pale colour, so that he doesn't have to wear the bandage.'

Her mother shows a discreet interest.

'Hmm,' she says, 'like the one we made for Viola when she hurt her paw.'

Mother and daughter are immersed in their conversation. Feeling neglected, Espol leaves and is accompanied to the door by a murmur of: 'No, I wouldn't use plain. I'd go for rib myself . . . You knit a few stitches then decrease, knit a few, then decrease . . .'

Walking mechanically across the invisible sands, Espol heads for his best friend's house. He finds him and tells him about this singular event. And his friend (why, no one will ever know) feels jealous and tries to change the subject: 'It's nothing, forget about it. Now something *really* extraordinary happened to me – about two years ago in May – one Monday . . . While he talks, he is thinking what *he* would do to make the most of a situation like that, and the unease he feels gradually stops the flow of words.

A silence falls, broken by the lightest of breezes rippling over the dunes. The friend pretends he's bored and doesn't even listen to his visitor who, as he's leaving, says:

'It's my life, you see. Here, look,' and he raises his fist and holds it at eye level. 'I can feel it right now, like a cricket. If I squeeze with my fingers, I start to feel breathless again.'

He leaves, because he needs some fresh air. It's a big city, and he is heading towards the east. On his way, he passes the shop of a bookseller whom he knows slightly. The bookseller, who is rather slow-witted, thinks long and hard . . . Then, he goes over to Espol and, with his forefinger, touches the fist.

'Does it hurt?'

'No.'

The man suddenly becomes very excited. With his face aglow, he takes Espol by the arm and says:

'Since time began, it has always been up to the individual to do what he thinks best, but, if I were you, I would go up onto the roof, take off the bandage and, when the first flock of pigeons flies by, I would open my hand.'

When he returns to the street again, its crowded solitude casts a shadow over his heart. He is reminded of a familiar address by the destination on the front of a bus, and he runs to catch it. A sister of his mother's lives in a house near Parque del Este. She is an old lady, who likes to live surrounded by marquetry work, by furniture inlaid with mother-of-pearl and by walls lined with red velvet. She whiles away the hours making wax fruit and figures of saints, which she places under glass domes with a mahogany base.

Espol kisses his aunt's hand and launches straight into his story. At first, his aunt takes a very firm line. She advises him to stop all this nonsense, to take off the bandage and unclench his fist this instant.

'But just the thought of it makes me feel sick.'

'Don't be so pathetic. A man must be a man and that's all there is to it. Do you intend going on like this? Life needs air, and if you carry it around shut up like that, you'll snuff yourself out like a candle, and no one will even notice.'

And she laughs, but her face is serious as she smooths her fingerless gloves.

'Take the bandage off, take it off . . .' A ray of light lends a strange glint to the woman's eyes and Espol experiences

74

his first mirage. Gradually, he begins to undo the bandage, but when his hand is free of it, he is brought to his senses by the sound of an aircraft engine overhead and he runs away.

Without the protective bandage, the fear inside him grows. He holds his fist more tightly shut and, to make quite sure, he puts his hand in his pocket.

The wind, which blows only for him, whips up the sand and Espol narrows his eyes against it. He leaves behind him on his right an island of palm trees, he crosses the park and begins to be tormented by thirst. He walks and walks, his feet sinking into the sand, and he feels the parched skin on his face creaking. In the arid desert of his thoughts, little lights come on only to be immediately extinguished. He is filled with a nostalgia for the time when he was not even aware of having a life, and the heat weighs on him.

The sound of distant music makes him look up and he sees a caravan of people and camels approaching. He feels somebody tugging at his jacket and, when he turns, he is met by the astonished gaze of a small beggar girl. In utter despair, Espol crouches down and tells the child everything, asks her what she would advise.

'If I were you,' says the girl, 'I would put my hand in a jug of water and then wait for a timeless sleep to begin.'

An inexplicable trick of the light plunges them into shadow and Espol continues on his way; in the desolate landscape that accompanies him, the desert wind causes things and ideas to flutter about him. The camels are slowly coming nearer and he sits down to watch them pass. A drumroll disperses the low mist of sand, and some red letters etch themselves on Espol's eyes: 'Circo Donamatti. 3-ring circus! Coming soon.'

He is just about to succumb to sleep, slightly turning his head to watch the caravan pass. A blonde trapeze artist, mounted on a horse, gives him a graceful wave, and Espol, distracted, responds, stretching up his right arm and opening his hand.

An amber-coloured ball escapes; startled, he tries to catch it, but fails. He slowly collapses, filled by the ineffable anxiety that he may have left the gas on at home.

© Pere Calders
Translated by Margaret Jull Costa

Pere Calders (Barcelona, 1912) started life as a commercial artist. In 1936, he published his first collection of stories, *El primer arlequí*. When civil war broke out, he enlisted as a military cartographer on the Republican side and, following the Nationalist victory, spent twenty-three years in exile in Mexico. There he found work as a graphic designer and continued to write and publish in Catalan. His first piece of fantasy literature, *Gaeli i l'home-déu* (1938) depicted a magical world in which supernatural powers prevailed over evil. In later books he explored his interest in time travel and science fiction: *Demà a les tres de la matinada* (1959) and *L'invasió subtil i altres contes* (1979; winner of the Lletra d'Or Prize). A selection of his stories is available in English translation (*The Virgin of the Railway and other stories*, tr. A. Bath, Aris & Phillips, 1991). This story is taken from *Cròniques de la veritat oculta* (Edicions 62, Barcelona, 1979).

Beyond Death

NOEL CLARASÓ

It is very hard to know what we are, but the problem does not end here; there is also what we were before and what we will be afterwards.

The owner of the hotel, a tall man with a contemptuous, indifferent air about him, was just explaining the affair to a few male customers who had called in for a drink. The hotel also has a café and a bar.

The story involves two newly-weds who arrived a few days ago. The husband claimed that he knew the mountains because he had been in Salardú before, although the owner of the hotel doesn't remember him. He said that he wanted to climb Beciberri, and the previous night he asked them to prepare some lunch for him. His wife says that he left alone, at dawn, and that he promised he would be back before seven o'clock in the evening. It is now ten'o clock at night.

The men consult their large pocket watches. One says it's a quarter to ten, one five past ten, the other seven minutes to. Each one declares that his watch is right, not that it really matters. One of them asks:

'Beciberri?'

They are slow on the uptake and have to have things explained to them three times before they understand.

'Yes.'

'Well, he should be back by now.'

Another man, who does a little hunting, calculates how long it would take.

'Seven hours to go up and five to come down, that makes twelve. If he left at dawn, that's more than enough time.'

An old man, who is no longer up to risking his life on steep slopes, asks:

'Does he know the route?'

'He said he did.'

All they know about her is that her name is Eulalia and that she is standing at the dining room window staring unceasingly out at the mountains. But night has fallen and she can see nothing now. She keeps looking, her eyes motionless. The outline of the landscape from which he will emerge is engraved on her eyes.

The other guests dare not approach. They do not know her. She has been at the hotel for three days, but no one has spoken to her. The couple did not take part in the general conversation. She keeps asking, as if out of habit, almost without taking her eyes off the darkness:

'What time is it?'

She began asking at eight o'clock and they told her it was eight, then that it was nine, and now no one dares to tell her that it is ten o'clock. She asks of no one in particular:

'What time might he be back?'

No one answers. Some don't know and those who do know don't want to say. The men are now talking about taking some sort of action, but they can't really be bothered. No one takes the initiative. The owner of the hotel sends a boy to Artíes to find a guide, just in case. They have a guide there, but not in Salardú.

All the guests have had supper by now, but they dare not go to bed. She has had no supper nor has she sat down at the table. The owner of the hotel has begged her two or three times to have something to eat and she says only that she wants to wait for her husband. At half past ten, the owner goes over to her and this time he doesn't suggest that she eats something, but that she goes to bed. She looks at him insolently, as if he had insulted her.

'What time is it?' she asks.

'Half past ten.'

'What time is he likely to be back?'

'I don't know. He can't be much longer.'

'I'll wait for him.'

'Perhaps he's got lost and has decided to spend the night on the mountain.'

Eulalia fixes her hard eyes on the owner of the hotel and asks him:

'Why don't they go and look for him?'

'They'll go later, they say. They've sent for the guide.'

Time passes implacably. Each minute weighs on Eulalia's heart. At eight o'clock, already impatient, she had decided to wait until half past eight. At half past eight, she had decided to wait until nine. And thus she has continued to divide up the time in search of boundaries to bind about her heart so that it does not break into pieces. From eleven o'clock onwards, though, she can wait no longer. Time has beaten her. Now all she wants is to see coming down the dim path the image of the man she loves. She can barely see the path in the black night and her eyes are wide open and staring, as she peers into the shadowless dark. At last, she sits down by the dining room window and covers her mouth with a handkerchief so that they do not hear her moans. The hotel owner's wife has tried several times to persuade her to go to bed, to no avail.

At midnight, the guide from Artíes arrives. He is lean and strong, a man of few words. He proposes that they wait a little longer and set off at two. There is no point in leaving any earlier because it would be a waste of time looking in the dark. Meanwhile, they organise the expedition. No one feels like joining in. They do not like the mountain. They know it because at some point they have all had to climb it, for their livelihood partly depends on the mountain. But they do not love it, they have no feeling for it. Nevertheless, they all offer their help, one after the other, the youngest first. Two foreigners offer to go as well. The guide chooses those who seem strongest and gets together a team of six men. He says that will be enough.

The women take care of Eulalia. The hotel owner's wife has still not managed to convince her to go to her room, but there are four or five women around her now, all insisting that she should go upstairs. She finally gives in because, from her room, you can also see the darkness surrounding the path. She remains standing at the window, her eyes fixed on the night. Her whole life depends on a physical shape that might condense out of the gloom. She has refused to go to bed or to eat anything. She couldn't. Her eyes are dry and she cannot speak. In the end, they all leave her. She no longer wants to know how much time has passed, but she does not lose hope. He said he would come back and he will. Perhaps he won't come back until the next day. Perhaps he has got lost and is waiting for dawn with fear in his heart. She accepts anything except the idea of death.

At two o'clock, the expedition leaves in silence. They do not tell her. They know she is watching from the window and they take a detour so that she does not see them. They do not turn on their lights until they are some distance away. The guide is at the head of the group. The owner of the hotel has not gone with them. They are all muttering amongst themselves. They do not go gladly. One says:

'He shouldn't have gone up there if he didn't know the area.'

The guide repeats the hotel owner's words:

'He said that he did.'

'What was he like?' asks another man.

And one of the guests describes him. He's tall, strong and very young. He looks as though he could get out of any scrape without help from anyone. But the mountain demands respect; they all know it and the guide says so too. He knows it better than anyone, for he knows all the mountain's tricks and traps.

'It's not to be treated lightly.'

And they walk on, unhurriedly but purposefully, taking long strides, their heads held high. They all savour the rare pleasure of breathing in the night air.

Now everyone in the hotel is asleep, apart from her. The women have lain down on their beds fully clothed, in case she needs them. She has promised that she will call them. She has not moved from where they left her. The room is in darkness. That is how she wanted it, because she believes she can see the night more clearly like that. She is alone and her eyes are wide open, staring at the black mountain. She cannot see the lights of the expedition. She cannot see anything.

Suddenly, she feels a presence near her. She had seen nothing on the path and she feels this presence inside the room, behind her. Before turning round, she knows that her heart is not mistaken. He is there! He is standing in the middle of the room, with his knapsack on and a rope slung over his shoulder. He is surrounded by a ghostly light and she can see him in the dark. She cannot cry out, she cannot move a step, she is frozen to the spot. He holds out a hand to her and calls her by her name.

'Eulalia!'

She hears that beloved, unmistakable voice. But she hears it not with her ears, but with her heart. She knows that he has called out to her and that she did not hear his voice. She knows that he is there and understands at the same time that he is also somewhere else.

He looks at her tenderly and she is not afraid, but she does not move, nor does she throw her arms about him or respond to his voice. The ghost repeats that dear name:

'Eulalia!'

And she realises that he has blood on his forehead.

'Did you fall?'

She knows that she has just asked this question, but she did not hear her own voice. He touches his forehead with one hand and the hand becomes stained with blood.

'Yes, I fell. I was left hanging on by my hands and then the stone crumbled. I fell from a great height and hit my head on the rocks.'

'Does it hurt?'

'No. It did at first, but not any more.'

'I told them to go and look for you.'

'They've already left. I saw them going up the mountain. They'll find me tomorrow when it's light. But don't tell them that you've seen me. They won't believe you. They and I no longer inhabit the same life.'

She looks and looks at him and does not dare to say

anything. She does not dare to say his name or to fall into his arms. She is not afraid, because he is her husband, and she cannot be afraid. But despite his beloved presence in the room, she begins to feel infinitely alone. He speaks to her tenderly.

'Eulalia, I've come to say goodbye to you. I couldn't leave without seeing you again. But if you wait for me, I will come back one day. I know that I will be able to come back. Wait for me always, always, always . . .'

She is holding out her hand and her mouth is open. but she cannot move her feet or cry out. The ghost slowly fades, but does so reluctantly, engaged in a terrible struggle to stay as long as possible. It becomes blurred. He is now no more than a vaguely luminous shape. All that are left are two eyes open like windows onto the infinite. At last, she feels her own heart stop and she falls to the floor at the ghost's non-existent feet.

The women go into her room first thing in the morning and they find her lying face down on the floor, unconscious. They pick her up and carry her to the bed. They rub her wrists and her temples. She remains for a long time with her eyes closed and when she finally opens them, she doesn't look at anyone or see anything around her in the room. A vision blocks her sight. They call to her and she does not reply. A dear, distant voice has robbed her of words.

They try to console her and she does not hear them. She knows that he is dead. She knew before anyone else did. The dead man visited her in the night to say goodbye. She knows it, but she knows too that she can tell no one. And she knows that she must wait always, always, because he will return one day.

When she comes to, when it is fully light, she asks a question that surprises the women.

'Haven't they brought him back to me yet?'

The expedition arrives at midday. They are carrying the body wrapped in a blanket. Four men carry him. They found him shortly after dawn, hanging from a rock. His forehead has been pierced by the nails of his climbing boots. It seems that, as he fell, he performed a strange pirouette.

She receives him in silence. There is no point in hiding anything from her because she already knows everything. She cannot cry or speak. They all respect her silent grief. They do not dare to keep her from her husband's body. She goes over to him fearlessly and uncovers his face. However, she does not see his disfigured face, but the face of the ghost who bore only a bloodstain on his forehead. She will always remember him like that, alive and more handsome than ever, but with that one bloodstain.

Then there are long unpleasant formalities to go through. Some men come for the widow and take her away in a car. They take the body too in another black car. Everything returns to normal in Salardú. The men and the women have another story to tell during the long winter nights.

Twenty years have passed. Eulalia had a daughter a few months after her husband's death and she has devoted her life to the girl. They are rich and live in a large house with a garden, in one of the exclusive areas of Barcelona.

The mother has always kept alive the memory of the husband who died so young on the mountain and who visited her that night to promise her that he would return. She knows that it was all an hallucination, but she has never stopped believing in the dead man's words and has continued to wait for him. She has never mentioned it to anyone, not even to her daughter. She knows that no one could understand the reason for that absurd hope.

The daughter is nineteen. She is lovely, as was her mother, but there is always something vaguely sad about her. Perhaps she has caught it from her mother. Sadness is an infectious disease. The daughter finds men rather comical. She still does not believe in love, despite her nineteen years. Her mother has often told her the story of how her father died, and the daughter thinks that the men who flirt with her are not like her father, even though she never knew him.

She has always liked the story. She found out about it when she was older. Her mother did not want to tell her when she was a child, so as not to frighten her. But one day, she told it to her and the daughter has since made her repeat it again and again. She likes the story. She has never been to Salardú and sometimes she says to her mother:

'Take me there one day.'

'I don't want to go.'

'Would you let me go without you?'

'Yes, if you go with other people.'

The mother does not like to be apart from her daughter, but she believes that her daughter's desire to go to Salardú is out of love for the father she never knew. And she gives in, out of respect for her daughter's love.

The daughter is also called Eulalia and one day she organises the trip with some friends. They are a married couple with a daughter and a son. The daughter is the same age as Eulalia, the son a little older. It seems that the son is in love with her, but Eulalia is not sure that she likes him. Something in her heart tells her that this is not the man for her.

Eulalia has a very vague idea of her father. There is a picture at home in a silver frame. It shows a young man with a pleasant face, but the photograph is rather blurred. It is not the work of a professional photographer, but an enlargement made from a smaller photograph, the one that her mother liked best. Young people do not think about death and have no interest in having a good photograph of themselves taken, of the sort that can be kept for ever as a souvenir.

The friends accompanying Eulalia know that her father died years ago in the mountains and that he fell to his death, but they do not know that it was there, in Salardú. Eulalia prefers them not to know and says nothing to them about it. She just wants to find out where her father died and to be in the room where her father stayed. She does not know that he also appeared there after his death. That secret has not been revealed to her. It was room number 2. Her mother has often told her that and she remembers it well.

'Number 2, the best room in the hotel.'

That is what her mother always said.

They reach Salardú and the hotel owner, who is older now, shows them the rooms. The hotel has changed little in twenty years. It has been renovated now and then, but the furniture is the same. Things change very little in twenty years.

Eulalia says to the hotel owner:

'I would like to stay in room number two.'

'Why?' asks the owner, who is astute and never gives his opinion without first asking a few questions.

'Some friends of mine stayed here years ago. They told me that it's a good room.'

'Yes, it's on a corner and has two windows, but all the rooms are good rooms. Besides, I can't let you have it because it's occupied. A gentleman is staying in it. I'll give you number four, which is next door.'

'Is he going to be here long?'

'He hasn't said. He only arrived yesterday.'

Eulalia installs herself in another room, number 4 next door to number 2. There is a continuous balcony that looks out onto the river and that connects all the rooms. She leaves her things and goes out on to the balcony to look. She knows that they carried her dead father down one of those paths. She looks across at the mountains on the other side of the river, hoping to see the peaks that soar to over three thousand metres. But you can't see them from there. Salardú lies between two secondary valleys and you have to go through them in order to reach the peaks. You can see only the meadows near the river and a slope covered in fir trees.

Eulalia walks along the balcony to the window of room number 2. The French windows are wide open. There is no one inside. She sees a suitcase under the bed, a coat hanging up and a few books on the table. The coat is a man's coat. On the glass shelf, next to the washbasin, there is a safety razor. Eulalia is deeply moved to think that, twenty years ago, in that very room, her mother spent that most dreadful of nights.

She goes further into the room. She is not interested in the objects, which belong, after all, to a stranger. She is interested in the room. On the table, next to the books, is an identity card with a photograph. Eulalia looks at the photo and is greatly struck by the stranger's face. She even closes her eyes in order to see it more clearly afterwards. There is an extraordinary similarity between that face and her father's face in the photograph in the silver frame. She examines the document and allows herself to imagine that she is going through the papers of her dead father. She smiles. Her father would be forty-five now. He would probably be a wonderful father. She reads the name on the documents. It's a perfectly ordinary name: Evaristo. She is amused by the name, but she doesn't like it. It is accompanied by two nondescript family names. She doesn't like either of them. Her father was called Felipe.

She looks at his date of birth: 18th July 1926. She closes her eyes again and then opens them to see better. It is the date of her father's death. Yes, her father died there on 18th July 1926. That peculiar stranger who arrived yesterday and took the room in which her father stayed before he died and whose face looks like the photograph of her dead father, was born the day her father died. Eulalia feels a strange presence near her. She goes out onto the balcony and hears the voices of her friends calling her.

They want to know if she's settled in. She shows them the room and the river and the distant trees.

'We should be all right here for a few days.'

'Yes, fine.'

They are all very happy and completely oblivious to the secret life that drifts through the thoughts of others. They laugh and go down to the dining room because it is already supper time.

Eulalia seems distracted at supper. They have to ask her everything twice and her replies seem rather odd. Her friend says to her:

'The mountain air obviously doesn't suit you.'

Eulalia laughs to disguise her feelings. It isn't the mountain air, it's because she is concentrating on the other guests. She is searching amongst those already seated at the tables for the stranger born on the very day her father died and she cannot find him. He's obviously not in the dining room. But Eulalia doesn't dare to ask for him.

Her friend's brother suggests going on a trip the next day.

She says yes, but she could just as easily have said no. She isn't thinking about what she's saying.

'Apparently there's a lake you can visit.'

'Well, let's go and see it then.'

'It's quite far.'

'We can go in the car.'

'They say you have to walk there.'

'I'm not sure I could manage a long walk. I'm not used to it and, besides, I've never been into the mountains before.'

Her friend tries to encourage her and says that they could even swim in the lake. She agrees to everything they say and they arrange to get up early the next day so as to do the trip at a leisurely pace.

They linger for a while over dessert and then, suddenly, the door opens and in walks a young hiker. He is tall, strong, with long, curly hair. Eulalia recognises him instantly. This is precisely the image she had of her father. The hiker has a knapsack over his shoulder and his skin is burned by the sun. He talks to the owner of the hotel and they both laugh. Then he washes his hands, puts his knapsack down in a corner and sits at a table set for one person. He doesn't say hello to anyone and Eulalia thinks: 'Of course, he only arrived yesterday.'

She no longer notices anything anyone says to her. She has eyes only for this stranger who is so like her father. She cannot imagine her father looking any other way. That is how he would have been, had he not died on the mountain. A little older perhaps, but with the same build and the same features.

When she says goodnight to her friends and goes into her room, she says:

'See you in the morning.'

'They'll call you at six.'

'Fine.'

But she has already formulated a plan. She won't get up. She won't go with them on the trip. All she cares about is meeting the man who looks like her father. And that night she can hardly sleep. She has strange visions and holds interminable conversations with the man whom she has only seen from afar, once, sitting at a table.

When they call her the next day, she doesn't get up. And when they come to find her in her room, she tells them that she slept very badly and isn't up to a walk. She begs them to let her sleep and she stays in bed. But she does not sleep or get up late. She goes out onto the balcony and sees the French windows of room number 2 standing wide open. But she does not dare to look inside. She stays there, waiting. She knows that the stranger will come out onto the balcony the moment he wakes up. He can't do anything else.

The stranger emerges when it is already quite late. Eulalia has gone to sleep on the balcony, sitting on the floor. The stranger sees her there and does not dare to speak to her, but he makes enough noise to wake her up. She wakes and sees him, they say good morning to each other and they have a bizarre dialogue that no one else would understand, indeed not even they do, and in which the words are the least important part. She says:

'We arrived yesterday.'

He takes all the usual questions as read and asks:

'Are you staying long?'

'Ten days.'

'Me too.'

Eulalia has got up and is standing next to the stranger, leaning her elbows on the balustrade; without moving her hands or her eyes, she exclaims:

'It's the river!'

'Yes, and there are the paths and beyond that the high peaks.'

'My name's Eulalia.'

'I would have liked to guess your name.'

'You'd never have guessed it.'

'Why not? You couldn't possibly be called anything else.'

'I might be called Teresa.'

'I wouldn't like you so much then and the only reason you are here is for me to like you immensely.'

And they talk and talk tirelessly. Then they have breakfast

together on the terrace and afterwards lie down in the meadow by the river and they swim in the river and they have lunch brought down to them there and they spend all day by the river lying in the meadow. By nightfall, when the hikers return from the lake, Eulalia has taken into her heart the one man she can truly love.

He wants to go with her to the mountain the next day and she agrees, but she is afraid to mention it to her friends. That night, before going to bed, she writes to her mother. She does not tell her about the stranger who is no longer a stranger. Nevertheless, her mother realises, when she reads the letter, that an irrevocable change has taken place in her daughter's heart. She knew that this would have to happen some day, but she is troubled by a strange presentiment. Why there exactly, in Salardú, where that other much-loved man had died so many years ago? Could it be an evil omen?

The following day, Eulalia gets up before dawn and leaves her room without making a sound. Evaristo is waiting for her at the door of the hotel, and the two of them go off to spend the day up the mountain. They are happy. There are no doubts or secrets between them now. The veil has been ripped away in a single day. This is true love, which always begins at once with love.

When, that night, Eulalia has to explain to her friends, all she can say are three words, round and hard as steel balls.

'I love him!'

'But you only met him yesterday.'

'It doesn't matter, I love him.'

'You don't even know who his parents are.'

'I don't care, I love him!'

'You don't even know if he's got any money.'

'I don't care, I love him!'

No solid reasons have ever triumphed over that brief, earnest argument. And her friends are finally convinced that she does, in fact, love him, and because they also love her, the woman decides to write to Eulalia's mother to tell her what has happened. Her mother reads the letter and is not in the least surprised. She knew it all already.

One day, the two of them are alone on the mountain, Evaristo and Eulalia. They have climbed one of the peaks, they have swum in a lake and are resting, waiting for the the sun finally to set. It is that unforgettable hour when people always tell the truth. They are holding hands, sitting very close together.

She asks him:

'What made you come here?'

'It was like an irresistible impulse. I'd never been here and I didn't even know this valley existed. One day, I was packing my suitcase to go and spend the summer at the beach with my family, as I always do, when, suddenly, this name 'Salardú' came into my mind. Where had I heard it before? I couldn't remember. But I became obsessed by the name and, the following day, instead of going to the sea, I came to the mountains. At home, everyone asked me if I had taken leave of my senses and I didn't reply because I might have had to tell them that I had.'

'How odd.'

'What's even odder is that when I reached the hotel, I had the feeling that I knew it already because I had been here before. Even the owner's face seemed familiar. I called him by name, without even realising it, and it was the right name. He asked me if we'd met before and I couldn't say yes or no. I was afraid that either answer might be a lie.'

'How odd.'

'Some even odder things happened to me after that. The following day, I went up the mountain for the first time in my life. I've always spent the summers by the sea, and yet a particular peak, unknown to me, drew me on irresistibly. I didn't know this peak, but I looked at it as if I had seen it before. I thought, I must have seen it in a dream. But it wasn't that. When I got to the peak, I saw that it was exactly as I remembered it, despite the fact that I had never seen it before. And as I climbed it, I had the feeling all the time that I knew the paths already. I didn't have to ask anyone the way and I didn't get lost.'

'How odd.'

'And there's another even odder thing. The second night after that strange walk up the mountain, I went to bed very tired and I fell asleep at once. I didn't dream. I never do. But I suddenly woke up with the definite feeling that there was a woman lying beside me. I would go so far as to say that I even touched her. And in the darkness I saw that woman's face. And it seemed to me that I had loved her for a long time and that this was not the first night I had spent with her.'

Frightened, Eulalia asked:

'What was this woman like?'

'She was like you, but she wasn't you.'

'My mother.'

The words came out involuntarily. Then she covers her mouth with her hand and bursts out laughing. She tries to change the subject. He has heard Eulalia's words, but they meant nothing to him and he gave them no importance. He is still immersed in remembering the inexplicable phenomena that took place during his first two days there. She realises that the inexplicable has just entered her life, she does not see what clear or defined role she has to play in it all and she begins to feel strangely troubled. Evaristo says:

'And the following morning, I came out and found you on the balcony.'

'That's not so odd.'

'For me, it's the oddest thing of all, because when I saw you, I immediately fell in love with you.'

'I loved you already from the night before, when I saw you in the dining room.'

And the conversation became one of those dialogues so common between lovers, in which everything has deep significance, except the words.

This story could go on for some time, but the end was swift and cruel and it is best to tell it quickly, with no rhetorical flourishes.

Evaristo is a medical student and belongs to a very good family. On that account, her mother can have no complaints. She thinks only that he is too young for her daughter. But her daughter is very much in love and, according to her, so is he, and they don't mind waiting.

Time passes and her mother has still not met him. Her daughter describes him to her, but that is not enough. She demands to meet him and her daughter always says the same thing:

'You will.'

But she carefully avoids a face-to-face meeting between Evaristo and her mother. Why? She doesn't quite know. Perhaps there is no reason. Nevertheless, she fears that nothing good will come of any interview between her fiancé and her mother.

Eulalia, the daughter, has never dared mention to her mother that her fiancé's face is identical to that of the man in the photo in the silver frame. Nor has she said that he was born on the same day her father died. She can't. She doesn't want her mother to know. Nor has she ever told her mother about the conversation that she and Evaristo had that afternoon on the mountain when he explained to her the strange impulse that had brought him there and the strange visions and incomprehensible memories he experienced there. Her mother must never know about any of that. But Eulalia does not know how to tell her fiancé that her mother must never know. What reason could she give?

Eulalia, the mother, has never spoken to her daughter about the apparition she had on that sad night, nor about her father's promise to return one day. If her daughter knew, she might be even more frightened. Evaristo is the only one who has no secrets, the only one who lets himself be carried along fearlessly by the impulses of his heart. Sometimes he is surprised by vague recollections of a former life he has never had, but he doesn't give it much importance. He is a medical student and he knows that there are many dark wells in the life of the spirit whose depths can never be plumbed.

It all happens very naturally. Eulalia, the mother, has not been very well. Now on the mend, she is sitting in an armchair next to the window, in the main living room on the first floor of the old house which was once her parents' house. Her daughter is in the garden with her fiancé. Her mother knows this and is sitting there, waiting, feeling a little sad that at last the moment has come to meet the man who will take her daughter away from her.

She hears the two of them coming up the stairs. It is a bright summer afternoon and the balcony doors are standing open. Eulalia, the mother, adopts a slightly affected pose and waits there, not moving, her eyes fixed on the distance. She hears footsteps approach and a dear voice calling to her:

'Mama!'

And what happens next can scarcely be described. It is all so quick and so tragic. The mother and her daughter's fiancé are brought face to face and for a moment they do not move. They stare at each other with wide eyes. They are no longer in control of their own wills. They are driven by apparently irrational, utterly irresistible impulses. The mother gets up and walks straight over to him. And the two of them fold each other in a long, close embrace, one of those almost legendary embraces that occur only between people who have loved each other very much and who have not seen each other for a long, long time. Eulalia, the daughter, sees her mother's face pressed against that of her fiancé and she goes over to the open balcony doors. She knows it is fatal. She cannot cry out and she cannot go on living. She falls, almost involuntarily, from the balcony onto the flagstones in the courtyard below and her head cracks open on the stones.

When the servants carry her dead body upstairs, Eulalia, the mother, and her daughter's fiancé are still locked in each other's arms.

© María Rosa Millás Vda de Clarasó
Translated by Margaret Jull Costa

Noel Clarasó (Alexandria, 1902–Barcelona, 1985) trained as a lawyer before dedicating himself to writing. He was also an enthusiastic traveller and amateur botanist. He began publishing in 1940 and his work encompasses short stories, crime novels and books on gardening. Among his publications are: *Seis autores en busca de un personaje* (1951), *Fruta prohibida* (1964) and *Seis vidas al margen del ley* (1965). 'Beyond death' is taken from *¡Miedo!* (1948).

No one

ISABEL DEL RÍO

The use of the first person allows the reader not so much to identify with the individual who is the subject of the text as to coexist with him: identification is less important than compassion, a feeling that one might experience, for example, when the fictional character makes the following confession: 'I am a creature whom no one looks at or wants to look at: abominably, improbably, impossibly human; I am, however, just like any other person and so I submit to my fate and accept it without complaint.'

The use of the first person evokes feelings that, to some degree, may also exist in the heart of the reader: 'I would like to mingle with the common people and sing their songs and join in their simple, uncomplicated conversations. But every time I approach, they recoil from me, they back away with a look of horror. I don't know if it's my face or my body that frightens them; sometimes I catch my reflection in shop-windows, but since it's dark and I am always covered up, it's almost impossible to know what I look like; the little I have seen, though, bears no resemblance to the people walking the streets.'

In this exercise, we will enter into a relationship of gradual intimacy with a character who has yet to metamorphose from a 'he' into an 'I', and will discuss the enormous effort involved in such a manoeuvre (in some cases, in parallel with what is, after all, purely a change of form, something terrible occurs with all the fury of a tempest). Sooner or later, everyone has to undergo a change that is almost as momentous as birth itself, and only when that happens can you be who you are and always have been: you have to stop referring to yourself as 'he' or 'she' or 'you' or 'they' (those who do so – out of altruism or self-denial or because it's an easy option – put others before themselves) and at last begin the reinstatement of the 'I'.

The first-person confession will be accompanied by information that merely describes the surroundings or the action, and then it doesn't matter if the third person is used: 'He lives in a house in a cul-de-sac, where there are no other houses, only the backs of various buildings that have their entrances in adjacent streets. It is a two-storey house, and not a single ray of light has ever shone into any of its rooms. The first memory he had was of nurses prodding him with pincers and other implements, making him moan with pain; then there was a long period of emptiness, during which he must have been under almost continual sedation. Finally, he was given this house; the State granted him a monthly allowance on condition that he only goes out very late at night, when everyone else is sleeping.'

To describe actual events, the narrative will continue in the third person without as yet a glimmer of emotion: 'Yesterday, in the street, despite the lateness of the hour, he came across a group of individuals talking loudly and deciding there and then, just like that, the fate of some poor devil who had stolen something – a wallet perhaps – and whom they had managed to corner; they were kicking and punching the boy. He approached the group and simply shouted out: 'No!' and they fled; it might have been his voice, cracked and shrill, that frightened them most, but it was almost certainly his appearance.

The supposed thief was lying on the pavement and his mouth and nose were bleeding; his eyes were swollen and he probably couldn't see anything. Our protagonist went to him and pressed a muslin handkerchief into his hand; the other man, despite his wounds, first wiped the blood from his face. The wallet was still lying on the ground; he examined it and found it empty: the other passers-by had run off with every last penny. He helped the young man to his feet and almost had to drag him to a bench where he lay him down; the wounded man told him that he had nowhere to go, that he came from a city a long way off, that he hadn't eaten for several days.

He decided to help him; he had never helped anyone before. He lifted him up as best he could, for he had never been strong, and dragged him the few yards to his house.

In a room on the ground floor there was an old bed and he laid the young man down on it as delicately as his own clumsy limbs would allow; he covered him with a blanket and the young man fell asleep. He was little more than an adolescent, but he was obviously hungry and in need of attention.'

Now the central character expresses his innermost thoughts, but still speaks of himself as someone removed from what is happening, and at no point does he mention the 'I': 'He went up to his bedroom and tried to go to sleep, to no avail: there was a living creature in his house, and he was filled by all kinds of sensations and feelings that he had never had before. So he went downstairs to look at him. The boy was breathing very fast and sweating. He barely touched him, but the boy's forehead was burning. He went into the kitchen and got several damp cloths which he placed on the boy's face, arms and legs in order to lower the fever. The boy also had an ugly wound on one temple and the man cleaned it as best he could. He had read about this in his books – which covered the majority of manifestations of human wisdom – and he at last had the opportunity to put that rudimentary knowledge into practice. He stayed there all night, just watching. Towards daybreak, the boy gave vent to the most terrible screams. He was delirious and was doubtless dreaming about what seemed to him to be hideous monsters . . .' Suddenly an 'I' creeps into the man's reasoning: 'My nightmares, on the other hand, are always filled with people.' However, he immediately returns to anonymity: 'The boy slept and slept. He was like that for three days, delirious, shouting out names, places, dates. Finally, on the night of the third day, he woke up, though he could still not open his eyes, because the swelling had not yet gone down. He remained lying on the bed, but said nothing. The man prepared him some food and helped him to eat it; the wounded boy devoured it all eagerly.

Then the boy sat up and, still blind, told him his story. He spoke for a long time; it was a monologue, but then the man had no idea how to respond anyway, since he had never spoken to anyone. Then the boy asked about him. Our protagonist was embarrassed; it occurred to him that he could make up a story about the person he would like to have been and about the places he would like to have visited. But he reasoned that the boy would recover his sight at any moment, and so it made no sense to lie. He told the boy that he would explain everything once he was restored to health. He found it hard to articulate words. On paper it was so easy for him, but it was agonizing to speak, and when he finished those few brief utterances, he felt exhausted.

And thus passed three more days which were filled with the boy's talk; he could still not get up and his eyelids remained sealed tight.

At the end of those three days, the boy said things to him that seemed incredible. He thanked him for his kindness, declared that he was the only person who had helped him in that cruel city; he heaped praise on him, comparing him to certain celestial beings, but this was one subject that was poorly covered in the man's library and so he was not quite sure what was meant. The boy even tried to hug him, sitting up and groping the air with his hands, but the other man eluded the embrace, making him lie down again, telling him that he should conserve his strength.'

The narrative suddenly changes; now the 'I' starts to invade the text; there is a gradual intensification of his state of somnolent unrest, triggered by a simple physiological event: 'I noticed a burning sensation in my eyes; I touched them and felt something wet: it was like water and tasted very salty; it kept falling in drops, one after the other, and I could do nothing to stop it. Then I remembered having read that when people can no longer contain their emotions, they weep. That confirmed to me that, in some way, I must be a human being, not a monster or some impossible creature as I had heard people call out when they saw me wandering the streets late at night.'

The call of the 'I' is irresistible, and the narrative will continue in that form: 'I took care of the boy, I fed him and washed him; he couldn't praise me enough and kept saying that he felt a rare affection for me.

One morning, he called to me from his room. I had only just woken up and I heard him saying: 'I can see again! I can see again!' I considered not going downstairs, I wanted to run away; if he saw me now, he would be terrified and leave for ever, the one person who had given meaning to my whole existence. Nevertheless, in deference to him, I decided to answer his call, despite the fear and shame gnawing at me inside. I went slowly down the stairs and got as far as his door.

The boy had his back to me. He was standing examining the planks of wood that had been nailed up at the windows, not to keep light out, but so that no one would look in from outside and see me. When I went into the room, I coughed in order to interrupt the thread of his thoughts and to warn him of my presence.'

The character in the story cannot, at that precise moment, withstand the turmoil he is feeling and so he again steps back from what is happening, to regain some distance: 'When he saw him, the boy ran to him and embraced him. He said that he was profoundly grateful, that he didn't know how he could ever repay such kindness; he spoke enthusiastically of his decision to go back to his village and work on the land with the other members of his family; he told him that he should come too because there the air was clean and the people were friendly, the days passed pleasantly and the seasons were less harsh; in short, he declared that life in his village was kinder than in the city and that people appreciated others for what they were. Again he embraced him.'

Having reached this point, he has no option but to confess all with the 'I': 'I was dumbstruck, I was so moved I could barely breathe, and I wondered how it was possible for the boy not to notice my face and body. I was on the point of asking what he thought of my physical appearance, but to do so would have been discourteous. Then he told me that he wanted to return to his village as soon as possible, and that, once there, he would write to me so that I could join him for a visit or to live if I chose. I gave him the money for his ticket back, and after some initial protests, the boy took it and left.

The house was empty again; I did not want to touch the bed, with its tangle of sheets and blankets; I did not even want to wash the muslin cloths with which I had cooled his fever. I looked at it all for hours at a time. For long days, I waited for his letter to arrive. The only correspondence to arrive punctually was my allowance from the State.

I have been waiting for several months and, although I have not entirely lost hope, I now have my doubts. Perhaps the boy was just saying those things, perhaps he *had* been frightened by my appearance, but, for some reason, had wanted to pretend otherwise . . . fear or money or prudence; perhaps it was all a nightmare and the most beautiful thing that ever happened to me never really happened at all.'

When the letter did finally arrive, so intense was his distress that he had to turn away from himself again: 'The envelope bore only the address, not the name (he had no valid name in any case). The page of tiny, blue, spontaneous handwriting was full of joyful expressions of gratitude, sincere apologies for the delay in contacting him. The young man invited him to go to his village: he wanted to show him the hills and the orchards, the river and the local paths, the reaping and the harvest, he wanted him to meet all the people who had helped him to understand who he was and where he should spend his life.'

For the conclusion, however, our character has no alternative but to be brave; he has the strength he needs (although, up until then, he had not known it) and he uses it convincingly (up until that moment, he had thought himself incapable of this); he will never again refer to himself with anything but an 'I': 'At that moment, I put the letter back in the envelope and I sealed it. In pencil, I wrote diagonally across it: 'NO LONGER LIVING AT THIS ADDRESS'. That night, while everyone was sleeping, I went out into the broad avenue where I had once seen a scarlet letter box. As I slipped the letter in through the slot, I took a deep breath, I felt an enormous sense of relief. Now I could simply go back to being the person I have always been. I too know where I should spend my life; I too know who I am.'

Translated by Margaret Jull Costa

The Key

ISABEL DEL RÍO

There are circumstances – when a silence suddenly falls, when the sun appears for a moment in a sky covered in dense cloud – that make us doubt the certainty of our surroundings, and it is precisely then that it occurs to us – as if there were no other possibility – that we might have invented the whole thing from start to finish. The story could thus begin simply (and the style too will have to be minimalist: short sentences, few adjectives, brief descriptions of real things, but none of any perceived emotional turmoil), with someone arriving home after a short walk, someone who knocks at the door, who knocks and knocks. No one opens it, though. The woman in the story is sure that someone is in, which is why she raps on the door so hard she almost skins her knuckles. It occurs to her that it is a day of celebration (during the brief hour that she was out of the house, the others have had time to prepare a party in her honour). There is no need to specify whether the person has gone out without her key or has lost it. She remembers, at that moment, that there is another key above the doorframe; she gropes for it blindly, but she is clumsy and the key falls soundlessly onto the doormat. There will be some description of the key, that it is a shiny, bronze-coloured key; it is an excessively small key to open such a heavy door. Despite that, however, she turns it just once in the lock and the door swings open. Once inside, she reads the message written on a banner that spans the corridor from wall to wall: HAPPY BIRTHDAY.

When she goes in, however, she is met by a stench – not of celebration – by the silence of a muted room, by an emptiness in which only the colours glitter in the shadows. Our character leaves the hall and goes down the corridor as far as the living room door; she enters the room and realises at once

103

what must have happened only a matter of moments ago: the inert, fallen bodies, one on top of the other, face down, blood still pouring from their backs. She can scarcely see their faces, she doesn't know what their last expression was, she doesn't want to; she looks only at the woman lying there; she has long black hair like hers that reaches down as far as the wound in her back and which is steeped, like the wick of a lamp, in blood; all that remains is a profile blurred by surprise; her eyes, which are the eyes of our protagonist, are wide open and bewildered, but no longer take anything in. In the half-light, this mound of death seems even more improbable, for above the corpses fly helium balloons and coloured streamers, beside them stand the tables with their white cloths, the cake and other delicacies, the sweets, the sparkling wine.

The woman goes out into the street, first closing the door and putting the key back in its hiding place. And it is only then that she is overwhelmed by grief; she does not know the reason behind the crime, or if there was perhaps a clue. She reaches the park and sits down on the grass, still thinking of possible motives. She decides that she must return to the scene of the crime, she must go back in order to raise the alarm, to notify the authorities.

She reaches the white building and goes up the ten steps that separate the house from the street. She again feels with her fingers above the doorframe and she touches something rough. How is it possible? The key is covered in rust, the colour of clay, and it is now so huge that it will barely fit in the lock. Our protagonist has to struggle to manipulate it and turns the key twice before the door gives. As the rusty hinges move, they emit a piercing noise.

Once inside, the air is the colour of amber, full of ancient perfumes and thousands of dust motes quivering in the slender cones of light coming in through the shutters. The various pieces of furniture are the ghosts of a remote past, covered in long white drapes; on the floor are the remains of letters and newspapers, the occasional kitchen utensil and fragments of photographs of unfamiliar men and women. The white shapes belong to furniture that does not correspond to hers.

There are no lifeless corpses there; now there are only dead objects.

She leaves again and walks about the streets. That place is no longer her home and she does not know where to go. For a long time, she walks and walks, aimlessly. At last, she stops; she decides that she has no option but to go back.

And on her return, everything is as it was . . . the birthday party, the joyful celebration, the coloured balloons; and she thinks about what might have been but was not, about what could happen on some not so distant day, she thinks that it might perhaps be best not to go out into the street, just in case.

© Isabel del Río
Translated by Margaret Jull Costa

Countdown

ISABEL DEL RÍO

My story is a brief one, so I won't take up much of your time. Besides, there is no time, not for me at least. I haven't a minute to lose, I have no more hours to spend. And if you're prepared to grant me one final wish, let it be this: that I should be the one to give the countdown. I am the only one with the right to do it, because it's my life that you have in your hands. So instead of the usual 'Ready, aim, etc.', I will be the one to give the order and I will do so with numbers. That will be my final tribute: I will count from ten to zero, as they do for any important event. And since I will be counting backwards, I will do likewise with the events that have led me to my present situation. No, I don't want a blindfold, really, I don't want to miss the spectacle that you have organised solely for me. I'll begin. Ten, here I am before you, and you still have your rifles trained on my heart. Nine, the local judge said that I was guilty of stealing a chicken. Eight, the police found me roasting a chicken leg over a fire that I had lit next to that dusty crossroads. Seven, I caught a chicken in a farmyard and split its head in two. Six, for days I travelled the parched roads that slice the mountains into green and black segments and I ended up at a farm where, at night, I broke into the henhouse. Five, early in the morning, with my pockets empty, I left the city on foot to take a close look at what awaited me. Four, I had a different dream from the one I dream every night, and in this new dream it was revealed to me that the solution was to flee the city and to wander the countryside with no plan, no forethought. Three, I fell asleep on the desk in my office, thinking about the many reports I had to finish for the next day. Two, I drank more than I should, I talked more than I usually talk, I regretted recounting what, until then, nobody knew. One, I explained for the first time in public that every night I had the same dream, I dreamed about the violet-red wallflowers that would grow on the grave dug for me, but I never found my grave in that dream cemetery however hard I looked, that is what I dreamed, doggedly, night after night, and today I lived through the whole incident when the police dragged me along the road, grazing my knees, me still grasping a chicken leg in one hand and a greasy wing in the other because I didn't want to let go of what was going to cost me my life, and I saw that very cemetery on the outskirts of this village, I recognised the landscape of my dream – look around if you like, no need to lower your rifles – the same single cypress tree in the middle and the same fountain with the sculpture of a fallen angel, the three white crosses on one side and the two black crosses on the other, to the left a bare mountain and a grove of trees in the middle of the plain of yellow earth, and I told the police when they arrested me, I told them I'd been through all this before, in a different way, of course, but I had nevertheless been through it all before, and I spoke to them of the circle about to close and of the end that is implicit in each beginning and they said they didn't know what I was talking about and told me to shut my mouth, and that is why I decided not to defend myself when they brought me before the judge, they heard me ask him *are you killing me on account of a chicken?* and they heard him reply *we're killing you because your hour has come,* and I'm going to explain something to you who are about to kill me for whatever the reason may be, always remember this: the most valuable thing I have done in my life is to track down the landscape of that insistent dream, which is why I'm giving this countdown now, the way they do on important occasions, like I said, even though what I've found will be my ruin, and my victory will be short-lived, even though everything I have done has come to nothing, and could accurately be described, in numerical terms, as zero . . .

© Isabel del Río
Translated by Margaret Jull Costa

Isabel del Río (Madrid, 1954) spent her childhood and most of her adult life in London. She has worked as a journalist and writer in Spain and in the UK, including working at the BBC World Service. She has also worked as a literary and commercial translator and currently works as a full-time translator for a UN agency in London. *La duda*, from which 'No one' and 'The Key' were taken, was shortlisted for the New Writers' Prize and the Icarus Prize in Spain. 'Countdown' was published in *Nomad as Nómadas* (1997), a collection of short stories and poems by Spanish and Latin American writers living in London. She writes poetry and prose, in English and Spanish, and is now working on two novels and a collection of short stories.

The Little Girl Who Had No Wings

PALOMA DÍAZ-MAS

'Once upon a time, before mankind had wings . . .'

That was how all my mother's stories began when I was a
little girl: harking back to an ancient or perhaps mythical time
when mankind had not yet acquired the ability to fly. I loved
hearing those stories, and I would beg her to tell me them
over and over again, even though I knew them all off by heart:
the one about the hero who, having no wings of his own,
made himself wings out of wax and bird feathers; but when he
flew too close to the sun the wax melted and he fell into the
sea and drowned. Or the one about the man who invented a
device made of canvas and wood that enabled him to launch
himself from the tops of mountains and glide over the valleys
of his country, taking advantage of the warm air currents,
something we all do today almost instinctively, yet hearing it
recounted made it seem strange and novel, as though I myself
had just discovered a phenomenon which is so common
nowadays we don't even notice it.

Little did I know as I listened to my mother's stories that,
one day, the lack of wings was something I would experience
very close to home, and the myth of those disfigured beings
would end up becoming part of my own life.

I never felt any great maternal instinct. I remember that
when we were teenagers, a lot of my friends yearned for the
day they would become mothers; they seemed to have no
other vocation in life, and I felt profoundly irritated by their
oohs and ahs and the silly faces they pulled every time they
saw a baby; they would surround the cot or the pram cooing
like doves and eventually they would ask the mother if they
could just hold the baby for a minute in their wings. When
the mother said yes and they gathered it to their breast and

wrapped it in their flight feathers, they looked so happy that I didn't know whether to set about them for being so wet and stupid, or myself for being so detached and insensitive. It made me feel odd to see them so carried away with something that left me cold.

In time I grew to understand that there was no obligation to be a mother. So as I approached the age of forty, happily married and with a fulfilling career, I had given up the idea of having children, but it was a sort of automatic decision: quite simply, motherhood did not enter into my plans. Then I discovered I was pregnant.

From the beginning, my husband and I were surprised by the doctor's intense solicitude, his insistence on examining me and doing tests, repeating some of them with the excuse that the results had not been clear enough. We had the impression something was not right, and so it turned out: I was just beginning the third month of my pregnancy when the doctor asked us to call at his surgery and gave us two pieces of news. The first was that the baby was a girl; the second was that in all probability she would be born without wings.

I was offered the option of terminating the pregnancy, but I refused. I, who had never felt the least attraction towards the idea of motherhood, was already in love with that unknown baby girl, even though I realised she would be a burden to me all my life. She was now my daughter and I would not give her up for anything in the world.

The birth was fine, surprisingly easy. It was as though that disfigured child came into the world full of the will to live, and as though the strength she ought to have in her non-existent wings had flowed to other parts of her body, especially her limbs: even during the pregnancy I had been surprised by how hard she kicked in the womb, and the staff in attendance at the birth all noticed how strong her arms and legs were.

When they brought her to me, still covered in blood and mucus, and put her to my breast, I cuddled her in my exhausted wings and noticed how warm her naked skin was. I thought she was the most beautiful baby in the world, all pink and clean, free of that cold tangle of downy feathers that other new-born babies have. Her nakedness moved me so much that the thought even crossed my mind that, ever since humanity has had wings, we have lost the warmth of that skin-to-skin contact, because there are always hard, dusty feathers between us. Who knows whether in gaining wings we have not lost many other things, as smooth and sweet as unprotected skin.

From that day on, my little girl was the centre of my life. The first few months were no problem; after all, a normal baby has such weak little wings that it can't use them to fly or do anything else, so my daughter seemed almost normal. She fed well, was a good sleeper and very soon learned to recognise us and smile and make little noises. When she saw me going over to her cot, instead of spreading her wings she would hold out her arms to me, asking me to pick her up. Apart from that small point, she was no different from any other little girl the same age.

Naturally, as the months passed, the differences began to be more noticeable. Between eight and ten months a normal child will begin to squat, or kneel down, spread their wings and begin to beat them, getting ready for their first flight. Instead of that, my daughter used to sit up and then rock to and fro, or she would get down on her hands and knees and try to walk like a dog or a cat. My husband could not bear to see her doing this; he would say she was like an animal. Other relatives suggested I should tie her to the bed to stop her doing it. I refused to do so. I defended her right to be different, to move and express herself in a different way from us and from other children. 'She has no wings, surely she has to move as best she can?' I would say to them. But nobody understood: they would say we ought to encourage her to move like other children, that when she was older maybe her problem could be overcome with artificial wings, that although we had to accept that she was different, we should not try to make her even more so. Day by day, the confrontations with my husband, relatives and friends grew more violent. None of them seemed to see that since the baby was different, it was only logical that she should do everything in a different way.

One day, I made a wonderful discovery. I had observed from old drawings and pictures that, in the days when mankind had no wings, women would hold their babies in their arms, instead of cradling them between the wing-feathers, as we do now. I remember that it was a winter's afternoon, I was alone with my daughter and she was crawling around the living-room carpet; at a certain point she sat up and held out her arms to me. Driven by an uncontrollable impulse, I too held out my arms and clasped her, then picked her up and put her on my knee. I cannot describe the feeling that swept over me at that moment: I had my baby on my lap, and my arms encircled her, from the right and from the left; and the most surprising thing of all was that she copied me, she put her little arms round my body and the two of us sat there like that for a long time, in this new and untried posture, facing each other, body to body, she with no wings and I with mine tucked away behind me, the two of us held together only by our intertwining arms.

From then on, I always picked her up in that way. At the beginning, I did it secretly, partly from shame and partly because I did not want to provoke any more quarrels with my husband, who was finding it more and more difficult to accept our daughter; but I soon began to hold her that way all the time at home, and then, later, I even began to do it in public. The first few times it took a tremendous effort to lift the baby up into my lap, but gradually my arms grew stronger from the repetition of this action, and I would say they even took on a different shape, as if some of the muscles were developing and rounding out in order to adapt to that movement. In the long hours spent with my baby in my arms I came to understand why old paintings depicting the subject of motherhood radiate an atmosphere of tenderness, incomprehensible to us, and fail to arouse the feelings of rejection one might expect, depicting as they do relationships between disfigured beings: the mother who holds her child in her arms communicates with the child as intensely as the mother who cradles it in her wings, perhaps even more intensely. Naturally, the few times I dared to voice such an opinion everyone looked away and fell silent, as pity for another's misfortune demands.

I gave up my job and devoted myself more and more to the child. Or perhaps I should say she devoted herself to me, because in fact she showed me a whole new world, a world at ground level. Instead of flying, she would crawl on the floor; then she began to stand up and take a few steps, advancing by holding on to the furniture and managing by this means to go all over the room; when there was nothing to hold on to, she would get down on the floor and support her body on the palms of her hands. Quite unlike other children, who first of all learn to fly, and then afterwards, when their wings are strong enough, begin to walk; that way their wings act like a parachute when they take their first steps, if they feel themselves falling all they have to do is spread them. My little girl, on the other hand, learned to walk much earlier than usual, and more surprisingly still, she could do it without the help of wings; it was astonishing to see how she contrived to keep her balance despite that very difficult posture, her back held straight with nothing to counterbalance it but the movement of her arms and head. I could hardly believe it when I saw her standing up in that way, tottering forward without falling and protecting herself, if she stumbled, by putting out her arms to cushion the blow.

I got into the habit of lying on the floor to be with her. My husband would fly into a rage when he saw me like that, face down on the carpet, my wings folded like those of a butterfly and leaning on my elbows to play with my daughter. But I enjoyed seeing things from down there, as she saw them, since she was unable to take flight and land on top of the wardrobe or observe the room from a corner of the ceiling. I gradually got out of the habit of flying.

All my friends and relatives said I must keep on flying, lead a normal life, get out more, I was burying myself alive. But I paid no attention; I was completely happy.

My husband went through several phases, from anger to indifference. By the time our daughter was two, we hardly spoke to each other, in fact we were seldom home at the same time: he always had loads of work and we would only see him at weekends, invariably in a bad mood; during the week, he would get home so late that he just slipped into bed in the dark, thinking I was asleep. Soon he had to work on Saturdays as well, then go off on business trips at weekends. His mood had improved, so I knew what was going on, but I didn't say anything: I didn't want my daughter to grow up without a father-figure, even if it was a purely symbolic one. A little girl like her needed all the protection we could give her.

By the time she was two, she could speak almost fluently; she was an extraordinarily bright child and I was very proud of her. But soon afterwards my torment began.

The first sign came one night while I was bathing her. I was rubbing soap on her back and suddenly noted a small rough patch just by her right shoulder blade. I examined it, thinking that perhaps she had hurt herself: all I could see was a red mark, and I forgot all about it.

A few days later there were two red marks, symmetrically placed on either side of her back. As I touched them, I felt a swelling beneath the skin. I was scared, but I didn't want to take her to the doctor, so I just put a bit of antiseptic cream on them. A week later, things had got worse; the swellings had got bigger and were now two lumps like abscesses, inflamed and apparently painful to the touch, since she protested when I ran my fingers over the surface.

I put on a dressing, with more antiseptic cream, but it had no effect; I changed the dressings twice a day and the lumps kept growing. So I got some bandages and elastoplast and bandaged the whole of her thorax, keeping the bandages firm, but not too tight. Luckily it was winter, so nobody noticed the bandages, hidden beneath her bulky clothes.

That was no good either. The lumps were getting bigger and harder all the time, like a dislocated bone threatening to burst through the skin. I didn't know what to do, or who to turn to.

Until one day, the inevitable happened. I went to get her up that morning and I found her face down in bed, which was unlike her. Beneath the bedclothes there was a suspicious shape, and I knew what it was before I pulled back the sheets.

There they were: incipient, but developed enough for there to be no doubt. They had sprouted in the night, tearing the skin, so that the bottom sheet was slightly stained with blood. My whole world collapsed about my ears.

I knew there was only one thing for it. I picked up my child, uncovered her body and bit with all the strength of rage and desperation. A foul taste of dust and mites filled my mouth; it's unbelievable how much filth a pair of wings can pick up in one night.

She didn't seem to feel any pain. Perhaps she felt a slight discomfort, because she cried a little, then stopped almost immediately. I took her to the bathroom to clean her up, and I managed to stop the bleeding, disinfect the wound and bandage it up.

She kept the dressings on for several days, though I changed them frequently. Every time I took them off, I examined the progress of the wound. I was relieved to see that it was healing quickly and within a few weeks it had closed completely.

Now you can hardly see it. All she has is a slight invisible scar, which you only notice if you touch it, or look very closely or know it's there. She's gone back to being what she was before, and I still devote all my attention to her. If people tell me I'm burying myself alive, that I should go back to work, that I've lost my husband, that I shouldn't be so tied to her, I tell them I'm happy doing what I'm doing and that it's a mother's duty to sacrifice everything for her daughter.

© Paloma Díaz-Mas
Translated by Annella McDermott

Paloma Díaz-Mas was born in Madrid in 1954, but lives now in Vitoria, where she lectures on Spanish Literature of the Golden Age and Sephardic Literature at the University of the Basque Country. She has written scholarly articles on

Sephardic themes, a book of short stories, *Nuestro milenio* (1987) and three novels, *El rapto del Santo Grial* (1984), *Tras las huellas de Artorius* (1985) and *El sueño de Venecia* (1992; winner of the Herralde Prize). *Una ciudad llamada Eugenio* (1992) relates her experiences in the United States. This story was first published in *Madres e hijas*, ed. Laura Freixas, Anagrama, 1996.

Concerning the Death of Bieito

RAFAEL DIESTE

It was near the cemetery that I first heard poor Bieito moving inside his coffin. (There were four pallbearers, and I was one of them.) Did I hear it or was it my imagination? At the time I couldn't be sure. It was such a gentle stirring! Like the tenacious woodworm that gnaws and gnaws through the night, that quiet movement has been gnawing at my fevered imagination ever since.

The thing is, friends, I wasn't sure, and for that reason — please understand, please listen — for that reason I could not, must not, say anything.

Imagine for a moment that I was to say:

Bieito's alive.

All the heads of the old men carrying candles would go up in astonishment and alarm. All the little children catching the drips from the candles in their hands would come buzzing around me. The women would crowd round the coffin. On every lip would be a strange, amazed, murmur:

Bieito's alive, Bieito's alive.

The weeping of mother and sisters would cease, and the brass instruments of the band intoning a solemn hymn would miss a beat. And I would be the one who revealed it, the saviour, the target of everyone's amazement and gratitude. And the sun on my face would take on an unexpected significance.

Ah! But what if later, when the coffin was opened, my suspicions proved false? Their utter amazement would turn to vast, macabre ridicule. The fervent gratitude of his mother and his sisters to contempt. The hammer falling once more on the coffin would have a unique, sinister sound in the stunned afternoon. Do you see what I mean? That's why I said nothing.

There was a moment when a slight expression of surprise crossed the face of one of my fellow pallbearers, as though he too noticed the slight stirring. But it was gone in a flash. His face cleared again. So I said nothing.

There was a moment when I nearly spoke up. Turning to the man by my side, and disguising the question with an amused smile, I murmured:

'What if Bieito was alive?'

The other man laughed slyly, as though to say, 'The things you come out with!' and I deliberately widened my joker's smile.

I also came close to saying something in the cemetery, when we had placed the coffin on the ground and the priest was murmuring the prayers.

'When the priest finishes,' I thought. But the priest finished and the coffin was lowered into the grave and still I could not find the words.

When the first handful of earth, kissed by a child, fell on the wood of the coffin inside the grave, the saving words rose to my lips . . . They were on the point of coming forth. But again there came to my mind the near certainty of making a horrible fool of myself and seeing the anger of the disappointed family, if Bieito turned out to be as dead as a doornail. Moreover, speaking up at such a late stage made the whole thing immensely more grotesque. How could I explain why I hadn't spoken up earlier? I know, I know, you can always find some excuse! Yes, yes, point taken! Only . . . what if he had died afterwards, after I heard him moving, and perhaps you could tell that from some sign? Then it was a crime, yes, a crime, to have kept silent. Already I could hear the accusations:

'The poor soul was asking for help and didn't get it.'

'He heard the weeping, tried to sit up and couldn't . . .'

'He died of terror, his heart gave out when he realised he was being lowered into his grave . . .'

'Just look at the dreadful expression on his face!'

'And that idiot knew, yet he acts as if nothing had happened, grinning like a clown.'

'Is he an imbecile or what?'

All that day, friends, I felt mad with remorse. I could see poor Bieito clawing at the coffin lid with the absolute terror, beyond consolation or resignation, of someone buried alive. I even began to think that everyone could read in my bleary, distant eyes my obsession with the crime.

So when it got to around midnight – I couldn't help it – I set off for the cemetery, with my collar turned up and keeping close to the shadow of the walls.

I arrived. On one side the wall was low: loose stones, held together by ivy and brambles. I jumped over and went straight to the place . . . I lay down, put my ear to the ground and what I heard immediately froze my blood. From deep in the earth, desperate nails were scratching at wood. Scratching? I don't know, I don't know. Nearby there was a hoe . . . I was just about to pick it up when I suddenly stopped. I could hear foot steps and the sound of voices on the path near the cemetery. There were people coming. In which case my presence there, at that hour and with a hoe in my hand, really would seem absurd, mad.

Was I to tell them I had let him be buried knowing he was alive?

I fled with my collar still turned up and keeping close to the shadow of the walls.

There was a full moon and dogs were barking in the distance.

© Carmen Muñoz Manzano Vda de Dieste
Translated by Annella McDermott

Rafael Dieste (Rianxo [A Coruña], 1899–Rianxo, 1981) was from the region of Galicia in northwestern Spain. He was a writer and philosopher, who, as well as poetry, short stories, plays and novels, published newspaper articles and books on mathematics and philosophy. A staunch supporter of the Galician language, he himself wrote both in Galician and Spanish, the latter probably in response to the fact that he spent a considerable part of his life outside Galicia. In 1939, following the Spanish Civil War, he moved first of all to Paris and eventually to Buenos Aires, where he lived in exile until 1961. Strongly influenced by the ideas of Tolstoy, he was attracted by the folk culture of Galicia, in which magical beliefs play a prominent role. Dieste's best-known works are *Dos arquivos do trasno* (1926), from which this story is taken, and *Historias e invenciones de Félix Muriel* (1943).

How My Six Cats Died

WENCESLAO FERNÁNDEZ FLÓREZ

Hermann Keyserling has written a book, *Immortality*, in which he suggests that there exists around us a supernatural world of which we are unware because we lack the necessary means of perception. I'm convinced that Keyserling is right and would even add my own unanswerable arguments to his. One of the enjoyable advantages of neurasthenia is precisely the ability it gives one to catch sight of many strange beings. One cannot always see them, but one can hear and, in some measure, feel them. More than once, while writing late into the night, in the silent solitude of my study, I've had the vivid impression that an invisible being was reading over my shoulder the very words that I was writing. This has never frightened me; I experienced only the uncomfortable feeling that I was being spied upon. When this happens, I usually pick up a piece of paper and scribble on it: 'Would you be so kind as to stop bothering me?' The invisible being disappears at once. I describe this experience because I know that a lot of people are troubled, in similar circumstances, by the same feeling of being watched.

Indeed, sometimes, you can even see them. You only get a brief look and there's nothing terrifying about it, as the cowardly might imagine. Sometimes, you see only lights, different-coloured lights.

Some people see birds; others, vague, shapeless shadows. I see only cats. For me the world of the unknown is populated with cats. They slink rapidly past, though only when I can just glimpse them out of the corner of my eye. They emerge out of one thick wall and disappear through another, or they suddenly appear at my feet. I stop and look and . . . there's nothing there.

They have never bothered me and I have absolutely nothing

to reproach them with. I love cats and it does not displease me to see them padding lightly across a room, even if they are mere ghosts.

Only once did they cause me any distress, but the cats in question were real, living, tangible cats.

This is what happened:

Guitián, my servant, told me that the cat had had six kittens.

'Too many,' I said.

'Too many,' he agreed. 'I wish I could say the same about the cow. The world really isn't very well organised. What shall we do with the creatures?'

'I don't know.'

'We'll have to kill them.'

'Poor things!'

Guitián raised his thick eyebrows:

'I don't like it any more than you do, sir. I certainly couldn't bring myself to kill them.'

I said decisively:

'We'll give the matter some thought, Guitián.'

And a month and a half passed. My servant complained:

'I don't know how to get rid of the wretched brood. Together they eat enough for two whole people and they're always getting under my feet. I've tried to give them away, but nobody wants them. In other places, people just throw them into the sea, but there isn't any sea here, not even a deep river.'

I had an idea.

'Take them into the mountains and leave them there.'

'All right,' he said.

And one morning, he went out with the six cats in a basket. He walked for more than a league and clapped his hands loudly to frighten them away. The little creatures raced off, tails bristling, and stopped at a prudent distance. In the end, he drove them into a maize field.

Then, thinking he could not be seen, he slung the basket over his arm and returned home with a light step. Along the way, he heard the busy rustle of shaken maize leaves. Guitián thought:

'They're following me.'

And he started running as fast as he could. Breathing hard, he stopped at the gate to our house and wiped away the abundant sweat from his brow. At that moment, from amongst a clump of wallflowers, a cat appeared before him, then another, and, finally, all six of them. And they started to miaow hungrily.

My servant was sunk in gloom for several days. One day, I saw him digging a ditch by the garden wall. He looked at me with furrowed brow and said:

'Today's the day.'

After supper, he came into my room. He stood silently before me, his lips set in a hard line; he kept rubbing his hands together nervously, mechanically, as if trying to wipe them clean of some disgusting substance.

'It's done!' he said.

He was deathly pale and, although he tried to smile, it was evident that some hideous, painful emotion was beating inside him. I thought he was going to fill me in on the details of the cats' execution, out of that need to confide that all criminals feel, so I hurriedly said:

'Don't tell me anything.'

He nodded and left. He may have committed that cruel deed, but . . . he was a good man.

The following day, when I was taking my morning stroll about the garden, I seemed to hear a faint mewing. I remembered the poor murdered creatures and I listened.

'It's pure obsession,' I said to myself.

And I continued my walk. Without intending to go there, I found myself near the wall, where the dug earth indicated the place where the six corpses had been buried. And then I heard the mewing again, quite distinctly.

I stopped, horrified. I heard more mewing.

I ran to find Guitián. I found him in the kitchen, his head in his hands and his hair all dishevelled.

'Guitián!' I cried.

He raised a distraught face to me.

'Guitián, there's a cat mewing underneath the earth in the flower border.'

He gave a crazed smile.

'It isn't a cat, sir.'

'Not a cat?'

'It's six cats. All six of them are mewing. I heard them too.'

He looked around him with a shudder. For a moment, I was dumbstruck.

'What have you done, Guitián?'

He made a vague, despairing gesture.

'I think I have lost my soul, sir.'

Quietly, he told me his story. He had lacked the courage to kill them. He put them in the basket to carry them to their grave and, to cut short his cruel task, he threw the basket into the grave and piled up earth on top of it.

'Was the basket closed?'

'Of course! If it was open, they would escape.'

'So they're alive inside the basket.'

'They are, sir.'

And, appalled, we both looked away.

★ ★ ★

Twenty-four hours later, the kittens were still mewing. To know this, I had only to look at Guitián, who was walking sombrely up and down in the remotest part of the garden.

'They're still there then?' I asked.

And he stopped, with his hands behind his back, and gave me a strange, hard look.

'Can't you hear them?' he replied. 'Is there a loud enough noise anywhere in the world to drown out the noise those poor wretches make? There are only five of them calling now; but the sound of their complaints reaches every corner. I hear them even with the sheets pulled up over my head, even if I move right away from the garden, even if I'm grinding coffee in the old coffee mill . . .'

There was a pause.

'You say there are only five of them now.'

'Yes, only five.'

'What happened to the sixth?'

He came over to me, eyes bulging, and said:

'They've eaten it, sir. I'm sure of it. They must have drawn lots. After the shipwreck of the *Arosa*, those of us still on the raft had to draw lots too . . .'

A generous soul! He was trembling with fever.

Maybe it was just his words that put the idea in my head, but, from then on, I too could hear the cats miaowing in every room, everywhere. I imagined them writhing around inside the crushed basket, their fur on end, their eyes shining fiercely in the thick darkness, besmirched by the earth that seeped in through the cracks.

Four days later, they were still calling. Guitián had lost so much weight that his clogs no longer fitted him. I sought him out in the corner of the kitchen where he went to be alone with his remorse. He was counting the cats as they stopped their mewing.

'There are two left. We must suffer for another forty-eight hours.'

And the following dawn:

'There's one left. Tomorrow . . . it will all be over.'

As soon as day broke, we ran out into the garden. A cat, a single cat was still mewing sadly, a tiny, mournful, heart-rending sound.

And it continued to do so for another day and another, for a week . . . Against all logic, its cries grew in volume. It was no longer like the crying of a newborn babe, heard through the wall. Sometimes, it was the furious miaowing of an angry tomcat and, at others, the long, plaintive, per-suasive call they utter beneath the January moon, when they are trying to convince some female cat to surrender to love.

Our sense of horror was mounting steadily. We were living through some ghastly tale by Edgar Allen Poe. My servant had said to me:

'This will end badly, sir.'

We were, indeed, convinced that the whole sad story would end in catastrophe, an outcome that we could sense only confusedly.

One afternoon, as we were walking along the road – we

127

avoided the house and garden as much as possible – I said to the melancholy skeleton at my side:

'Guitián, I can't understand how the poor creature' (we spoke of it with compassion and affection) 'can still survive. It was buried almost a month ago; even if some air were still getting through, what can it eat? No animal could last that long in those conditions.'

'It's eating its own tail, sir.'

'Its own tail?'

'As you know, cats' tails keep growing, especially when they're young, like the poor creature in there. It will eat a little each day and each day another bit will grow.'

'That's ridiculous, Guitián.'

'What else can the poor wretch do, sir?'

'Guitián.'

'Yes, sir.'

'We've got to do something . . .'

'What?'

'We've got to . . . finish the creature off.'

'But how?'

'We'll tamp down the earth covering its body.'

'I don't know if I've got it in me to do that.'

'I'll help you. Shall we do it now?'

He drew one hand across his brow, and said:

'Yes, let's finish it.'

We ran to the garden. In the toolshed we found the tamper that was used to smooth the paths, and we carried it off to the terrible, familiar place by the garden wall.

I fell back a little, shaken by some vague, supernatural idea.

'Go on then!' I ordered.

The man lifted the tamper, still uncertain.

'Go on!' I shouted boldly.

And the heavy instrument fell upon the earth with a dull thud. His eyes wild, his mouth set in a grimace, Guitián rained down blows on the earth, all the while crying:

'Forgive me, forgive me, poor creature! Unlucky martyr, more martyred than all the martyrs put together! Forgive me, forgive me! Please die! I'm killing you for your own good, poor, sad creature. I'm only following my master's orders!'

I had to flee the scene, because I thought I might go mad.

★ ★ ★

From that moment, the cat miaowed more obstinately and furiously than ever.

A devastated Guitián came to me and said:

'Sir, I've come to say goodbye.'

I nodded.

'I understand, my faithful friend, I understand. This torment has become unbearable.'

'If you mean the miaowing of the six cats – because now the six of them have started up again – I've some good news for you. In half an hour, they can miaow all they like, because I won't hear them.'

'Are you leaving the village?'

'I'm going to kill myself, sir. I can't stand it any longer. They have poisoned my life, as the priest said when the doctors forbade him to have more than six helpings at mealtimes. I just wanted to ask you if you would mind very much if I hanged myself from that chestnut tree near the gate. It doesn't really matter to me which tree I use, but that one is the strongest.'

'My friend,' I said, moved, 'choose whichever tree you like, even the peach tree, although you know how badly it reacts to having its branches broken. But since it's you . . . Before I let you do it, though, I have a proposal.'

'There's nothing more to be done.'

'Let's fight one last battle.'

'No. Goodbye, sir. Enjoy life . . . if you can.'

He left.

'Guitián,' I shouted from the gate, 'we've got one final card to play.'

'What's that?'

'Why don't we dig them up?'

He hesitated for a moment. Then I dragged him with me and placed a hoe in his hand. The miaowing was more

129

terrifying than ever, like a spine-chilling concerto. We dug and dug . . . We thought we would encounter monstrous, shapeless creatures covered in earth, their eyes too . . . We dug and dug . . .

The hoe struck the crumbling, rotten basket.

We dug again.

And there was the small, jumbled pile of cats, their bodies beginning to mingle with the earth. They were all quite dead, putrefying and . . . silent.

Translated by Margaret Jull Costa

Wenceslao Fernández Flórez (La Coruña, 1885 – Madrid, 1964) started out as a journalist on various Galician newspapers and then moved to Madrid where he achieved fame with his chronicles of parliamentary life: *Acotaciones de un oyente* published in the Madrid newspaper *ABC*. His books – including *Volvoreta* (1917), *El secreto de Barba Azul* (1923) and *Las siete columnas* (1926) – were immensely popular in their day, though his work is now little known. His many incursions into the world of the fantastic produced a large number of remarkable short stories and novels, including *La casa de la lluvia* (1925), *Fantasmas* (1930) and *El bosque animado* (1943). This story is taken from *Visiones de neurastenia* (1924).

How the Tailor Bieito Returned to Hell

ÁNXEL FOLE

I hope my readers will forgive me if I write Hell with a capital H. I also write Devil, Cemetery and Cathedral with capitals, just to be different. We so rarely use capital letters. Of a gentleman whose surname was Carballo, but who wrote it Carvallo, they say he did so in order to save on ink.

Now I chanced to find myself in the town of Ferreira in 1945, the year that the Second World War ended. Everyone was talking about what had happened. When the new grave-digger set about opening a niche in the Cemetery, he had nearly had to demolish the tomb next to it. He had to lay it completely open. And . . .

To his great surprise, he saw that in the tomb to the right there was a skeleton lying outside the coffin . . . and the coffin was empty. The frontal bone of the skull was caved in and two ribs were broken. Otherwise, the skeleton was that of a small man.

The gravedigger reported the case to the mayor and the mayor imparted the news to the Investigating Magistrate who immediately ordered an official investigation.

Incidentally, calling the town Ferreira is a mere convention. It could just as easily be Monforte, Ribadavia or Orense.

According to records in the Municipal Archive, the remains belonged to a man who had been buried in 1918, at the time of the flu epidemic, and the gravedigger was nicknamed Foulmouth because he was always cursing.

With that sparse information, I began my investigation, and my stay in Ferreira lasted for three months. When I finished, I wrote a report which I sent to the Royal Academy of History. But the years passed and I received no reply from the Academy, not even a word, either directly or indirectly, which forced me to conclude that the Academy must think me mad.

The reader will be aware that during the 1918 flu epidemic gravediggers and undertakers had a great deal of work to do, as did the doctors, the priests and the pharmacists.

In 1918, for example, in Lugo, the gravediggers would normally bury two people a day, but a month and a half into the epidemic, they were burying twelve or fourteen a day. In Ferreira it was much the same.

★ ★ ★ ★

Bieito Fernández was the hardest-working tailor in Ferreira. According to the rumourmongers, he had grown rich, indeed very rich, by lending money at twelve per cent interest. He had given his children a good start in life: he had four sons and one daughter. The eldest son was studying medicine in Santiago and one day brought a musical group composed of fellow students on a visit to Ferreira, and was even feted by the mayor. He was feted for his good looks too, which he got from his mother.

Bieito was positively drooling, as they say, when he saw Bieito Junior leaving the local social club in the company of the notary's son and the nephew of the owner of the local hotel.

His mother would ask him who he had danced with at the club. Was it that nice blonde girl: the daughter of the Secretary to the Town Hall, or the girl from the corner shop whose father had made more than two million *reales* exporting chestnuts and hams to France?

Bieito Junior's father was definitely drooling.

Then in 1918, the flu epidemic started and carried off thousands to the next world. The gravedigger, Foulmouth, couldn't cope with all the graves he had to dig.

They called him Foulmouth because he didn't have a good word to say about anyone. When a monk was buried, he was told that the man had died 'in the odour of sanctity'; Foulmouth replied that he had buried him himself and that the monk had stunk to high heaven.

'He reeked of rotting flesh, just like everyone else.'

One day, during the time of the epidemic, he had to dig seven graves. He went to the mayor and said:

'Look, Don Juan, I can't cope with all this work and I get paid a pittance. You'd better make my eldest son my assistant; he's seventeen now.'

The mayor deemed his request to be a fair one.

'So be it. You shall each wear a peaked cap bearing an 'M' and an 'S' standing for Municipal Services, because you both serve the municipality.'

Foulmouth showed his teeth and smiled much as a gorilla might smile. There wasn't an uglier man for twenty leagues around. He had a short, fat neck.

Once, a man said to him: 'You haven't got much to thank God for' and Foulmouth stabbed him and almost killed him.

If the father was proud of the cap he had to wear, his son, Benjamín, was even prouder. He would go into the taverns just to show it off. When he arrived, the other boys would cover their noses with their hands, and when he left, they would say: 'Foulmouth's son stinks of rotting flesh.'

Everyone in Ferreira knew that the tailor Bieito had fallen ill with the flu and that it had turned into pneumonia. He died one Wednesday.

Foulmouth had it in for him, probably because Bieito had taken him to court once over some money he owed him for a suit he had made.

They buried him on the Thursday. He was laid out at home for just twenty-four hours.

Some said:

'There's never been a better year for doctors, priests and pharmacists.'

Foulmouth and Benjamín buried the pharmacist first. While they were covering him with spadefuls of earth, the gravedigger said:

'You could have kept a whole family on what this greedy pig shelled out on cakes. I hope he spends the next hundred years in Purgatory.'

Then came the body of the tailor Bieito. The cortège consisted only of the priest, the altar boy and about twenty or so followers. The gravedigger rubbed his hands and smiled. The priest read the prayer for the dead and blessed

133

the earth that the gravedigger and his son were throwing onto the coffin.

At that same moment, they noticed a great cloud of smoke in the sky. A little boy appeared at the Cemetery gates shouting:

'The priest's house is burning down!'

When the priest heard those words, he took off his chasuble and stood there in his robe, yelling:

'I just hope that jar of notes I left on the mantelpiece hasn't caught fire.'

And with that he bounded off, leaping over the graves. There was no one left in the Cemetery.

Foulmouth was roaring with laughter.

'It would just serve that old moneylender right as well, if all his thousand *real* notes burned up. He did nothing but hoard them all his life.'

Father and son picked up the wine bottle and each took a long swig.

'Your turn now, tailor. We don't want you complaining that you haven't got enough earth on you.'

The same boy who had come to the Cemetery gates before, shouted:

'It's Raposa's oven that's on fire!'

But, by then, the Cemetery was empty.

When the gravedigger picked up the hoe, he saw that Bieito had got out of his coffin.

'I thought you were supposed to be dead, tailor. Everyone they bring here has got to be properly dead.'

'With a certificate signed by the relevant authority,' added his son.

Bieito said in a plaintive voice:

'Would you mind very much explaining to me what's going on? What am I doing here wearing a Franciscan habit?'

'We haven't got time for explanations, we've got too much work to do. We still have a lot of other unfortunates to bury.'

But the son saw things differently and he asked Bieito:

'Have you got a certificate from Satan to say you've been

resuscitated? Because if you haven't, there's nothing we can do. It's back into the grave with you.'

'Can't you see I'm alive?'

'Alive? You got the flu which developed into pneumonia and you died. Or do you think you know more than the doctor who wrote out your death certificate?'

And he dealt Bieito such a blow on the head with the hoe that he split his head open.

'Finish him off, Benjamín, finish him off.'

'I'm an obedient son, so I will.'

And he hit Bieito so hard that he crushed his skull and his brains spilled out.

'Now cover him up with plenty of earth, that's it.'

I certainly had my work cut out for me, thanks to that wretch Foulmouth.

Anxel Fole (Lugo, 1903 – Lugo, 1986) was a writer and journalist and, until the outbreak of Civil War in 1936, worked with the Partido Galleguista (the Galician party). His writing is steeped in the world of rural Galicia and his stories are often retellings of stories he himself was told: tales of rural grotesques, ghosts, mysteries and premonitions. He wrote in both Galician and Castilian, his best-known works being: *A lús do candil* (1953), *Terra brava* (1955) *Contos da néboa* (1973) and *Histórias que ninguén cré* (1981). This story was originally published in Galician as 'De como o xastre Bieito volveu pro inferno' in *Contos da néboa* (1973).

A Face

PERE GIMFERRER

Supper was served at ten beneath the solemn gold of the candelabra. The six of us sat down at the table. Everything, the china, the gleaming cutlery, ourselves, had its double in the glass table top. I was the first to notice that the sinister pane of glass reflected back at us not six faces but seven. The intruding face was situated to the right, slightly towards the centre, between Miguel and Mercedes. It could have been there for several days. The glass hadn't been cleaned since Saturday, we had no proof – the maid was new – that the cleaning had been carried out particularly thoroughly, and we all know how easy it is to eat mechanically, not once, but many times, without pausing to look for your double in the glass. So it was perfectly possible that the face had been there for five or six days. Other questions arose: had it been there for twenty-four hours every day? during that time had its position at the table varied? had the face been different every day? Not forgetting, of course, the most immediate and obvious questions: the identity of the face and the reason for its unusual presence there. I think the moment has come to describe the object of our questions. The face could have been about thirty or thirty-five. Everything about it bespoke serenity or, rather, indifference. Its regular features belonged to an individual of the male gender. It had blond hair. Beneath the arch of the eyebrows, you could just make out a pair of dark eyes. Was it looking at us? I moved my hand in front of the face; it took no notice. Perhaps it was pretending. I did not dare to touch it, even though I knew that to do so might make it disappear. After all, it was a living face. Removing the glass would be another solution, though I was quick to see that it would be a false one. The face might remain stuck to the glass or rise up from the bare table. I found neither of those two possibilities to my liking, not to mention the awful sense of mutilation that would mark any such ceremony. Anyway, the face did not appear to be hostile. It clearly wanted nothing from us – if indeed it had even noticed our presence – only to remain in the place where, to our astonishment, we had found it. We would have to move our supper to the drawing-room. I hesitated for a moment on the threshold: obviously we would have to close the door, but I felt uneasy about switching off all the lights. The thought that this otherwise harmless measure might put the face to flight prompted me instead to abandon it to the half-light. That was a mistake, for, night after night, it remained on the glass. For us, eating in the drawing-room became a habit. Eventually, we abandoned the dining room – almost always closed and in darkness – to the face. The last time I went in there, I didn't actually see it. Dust had accumulated on the table, forming the kind of vegetation you normally find under beds. Grown accustomed to the dark, the dining room seemed strangely opaque. In that neglected, dirty state, there was a wildness about it. Maybe the face isn't even there any more.

© Pere Gimferrer
Translated by Margaret Jull Costa

Pere Gimferrer (Barcelona, 1945) published two books of poetry in Castilian – *Arde el mar* (1966), for which he won the Premio Nacional de Poesía, and *La muerte en Beverley Hills* (1968). Subsequently he has written exclusively in Catalan, translating his own work into Castilian. His novel *Fortuny* won the Spanish Critics' Prize in 1983. Amongst his publications since then are *Mascarada* (1996) and *L'agent provocador* (1998). He has also written a book of film criticism as well as essays on Magritte, Ernst, Miró, Toulouse-Lautrec and De Chirico (published in English by Academy Editions). 'A Face' is one of five stories in the fantastic genre which he wrote in 1965, four of them published in the magazine *Papeles de Son Armadans* and one in the literary review *Ínsula*.

The Stork-men

JUAN GOYTISOLO

I'm a fan of magic realism, an avid reader of García Márquez, Isabel Allende and their illustrious followers. I love novels and stories that are rich in fantastical characters and fabulous happenings: wise grandmothers, blood falling as rain, flying children, galleons mysteriously stranded amidst the greenery of the virgin jungle. These 'romans de pays chauds', as they were labelled by one defender of outmoded, anaemic literary values, represent fresh energy and vitality, and bring an element of poetry into the prosaic narrowness of our lives. So, when I heard the tale of the *Thousand Minus One Nights* of my esteemed colleague from the Circle, with its reference to the stork's nest next to the little house Eusebio rented in the Alcazaba district, by the *mechouar*, I recalled certain paragraphs by my fellow Spaniard, Alí Bey, on the subject of these migratory waders whose company he enjoyed in Marrakech thanks to the Sultan's credulity.

According to an old Moroccan tradition, Berber peasants believe that storks are human beings who adopt that form temporarily in order to travel and experience other lands, and then, when they return to their own country, they recover their original shape. So, on my arrival in Marrakech in pursuit of the elusive Eusebio, I decided to abandon risky and fruitless enquiries, and with the help of the historian Hamid Triki I made my way to the ancient stork refuge next to the Mosque of Ibn Yusef.

After a great deal of searching and asking for directions, I came upon Dar Belarx and managed to find the guide. Encouraged by my generous tip, he produced a bunch of keys and led me through a side door, along a gloomy corridor and into a large, magnificent patio, though dirty and neglected. Heaps of rubble covered the central area, adorned with a fountain; but the fine arcades, the mouldings in the side rooms and the tile friezes had resisted the ravages of time. There were piles of feathers and pigeon droppings, and even the recent corpse of one of those birds, attracted, like her companions, by the silence and benevolence of the spot. The refuge had been closed up a century earlier, on the death of a grandson of its founder.

I mentioned to my escort the legend of the stork-men. To my great surprise, he corrected my terminology. It was no legend, but the absolute truth. He himself knew someone who emigrated in that fashion to Europe and returned home a few months later, having recovered his former shape. The man lived in that very alley, and my guide needed no prompting to introduce me to him.

The quick-change artist – how else to describe him? – was a placid, serene old man, of a very similar appearance to the one my colleagues have attributed to Eusebio, with intensely blue eyes and a carefully-tended white beard, sitting at the door of his house, his right hand resting on the handle of his stick. To avoid any boring preamble I will let him tell his own story; I don't know if it's true, or his own invention, or taken from folklore.

'Some forty years ago, my wife – may she be with God! – managed to get a contract to work in a thread mill in France and so she emigrated in order to improve our modest fortunes, leaving me behind to take care of the children. At first, we received regular news of her, together with a postal order representing her savings for the month; but gradually the money began to arrive on its own, with no accompanying letter. This strange, long silence, pregnant with fears and doubts, plunged me into a profound melancholy. My own letters went unanswered; as did my requests for her to telephone. I wrote enquiring after her to a neighbour who had also gone to work in a thread mill in the same area. Her laconic telegram – 'all well your wife working' – far from dispelling my unease, only increased it. If all was so well, why the silence? Had she forgotten her position as wife and mother of four children? At night I would toss and turn in my bed, unable to sleep. Meanwhile, the chances of getting a passport had decreased: the economic crisis and unemployment in the Christian countries meant all doors were closed to foreigners, and the French consulate did not issue tourist visas to poor artisans like me: a humble cobbler. They asked me for a bank reference and goodness knows what else. In short: I had to give up the idea. But I still yearned to make the trip and one day, as I was gazing at the storks nesting on the top of the walls of the royal palace, I thought to myself, if only I could be like them and fly to where my wife is working in her thread mill in faraway Épinal. As though led by a presentiment, I went to see my eldest brother: I told him I had decided to go to Europe and I gave him temporary charge of the care and education of my children. That uneasy period of my life came to a sudden end.

The next day, I was on my way with a flight of storks, in a state of bliss and delight difficult to express in words. The world was both tiny and immense: landscapes and towns like toys, seas glinting like mirrors, white mountains . . . Height, weightlessness, speed of movement, made me feel superior to humans, slow as tortoises, tiny as insects. I was flying with a sense of utter happiness towards the prosperous and enlightened continent from which Christians had ventured forth in order, apparently, to educate us, and incidentally offer us work, distracted by the rapture of soaring from the precise purpose of my journey. Those were weeks of freedom and contentment, untrammelled by borders and official stamps. Carrying no papers of any kind, we crossed the boundaries of separate territories, we broke their petty laws, eluded customs barriers and police checks, laughed at the mean discrimination represented by visas. Once we had passed a huge chain of mountains, covered with snow like the Atlas range, the view changed: the fields were greener, woods more frequent and thicker, the towns with ochre tiles gave way to others with roofs of grey slate. We were following the course of a river on whose banks stood cities and factories. A few days later, after many a long day's flight, halting by night on towers and belfries, I felt my drive weaken, I could not keep up with my companions, I was falling hopelessly behind, I could scarcely move my wings. Unable even to hover, I nearly plummeted to the ground, but landed as best I could in a garden.

My appearance startled the owner of the house, a Frenchman of about forty who was pruning some trees and trimming the lawn with shears. 'Look, Aicha, a stork,' he cried. The name of my beloved wife set my heart fluttering wildly. Who was this fellow, and how dare he address her so intimately? When she appeared at the door, I was ready to faint. I kept staring at her and my eyes flooded with tears. 'That's incredible,' she said in French. 'There are lots of them in my country. I'm sure that's where it's come from.' She came over to me, without recognising me, and stroked my feathers. 'How tame it is! It has probably fallen ill and can't fly on. I'm going to take care of it and feed it raw fish. Where I come from they say it brings good luck; it's a guest out of the blue and it deserves our respect and hospitality.'

Aicha's sweet, welcoming words, instead of easing my pain, increased it. Her use of 'our' and her obvious intimacy with the man confirmed my suspicions: she was living with him as man and wife, sharing his bed and table. Still bewildered, and full of bitterness, I wondered whether they had children. I was afraid I might hear a baby crying, and I scrutinised the washing line, fortunately without spotting any nappies or baby clothes. But the sense of superiority and pride I had previously felt, up in the sky, gave way to feelings of impotence and rage. I was two steps away from my wife and her lover, incapable of responding to her adultery, with my awkward wader's movements and my discordant squawks. The affection and maternal instinct Aicha showed, her eagerness to care for me, choose my food, build me a kind of nest on the roof of a shed, degraded, rather than exalted, my temporary status as a bird. The sight of me reminded her of home, she covered me with kisses and caresses, but at night when they both came back from work – she from her thread mill, he from a branch of a major bank – they would go inside and close the door, leaving me standing one-legged on my nest.

After the first weeks of sadness, I grew bolder: I resolved to go on the offensive. I left my wretched nest and, without further ado, stalked into the house. At first, the intruder tried to shoo me away, but she stopped him.

'This stork is a blessed creature which reminds me of everything I left behind. If it wants to live in the house it shall live in the house. God sent it to us, his will be done.'

The fellow oozed bad temper. 'That's all very poetic, but who's going to clean up its droppings?'

'I will! Haven't I told you a thousand times it's a sacred animal?'

He muttered something about India and its sacred cows, she shrugged her shoulders and got her own way. From now on, if I wanted, I would share their home day and night.

The new situation brought about by my wife's energy and determination favoured my plans for revenge. Taking advantage of their absence during working hours, I rifled through the drawers and poked around in every corner of the house; I discovered that Aicha treasured her children's photos, paid her entire wages into a savings account and regularly sent a proportion of this money to my address. The shopping – including the fish and maggots intended for me – and the gas and electricity bills, were all paid by the intruder. This evidence of provision for our future, together with her kindness towards me, made me bolder: I increased the frequency with which I soiled objects and garments belonging to the intruder; I parked myself on their bed.

As I had hoped, the rows and domestic quarrels got worse.

'Surely you're not going to let it dirty the sheets!'

'If she does, I'll wash them. (She often referred to me in the feminine.) The poor soul, she's had a long journey, then she fell ill, and she feels comfortable here, she's part of the family.'

I pretended to give in to the fellow's irritation, and surrendered the field in a dignified manner. I waited till they had turned off the light and he had begun to move around and touch her, then I hopped onto the bedspread and soiled it. He immediately snapped on the bedside light.

'Right, that's it! This time it's gone too far! Enough is enough!'

'If you so much as touch a feather on that bird, you'll be sorry! If you must know, I'm tired of you mauling me. I just want to get to sleep!'

'If you want to sleep, sleep, but not with that creature. I've told you a thousand times, I can't stand it.'

'In that case, go and sleep on the sofa. I'm staying here.'

'Honestly, anyone would think you were married to it. Ever since it arrived, you've been behaving oddly. These mad ideas and superstitions may be all very well where you come from, but they don't suit a modern, civilised nation.'

'My country is better than yours, do you hear? This stork belongs to me, and if you don't like it, I'll leave and that'll be that.'

From then on, there were quarrels every day. I wanted to sleep on the bed with my wife, and the intruder was beginning to give in and migrate to the sofa. I could feel that Aicha preferred me and was thinking about me. Sometimes she would sit at the kitchen table and write letters home, to the house next to the stork refuge founded centuries ago. She and the *nsrani* fought like cat and dog. When she was out, I would fly to the roof of the shed and take up my position on the nest. I feared the intruder might slit my throat with a knife, or club me to death. My success was reassuring and I began to recover my pleasure in flying. One day, after swallowing my ration of fish, I bade a silent goodbye to Aicha, waited till my flock came into view, joined them and began the flight back to Marrakech.

As soon as I arrived there, I regained my human form. I turned up at my house as though I had only just left it and embraced my children. My brother had taken good care of them, they were attending school, and they danced for joy to see me. Beside the clock in my bedroom there was a pile of letters from Aicha. They spoke of the stork's visit, of her deep longing for her homeland and her family. She was still working in the thread mill in order to save enough to buy a little business on her return. When she did return, two years later, she was radiant with joy and came loaded down with presents. I forgave her, of course I forgave her: I forgot her betrayal and

144

lived happily with her until God called her to His side and we buried her in Bab Dukala.

I never told her about my visit, nor did I tell anyone else, except one neighbour and also a gentleman of European origin living in the neighbourhood, whose Moroccan friend was killed in a traffic accident and who ever since then had withdrawn from the world; he wrote poetry and in the evenings would go and sit quietly in the Mosque of Ibn Yusef. His name was Eusebio.

I remember that he listened to me attentively and then he wrote down word for word the same story that I have just related to you.'

© Juan Goytisolo
Translated by Annella McDermott

Juan Goytisolo (Barcelona, 1931), essayist, travel writer and novelist, is probably the best-known Spanish writer and intellectual commentator of today, though he has spent long periods living out of Spain, initially in Paris, from 1957 onwards, and latterly in both Paris and Marrakech. Some of the defining traits of his personality as a writer have been his left-wing politics, his discovery and exploration of his homosexuality and his great love of North African culture. A large number of Goytisolo's books are available in English: Serpent's Tail have published, amongst others, *Landscapes After the Battle* (1987; tr. Helen Lane) and *Marks of Identity* (1988; tr. Gregory Rabassa), Quartet *Realms of Strife* (1990; tr. Peter Bush) and *Saracen Chronicles* (1992; tr. Helen Lane), and Faber *The Marx Family Saga* (1996, tr. Peter Bush). This story is taken from *Las semanas del jardín* (1997; an English translation by Peter Bush is to be published soon by Serpent's Tail).

The Shooting Gallery

ALBERTO INSÚA

The shooting gallery was located in the stern, to starboard: a brilliantly lit wooden stall painted with red and green stripes. The hollow eggs, glass butterflies and clay pipes went round and round in front of the black backcloth. For target shooters, there were two sets of those horizontal zinc tubes with bits of cardboard at the end, which always look like telescopes that have swallowed a star. A blue-and-yellow celluloid ball bobbed up and down on the plume of water spouting from a fountain. There was a cutout skeleton that performed a ghostly, dislocated tarantella when hit between the eye sockets. A black woman, made out of cardboard, writhed about like Josephine Baker when a bullet struck her belly button. There were other dolls as well . . .

A man and a woman, dressed up like circus sharpshooters, were loading the pistols and rifles. That was where Arcadio found Prince Emilio. He was the one who, to the great admiration of onlookers, never failed to shatter the hollow eggs, the glass butterflies and the clay pipes. He was a superb shot, the bullet seemed to follow his eye exactly. And he stood and moved so elegantly. Now he was taking on the skeleton. Arcadio went over to the stall. The Prince aimed, fired and the mechanism broke into a crazy dance of vertebrae and bones. Everyone applauded and laughed. Then the man who ran the stall pressed a button and restored everything to its proper place. La Molinari was at the Prince's side, exclaiming enthusiastically:

'That's amazing! I've never seen anyone shoot better than that.'

And the Prince replied modestly:

'Mere child's play, Lina.'

'Now try and hit the black woman.'

'All right.'

The Prince hit the black woman in the navel and the black woman danced. There was applause and loud laughter. Suddenly, though, the Prince turned pale, and the hand holding the pistol shook. Amongst the 'audience' he had just spotted the ironic gaze of Strong. The Prince turned from white to scarlet, and the mocking curl of his lips became an angry scowl.

'Come on, set up the targets, quickly!'

They loaded a rifle for him. He fired, once, twice, several times, aiming through the tube at the cardboard rectangle. The shots reverberated in the metal chamber with a thunderous roar.

'Bring it over here.'

The man pushed the target round on some rails. There was a crown of holes and, in the middle, a cross. The Prince, deaf to the applause and oblivious to the kiss blown to him by La Molinari, took the target and held it up against the light so that everyone could see the perfection of the design he had made with the bullet holes; holding it out to the blond gentleman, he said:

'Could you do the same?'

It was a challenge. Arcadio feared for the Prince. The Prince's eyes blazed, but the look in Strong's eyes was purely and simply one of pity. Everyone awaited the Englishman's response. Anxiously. Everyone had sensed that there was some kind of duel or drama going on between the two men. The wheel stopped abruptly, as did the music. Around the shooting gallery a profound silence fell; one could hear in the distance the dull tumult of another party in full swing. Nazarof, Lorenzi, Mr Steinert and Don Manuelín suddenly appeared at Arcadio's side. They were panting. They had run there, in obedience to some mysterious order. And Commander Wolf, the superintendent and the purser had also inexplicably appeared. Strong took a while to reply. He did so with a placid, pitying smile, and reached out to take the Prince's trophy in one pale, perfect hand. Meanwhile, all the passengers from the staterooms were flocking to that part of the deck, pushing and shoving, all anxious to get close to Prince Emilio and to the stranger, for, apart from 'the seven', no one knew Ángel Strong's name nor who he was. He took the pierced piece of card. He looked at it, held it up to the lights on the stall, so that everyone could see it, radiant . . . And while he was slowly giving it back to the illustrious marksman, he said:

'That's nothing.'

The Prince could not contain himself.

'Nothing! Now look here, I'm the sort who could hit William Tell's apple, or miss it altogether if necessary . . .'

Strong retorted:

'I'm the sort that never misses. This is just a game. You've hit every target on the stall and left none for me.'

'What about this one?'

The Prince struck his own chest, or, rather, his shirt front.

'A challenge? No, sir. We'll just have to look for a more difficult target.'

Paying no heed to the Prince's impatience or to the murmurings and shouts that warned of the crowd's hostility towards him, he looked up, opened his eyes wide and stared at the moon.

'Give me a pistol! I'll take the moon as my target.'

La Molinari let out a musical laugh. Others followed suit. Some whistled.

'He's a fraud!'

'He's making fun of us!'

'Go on, shoot then!'

'Ladies, gentlemen . . .' said the Commander calmly.

The Prince was trembling with rage, Arcadio with fear. Mr Steinert was paler than the moon itself. Lorenzi was the colour of quicksilver. And the laughter had frozen on Don Manuelín's lips.

'Gentlemen, let him do it. Let him shoot at the moon and hit it. He is neither a fraud nor a madman. Give him a pistol, now!' said a cracked, hysterical voice. It belonged to Dr Demetrius.

The stallholder looked at the Commander and hesitated, the empty gun in his hand.

'Load it!'

And turning to the group, the Commander said:

'Gentlemen, why all this upset? You mistake a mere joke for a threat. It's all right, Your Majesty. Calm yourself, doctor. I myself will place the gun in the gentleman's hand.'

He did so. Ángel Strong stretched out his arm, screwed up one eye and aimed at the vast, perfect moon. The moon was not a silver moon, but blonde, almost golden. The stars encircling it were growing pale, its gold dripped onto the waters of the sea. It was a beautiful moon, young and lovely, that did not deserve to die. Inexorably – and smiling diabolically – Strong was aiming between its eyes – the moon's large, grey eyes, the eyes of one in love.

'One, two . . .' the commander was saying.

When he said 'three', the shot was fired. And everyone – all those who could withstand the terrible lurch the ship gave, as if it were about to be sucked under by a sudden whirlwind; all those who could withstand the apocalyptic yet harmonious din, a sound like a vast glass tower crumbling – everyone witnessed the marvel of seeing the moon pierced, cracked, shattered like a mirror by a bullet. Phosphorescent fragments of moon were sinking into the ocean. The light from the moon and stars was replaced by a profound, icy gloom. Almost all the witnesses to the catastrophe were lying on the floor, some stiff as corpses, others in the grip of an epileptic fit. Mournful voices and cries of terror arose while the *Amphitrite* righted itself, recovered its equilibrium and regained its previous solid stillness, like an islet newly born out of the stormy womb of the sea. Meanwhile, Ángel Strong was laughing. He alone was roaring with laughter. No one had the strength to rebuke him or to stop his laughter. Then, suddenly, as if the feeble, terrified crowd filled him with pity or disdain, he said:

'Don't worry, I've got plenty of spare moons.'

And then the second marvel happened. With the skill and dexterity of a magician he drew from the inside pocket of his dinner jacket a small, shining disc, which he stroked and turned in his fingers, before throwing it into the air. They saw the disc describe a perfect parabola and then watched it growing and growing until it was the same illusory size as the moon. The disc came to rest in exactly the spot where the moon had been. And there it was once more, the blonde, almost golden moon dripping its honey onto the sea.

Translated by Margaret Jull Costa

Alberto Insúa (Havana, 1885-Madrid, 1963) was the pseudonym of Alberto Galt y Escobar. Born of a Spanish father and a Cuban mother, Insúa was educated by Jesuits in Havana and only came to Spain when he was fifteen. There he studied law, but soon became immersed in the worlds of literature and journalism. During the First World War, he was correspondent in Paris for the Madrid newspaper *ABC* and, after the war, was awarded the Legion of Honour by the French government. The openly erotic nature of his first novel, *La mujer fácil* (1909) caused a huge scandal and the book became a bestseller. *El negro que tenía el alma blanca* (1922) was his most famous work and was adapted for both stage and screen. He wrote more than seventy novels, as well as two volumes of memoirs (*Memorias*, 1951–52). This story is taken from a novel entitled *El barco embrujado* (1929).

The Yellow Rain

(an extract)

JULIO LLAMAZARES

Ever since then, death has continued its slow, tenacious
advance through the foundations and the interior beams of
the house. Calmly. Unhurriedly. Pitilessly. In only four
years, the ivy has buried the oven and the grainstore, and
the woodworm has entirely eaten away the beams support-
ing the doorway and the shed. In only four years, the ivy
and the woodworm have destroyed the work of a whole
family, a whole century. And now the two are advancing
together, along the rotting wood in the old corridor and
the roof, searching out the last substances that still bear the
house's weight and memory. Those old substances, tired,
yellow – like the rain falling on the mill that night, like my
heart now and my memory – which, one day, possibly very
soon now, will also decay into nothing and collapse, at last,
into the snow, perhaps with me still inside the house.

With me still inside the house, and with the dog howling sadly
at the door, death has, in fact, already often come to visit
me. It came when my daughter made a surprise return one
night to occupy the room that had remained padlocked
since the day of her death. It came when Sabina rose from
the dead one New Year's Eve in the old photo that the
flames slowly consumed and when she kept watch over my
suffering, as I lay burning up between these same sheets,
devoured by fever and madness. And it came to stay with
me for good on the night that my mother suddenly
appeared in the kitchen, all those years after she was buried.

Until that night, I still doubted my own eyes and even the
very shadows and silences in the house. However vivid

those experiences had been, up until then, I still believed, or, at least, tried to believe, that fever and fear had provoked and given shape to images that existed only as memories. But that night, reality, brutal and irrefutable, overcame any doubts. That night, when my mother opened the door and was suddenly there in the kitchen, I was sitting by the fire, opposite her, awake, unable to sleep, as I am now, and when I saw her, I didn't even feel afraid.

Despite all the years that had passed, I had little difficulty recognising her. My mother was just as I remembered her, exactly the same as when she was alive and wandered about the house, day and night, tending to the livestock and to the whole family. She was still wearing the dress that Sabina and my sister had put on her after she died and the black scarf that she never took off. And now, sitting on the bench by the fire, her usual still, silent self, she seemed to have come to prove to me that it was not her but time that had died.

All that night, the dog sat howling at the door, wakeful and frightened, as she did when the people in Ainielle still used to keep vigil over their dead or when smugglers or wolves came down into the village. All night, my mother and I sat in silence watching the flames consuming the gorse twigs on the fire and, with them, our memories. After all those years, after all that time separated by death, the two of us were once again face to face, yet, despite that, we dared not resume a conversation that had been suddenly interrupted a long time ago. I did not even dare look at her. I knew she was still in the kitchen because of the dog's frightened barking and because of the strange, unmoving shadow that the flames cast on the floor by the bench. But, at no point, did I feel afraid. Not for a moment did I allow myself to think that my mother had come to keep vigil over my own death. Only at dawn, when, still sitting by the fire, I was woken by the warm light and realised she was no longer with me in the kitchen, did a black shudder run through me for the first time, when the calendar reminded me that the night ebbing away behind the trees was the last night of February: the exact same date on which my mother had died forty years before.

After that, my mother often came to keep me company. She always arrived around midnight, when sleep was already beginning to overwhelm me and the logs were starting to burn down amongst the embers in the hearth. She always appeared in the kitchen suddenly, with no noise, no sound of footsteps, without the front door or the door from the corridor announcing her arrival. But before she came into the kitchen, even before her shadow appeared in the narrow street outside, I could tell from the dog's frightened yelps that my mother was approaching. And sometimes, when my loneliness was stronger than the night, when my memories became too full of tiredness and madness, I would run to my bed and pull the blankets up over my head, like a child, so as not to have to mingle those memories with hers.

One night, however, around two or three in the morning, a strange murmuring made me sit up suddenly in my bed. It was a cold night, towards the end of autumn, and, as now, the window was blinded by the yellow rain. At first, I thought the murmuring was coming from outside the house, that it was the noise of the wind dragging the dead leaves along the street. I soon realised I was wrong. The strange murmuring was not coming from the street, but from somewhere in the house, and it was the sound of voices, of words being spoken nearby, as if there were someone talking to my mother in the kitchen.

Lying absolutely still in my bed, I listened for a long time before deciding to get up. The dog had stopped barking and her silence alarmed me even more than that strange echo of words. Even more than the rain of dead leaves that was staining the whole window yellow. When I went out into the corridor, the murmuring abruptly stopped, as if they had heard me from the kitchen. I had already picked up the knife which, ever since the day Sabina died, I always carry in my jacket, and I went down the stairs determined to find out who was in the kitchen with my mother. I didn't need the knife. It wouldn't have been any use to me anyway. Sitting in a circle round the kitchen fire with my mother there were only silent, dead shadows, who all turned as one to look at me when I flung open the door behind them, and amongst them I immediately recognised the faces of Sabina and of all the dead of the house.

I rushed out into the street, not even bothering to close the door behind me. I remember that, as I left, a cold wind struck my face. The whole street was full of dead leaves and the wind was whirling them up in the gardens and court-yards of the houses. When I reached Bescós' old house, I stopped to catch my breath. It had all happened so fast, it was all so sudden and confused, that I was still not entirely sure that I wasn't in the middle of a dream: I could still feel the warmth of the sheets on my skin, the wind was blinding and buffeting me and, above the rooftops and the walls of the houses, the sky was the yellow of nightmares. But no, it wasn't a dream. What I had seen and heard in the kitchen in my house was as real as me standing at that moment in the middle of the street, stockstill and terrified, again hearing strange voices behind me.

For a few seconds, I stood there, paralysed. During those seconds – interminable seconds made longer by the wind rattling the windows and doors of the houses – I thought my heart was going to burst. I had just fled my own house, I had just left behind me the cold of death, death's gaze, and now, though how I didn't know, I found myself once more face to face with death. It was sitting on the bench in Bescós' kitchen by a non-existent fire, watching over the memory of a house that no one even remembered any

156

more, on the other side of the window against which I just happened to be leaning.

Terrified, I started running down the middle of the street, with no idea where I was going. My whole body broke out in a cold sweat and the leaves and the wind were blinding me. Suddenly, the entire village seemed to have been set in motion: the walls moved silently aside as I passed, the roofs floated in the air like shadows torn from their bodies and, above the infinite vertex of the night, the sky was now entirely yellow. I passed the church without stopping. I didn't think for a moment of taking refuge there. The belfry leaned menacingly towards me and the bells began to ring again as if they were still alive beneath the earth. Yet in Calleja de Gavín, the fountain seemed abruptly to have died. Water had ceasing pouring from the spout and, amongst the black shadows of the algae and the watercress, the water was as yellow as the sky. I ran towards Lauro's old house, battling against the wind. The nettles stung me and the brambles wrapped about my legs as if they too wanted to hold me back. But I got there. Exhausted. Panting. Several times I nearly fell. And when I was finally out in the open country, far from the houses and the garden walls, I stopped to see what was happening around me: the sky and the rooftops were burning, fused into one incandescent brightness, the wind was battering the windows and doors of the houses and, in the midst of the night, amongst the endless howling of leaves and doors, the whole village was filled by an incessant lament. I did not need to retrace my steps to know that every kitchen was inhabited by the dead.

During the whole of that night, I wandered the roads, not daring to return to my own dead. For more than five hours, I waited for dawn, afraid that it might perhaps never come. Fear dragged me aimlessly, senselessly through the hills, and the thorns snatched at my clothes, gradually eating away at my courage and my strength, not that I was aware of them.

Blinded by the wind, I could barely see them, and madness propelled me beyond the night and beyond despair. And so, when dawn finally arrived, I was far from the village, on the top of Erata hill, by the abandoned watering hole of a flock that had not been seen for several years.

I continued to wait, though, sitting amongst the brambles, until the sun came out. I knew that no one would now be waiting for me in the village – my mother always left with the dawn – but I was so tired I could barely stand. Gradually, though, my strength returned – I may even have managed to sleep for a while – and when the sun finally broke through the black clouds over Erata, I set off again, ready to go back. Downhill and in the full light of day, it did not take me long to cover the distance walked that night. The wind had dropped and a deep calm was spreading softly over the hills. Down below, in the river valley, the rooftops of Ainielle were floating in the mist as sweetly as at any dawn. As I came within sight of the houses, the dog joined me. She appeared suddenly at the side of the road, from amongst some bushes, still trembling with fear and emotion. The poor creature had spent the night there, hiding, and now, when she found me, she looked at me in silence, struggling to understand. But I could tell her nothing. Even if she had been able to comprehend my words, I could not explain something that I myself could not grasp. Perhaps it really had been nothing more than a dream, a murky, tormented nightmare born of insomnia and solitude. Or perhaps not. Perhaps I really had seen and heard everything that I saw and heard that night – just as now I could see the garden walls and hear around me the cries of the birds – and those black shadows were perhaps still waiting for me to return to the kitchen. The presence of the dog gave me courage, however, to walk past the houses and go towards my own. The street door was still open, just as I had left it, and, as always, a profound silence welled up from the far end of the corridor. I did not hesitate for a second. I did not even stop to remember the things I thought I had experienced during the night and on many other previous nights. I went in through the door and entered the house convinced that it was all a lie, that there was no one waiting in the kitchen and that everything that had happened had been merely the nightmarish fruit of insomnia and madness. Indeed, no one was in the kitchen. The bench was empty, as it always was, touched by the first light of day coming in through the window. In the fireplace, though, quite inexplicably, the fire I had doused before I went to bed was still burning, still wrapped in a strange, mysterious glow.

Several months passed and there was no recurrence of these events. I sat waiting in the kitchen every night, alert to the slightest sound, fearing that the door would again open of its own accord and that my mother would appear once more before me. But the winter passed and nothing happened, nothing disturbed the peace of the kitchen and of my heart. And so, when the spring arrived, when the snows began to melt and the days to grow longer, I was sure that she would never return, because her ghost had only ever existed in my imagination.

But she did return. At night, completely unexpectedly, while it was raining. I recall that November was drawing to a close and that, outside the windows, the air was yellow. She sat down on the bench and looked at me in silence, just as she had that first day.

Since then, my mother has returned on many nights. Sometimes, with Sabina. Sometimes, surrounded by the whole family. For a long time, so as not to see them, I would hide somewhere in the village, or else spend hours aimlessly, senselessly wandering the hills. For a long time, I preferred to shun their company. But they kept coming, more and more often, and, in the end, I had no option but to resign myself to sharing with them my memories and the warmth of the kitchen. And now that death is prowling outside the door of this room and the air is gradually staining my eyes with yellow, it actually consoles me to think of them there, sitting by the fire, awaiting the moment when my shadow will join theirs for ever.

Julio Llamazares (1955) was born in the now non-existent village of Vegamián near León and currently lives in Madrid. Initially he trained and worked as a lawyer, but soon abandoned that career to work as a newspaper, TV and radio journalist. He has published two books of poetry: *La lentitud de los bueyes* (1979) and *Memoria de la nieve* (1982), for which he won the Jorge Guillén Prize. He has also written two books about his childhood and the area where he was born – *El río del olvido* (1990) and *Escenas de cine mudo* (1994) – and two remarkable novels: *Luna de lobos* (1985) and *La lluvia amarilla* (1993), winner of the Premio Nonino for the best foreign novel published in Italy. The latter, from which this extract is taken, is an elegiac account of an abandoned village near the Spanish Pyrenees, of which the narrator and his dog are the sole remaining inhabitants.

Gualta

JAVIER MARÍAS

Until I was thirty years old, I lived quietly and virtuously and in accordance with my own biography, and it had never occurred to me that forgotten characters from books read in adolescence might resurface in my life, or even in other people's lives. Of course, I had heard people speak of momentary identity crises provoked by a coincidence of names uncovered in youth (for example, my friend Rafa Zarza doubted his own existence when he was introduced to *another* Rafa Zarza). But I never expected to find myself transformed into a bloodless William Wilson, or a de-dramatised portrait of Dorian Gray, or a Jekyll whose Hyde was merely another Jekyll.

His name was Xavier de Gualta – a Catalan, as his name indicates – and he worked in the Barcelona office of the same company I worked for. His (highly) responsible position was similar to mine in Madrid where we met at a supper intended for the dual purpose of business and fraternisation, which is why we both arrived there accompanied by our respective wives. Only our first names were interchangeable (my name is Javier Santín), but we coincided in absolutely everything else. I still remember the look of stupefaction on Gualta's face (which was doubtless also on mine), when the head waiter who brought him to our table stood to one side, allowing him to see my face for the first time. Gualta and I were physically identical, like twins in the cinema, but it wasn't just that: we even made the same gestures at the same time and used the same words (we took the words out of each other's mouths, as the saying goes), and our hands would reach for the bottle of wine (Rhine) or the mineral water (still), or our forehead, or the sugar spoon, or the bread, or the fork beneath the fondue dish, in perfect unison, simultaneously. We narrowly missed colliding. It was as if our heads, which were identical outside, were also thinking the same thing and at the same time. It was like dining opposite a mirror made flesh. Needless to say, we agreed about everything and, although I tried not to ask too many questions, such was my disgust, my sense of vertigo, our lives, both professional and personal, had run along parallel lines. This extraordinary similarity was, of course, noted and commented on by our wives and by us ('It's extraordinary,' they said. 'Yes, extraordinary,' we said), yet, after our first initial amazement, the four of us, somewhat taken aback by this entirely anomalous situation and conscious that we had to think of the good of the company that had brought us together for that supper, ignored the remarkable fact and did our best to behave naturally. We tended to concentrate more on business than on fraternisation. The only thing about us that was not the same were our wives (but they are not in fact part of us, just as we are not part of them). Mine, if I may be so vulgar, is a real stunner, whilst Gualta's wife, though distinguished-looking, was a complete nonentity, temporarily embellished and emboldened by the success of her go-getting spouse.

The worst thing, though, was not the resemblance itself (after all, other people have learned to live with it). Until then, I had never seen myself. I mean, a photo immobilises us, and in the mirror we always see ourselves the other way round (for example, I always part my hair on the right, like Cary Grant, but in the mirror, I am someone who parts his hair on the left, like Clark Gable); and, since I am not famous and have never been interested in movie cameras, I had never seen myself on television or on video either. In Gualta, therefore, I saw myself for the first time, talking, moving, gesticulating, pausing, laughing, in profile, wiping my mouth with my napkin, and scratching my nose. It was my first real experience of myself as object, something which is normally enjoyed only by the famous or by those with a video camera to play with.

And I hated myself. That is, I hated Gualta, who was identical to me. That smooth Catalan not only struck me as entirely lacking in charm (although my wife – who is gorgeous – said

162

to me later at home, I imagine merely to flatter me, that she had found him attractive), he seemed affected, prissy, overbearing in his views, mannered in his gestures, full of his own charisma (mercantile charisma, I mean), openly right-wing in his views (we both, of course, voted for the same party), pretentious in his choice of vocabulary and unscrupulous in matters of business. We were even official supporters of the most conservative football clubs in our respective cities: he of Español and I of Atlético. I saw myself in Gualta and in Gualta I saw an utterly repellent individual, capable of anything, potential firing squad material. As I say, I unhesitatingly hated myself.

And it was from that night, without even informing my wife of my intentions, that I began to change. Not only had I discovered that in the city of Barcelona there existed a being identical to myself whom I detested, I was afraid too that, in each and every sphere of life, at each and every moment of the day, that being would think, do and say exactly the same as me. I knew that we had the same office hours, that he lived alone, without children, with his wife, exactly like me. There was nothing to stop him living my life. I thought: 'Everything I do, every step I take, every hand I shake, every word I say, every letter I dictate, every thought I have, every kiss I give my wife, will be being done, taken, shaken, said, dictated, had, given by Gualta to *his* wife. This can't go on.'

After that unfortunate encounter, I knew that we would meet again four months later, at the big party being given to celebrate the fifth anniversary of our company, American in origin, being set up in Spain. And during that time, I applied myself to the task of modifying my appearance: I cultivated a moustache, which took a long while to grow; sometimes, instead of a tie, I would wear an elegant cravat; I started smoking (English cigarettes); and I even tried to disguise my receding hairline with a discreet Japanese hair implant (the kind of self-conscious, effeminate thing that neither Gualta nor my former self would ever have allowed themselves to do). As for my behaviour, I spoke more robustly, I avoided expressions such as 'horizontal integration' or 'package deal dynamics'

163

once so dear to Gualta and myself; I stopped pouring wine for ladies during supper; I stopped helping them on with their coats; I would utter the occasional swear word.

Four months later, at that Barcelona celebration, I met a Gualta who was sporting a stunted moustache and who appeared to have more hair than I remembered; he was chain-smoking John Players and instead of a tie, he was wearing a bow-tie; he kept slapping his thighs when he laughed, digging people with his elbow, and exclaiming frequently: 'bloody hell!' I found him just as hateful as before. That night, I too was wearing a bow-tie.

It was from then on that the process of change in my own abominable person really took off. I conscientiously sought out everything that an excessively suave, smooth, serious, sententious man like Gualta (he was also very devout) could never have brought himself to do, and at times and in places when it was most unlikely that Gualta, in Barcelona, would be devoting his time and space to committing the same excesses as me. I began arriving late at work and leaving early, making coarse remarks to the secretaries, I would fly into a rage at the slightest thing and frequently insult the staff who worked for me, and I would even make mistakes, never very serious ones, but which a man like Gualta, however – so punctilious, such a perfectionist – would never have made. And that was just my work. As for my wife, whom I always treated with extreme respect and veneration (until I turned thirty), I managed, gradually, subtly, to persuade her not only to have sex at odd times and in unsuitable places ('I bet Gualta is never this daring,' I thought one night as we lay together, in some haste, on the roof of a newspaper kiosk in Calle Príncipe de Vergara), but also to engage in sexual deviations that only months before, in the unlikely event of our ever actually having heard of them (through someone else, of course), we would have described as sexual humiliations or sexual atrocities. We committed unnatural acts, that beautiful woman and I.

After three months, I awaited with impatience a further encounter with Gualta, confident that now he would be very different from me. However, the occasion did not arise and, finally, one weekend, I decided to go to Barcelona myself with the intention of watching his house in order to discover, albeit from afar, any possible changes in his person or in his personality. Or, rather, to confirm the efficacy of the changes I had made to myself.

For eighteen hours (spread over Saturday and Sunday) I took refuge in a café from which I could watch Gualta's house and there I waited for him to come out. He did not appear, however, and, just when I was wondering whether I should return defeated to Madrid or go up to his apartment, even if I risked possibly bumping into him, I suddenly saw his non-entity of a wife come out of the front door. She was rather carelessly dressed, as if her spouse's success were no longer sufficient to embellish her artificially or as if its effect did not extend to weekends. On the other hand, though, it seemed to me, as she walked past the darkened glass concealing me, that she was somehow more provocative than the woman I had seen at the supper in Madrid and at the party in Barcelona. The reason was very simple and it was enough to make me realise that I had not been as original as I thought nor had the measures I had taken been wise: the look on her face was that of a salacious, sexually dissolute woman. Though very different, she had the same slight (and very attractive) squint, the same troubling, clouded gaze as my own stunner of a wife.

I returned to Madrid convinced that the reason Gualta had not left his apartment all weekend was because that same weekend he had travelled to Madrid and had spent hours sitting in La Orotava, the café opposite my own house, waiting for me to leave, which I had not done because I was in Barcelona watching his house which he had not left because he was in Madrid watching mine. There was no escape.

I made a few further, by now rather half-hearted, attempts. Minor details to complete the transformation, like becoming an official supporter of Real Madrid, in the belief that no supporter of Español would ever be allowed into Barça; or else I would order anisette or aniseed liqueur – drinks I find repugnant – in some dingy bar on the outskirts, sure that a man of Gualta's refined tastes would not be prepared to make

165

such sacrifices; I also started insulting the Pope in public, certain that my rival, a fervent Catholic, would never go that far. In fact, I wasn't sure of anything and I think that now I never will be. A year and a half after I first met Gualta, my fast-track career in the company for which I still work has come to an abrupt halt, and I await my dismissal (with severance pay, of course) any week now. A little while ago, without any explanation, my wife – either because she had grown weary of perversion or else, on the contrary, because my fantasies no longer sufficed and she needed to go in search of fresh dissipations – left me. Will Gualta's nonentity of a wife have done the same? Is his position in the company as precarious as mine? I will never know, because, as I said, I now prefer not to. For the moment has arrived when, if I did arrange to meet Gualta, two things could happen, both equally terrifying, at least, more terrifying than uncertainty: I could find a man utterly different from the one I first met and identical to the current me (scruffy, demoralised, shiftless, boorish, a blasphemer and a pervert) whom I will, however, possibly find just as awful as the Xavier de Gualta I met the first time. As regards the other possibility, that is even worse: I might find the same Gualta I first met, unchanged: impassive, courteous, boastful, elegant, devout and successful. And if that were the case, I would have to ask myself, with a bitterness I could not bear, why, of the two of us, was I the one to abandon and renounce my own biography?

Javier Marías (Madrid, 1951) wrote his first novel when he was eighteen (*Los dominios del lobo* (1971) and has since published eight more, amongst them: *Todas las almas* (1989; *All Souls*, Harvill/HarperCollins, 1992), *Corazón tan blanco* (1992; *A Heart So White*, Harvill, 1995), *Mañana en la batalla piensa en mí* (1994; *Tomorrow in the Battle Think on Me*, Harvill, 1996), *Cuando fui mortal* (short stories) (1996; *When I was Mortal*,

Harvill, 1999 – all English translations by Margaret Jull Costa) and *Negra espalda del tiempo* (1998). He is also a prize-winning translator, notably of Laurence Sterne's *Tristram Shandy*. His own work has been translated into twenty-three languages and has won numerous prizes both in Spain and abroad; these include the 1993 Spanish Critics' prize 1993, the 1995 Rómulo Gallegos International Prize for the Novel, the 1996 Prix Femina for best foreign novel and the 1997 International IMPAC Dublin Literary Award. This story is from a collection entitled *Mientras ellas duermen* (1990).

No News from Gurb

EDUARDO MENDOZA

DAY 9

0.01 (local time)　Landing executed without difficulty. Conventional propulsion (augmented). Speed of landing: 6.30 on the conventional scale (restricted). Speed on touchdown: 4 on the Minus-UI scale, or 9 on the Molina-Clavo scale. Cubic capacity: AZ-0.3.
Landing-place: 63Ω (IIβ) 284763947836394739937492749.
Local name for landing-place: Sardanyola, Catalonia, Spain.

07.00　In response to orders (mine) Gurb preparing to initiate contact with local life-forms (real and potential). As we are travelling in acorporeal mode (pure intelligence – analytical factor 4800) arrange for him to adopt a form analogous to that of the inhabitants of the area. Objective: to avoid attracting the attention of native fauna (real and potential). Having consulted the *Astral Catalogue of Assimilable Forms (Earth) ACAF(E),* select for Gurb the form of the human being designated Marta Sánchez.

07.15　Gurb exits spaceship via hatchway 4. Weather fine, light southern wind; temperature, 15 degrees centigrade; comparative humidity, 56 per cent; sea, calm.

07.21　First contact with an inhabitant of the area. Information received from Gurb: height of individual, 170 centimetres; cranial circumference, 57 centimetres; number of eyes: two; length of tail, 0.00 centimetres (no tail). It communicates by means of a language of tremendous structural simplicity, but immensely complex utterance, since enunciation *involves*

169

the use of internal organs. Level of conceptualisation minimal. Designation of individual, Lluc Puig i Roig (reception probably defective or incomplete). Biological function of individual: professor (fully-tenured) at the Autonomous University in Bellaterra. Level of docility: low. Uses a vehicle of tremendous structural simplicity, but poor manoeuvrability, known as a Ford Fiesta.

07.23   Gurb invited by the individual to climb into his vehicle. Requests instructions. Order him to accept the invitation. Principal objective: avoid attracting attention of local fauna (real and potential).

07.30   No news from Gurb.

0.800   No news from Gurb.

09.00   No news from Gurb.

12.30   No news from Gurb.

20.30   No news from Gurb.

DAY 10

07.00   Decide to go out in search of Gurb. Before leaving, disguise spaceship to prevent reconnoitring and inspection by local fauna. Having consulted the *Catalogue*, decide to turn spaceship into attr. semi-det. res. 3 bdrms, 2 bthrms, balcony, comml. sw.pool., 2 prkg spces, mrtge avail.

07.30   Decide to adopt appearance of individualised human being. Having consulted the *Catalogue*, opt for the Count-Duke of Olivares.

07.30   Rather than leave the ship by the hatch (now turned into a panelled wood door of tremendous structural simplicity

170

but poor manoeuvrability), decide to beam down in a spot where the concentration of human beings is densest, in order to avoid attracting attention.

08.00   Beam down at a spot known as corner of Diagonal and Paseo de Gracia. Knocked down by no. 17 bus, Barceloneta to Vall d'Hebron. Obliged to retrieve head, which fell off as a result of accident. Operation difficult due to large number of vehicles.

08.01   Knocked down by an Opel Corsa.

08.02   Knocked down by a delivery truck.

08.03   Knocked down by a taxi.

08.04   Manage to recover head and wash it in a fountain situated close to the scene of the accident. Take advantage of the opportunity to analyse the composition of the local water: hydrogen, oxygen and faeces.

08.15   In view of large number of individuals, it may prove difficult to locate Gurb by *sight,* but wish to avoid sensorial location, as am unsure of effect it could have on ecological balance of area and, by extension, on inhabitants. Human beings are creatures of variable height. The smallest among them are so tiny that if they were not conveyed by taller ones in carriages they would soon be trampled underfoot (with possible loss of head) by tall ones. The tallest rarely exceed 200 centimetres. A curious detail is that when they lie flat *they remain exactly the same length.* Some have a moustache; others, beard and moustache. Almost all have two eyes, which may be situated at the front or the back of the head, depending on how they are facing. When walking they move in a forward direction, and are thus forced to counteract the movement of the legs by means of *vigorous arm swinging.* Those in the greatest hurry reinforce this arm movement by means of briefcases made of plastic or leather or a material called

Samsonite, which comes from another planet. The traction principle used in their cars (four aligned wheels filled with evil-smelling air) is more rational, and permits the attainment of higher speeds. Must remember not to fly or walk on my head if wish to avoid being taken for an eccentric. NB Must remember always to keep one foot touching the ground – immaterial which one – or if not, the external organ known as the bottom.

11.00   Have been waiting for three hours to spot Gurb. A waste of time. Flow of persons past this point in this city shows no decrease. Rather the reverse. Calculate that the odds against Gurb passing without me seeing him are of the order of seventy-three to one. However, to this calculation, one would have to append two variables:
a) Gurb doesn't pass this spot
b) Gurb passes this spot, but *having modified his external appearance.* In latter case odds against my spotting him go up to nine trillion to one.

12.00   The hour of the *Angelus.* Meditate for an instant in silent prayer, trusting that Gurb is not going to choose that exact moment to pass in front of me.

13.00   The erect position in which I have held my body for the last five hours is beginning to tire me. Apart from the stiffness in the muscles, I must make a continuous effort to inhale and exhale air. Once when I forgot to do it for five minutes, my face went purple and my eyes popped out of my head, and I had to go and retrieve them from amongst the cars. If this goes on, I'll end up drawing attention to myself. It seems that human beings inhale and exhale air in an automatic fashion, which they call *breathing.* This automatic functioning, which is repugnant to any civilised being, and which I note here for purely scientific motives, characterises not only breathing but many corporeal functions, such as the circulation of the blood, digestion, blinking – which unlike the two previously mentioned actions can be consciously controlled,

172

in which case it is known as *winking* – the growth of the nails and so on. So subject are humans to the automatic functioning of their organs (and organisms) that they would soil themselves, if they were not trained as children to subordinate nature to decorum.

14.00   Have reached the limit of my physical resistance. Rest by getting down on the ground, stretching my left leg out behind me and my right leg in front. Seeing me in this posture, a woman gives me a 25-peseta coin, which I immediately swallow in order not to appear impolite. Temperature, 20 degrees centigrade; comparative humidity, 64 per cent; light southerly winds; sea, calm.

14.30   Density of traffic, both vehicular and pedestrian, diminishing slightly. Still no news from Gurb. Even at the risk of disturbing the precarious ecological balance of the planet, decide to establish sensorial contact. Taking advantage of the fact that there is no bus passing, make my mind a blank and emit waves on frequency H76420ba, rising gradually to H76420ba400010.

At the second attempt receive a response signal which is weak at first but gradually clears. Decode the signal, which appears to be coming from two different points, though close together in terms of the earth's axis. Text of the signal (decoded):

Where are you calling from, Señora Cargols?
From Sant Joan Despí.
Can you give me that again?
From Sant Joan Despí. Sant Joan Despí. Hello? Can you
    hear me?
We seem to be having some technical problems here in the
    studio, Señora Cargols. Can you hear us?
What did you say?
I asked if you're hearing us. Señora Cargols?
Yes, carry on. I'm hearing you clearly.
Señora Cargols, can you hear us?

173

Yes, very well. I can hear you.

And where are you calling from, Señora Cargols?

From Sant Joan Despí.

From Sant Joan Despí. And can you hear us clearly in Sant Joan Despí, Señora. Cargols?

Yes, I can hear you fine. What about you? Can you hear me?

Yes, very well. Now, where are you calling from?

I sense it is going to be harder than I thought to locate Gurb.

15.00   Decide to search the city systematically, rather than remaining in one spot. By doing so, I reduce the odds against finding Gurb by one trillion, but even so, success remains uncertain. Set off, following the automatic self-correcting heliographic map which I incorporated into my internal circuits on leaving the spaceship. Fall into a hole in the road left by the Catalan Gas Company.

15.02   Fall into a hole in the road left by the Barcelona Water company.

15.03   Fall into a hole in the road left by National Telecommunications.

15.03   Fall into a hole in the road left by the Residents' Association on Calle Córcega.

15.06   Decide to proceed without the automatic self-correcting heliographic map and instead look where I'm going.

19.00   Have been walking for four hours. No idea where I am, and my legs can hardly carry me. The city is huge: the crowds, constant; the noise, incredible. Surprised not to find the usual monuments, such as a Cenotaph to Blessed Mother Pilar, which would aid orientation. I stopped a pedestrian and asked him how I could set about finding somebody who was lost. He asked me how old the person was. When I said six thousand, five hundred and thirty years, he said try the *Corte Inglés* department store. The worst thing is having to breathe this air, which is thick with succulent particles. It is a well-known fact that in some parts of the city the density of the air is such that the residents have forced it into skins and exported it as *black pudding*. My eyes are smarting, my nose is blocked, my mouth is dry. The quality of life is so much better in Sardanyola!

20.30   After sunset the atmospheric conditions would have improved greatly if the human beings had not had the bright idea of switching on the street lighting. It seems they require it when they're out of doors, because although the majority of them have unattractive, or even frankly ugly features, they feel the need to see one another. Even the cars switch on their lights and attack each other with them. Temperature, 17 degrees centigrade; humidity, 62 per cent; light south-easterly winds; sea, choppy.

21.30   Have had enough! Cannot take another step. Have suffered considerable physical deterioration. Have lost an arm, a leg, and both ears, and my tongue is hanging out so far that I've had to tie it to my belt, after I had picked up four dog turds and I don't know how many cigarette ends. Given the conditions, it would be better to postpone my search until tomorrow. Hide under a lorry, disintegrate and beam down inside the spaceship.

21.45   Energy recharge.

21.50   Put on my pyjamas. Gurb's absence weighs on my spirits. As we have spent all our evenings together for the last eight hundred years, am at a loss as to how to kill the time between now and sleep. I could watch local television, or read the latest comic strip adventure of Lolita Galaxia, but neither appeals. Cannot understand Gurb's absence, and even less his silence. Have never been an unreasonable superior. Have

175

always allowed the crew, i.e. Gurb, complete freedom to come and go as he pleases (in his time off), but if he knows he won't be back, or he's going to be late, surely the least he could do is let me know?

DAY 11

08.00   Still no news from Gurb. Try again to establish sensorial contact. Get an angry voice demanding in the name of *decent people everywhere*, whom it claims to represent, a full and detailed inquiry into allegations of sleaze against a certain Señor Guerra. Decide to abandon sensorial contact.

08.30   Leave the spaceship and in the form of a grebe take a look at the area from the air.

09.30   Having completed the operation, return to the spaceship. If the cities are tortuous and irrational in their design, the countryside around them is worse. Nothing is flat or regular, on the contrary it seems to have been deliberately planned so as to be inconvenient. As for the coastline, it looks like the work of a madman.

09.45   After a detailed study of a map of the city (the double elliptical-axis cartographic version), decide to continue my search for Gurb in a zone on the periphery inhabited by a species of human being known as *poor people*. As the *Catalogue* assigns them a level of docility somewhat lower than that of the variety known as *rich people,* and considerably lower than the variety known as *the middle classes*, opt for the appearance of the individual designated Gary Cooper.

10.00   Beam down in an apparently deserted street in the San Cosme district. Doubt if Gurb would come to live here of his own accord, though he is not what you would call the sharpest arrow in the quiver.

10.01   A group of youths with knives take my wallet.

10.02   A group of youths with knives take my gun and my sheriff's badge.

10.03   A group of youths with knives take my waistcoat, shirt and trousers.

10.04   A group of youths with knives take my boots, spurs and the harmonica.

10.10   A patrol car draws up beside me. A policeman gets out, informs me of my rights under the Constitution, hand-cuffs me and shoves me in the car. Temperature, 21 degrees centigrade; humidity, 75 per cent; winds gusting from the south; heavy seas.

10.30   Put into a cell at the police station. In the same cell there is an individual of shabby appearance, to whom I intro-duce myself and give an account of the vicissitudes that have brought me to this unhappy pass.

10.45   Once he has overcome the initial distrust that human beings invariably feel towards other members of their species, the individual whom fate has placed in my path decides to initiate a conversation with me. He gives me his card which reads as follows:

JETULIO PENCAS
Consultant Beggar
I read tarot, I play the violin, I inspire pity
Service in your own home if required

10.50   My new friend explains that he has been *banged up* in error, because he never broke into a car to steal nothing, he earns an honest living begging, and the substance they found on him wasn't what they said it was, but the ashes of his late father, God rest his soul, which he was taking that very day to

177

scatter them over the city from a well-known beauty spot. He then adds that everything he's just told me is a lie, but, in any case, it won't do him any good, because there's no such thing as justice in this country, and even though they've got no proof and no witnesses, they'll probably take us and lock us up in the *slammer* just because of the way we look and when we get out we'll have fleas and AIDS. I tell him I don't understand, and he replies that there's nothing *to* understand, calls me *mate,* adds that *such is life* and remarks that the crux of the matter is the unequal distribution of wealth in this country. By way of an example, he cites the case of an individual whose name I forget, who has built himself a house with twenty-two toilets, adding that he hopes he gets diarrhoea sometime when they're all occupied. He then climbs onto his bed and announces that when the glorious day dawns (what glorious day does he have in mind?) he'll force the individual in question to do his business out in the yard with the chickens and will distribute the twenty-two toilets to a similar number of families on income support. That way, he says, they'll have something to occupy their time with till they're given a job, as promised. At this point he falls off the bed and bangs his head.

11.30   A different policeman from the one previously mentioned opens the cell door and orders us to follow him, apparently with the aim of charging us. Fearful after my new friend's warnings, decide to adopt a more respectable appearance, so turn into Don José Ortega y Gasset and as a gesture of solidarity turn my friend into Don Miguel de Unamuno.

11.35   Taken to the sergeant, who looks us over, scratches his head, says why go looking for problems and tells us we're free to go.

11.40   Say goodbye to my new friend outside the police station. Before we go our separate ways, friend asks me to restore him to his old appearance, because the way he looks now, nobody's going to give him a penny, even if he sticks on some artificial ulcers that make him look absolutely stomach-churning. Do as he asks and he leaves.

11.45   Renew my search.

14.30   Still no news from Gurb. Following the example of everyone around me, decide to eat. As all the shops are closed, except ones called *restaurants,* deduce that food served in these. Sniff the rubbish outside several *restaurants* till I find one that appeals.

14.45   Go into the *restaurant* and a gentleman dressed in black asks me in a disdainful tone whether I have a reservation. Tell him I haven't, but add that I am having a house built with twenty-two toilets. Ushered immediately to a table decorated with a bunch of flowers, which I promptly eat, in order not to appear impolite. They give me the menu (uncoded), I read it and order melon, melon with ham, and ham. They ask me what I want to drink. To avoid attracting attention, I order the liquid most commonly found among humans: urine.

16.15   Have coffee. Am offered a glass of pear liqueur *on the house.* They then bring me the bill, which comes to six thousand eight hundred and thirty-four pesetas. I have no money of any kind.

16.35   Smoke a Montecristo Number Two (2) while trying to think how to get out of embarrassing situation. I could disintegrate, but reject this idea because a) it might attract the attention of waiters and other customers and b) it would be unfair if the consequences of my lack of forethought were to fall on these amiable people, who have offered me a glass of pear liqueur *on the house.*

16.40   On pretext of having left something in my car, leave restaurant, go to news kiosk and buy tickets and cards for the various lotteries on offer.

179

16.45   Manipulating the numbers by means of elementary formulae, win 122 million pesetas. Go back to restaurant, pay bill and leave one hundred thousand peseta tip.

16.55   Resume search for Gurb by only means known to me: walking the streets.

20.00   Have walked so much there is smoke rising from the soles of my shoes. The heel has fallen off one shoe, forcing me to hobble along in a ridiculous and tiring fashion. Throw the shoes away, go into a shop and with the money left over from the *restaurant* buy a new pair of shoes, less comfortable than the other ones, but made of very strong material. Wearing these new shoes, known as *skis*, begin to search the Pedralbes district of the city.

21.00   Complete the search of Pedralbes without finding Gurb, but very pleasantly impressed by the elegant houses, the secluded streets, the smooth lawns, the deep swimming pools. Cannot understand why some people prefer to live in deplorable districts like San Cosme, when they could live in places like Pedralbes. Possibly not a question of preference so much as money.

It would appear that human beings are divided into various categories, one of which is rich and poor. This is a division which they consider very important, for reasons that are unclear. The fundamental difference between the two seems to be this: wherever they go, the rich don't pay, however much they acquire or consume. The poor, on the other hand, practically have to pay for the privilege of breathing. This exemption enjoyed by the rich may be something that goes back a long way, or it may be a recent thing, it may be temporary, it may even be a pretence; it doesn't matter. From a statistical viewpoint, it seems clear that the rich live longer and better than the poor, they are taller, healthier and better-looking, they have a more exciting time, they get to travel to more exotic places, receive a better education, work shorter hours, live in greater comfort, have more clothes, in particular more spring outfits, are offered better health care and more elaborate funerals and are remembered for longer. They are also more likely to have their photograph appear in newspapers and magazines and on calendars.

21.30   Decide to go back to the spaceship. Disintegrate in front of the entrance to the Monastery of Pedralbes, to the astonishment of the nun who at that precise moment is putting out the rubbish.

22.00   Energy recharge. Get ready to spend another evening alone. Read a comic strip about Lolita Galaxia, but usually do this with Gurb, to whom I have to explain the more risqué jokes, because he's not what you'd call quick on the uptake, so instead of cheering me up, it just makes me feel sad.

22.30   Tired of walking up and down inside the spaceship, decide to turn in for the night. It's been a long day. Put on pyjamas, say prayers and get into bed.

© Eduardo Mendoza
Translated by Annella McDermott

Eduardo Mendoza (Barcelona, 1943) is a key writer in the genre of new detective fiction which has emerged in Spain since the 1970s, author of *La verdad sobre el caso Savolta* (1975; *The Truth about the Savolta Case*, tr. Alfred Macadam, Harvill, 1993), *El misterio de la cripta embrujada* (1979), *El laberinto de las aceitunas* (1982) and *Una comedia ligera* (1996). *La ciudad de los prodigios* (1986; *City of Marvels*, tr. Bernard Molloy, Harvill, 1988) is a period novel, set in Barcelona in the 1920s. *La isla inaudita* (1989), unusually for Mendoza, is set in Venice. *El año del diluvio* (1992; *The Year of the Flood*, tr. N. Caistor, Harvill, 1995) tells the story of a relationship between a nun and a rich landowner in rural Catalonia. Mendoza is also the author of a play, *Restauració* (1990) and of an engaging tale of aliens landing in Barcelona, *Sin noticias de Gurb* (1991), from which this extract is taken.

The Companion

JOSÉ MARÍA MERINO

I saw him by chance. Pacing around the room, killing time while I waited for Juanjo to finish signing the minutes, I had gone over to the window, and I saw the tall, thin figure of a man dressed in a dark suit, and Paquita approaching with a certain air of timidity. He took her by the arm and they walked off. I followed their vague outline in the fading evening light, till they disappeared into the bustle of the street, beyond the railings of the playground.

'Who's that?' I asked.

Juanjo looked at me, with his pen still poised.

'A man who was waiting for Paquita,' I added.

Juanjo took advantage of the pause to stretch his legs. He put his pen down on the table, lit a cigarette and joined me by the window. We both stared at the playground, so strange at that time of day, silent and full of shadows, devoid of the presence and voices of children.

'Oh, I know who it is,' said Juanjo. 'A tall thin chap she goes out with.'

He smiled. Paquita was getting on a bit now, she was rather plain, and she was shy to the point of unsociability, though totally dedicated to the school and her pupils.

'We may hear wedding bells yet.'

I wasn't laughing, however. I had recognised the man immediately. His pale, angular face had not changed, nor the wiry black hair against which his big ears stood out. I knew what was going to happen and I was surprised at my own casual reaction, my lack of alarm.

'If she does decide to get married, you'll have to start doing a full timetable,' Juanjo added slyly.

No, he hadn't changed one bit. I could remember the first time I saw him with Marisa, inclining his head with its big ears to look at her. It was then, remembering Marisa – with an instantaneous clarity that I would never have thought I could recover – that I felt the alarm I had not experienced earlier. I must have let my unexpected emotion show, because Juanjo put an arm round my shoulder.

'What's wrong?' he asked.

I muttered some excuse and sat down. It was perfectly true, though, that I did not feel well. Juanjo went back to the table, stubbed out his cigarette in the ashtray and went on with the minutes. A little later we left. I asked him again about the man who was with Paquita.

'Don't you remember him?'

'Never seen him before in my life,' he replied.

We were wandering around in the maze of old streets that twisted and turned past almost deserted buildings, with patches of crumbling plaster and paint peeling off like scabs. From some flats there came a smell of vegetables cooking and, at street level, a few humble, rundown bars still clung to existence. Yet above our hesitant steps and the dingy surroundings, the June twilight was full of the balmy scent of trees, wafting down from above.

I had already met Marisa, but I really only got to know her properly after she began work as an assistant in a store that had opened to a fanfare of publicity on Calle Ordoño, where they sold all the latest items, like record players, radios, electric irons, washing machines, the kind of goods that have since become so commonplace. She was tall and willowy, with dark brown hair and eyes the colour of ruby-red honey.

Walking along the avenue in the evenings, I used to watch her through the shop window, warmed, for it was winter, by some red bars that provided modern, electric heating for the passers-by who stopped to look at the display of goods.

I spoke to her at the town's annual *fiesta,* taking advantage of some friendly jostling over a dodgem car. A couple of days later, we were going out together. She liked me too. I used to wait for her when she came out of work and walk her to the entrance of her block of flats. Sometimes her sister would come along; she was shorter than Marisa and rather thick-set, but she made up for her lack of beauty by her affectionate and open personality.

Marisa and I scarcely spoke. Whenever she had a day off work, we used to search out the shadows of the park and hold hands. Around that time I read some essays on love. I think that my distrust of those who are considered experts on the matter dates from then. A teacher lent me some books on the subject, but I read them with as little enthusiasm as if they were texts I had to study for an exam. None of those austere thinkers seemed to express the way I saw Marisa as the sole radiant source of light, the way my insides melted when I looked at her face, the strange feeling of nostalgia that came over me when we were apart and even, perhaps more acutely, when we were together.

The summer passed in a flash. We wrote to each other, and I would send long missives telling her about the village where my grandparents lived, with its simple pleasures and its rural values. She wrote much less assiduously. Her replies to my frequent letters were often short and awkward and their recounting of trivial events displayed, both in the spelling and the style of narration, a notable departure from the standard of written communication I was accustomed to in my family and at school.

That year's *fiesta*, the letters we wrote over the summer, and the following autumn, were, I think, the happiest days of our relationship. Once the following term had got under way, a series of circumstances combined to make things more difficult.

I was so wrapped up in my passion that I began rather to neglect my studies and instead of staying in the *pensión*, as I had always done before, poring over my books next to the stove which Doña Valeriana fussed over constantly, I began to wander around the streets almost compulsively, sometimes in Marisa's company, but at other times alone, watching my shadow as it slipped over walls, shop windows and the corners of streets.

One day, when I arrived back for lunch, I found my mother waiting. She had come by bus from Martiniano and she told me, with a very solemn expression on her face, that she needed to have a serious chat with me. After the meal we went to my room. She sat on my roommate's bed – guessing what was happening he had lingered in the dining room – and I sat on mine.

She immediately started to cry, as though she had been holding back floods of tears all this time. As she cried and blew her nose, she launched into a long tirade, so incoherent that it took me some time to understand her words, though I soon guessed the reason for her distress. She and my father worked as schoolteachers in a remote part of the province and were having to struggle to earn enough money so that I could look forward to a better life than they had; meanwhile, I was demonstrating my lack of gratitude for those efforts by neglecting my studies, taking up with girls in a way that was inappropriate at my age, roaming the streets, and behaving in a completely selfish and irresponsible fashion.

That visit from my mother is imprinted on my memory like a scar. I too burst into tears, and promised I'd do anything she asked.

When I calmed down, I began to speculate as to the possible identity of her secret informants. I quickly ruled out my teachers, obscure, weary individuals, with absolutely no interest in the lives of their pupils, and I was inclined to blame Doña Valeriana and her daughter, who were from the village where my parents taught, that being, in fact, the reason for my choice of lodgings.

That conjecture, associated with one of the first bitter experiences of my adolescence, forced me to learn the rudiments of hypocrisy. I believe now that this suspicion, with its inevitable accompaniment of deceit and the search for safer meeting places, subtly altered the natural spontaneity of my relationship with Marisa. I was filled with anxiety at the thought of a possible repeat visit from my mother, but I could sense that my secretiveness made Marisa uneasy, and that she resented it. Nevertheless, our relationship grew and I was quite convinced that my destiny, after my University career and the consequent attainment of a professional situation – for that was what my parents had always planned for me, and I had accepted it since childhood – would be intimately linked to hers. Marisa would be my wife. I used to swear this to her, and she would smile. Once, a gypsy who was reading palms confirmed it.

But in the next summer holidays things changed. I wrote with the same fervour as the year before. I told her about the *fiestas,* fishing for crabs, the long games of skittles. She, on the other hand, wrote me only one letter, at the beginning of the summer.

Her silence condemned me to a permanent state of anxious anticipation, darkened by a cloud of gloomy premonitions. So when I returned to the city, I was afraid to meet Marisa. All the same, I went to see her the very day I arrived.

The weather was still warm and the glass doors were wide open. I saw her at the back of the shop, leaning over the counter next to the girl on the till. It was not long until closing time. Suddenly she raised her eyes and looked at me through the window. I smiled timidly, and raised my hand in a conciliatory gesture, rather than a greeting. She then ran through the shop, out into the street, and came over to me. She looked beautiful. The sun had not darkened that white, lunar visage. Her hair was shiny and combed tightly back, held at the nape of her neck by a small bow.

Her eyes betrayed a touch of annoyance. She spoke rapidly, without preamble, as though we had seen each other minutes earlier and there was still the tension of some quarrel between us.

'Look,' she said, in a low, brusque voice. 'Please go away. Don't wait for me. I won't be going with you.'

I can still recall the feeling clearly: everything swam before my eyes, and I felt a sudden burning sensation, as though some bodily substance was racing through my limbs, my chest, my cheeks and covering my eyes with a sudden opacity. I was incapable of replying.

'Don't come to meet me after work any more.'

I stood there for a bit, overwhelmed, hearing a curious whistling in my ears, like some mysterious locomotive. When

187

I came to, I saw that she was once again busying herself by the counter, glancing at me from time to time out of the corner of her eye, visibly irritated.

So I left, dragging my feet. On the one hand, a forlorn, obedient impulse urged me to get out of her sight, since that was clearly what she wanted; on the other hand, every step I took, carrying me away from her, seemed like a kilometre of sadness. In the end, after wandering around in the area near the shop, I crossed the road and stood on the pavement on the other side, glued to the spot, staring fixedly at the entrance.

That was when I first saw him. Initially, my gaze was fastened on the figure of Marisa, whom I glimpsed through the huge windows, getting the final tasks of the day done. I only noticed him when she came out of the shop and went towards him. It was the same individual: tall, thin, with very thick hair, dressed in a dark suit.

From the opposite pavement it was difficult to make out his face: his pallor stood out, like a white smudge, otherwise the giant ears were his only striking feature.

Marisa took his arm and they began to walk. I followed them for a bit, until they drew near to the park. The twilight was full of the sweet scent of river and roses. At that moment I felt a searing pain as though my soul were raw flesh, a feeling of despair such as I have never again experienced in my life, and I turned away.

I followed them on other occasions, as they walked towards the old haunts of my first love affair. I would lurk amidst the shade of the giant chestnut trees, and spy on them. They would sit still and quiet, never speaking a word, as though listening to some sound inaudible to my ear. Later, he would walk her home.

Once, in a rage, I followed him. We walked for ages, leaving behind us Pinilla, where Marisa lived, and crossing the district of Crucero, Calle Astorga, the station, the bridge, Calle Guzmán, the Papalaguinda district and the bullring. We had gone past Avenida Hispánica and were approaching Avenida Venatoria. It was very dark. I was weary of the long

188

walk, where he had set the pace, marching along like a robot.

I loathed his height, his thin angularity, his elderly air, but, above all, I hated that head flanked by the two great white ears.

We were alone in that long darkness which the feeble bulbs of infrequent streetlights did little to attenuate. I picked up a stone from the ground and began to run towards him. I stopped a few paces away and threw it at him with all my might. However, my aggression was diluted by the sheer futility of my gesture; the stone appeared to miss him, and I heard it fall further on, raising slight echoes along the road.

Yet there was something in the event that filled me with confusion: I was certain I had hit him with the stone, right between the shoulderblades; yet that certainty was complemented by another; the stone had continued on its way as though it had met no obstacle. My confusion turned to fear, for I was convinced I had seen the stone pass through that dark figure without causing him to falter. So I stood still, watching him disappear into the darkness that thickened in the distance, at the place where the two rivers meet.

One day, I was told that Marisa had a dreadful illness. At my lodgings they seemed to have forgotten their previous dislike of her and Doña Valeriana would make the sign of the cross whenever she spoke of the disease, lamenting the fact that it should strike such a young girl. As soon as I heard about it, I went to the shop on Calle Ordoño, but Marisa wasn't there.

I never saw her again. She died a few months later. A lot of people from the town went to the funeral. The service was in the church of San Francisco. It was a Saturday in spring, and there was a thick mist. I walked as far as Puente Castro and carried on to the cemetery. The physical exercise brought me some relief from my pain. When I got to the cemetery, everyone else had left, but I knew immediately where they had placed Marisa's body, for he was there, standing by the recently dug grave with its fresh bunches of flowers.

The afternoon had turned grey. I watched him in silence. He was motionless, paler than usual. I approached until I was within six steps of him. I gazed avidly at his ashen face, full of angularities and his hair like the bristles of an animal. I don't know how long I stared, but slowly I began to realise that my hatred during all those months made no sense.

Marisa's companion, my rival, stood there like the rusting equipment used for lowering the coffins, the worn head-stones, the remnants of wreaths, the empty candle-holders. In that absolute silence, with neither birdsong nor voices, I understood that Marisa belonged to him much more than she would ever have belonged to me. Then, very gradually, I saw his dark, thin figure begin to dissolve, fading into the mist in long grey wisps, until he had disappeared completely.

We had gone into Benito's bar and Juanjo was staring at his glass like someone examining a particularly strange object.

'Let's hope things work out for her,' he said.

I looked at him, puzzled.

'Paquita,' he said. 'She's a good sort.'

'Sure,' I said, picking up my own glass from the counter.

'By the way,' he added. 'You'll have to go to the meeting on Monday instead of her, because she's got a doctor's appointment. She tells me she's been getting some bad headaches recently.'

© José María Merino
Translated by Annella McDermott

The Lost Traveller

JOSÉ MARÍA MERINO

Driving rain was bouncing noisily off the road, creating ripples of shimmering whiteness against the silvery reflection of the surface. The man appeared out of nowhere and stopped suddenly in front of him; he instinctively retreated, seeking the protection of the doorway where he had taken shelter. The man was carrying a small suitcase in his right hand and in the other a canvas bag. Water streamed from his hair onto his collar, his scarf and the lapels of his gabardine raincoat, which was soaked through.

'Excuse me,' said the man.

He was taken by surprise, and did not answer. The man was staring at him with wide eyes, above which his forehead glinted, while water streamed down over his eyebrows.

'Excuse me,' the man said again.

Rain was also pouring from his cuffs over the luggage he was carrying in his hands.

'What can I do for you?' he responded.

'I'm lost,' said the man.

He was breathing hard as though he had been running.

'I'm lost. I need to get to the railway station. I have a train to catch at twelve o'clock.'

'It's a long way. You'd better take a taxi.'

'There are none to be had,' the man answered. 'I've been trying for the last hour to get hold of a taxi, but I can't find one.'

'Well, the Metro is just there,' he said.

He pointed to the end of the street, invisible through the leaden grey of the rain.

'Down there, on this side of the road.'

The man's eyes had not lost their petrified expression.

'I'm a stranger here,' he said.

191

'The station has a lot of steps,' he added. 'You'd better hurry. It'll take you close on half an hour.'

The man stammered his thanks and walked off through the rain.

When he got back home with his newspaper and the shopping, this encounter stuck in his mind: the man's tense expression, his apprehensive gaze, that slight hesitation when he spoke. Nor did the memory of the traveller fade from his mind as he finished his tasks for the morning, adding a few sentences to the article on fiction in the last decade, and putting onto the computer nearly half of the interview with the Mexican academic, nor during lunch – he ate at home, since the rain was still bucketing down – nor during the editorial meeting at the magazine, which took up the whole of the afternoon and the early part of the evening.

He got home around half-past eight. Berta was not there, and she rang shortly afterwards to say she would be home late. He poured himself a drink and lay down on the sofa, staring at the blank television screen. The image of that petrified face above the drenched raincoat persisted, gradually taking on the vague coherence of a scene from a novel. He got up, fetched his notebook and a pen and drafted a few notes. A man walks through a strange city. A man walks in fear through an unfamiliar city.

At a quarter to ten, Berta rang again.

'I'll be a while yet.'

He poured himself another drink, went to his study, switched on the computer, put in his short stories disk and began to write. Finally, after all this time, he had an idea. He was excited, almost happy, his head clear.

A man walks around a city at twilight. A seasoned traveller, he is from a faraway country and is a complete stranger to these streets where the wind catches up discarded lottery tickets, leaves and cigarette ends. In his eyes there is an expression of such immutable desolation that the people passing stare in surprise, and even the street-vendors and beggars look at him suspiciously, though without daring to speak. The man is not strolling, he is drifting, with his hands in his pockets, his body slightly bent and taking long, slow steps. Sometimes he pauses in front of shop windows, but he does not look at the goods on offer; instead he stares at the glass, searching for an angle that will allow him to see his own reflection, as though trying to recognise himself.

After working for about an hour he printed out what he had written and went back to the sitting room with the empty glass. It felt good to be writing again. He turned on the television set, but he was staring at it distractedly and, through the moving images, he could still picture the anguish of that traveller, not now the one he had met in the morning, but the one in the story he had recently begun.

'He's trapped,' he murmured. 'He's terrified. As though something terrible was about to happen to him.'

It was after half-past eleven when Berta got back, and he was on his fourth drink. She looked fed up and seemed physically exhausted.

'Aren't you going to give me a kiss?' he said, hugging her.

'Have you had a lot to drink?'

'I'm writing a story.'

She looked at him as though she hadn't heard and went off into the bedroom. When she appeared again she had taken off her coat and was slipping out of her skirt as she went towards the bathroom. He heard her peeing loudly, heaving a sigh of relief.

'Didn't you hear what I said? I'm writing a story.'

She came out of the bathroom without her skirt, went to the bedroom and carried on undressing.

'Have you had dinner?' she asked.

'No.'

'Nor have I. I just couldn't get away. Have we got anything to eat?'

He shrugged. He felt happy.

'There must be something,' he exclaimed.

He told her about it again the next day, again at the end of the day's work, when they were both home. Berta, who was leafing through her diary, just stared at him.

'A story?'

'I told you yesterday. You didn't hear me.'

'I was worn out. I don't know if I can take this blasted reorganisation.'

She lit a cigarette and continued the conversation with interest.

'So you're writing?'

'Yes, although I've got lots of other work I should be doing. Yesterday, I came across a guy soaked to the skin and it sparked off an idea.'

'What's it about?'

He fetched what he had written so far.

'I've just sketched out the idea,' he said. 'A man wanders through a distant city, in which he's lost and scared, as if he's being followed.'

He read out the brief text. When he had finished, he looked at her. She still had her eyes fixed on him, engrossed.

'What do you think?'

Berta did not answer.

'Maybe there is no external pursuer and his fear comes purely from himself, from his own demons,' he added. 'The man has clearly experienced a personal tragedy and maybe he's forced to travel because of his job. He's constantly changing cities, climates, customs. As the years go by, these perpetual rapid changes and the persistent, troubling memories gradually begin to induce a strange anxiety in his mind. Perhaps he's afraid that one day, in one of these strange cities, he'll forget how to get back to his hotel, and may even forget who he is. Perhaps he fears he'll be taken over by the places he goes to, which he always experiences as strange and unwelcoming, and yet their hostility feels right, somehow, because it reflects the intense grief living inside him.'

'What happens to him?' she asked.

'I don't know yet,' he answered. 'I'm going to think it over, calmly. I've got him there, wandering round and round in circles, like in a maze, and it's an image which, far from

194

upsetting me, calms me down. It's as though his anxiety, whose cause I don't yet know, was swallowing up all my own worries. I haven't felt this good for months. Anyway, I'll certainly carry on with it.'

She nodded.

'Yes, you must carry on. You couldn't be that cruel.'

'Cruel?'

'To your character.'

He was disconcerted.

'Who knows, maybe there's worse in store for him yet,' he said finally, and they both laughed.

At the end of March, he was asked to write a report on a critical symposium and then several other things came up, so he put the story to one side. She, however, did not forget it and she asked him several times how it was shaping up. Her questions troubled him.

'I haven't had time to go back to it,' he would reply.

She would blink rapidly, as she always did in reaction to anything strange or unresolved, then the gesture would change to a smile that implied, not altogether convincingly, that the reproach was jocular.

'So you're keeping him running round and round in circles?

One night he woke up, startled by a cry from her. He groped for the light switch on the bedside table. From the other bed, Berta was staring at him with a look of such fear on her face that he too was overcome by a wave of alarm. He threw off the bedclothes and went over to lie beside her, hugging her tightly.

'What is it? What on earth is wrong?'

Berta's forehead was bathed in sweat and tears as thick as mucus welled up in her eyes. She spoke in a halting voice, with frequent sobs.

'There was somebody looking at me. A man. His face was right up against mine. A man was looking at me with a horrible expression on his face.'

From then on, he was woken on several nights by Berta's

terrified cries. Berta always said that she had seen right up close to her the face of a man whose eyes were filled with fear. A man in a grey street, with ugly low houses, in a dusty city.

On one of those occasions, Berta said accusingly:

'It's the man in your story. It's the same lost traveller, petrified with fear.'

He couldn't think what to say.

'You have to get him out of there.'

He switched off the light and lay there uneasily. Berta couldn't sleep.

'You have to get him out of there,' she repeated.

He sat up and spoke in her direction, and though he knew she was near, he noticed in himself a vague fear of the darkness.

'OK, I'll get him out. Now go back to sleep.'

But she would not be pacified.

'You have to get him out of there.'

'Calm down. I promise I'll do it.'

'How?'

At that point, the idea came to him, suddenly yet with deliberation, as though it had emerged from deep down and had always been there inside him.

'A meeting. He'll meet somebody and escape from the maze.'

He didn't write it. In the mornings, he was too busy with other things and had no time to go back to the story; also, spring had come and he usually spent the afternoons chatting to friends in bars or going for a stroll. However, from the time he told Berta that the traveller in the story would escape from his fear because of a meeting with someone, she never again had that nightmare about the face staring at her.

In the second week of May, Berta had to go on a trip to negotiate a tender. She was growing more and more fed up with the company and the jockeying for position in the office. Also, she believed that she was liable to be the loser in the constant wars, because the other potential directors were all men and the one thing they seemed to agree on, concerning

196

the changes in the wake of the reorganisation, was that she was not in line for any promotion.

The trip was awkward in some ways, because she was going to North Africa, a journey involving stopovers and waiting for connections, and Berta was eager to get it over as quickly as possible; she planned to leave on Thursday morning and be back by Friday evening.

She went off very early, and that night he missed her sorely. After one failed marriage and a few unsatisfactory affairs, this relationship, in spite of the problems that had been making Berta so edgy in the last few months, had given him a balance he had never found before, and introduced him to a more regular lifestyle. He drank a lot less, the only thing he smoked were cigarettes, he was up to date with his reading, he was meeting all his deadlines and he had even lost the rage he used to feel, the bitterness that would rise in him as he saw the days and months pass without him being able to write a story. The sight of her undisturbed bed upset him so much that he ended up sleeping on the sofa in the living room, like a guest invited to stay the night.

Berta called him the next day, just after lunch, as he was on his way out. Apparently there were high winds in Melilla and it was likely that all flights that afternoon would be cancelled. Her voice sounded tired. She couldn't come home yet.

'What are you going to do?' he asked, disguising the sudden unease that the news had aroused in him.

'I don't know. There's a boat leaving at eleven o'clock at night.'

'A boat?'

'It goes to Málaga, and I'd have to get a plane from there. But it's an all-night crossing, and they say the sea is rough as well.'

Silence separated them as though the line had been cut.

'Berta, Berta,' he said urgently.

'I'm here.'

'What about tomorrow?'

'There are several flights, but the high winds may continue and the planes will still be unable to take off. Don't worry about me,' she finally added, 'I'm fine. I'll read a couple of detective novels.'

'Call me the minute you have some news,' he replied, and she rang off with a promise that she would.

He did not go out after lunch. He was seized by a pressing need to continue the story he had begun so many months before. He discovered that his character was trapped in a remote city on the other side of the ocean. The winds were rising, his plane could not take off, and flight after flight was cancelled. Amidst that wind with its burden of dust and sand, snatching up pieces of newspaper and plastic, the traveller was filled with a sense of deep confusion and had to make an effort not to lose consciousness. He had gone up to the old quarter, but the houses, uninhabited or ruined, only increased his unease, so he made his way back to the airport.

Sitting on one of the seats, with a small, dark suitcase placed carefully at her feet, and her handbag on the seat next to her, was the woman he had noticed earlier in the queue of passengers. The traveller joined the group of people standing by the check-in desk listening to the explanations of the airline representative. He was talking about a phone call that would come shortly from Spain, to say whether the last flight of the day could take off, but it was clear that the verdict was unlikely to be favourable.

He hesitated for an instant, though his first impulse had been to go back outside, where the bushes around the glass building were bending in the wind. Finally, he went over to the seats, took the empty chair nearest to the woman, and stayed there gazing at her profile as she sat motionless with her hands around a closed book. Her legs were pressed together, and her posture was slightly forced, possibly a sign of her impatience.

He was staring at her so hard that the woman felt it and turned her head. When her eyes fell on the traveller, she gave a start, as if something in his face had surprised or even alarmed her. In her apprehension, she suddenly stood up and the book fell to the ground. The man disguised his own confusion by bending down to pick it up, but she was quicker. There was a suggestion of displeasure in the woman's attitude, as though she felt threatened. The man stood up too, and, making a tremendous effort to remain calm, he spoke to her. Although his words referred to the storm which was delaying all of them, he attempted, by his particularly respectful tone, to apologise for the alarm his presence had caused her, and also to initiate a conversation which, however trivial the pretext, would distract him for a time from his anguished wanderings.

He carried on writing till very late, waiting for Berta's phone call, which never came. He tried hard not to worry, blaming the lack of news on various trivial causes. Eventually he went to bed – the sofa again – and lay awake for a long time. When he fell asleep, he dreamed he was back again sheltering from the rain in a doorway and that the same passer-by, drenched to the skin and carrying two pieces of luggage, came over to him and repeated the same questions. However, just as he was about to answer – in his dream the scene did not seem like a memory, so vivid was it, and so real the sound and the metallic gleam of the rain and the feeling of dampness – Berta appeared. He tried to speak to her, but Berta did not even look at him: she was speaking solicitously to the traveller, urging him to take shelter under an awning covering the doorway, and she was drying his face, his neck, his hands, with a white cloth she had taken from her handbag, and with evident care and fondness. He could discern in Berta's eyes and in her movements a loving tenderness which he believed she had never shown to himself. He could feel sadness paralysing his body and he was sure that he would be stuck forever, motionless and alone, in that doorway, looking out at the rain.

He awoke at dawn and immediately sat down to continue the story.

At the airport, the lost traveller has met a woman, forced, like him, to wait until the wind dies down. Some initial remarks on the problem affecting them have opened the gates to a long conversation. After a while, they are told that the last flight of the day has been cancelled. Together the two travellers leave the airport and walk around the city, absorbed in their conversation.

That strange distant city and all the circumstances of their peculiar shipwreck conspire to awaken in each of them a frankness that grows as the hours pass. At first, the traveller talks about his job, recalling the early days when all that nonstop travel held a promise of adventure, and he arrived in each city eager to discover some of its secrets. In turn, she told him about her first years in her job when she saw each new project as a story, always with the promise of a happy ending.

Later, he tells her all the details of his progressive anxiety, how as the years and the journeys have passed, he has begun to fear that one day he will forget his name and will become irredeemably lost in the streets of a city like this one, surrounded by shops selling kimonos, tape recorders and quartz watches. She then tells him about her struggles in the company over the last year, her growing weariness with the infighting.

They both rejected the crossing in the boat that was to leave at eleven. They hoped that the wind would die down in the night and that flights to Spain would be resumed in the morning. They had dinner together and, later, they sat in one of the cafés near the plaza, where they stayed till closing time. The wind had died down.

On one side of the huge circular plaza, built as a backdrop for military ceremonies and parades, was the park with its tall palm trees, its ghostly walls, its deserted white paths along which only they now strolled. They walked and chatted for another hour, then went back to the hotel where they were both staying. The sleepy night porter handed them the keys. They had both been drinking and were talkative and wide awake. She remembered that she had in her room a couple of bottles of whisky that she had bought in an Indian shop as potential presents, and invited him in for a drink.

So they went on till dawn, drinking and talking. The sky was growing light over the port when she told him about her various disappointments in love, and spoke about her present partner, with whom she stayed mainly out of friendship and the fear of loneliness. 'Yet I'm still lonely,' she confessed. He moved closer and told her how he had lost his wife in an accident, in the winter rain. 'I'm haunted by the memory,' he said. 'I can't forget her, I can't forget what happened. I carry it around inside me all the time, like a demon that won't let go.' Like a beast gnawing at his imagination, constantly opening fresh wounds.

They separated after breakfast, to catch a few hours' sleep before going out to the airport. However, with morning the wind had regained its strength and was gusting over the city, veiling in dust the outline of the distant mountains.

By midday, Berta had still not called. The story had advanced a lot, but as he re-read it he felt a detachment, even an antipathy, towards what he had written and realised that he could not go on; he did not like the way the story was developing; it was too much of a cliché; the enigma of the lost traveller could not be resolved by an encounter with a woman, however attractive, so he tried to reshape it completely from the point where the man begins to speak with the woman in the airport lounge, attempting to substitute for the relationship between them – after her shock at seeing that face – events with a completely different meaning.

Instead of engaging in conversation with the traveller, the woman would get to her feet, pick up her luggage and hurry away. Thus the relationship between them could never arise; the growing intimacy would be transformed into distance and only a few brief interchanges would link them intermittently over the course of a night in which she would flee while he tried vainly to pursue her.

However, the story would not bend in the new direction he had decided to give it. He changed the text numerous times, but successive readings of the new versions forced him to accept that, despite his dislike of the original plot, the meeting between the two travellers and their subsequent intimacy was no more melodramatic and clichéd than keeping them apart.

Moreover, during the long conversation, some elements

could be introduced which would give the whole thing a sense of destiny, because it occurred to him that the traveller might begin to suspect, behind the behaviour and appearance of the woman, some mystery relevant to himself.

It was Saturday afternoon, and he felt resentful. 'It's a ridiculous tale,' he thought, knowing that he was enslaved to the story, which was determined to develop in ways that defied his will.

All he had eaten was some biscuits and fruit and he felt low and sluggish, but he clung to the story as to a vow whose abandonment might bring down on his head all kinds of grief and misfortune. He felt very alone, on an interminable day full of evil omens, and the story, though resistant to some of his intentions, was at least a testimony to reality and coherence.

The two travellers remained for a further day in the city. Their prolonged conversation had brought them closer and they enjoyed each other's company. The wind continued and flights were still suspended, so that night they bought tickets for the boat, being obliged to share a cabin. With an unease that was simultaneously frightening and pleasurable, the traveller noticed that the woman was beginning to seem eerily familiar to him.

They sat in the main lounge, where some people were dancing under the fluorescent lights. Only an hour or so had gone by when dancing became very difficult because of the rolling of the ship amid the rough seas. One of the dancers fell against a table, glasses shattered, there were hysterical shrieks that marked the end of the evening and everyone went off to bed.

The lights were dim and the cabin looked like some ancient crypt recently uncovered thanks to luck and the skill of the archaeologists. She sat on one of the bunks and took off her shoes with a gesture in which the traveller found the definitive key to his unease.

She had her head bent and her hair concealed her face, but the traveller was sure now who she was: only some ancient misunderstanding or the persistence of an incomprehensible

202

delusion – unless it was a dream from which he was now emerging, only to realise it was a lie – could have led him to believe she was dead. When the woman looked up at him, his hope turned to joy as he unhesitatingly recognised every single feature of her face.

That twist in the plot, an unexpected flash of imagination, put a sudden end to his efforts. In amazement he re-read the last passage. For reasons he could not fathom, the lost traveller had irrupted into places never suspected or foreseen by the author.

It was the middle of the night by now, and only the inter-mitten frenzy of Saturday-night drivers disturbed the darkness of the streets. He decided not to write any more and went to the living room, where he stood for a long time, immersed in the bafflement induced by the way his story had developed, apparently heading nowhere but into confusion and mad-ness. His growing disappointment led him eventually to an implacable sense of his own solitude.

It took him a long time to fall asleep and, at nine o'clock the next morning, he was woken abruptly by the ringing of the telephone. It was Berta, back in Spain after taking the boat. Her voice was hoarse with lack of sleep and sounded vaguely uneasy.

'Are you OK?' he asked anxiously.

'Fine,' she said, in an evasive tone.

'When will you get here?'

She told him that she would be taking the plane at midday.

'I need to talk to you about something,' she added finally.

He felt an obscure threat in her tone and could not think what to reply. He simply said that he would be waiting at the airport. He felt very restless, so he went out. It was Sunday and the streets were deserted and quiet. He began to wander around, oblivious to the brightness of the sun, just going where his feet led him. He tried not to think about Berta, prey to a gloomy premonition that echoed the feelings of his dream of the night before last, when he had seen her lavish such tenderness on a stranger. Nor did he want to think about the story that lay in his office awaiting its ending. Yet he could not forget it either, as he strode on, with wide, staring eyes, provoking surprise and even alarm in the few people who crossed his path.

He had walked a great distance, when he became aware that it was time to set off for the airport. Yet an obscure impulse drove him back home. He turned on the computer, put in his short stories disk, searched in the directory for the story he had been writing for so many months and clicked the command that would make it disappear. When the story had been deleted, he heaved a sigh.

Once again, he had been unable to finish a story and maybe this time, too, the memory of the unresolved plot would fester in his mind, preventing him for a long time from constructing another one. But the plane would be landing soon and he hurried out of the flat.

© José María Merino
Translated by Annella McDermott

José María Merino was born in La Coruña in 1941, but lived for many years in León. At present, he is resident in Madrid. Merino's first work of fiction was *Novela de Andrés Choz* (1976). His novel *La orilla oscura* (1985) won the Spanish Critics' Prize and *Las visiones de Lucrecia y la ruina de la Nueva Restauración* (1996) was awarded the Miguel Delibes Prize. 'The Companion' is from *Cuentos del reino secreto* (1982) and 'The Lost Traveller' is the title story of *El viajero perdido* (1990).

The One Where She Tells Him A Story

JUAN JOSÉ MILLÁS

She smiled at him from one end of the sofa. She was wearing a very short black skirt and a tight grey sweater. It was dark in the sitting room and out in the street the evening was beginning its leisurely decline.

'Are you sure your parents aren't going to turn up any minute?' he asked.

'If you're going to be like that, we'll go out,' she replied.

'I just feel really uptight,' he said.

'Why?' she asked.

He passed her the joint and did not respond at once. Finally, his gaze lost in the geometry of a piece of porcelain, he said:

'I get like this sometimes, I get a sort of knot in my chest, just here. And it doesn't go away until something happens.'

'What sort of something?' she asked, stubbing out the joint in a copper ashtray.

'Something bad,' he said.

It was a very spacious living room, full of over-large furniture and objects that harked back to a solid but inglorious past. The boy, who was sitting at the other end of the sofa, smiled at the girl and tried in vain to evoke some exciting fantasy. The minutes passed noisily on a pendulum clock. For the second time, she asked him if she should put some music on and he again said no.

'If they tried to open the door or if they rang the bell, we wouldn't hear them,' he argued.

'So you spend the whole day just waiting for something to happen,' she said.

'Yes,' he said shyly.

At that moment, the phone rang and he almost jumped off the sofa, causing her to collapse in laughter.

'Aren't you going to pick it up?' he asked.

'I can't, we're not here,' she said.

'Where are we?'

'At the cinema or having a few beers somewhere.'

'What if it's your parents and they've decided to come back?'

'Don't start that again.'

The phone continued to ring throughout this conversation and then stopped. Night was falling on the other side of the windows, although the living room had been in darkness for some time. The boy was sweating; he switched on the table lamp to his left, and a few objects recovered their shapes.

'Imagine it was true what you said before: that we're not here.'

She crossed her legs and lit a cigarette. Then she screwed up her eyes and pursed her lips; the shadow of a smile flickered across her mouth.

'It's possible,' she said at last, 'we might well be somewhere else, but, for some reason, we might believe that we were here.'

'That would be great,' he said, as if relieved of an enormous burden. 'That way, even if your parents did come back, nothing would happen.'

'Have you ever seen a film called *The Boston Strangler*?'

'No,' he said.

She changed position, put out her cigarette and proceeded to roll another joint while she summarised the plot for him.

'It's based on real events, I think. It's about this really normal guy who worked as a plumber or something. The thing is, the guy was a murderer, only he didn't know it. There was a murky area in his life that he knew nothing about, and when he was in that murky area, he used to strangle women. There's a really moving bit when the police discover that he's the murderer, but at the same time realise that he doesn't know it. Like I said, he was a model family man and all that. Anyway, they arrest him, but they don't tell him what he's been accused of, instead they call in some psychiatrists to see if they can make him remember his crimes. The man is completely baffled, of course, because he has no idea what's going on. Then the psychiatrists start working with him and there's one really chilling moment. Just thinking about it makes my hair stand on end. I'm going to put the centre light on.'

She handed him the joint and got up to turn on the main light. The shadows, far from diminishing, grew thicker in the most densely furnished parts of the room. The boy took a rather anxious drag on the joint. He seemed to have grown thinner in the last few minutes, but that was due to the intensity of his gaze and the effect of the light on his face.

'And where did he think he was when he was killing these women?' he asked.

'He wasn't anywhere,' she replied, 'the crimes were parentheses, black holes. That's what I think anyway. So, I was telling you about this one moment, when he's with the psychiatrists, when an event surfaces in his memory that he has no knowledge of having been part of. He sees himself climbing furtively down the drainpipe in some inner courtyard somewhere. Then you get a close-up of his face on the screen and it shows the utter horror he feels at remembering something that, as far as he was concerned, never happened. Can you imagine what it must feel like to remember things that haven't happened or that you believe haven't happened?'

'How did it end?'

'I can't remember.'

'Those things usually end badly.'

'Have you still got the knot in your chest?'

'It's got much worse now. That story about the plumber has made me feel really strange.'

She changed position and sat looking up at the ceiling, watching the smoke from the joint rise up and disperse. The boy could not find a position in which he could sit comfortably for more than half a minute. After a while, he said:

'Why have you gone all silent?'

'I'm enjoying myself just imagining things,' she replied.

'What are you imagining now?'

'That what you said about the knot is true, that it warns you when something bad is going to happen.'

'It's true, I told you it was.'

'The same thing happens to my father when he dreams that he's smoking a cigarette. He gave it up fifteen years ago, but sometimes, in dreams, he sees himself smoking again and the following day something always happens.'

The girl stopped speaking and the tick-tock from the pendulum clock took on vast proportions.

'Keep talking, please,' he said, 'when you stop talking, I feel even more anxious.'

'Did I tell you what happened to my grandmother when my Uncle Fernando died, my father's twin brother?'

'Don't tell me any more stories like that.'

'All right. Do you want to go to my room then?'

'Not yet. I just need to calm down a bit first.'

She excused herself and left the living room. When she got to the bathroom, she looked at herself in the mirror and her eyes were shining. She sent herself a knowing smile and unhurriedly retouched her lipstick. Then she brushed her hair, tried out a few horrified expressions and returned to the living room.

'It was awful,' she said, 'it was in the house opposite, I saw it from the bathroom window: a woman just leapt into space.'

'What do you mean?'

'She killed herself. The people next door have picked up the body and put it in a car.'

The boy sat very still, his eyes fixed on the ashtray, as if listening to some internal event.

'That's probably the thing you sensed was about to happen,' she added.

'That's exactly what I was going to say,' he said, 'the knot in my chest is gradually dissolving.'

After a while, he got up, put his arm around the girl's waist and they made their way to the bedroom kissing. From the street came a scream that penetrated the windows, but they were too busy exploring each other's bodies to notice. The pendulum clock struck ten.

Ah, well.

Juan José Millás (Valencia, 1946) is both a writer of short stories and novels and a journalist. His first novel, *Cerbero son las sombras* won the Sésamo Prize in 1974 and since then he has published *Visión del ahogado* (1977), *Papel mojado* (1983), *Letra muerta* (1983), *El desorden de tu nombre* (1988), *La soledad era esto* (1990; winner of the Nadal Prize), *Volver a casa* (1990) and *El orden alfabético* (1998). This story is taken from *Primavera de luto y otros cuentos* (1989) in which all the stories end with the same resigned, anticlimactic 'Ah, well.'

Family Life

QUIM MONZÓ

Armand ran into the workshop making a noise like a car and trampling the shavings on the floor, crunching over them as noisily as he could. He circled the carpenter's bench twice, and looked at the saws, gouges, clamps and planes hanging up, all in perfect order, each tool in its proper place (marked by the appropriate outline sketched on the wall), then went off down the passage at the end of which the actual house began. Uncle Reguard had his workshop at the back of the house and although the grown-ups always used the front entrance, Armand preferred to go in through the workshop. He was fascinated by the fact that his uncle's workshop was just behind the house. He lived in a flat and his father's workshop was on the ground floor of another building, four blocks away. His cousins all felt the same. Uncle Reguard was the only member of the family to have his house and his workshop together; there was a little room that served to separate the two, and also served as a lumber room. Immediately after it, if you were approaching from the workshop, came the dining room, with the big table, the chandelier, and the armchairs, then the corridors with doors to the other rooms.

When Armand got to the dining room the others were already there, exchanging kisses, laughing, and shouting louder and louder all the time in order to be heard; his father, his mother, his cousins, his uncle, his aunts, the other aunt and uncle, and the other group of more distant cousins, who in fact weren't cousins at all, he just called them cousins because they belonged to such distant branches of the family that he didn't know exactly how to classify them.

They ate a meal that went on for hours, then sat around afterwards, with cigar smoke filling the room. The empty champagne bottles began to pile up in the lumber room, between the house and the workshop, the aunts cut cake non-stop and the older cousins played records. The air was thick and smelled of chocolate. The younger cousins (Armand, Guinovarda, Gisela, Guitard, Llopard) asked to be allowed to get down from the table, then ran to Eguinard's room to play with the wooden houses, which had roofs and doors and windows all painted in different colours. With the door ajar, Armand could see a corner of the passageway and in that corner the harp.

It was a harp that Uncle Reguard had made thirty years ago, and it was a source of great pride in the family, because (as Armand's father always said) it showed that carpentry and instrument-making were not so very different. As far back as he could remember, Armand had seen the harp in Uncle Reguard's house, always in the same place: the corner where the passage way bent round. He found it much more beautiful than any of the drawings or photographs of other harps that he cut out of magazines and kept in a blue folder: a harp in the hands of a mythological god, a Sumerian harp topped with the carved head of an animal he was unable to identify, a badge from Ireland, two Norwegian harps (one had a dragon's head, the other the head of a woman with a blindfold over her eyes), and one made from a branch of a tree, being played by Harpo Marx.

His cousin Reguard came into the room tearful and smiling, surrounded by grown-ups congratulating him. In his right hand he had a chocolate mint ice cream; his left hand was wrapped in a bandage. It was a scene that Armand had witnessed over and over again, every time the family got together, sometimes at his house, sometimes at the house of the real cousins, occasionally in the houses of the other, distant cousins, some of whom even lived in different cities. A child always appeared with his left hand in a bandage. The bandage was thickest in the area of the ring finger: Armand knew that there was no longer a finger under the bandage, and that when the bandage came off there would be nothing there but a tiny little stump, completely healed. Once again, Armand looked round his relatives' hands. As he had gradually begun to notice some time ago, everyone over nine years of age was missing the ring finger of their left hand.

Armand was seven when he first realised that it was no coincidence that every time there was a party, one of the children had a finger cut off. Naturally, he had noticed that the older children had a finger missing, but it seemed entirely normal. All his adult relatives had a finger missing, for reasons which escaped him and to which he was indifferent; so many things escaped his knowledge, things he knew he would not understand until he was grown up, that he paid very little attention to this issue, which was trivial in comparison to other matters that occupied his mind: the spirit of self-sacrifice of the St Bernard dog, the origins of life or the rules governing offside in football. So far as he was concerned, in order to become a teenager, leaving behind the world of the child, you had to lose the finger of your left hand. It seemed as acceptable, normal and desirable as losing your milk teeth.

When he had first gone to school, he had been surprised to see that many grown-ups still had five fingers on each hand, and they seemed unperturbed by it. This he found remarkable, odd and rather unpleasant, and he felt proud to belong to a logical family. As the months passed, contact with other children led him to think that perhaps it was some sort of coincidence that all his relatives suffered accidents to their left hand and the accidents always resulted in the loss of the ring finger. The boy sitting at the desk next to his explained that losing a finger was typical of carpenters. The carpenter in his neighbourhood (he recounted) had lost three fingers. His mother had told him that the same thing happens to lots of carpenters, because sooner or later, the blade of the circular saw lops off a finger or two. Armand knew this was not exactly the case in his family. They were carpenters, but the loss of their finger was no fault of the circular saw, and it was no accident. At nine years of age, the children were not yet carpenters, and they did not even know if they would be carpenters when they grew up; although generally speaking, from time immemorial, all the members of the family had shown a marked preference for that trade and apart from a few exceptional cases, they all ended up as carpenters.

Armand spent many nights puzzling over the matter. Was there some professional obligation to have your finger cut off? He came to a conclusion for which he would have liked confirmation: the family cut that first finger off so that the children would begin to get used to the idea. The loss of that first finger made them lose their fear of losing another. It made them realise it was not such a big deal; it gave them courage and helped them to face their work bravely. One thing still nagged at him: he had met the father of a schoolfriend from another class, who was also a carpenter, yet (as he noticed every time the man came to pick up his son from school) he had no fingers missing from his hand.

As the adults did not make a tragedy out of it and, indeed, seemed particularly happy at the time the finger was cut off (especially the parents of the child who was being amputated), Armand saw nothing tragic about it either. Until that day, two years earlier, when he had first realised that some time in their ninth year, all the members of the family had a finger cut off, and it would happen to him one day: then he felt afraid. He was in the bedroom with his cousins, playing with the wooden houses. Eguinard, Gisela and Gimfreu had already lost a finger. Llopart and he still had five fingers, which meant that they were still children. At one point, when Eguinard stopped playing for a minute, Armand went over to him, swallowed hard and asked him what was all this business about fingers. Llopart, Gisela and Gimfreu looked round, just for a second, then carried on running in and out of the wooden houses. Eguinard asked him to repeat his question, perhaps playing for time while he thought up a reply. Armand amplified it: what was this business of the fingers; they had cut off his cousin Renguard's finger that day, and they cut off everybody's finger, sooner or later, once they reached nine. Llopart was looking at him in bewilderment. Eguinard stood up, tousled Armand's hair and gently drew him out of the room. Armand continued to insist: how come everybody in the family had the same finger missing from their left hand, and other people, who were not in the family, did not? Armand stared at Eguinard's finger, which was cut off at the base. There was a clean scar, for it had been done very well.

Moreover, why the ring finger of the left hand and not the little finger on the right hand, or one of the index fingers? Did it relate to some question of hygiene, the meaning of which had been lost down the centuries? It was clearly an ancestral custom, but what was its origin? Had they been doing it for centuries? Or just decades? The day he turned nine, his father found him crying in bed.

'I don't want to have my finger cut off.'

'What nonsense!'

'I want to be normal like the other children in school.'

'Being normal has nothing to do with the number of fingers you have.'

He dried his son's tears, and explained that normality is a cultural construct, and therefore relative; some people cut their hair short, others let it grow, some people have a beard and a moustache, some just a moustache, some just a beard, some are clean-shaven; there are societies where both men and women shave their body hair, other societies where only the women do so. We cut our nails, which differentiates us from animals and primitive peoples, who let theirs grow long. Armand did not accept these analogies: nails and hair grow back again, fingers don't. The sun streamed in the window; father and son stared at the warm rays as they fell across the floor.

'There's no need to decide immediately.'

'I have decided, and I don't want it.'

'Why?'

'Because you can't play the harp with a finger missing.'

Even he was surprised by this reply. He had spoken the words without thinking. However, even if he didn't know it, even if the thought had never actually crossed his mind, as far as other people were concerned, including his father, it was quite possible that he might really want to be a harpist, and so he clung to the idea. A few months earlier he had seen a programme on television with Nicanor Zabaleta playing the harp and he was quite sure that you needed all your fingers. A harpist needs them all. His father looked at him gravely. He had never seen his father look so stern.

'If you like music, there are all sorts of instruments. It doesn't necessarily have to be the harp.'

'I like the harp.'

'You've got that idea into your head because of your uncle's harp. But it's not the only instrument in the world. There are plenty of others: kettledrum, bass drum, cymbals, tambourine, bongo drums, the triangle . . .' Armand displayed no great enthusiasm. 'I could understand if you weren't too keen on the maracas, but what about a drum kit? A drum kit is a really complex set of instruments: the bass drum, the small tom-tom, the large tom-tom, cymbals, the large cymbal. Or what would you say to the vibraphone?'

Armand felt uneasy during the next few months. A story had always been jokingly bandied round the family that, one day, a child would have his finger cut off and it would grow again after a couple of months. Some said it would be a sign of something or other, but they could never agree on what exactly. Others accepted that, one day, an amputated finger would grow again, but denied it would be a sign of anything. For Armand that story raised a new dilemma: what if he refused to let them cut his finger off, and it turned out that he was the chosen one whose finger would grow back again? What an absurd situation! By refusing he was preventing the possible fulfilment of the prophecy.

He grew obsessed with fingers. He became aware that some people wore their ring on a particular finger of their left hand. Since in his family nobody had that ring finger, they wore their ring on their little finger and when there was a wedding the priest always looked very serious when the bride and groom came to exchange rings. Once, in the street, Armand saw a stranger with his left-hand ring finger missing and he spent days trying to find out if he was some distant relative, too far removed for him to know. Did other families follow the same custom? Or other similar customs: amputating

216

different fingers or other parts of the body, in order to . . . ? What? Where was the sense in it? What did they do with the amputated fingers? Bury them? Armand imagined them buried upright, like stems of asparagus, in little finger cemeteries. Maybe they cremated them.

Gradually he began to see his parents, and his other relatives, in a new light. What sort of macabre tradition was this, and how could they accept it so unfeelingly? Since he could not trust them, he used to sleep with his left hand under his pillow, and his head on top. He had worked out that it was completely impossible for them to get hold of his finger to cut it off by raising his head, removing the pillow and taking hold of his hand, without him waking. Sometimes he would dream that despite these precautions, his parents (wearing beatific smiles) managed to lift his head and the pillow, grasp his hand, and with one deft stroke of a butcher's knife lop off his finger.

When he heard that there was to be another family get-together on the following Sunday, he flew into a panic. For the first time, he was a candidate for losing a finger. Out of all the cousins, he and Guitard were the most likely cases. Both had reached nine years of age. He three months earlier, Guitard seven. If it went by seniority, then it was Guitard's turn. However, the amputations were not always done in order of age, so it might very well be him.

Sunday came and neither of them lost a finger, instead it was Teodard, a cousin who wasn't even nine yet (he had a month to go) and so in theory was not even in the running. Guitard was furious. It was his finger that should have been cut off, not his cousin's. It was explained that the event had been brought forward for a very simple reason: Teodard's mother was expecting a baby and they wanted to get it over with, so that when the new baby was born they would not have to be thinking about the amputation of the older child's finger. Armand was fascinated by Guitard's indignation. He asked him if he did not mind his finger being cut off. Why should he mind? On the contrary, not only could he not see any problem, he was astonished by Armand's question.

217

'It's not your head they cut off. Just a finger, and not even the most important one.'

Guitard was dying to be a grown-up: which is why, at the next family get-together, he ran into the room where the other children were playing with a train set, triumphantly brandishing his bandaged hand.

When the new little cousin was born (they named him Abelard), there was great agitation, whispered comments, then sudden silences, whenever a child came into the room. Naturally, this secretiveness aroused Armand's curiosity. Yet three days went by before he found out that Abelard had been born with six fingers on his left hand.

The whole family was alarmed. What were they to do when Abelard reached nine? If they cut off a finger, he would have ten, not nine like everyone else. Some took the view that this might be seen as unfair, and that he would have to lose two fingers, to be on the same footing as the rest of the family. However, others felt it was too much to cut off two of his fingers if the rest of the family lost just one. Only one should be cut off. That is what had always been done, and there was no reason to change the custom. The arguments branched off into other areas, expanded, came back to the point of departure. Finally they reached the obvious conclusion, that this was an exceptional case, and, as such, demanded an exceptional solution. Moreover, there was no need for haste. There was a long time to go before Abelard would be nine, when the decision would have to be taken.

This comforting stance collapsed, however, a few weeks later, when little cousin Gerarda was born: again with an extra finger, which again was on her left hand. The case therefore was no longer exceptional and the first serious doubts were raised. Postponing the decision until Abelard and Gerarda were nine no longer made sense. An uncle, who was a short-hand typist and keen on French jazz, was brave enough to ask if there was any point in carrying on with that absurd tradition. It was the provocation the family needed. The reaction was unanimous. A tradition going back centuries could not be questioned just because two children happened to be born with six fingers. The dissident was made to feel that his question was unnecessary and inopportune and, with great solemnity and resolve, the date was fixed for the next get-together, in one month's time, at the beginning of December.

A week later, however, came the news that in Barbastro a third cousin (more or less removed) had been born with six fingers. Suddenly it became clear that it was inappropriate to speak of chance and that putting off the decision for nine years would not solve anything. Some members of the family took the view that there was no need for alarm: the appearance in the family of children with six fingers on one hand was the product of a logical evolution. Uncle Reguard himself suggested that many centuries (some said millennia) of cutting off the left-hand ring finger were eventually giving rise to a mutation whereby, in order to compensate for the finger they would lose at nine, they were being given an extra finger at birth. This idea was considered absurd by other members of the family, who rejected the notion that such a large mutation could take place over a short period such as centuries or millennia. Actually, it was irrelevant who was right. For the first time, there was a profound schism within the family, capable of splitting it apart. On one side, those who believed that children born with six fingers had to have two fingers removed (the ring finger, as usual, and this new finger between the ring finger and the middle finger which has no name) and that there was no need to wait till the children were nine; instead it should be done now, as a show of force to stifle dissent. On the other side, those who held that if tradition dictated the removal of one finger, then no matter what anatomical modifications appeared, they should carry on being faithful to the tradition and cut off just one finger. When the debate was at its height, a third stance, initially a minority one, was adopted by the shorthand typist uncle and two sisters-in-law, who denounced the custom itself as an act of barbarity.

The fact that it was the sisters-in-law who put forward this denunciation was particularly serious, because people who married into the family had always been the most fervent defenders of the customs, having become convinced of its merits during courtship. In fact, one of the key moments in any courtship (and a common source of jokes on family occasions), was when the family member, thinking things were getting serious, approached their future spouse to say that, before they got engaged, there was something they should know. Something that would almost certainly seem very strange at first, though in actual fact it wasn't, and which would have to be taken into consideration if they were to have a future together. Then they said it: 'When the children in the family get to the age of nine, we cut off the ring finger of their left hand.'

The initial reaction was always hesitation (was it a joke?), and then afterwards (when it was clear it was not a joke) horror. The same objections were always raised: 'How can such a barbarous custom survive in this day and age?' 'What's the point?' 'I hope you don't think you're doing that to our children!' So the task of persuasion would begin, hours of conversation, of justification. Days and days drawing subtle distinctions, clarifying details and explaining, until the future partner finally understood. From that point on, they turned into the most ardent defenders of the practice and even (though in theory nobody asked them to do so) offered their own ring fingers, in order really to become part of the family. They were also the first to demand, when their children turned nine, that the ceremony should be carried out immediately, strictly according to custom, and the first to volunteer to hold down the hand.

Hence it was a serious matter that the revisionist tendency should emerge from that faction of the family, the converts, apparently the most ardent devotees of the custom. However, that consideration began to lose its importance: soon there were no differences and the initial faction formed by the shorthand typist and the two sisters-in-law was joined by everyone else. A fourth cousin was born with six fingers. Crisis point had been reached. People were

220

beginning to drift apart and the get-together that had been arranged for the beginning of December was postponed *sine die.* 'Until a definite decision is reached.' However, many suspected that this was just a polite formula and that this would be the only decision taken, although it appeared not to be a decision.

Armand was given a harp. He was enrolled for music and harp lessons, every Tuesday and Thursday, after school. He practised every weekend, with a diligence and conviction not always rewarded by the results. Once it became clear that the family custom of cutting off fingers was a thing of the past, Armand's interest gradually waned and the harp ended up in a corner gathering dust until years later, when Elisard, one of the cousins with six fingers, showed an interest in it. Every time there was a meal at Armand's house (nowadays there would only be six or eight people, whereas before there had always been more than twenty), Elisard would go off to Armand's room to play the harp. Each time he came, his playing got better, until he could play pieces by Halffter, Milhaud and Ginastera and (to please the family) some Paraguayan tunes and a little Mexican number that he played over and over again, each time with more brio. Armand's parents suggested giving him the harp. Armand took this as a criticism (reproaching him for having first made such a thing of his vocation as a harpist, then losing all interest in it); to avoid giving them the satisfaction, he said he couldn't care less what they did with the harp. His parents decided they would give it to Elisard the next time he came.

But Elisard never visited Armand's house again. Gradually, without the ceremony to bind them together, the family reunions came to be held less and less frequently; those that took place attracted fewer and fewer people and soon everybody began to make excuses not to attend: if it was winter, they were going skiing; in summer, they were off to the beach; and at any other time of the year, they had a previous engagement they could not possibly cancel. Within a few years, family reunions had become a thing of the past and even the closest relatives were strangers who spoke once a year, if that, and then only on the phone.

Elisard was the only relative of whom everyone continued to have news all the time, for over the years (some said his anatomical peculiarity was a factor) he became an outstanding harpist, who restored to the instrument the status and prestige it had lost through the excessively simple use made of it in previous decades. Armand took a different view. He considered him a child prodigy who had had a brilliant period but who, as he grew older, had become a pathetic figure: him, his harp and those ghastly tunes. Leaning on the bar counter, Armand sees Elisard yet again on the television set next to the line of bottles. He turns round, heaves an exaggerated sigh, makes some slighting remarks in a loud voice and proposes a revival of the custom of cutting off ring fingers, beginning with the celebrated harpist. The other people in the bar don't even look at him. Since nobody is paying him any attention, he tells the story of his family. A couple of people who do finally listen to what he is saying take him for a drunk or a madman or both. Just one girl looks at him with a certain interest, and when he finishes, she comes over. She's beautiful, with an attractive smile and a lock of chestnut hair falling over her face, in that style some women use to disguise the fact that they have one glass eye.

© Joaquim Monzó
Translated by Annella McDermott

Gregor

QUIM MONZÓ

One morning the beetle emerged from its pupal state, and found itself transformed into a chubby boy. He was lying on his back, which was surprisingly soft and vulnerable, and if he raised his head a little, he could see his pale, swollen belly. The number of limbs was drastically reduced and the few he could feel (four, he would later count) were painfully fleshy and so thick and heavy that he just could not move them.

What had happened to him? The room now seemed tiny and the smell of damp less penetrating than before. On the wall there were hooks to hang the broom and mop. In a corner, two buckets. Up against another of the walls, a set of shelves with bags, boxes, jars, a vacuum cleaner and, leaning against them, an ironing board. How small those things looked, yet before they had been so huge he could hardly take them in. He moved his head. He tried to move to the right, but his now gigantic body was too heavy and he could not manage it. He tried again, and a third time. After that, he was exhausted and had to rest.

He opened his eyes again, anxiously. What about his family? He turned his head to the left and there they were, at a distance difficult to estimate, staring at him in alarm and fear. He was sorry they were scared; if he could, he would have apologised for the awful experience he was putting them through. His attempts to move and approach them were grotesque. He found it particularly difficult to crawl along on his back. Instinct told him that if he turned face downward he might find it easier, although with only four legs (and those not particularly agile) he was not sure how he was going to manage to advance. Luckily there were no noises to suggest there were humans in the house. The room had a window

223

and a door. He could hear raindrops drumming on the metal window sill. He hesitated whether to make first for the door or the window and finally decided to make for the window because from there he could see exactly where he was, though he was not sure what good it would do him to know exactly where he was. With all the strength he could muster, he attempted to turn over. He was strong, but it was clear that he did not know how to control his strength; each movement was separate and disjointed, there was no coordination. Once he learned to use his limbs, things would be so much better, he would be able to join his family. Suddenly, he realised he was thinking, and that made him wonder if he had also thought previously. He would have said he did, but in comparison to now, the earlier thinking was decidedly elementary.

After many failed attempts, he managed to put his right arm over his body; having done that, he threw all his weight onto his left side and, with one final effort, managed to turn his body over and slump heavily face down. His family quickly moved out of the way; they stopped some way off, afraid he might make another sudden movement and crush them. Feeling sorry for them, he laid his left cheek against the floor and stayed still. His relatives came to within millimetres of his eyes. He could see their antennae waving, their jaws clamped in a grimace of consternation. He felt afraid of losing them. What if they rejected him? As if she had heard what he was thinking, his mother stroked his eyelashes with her antennae. Of course, he thought, it's what she must find least changed in me. Moved (a tear ran down his cheek and formed a pool around his sister's legs), he tried to respond to the caress; he moved his right arm, lifted it and then, unable to control it, he let it fall heavily, whereupon his relations ran off and took refuge behind a bottle of fabric softener. His father poked his head out, cautiously. He was convinced they knew he meant them no harm, and understood that all those dangerous movements were the result of his lack of skill in controlling the monstrous body. This was confirmed when they approached him once more. How tiny they looked, how small and (he found it hard to accept this) distant, as though his life and theirs were about to set off in two fundamentally different directions. He would have liked to ask them not to leave him, to stay until he could go with them, but he did not know how. He would have liked to stroke their antennae without that caress destroying them but, as events had just shown, his awkward movements posed an obvious risk. Face down, he began the move towards the window. Slowly, with the help of his limbs, he crawled across the room (his family still on the lookout) till he reached the window. But the window was very high up and he had no idea how to reach it. He yearned for his former body, small, agile, hard and with plenty of legs, which would have allowed him to move easily and quickly, and another tear rolled down his cheek, this time a tear of impotence.

As the minutes passed, he learned to move his limbs, to coordinate, to apply the right pressure with each arm. He learned to move his fingers and used them to grasp the window ledge. Some time later, he eventually managed to raise his trunk. He considered that a triumph. Now he was sitting, with his legs under him and his left shoulder leaning on the stretch of wall under the window. His family were watching him from a corner with a mixture of admiration and panic. Finally, he knelt and, with his hands on the window ledge so as not to fall, he looked out of the window. On the other side of the road he could clearly make out a part of the building opposite, a long building, made of dark material, with symmetrical windows to relieve the monotony of the façade. The rain had not stopped, but it was falling now in isolated drops that could be seen splashing onto the pavement. With one last effort he managed to push himself up and stand. This vertical posture delighted and alarmed him. He felt dizzy, and he had to lean on the wall to avoid falling; suddenly his legs felt weak, so he sank gently down until he was kneeling on the floor once again. He began to walk on his hands and knees towards the door. It was ajar. He swung it open, with such force (he had problems working out the exact effort required for each movement) that it hit the wall, rebounded and nearly closed.

He tried again, less brusquely this time. Once he had got the door open, he went out into the corridor, still on his hands and knees.

Would there be humans in any part of the house? If he met some now (he supposed) they would not do him any harm: he looked like one of them. The idea fascinated him. He would not have to run away for fear they would trample him underfoot. It was the first positive aspect of his transformation. He could see only one drawback: they would want to speak to him and he would be unable to answer. Out in the corridor, with the help of his arms, he pulled himself upright again. This time he did not feel so dizzy. Little by little (his legs were taking his weight better now), he walked along the corridor, his confidence growing. At the end of the corridor there was a door. He opened it. There was the bathroom. The toilet, the bidet, the bathtub, and two washbasins, each with its own mirror. He had never seen himself, but he knew right away that this was him, naked, fat and soft. Judging by the height his face came up to on the mirror, he was not an adult. Was he a child? A teenager? It was odd to see himself naked, though he could not explain why, because walking around naked had never bothered him before. Was it the grotesqueness of his body, all those kilos and kilos of flesh and that flabby face covered in acne? Who was he? What did he do? He wandered through the house, growing steadier on his feet. He opened the door of the room next to the bathroom. There was a pair of skates by the bed. And loads of pennants on the wall. There was also a desk, exercise books and school books. And a set of shelves with comics, a football and photos. One was a photo of him (he recognised himself immediately, looking just as he did in the bathroom, plump, with acne, dressed for five-a-side football, in a blue jersey with a white stripe down each sleeve). In the cupboard he found some clothes. He took out a pair of underpants, a vest, a sports shirt, tracksuit bottoms, socks and gym shoes. He put them on.

When he got to the door of the flat, he looked out through the spy hole. Outside there was a landing, and the doors to three more flats. He went back to the living room and ran his

226

finger along the spines of the few books on the shelves. He
stroked a china vase. He pressed a button on the radio. The
music was loud, and the words incomprehensible:

> *unforgettable*
> *Unforgettable as those days*
> *When the rain coming down from the hills*
> *Stopped us from going to Zapooooo . . . pan.*

He pressed the button again. Silence. He sat on the sofa.
Picked up the remote control. Turned on the TV. He flipped
through the channels, sharpened the colour contrast as far as it
would go, turned the volume up to maximum. Then down to
minimum. It was easy. A book lay open on the sofa. He picked
it up, convinced he would not understand a word, and yet as
soon as he laid eyes on it he read it with no great difficulty. 'I
have moved. I used to live in the Hotel Duke on a corner of
Washington Square. My family has lived there for generations
and I mean at least two or three hundred generations.' He
closed the book, and just as he was putting it back where it
had been, he remembered that he had found it open, not
closed. He picked it up again and, as he was searching for the
right page, he heard the sound of a key in the lock. It was a
man and a woman, clearly adults. The man said 'Hi'. The
woman came over to him, kissed him on the cheek, looked
him over and asked: 'How come your trousers are inside out?'
He looked at the tracksuit bottoms. How was he to know they
were inside out? He shrugged. 'Have you done your homework?' asked the man. Oh no, homework! He imagined (it
was as if he remembered) an earlier time in which there was
no homework and no trousers inside out. 'Hurry up.' It was
the woman again. He stood up reluctantly. Before going to
the bedroom to do the homework, he went to the kitchen,
opened the fridge, took out a bottle of Diet Pepsi and, as he
was struggling to open it (he was still clumsy with his hands),
he spilled half of it over the floor. Before they could tell him
off, he went to the broom cupboard and, as he was getting out
a mop, he saw cowering against the wall three beetles, which

froze for a moment then tried to run away. With a certain distaste, he put his right foot on top of them and pressed down hard until he heard the crunch.

© Joaquim Monzó
Translated by Annella McDermott

Quim Monzó (Barcelona, 1952) has been a cartoonist, scriptwriter for radio, films and television, graphic designer and war correspondent. He writes in both Catalan and Castilian and has won several important literary prizes, the most recent being the Premio de la Crítica Serra d'Or. Monzó has published several collections of articles, three novels: *L'udol del griso al aire de les clavegueres* (1976), *Benzina* (1983) and *La magnitud de la tragedia* (1989), as well as several collections of short stories: *Self Service* (1977), *Uf, va dir ell* (1978), *Olivetti, Moulinex, Chaffoteaux et Maury* (1980), *L'illa de Maians* (1985), *El perquè de tot plegat* (1992). These two stories were first published in Catalan in *Guadalajara* (Quaderns Crema, 1996).

The Preacher

CARLOS EDMUNDO DE ORY

One day, a preacher belonging to one of the many minor
religions that people the earth, too small to be statistically
interesting, but whose membership had recently grown considerably (enough to cause alarm amongst the supporters of
other sects), started preaching at the top of his voice to a
packed audience of keen new adherents, who, hanging on his
every prophetic word, felt enlightenment gradually growing
within them and finally fell into an ecstatic trance.

This happened one Sunday morning in a large enclosed
space to which only members of the faith had access. The
preacher was the most worthy custodian of that faith, quite
rightly, since he was both its current leader and its keenest
disseminator.

The formal service provided a break in the ceremony that
took place every Sunday at the same time, and the believers
gathered there sat down as usual on their respective benches
in order to listen attentively, in a relaxed manner, to the words
addressed to them.

The fiery preacher had barely raised his arms and hurled
forth the flames of his first words – fire in his very voice –
when, doubtless filled by a unanimous fervour, as if impelled
by an invisible force, the congregation again fell to their knees
and remained there, motionless, their heads bowed, their
hands covering their faces, while the mystic apostle continued
his sublime sermon as he had begun it, with all the untamed
energy of a wild waterfall.

Drunk on celestial choler, full of an irresistible authority,
giving ceaseless vent to the lava of his thoughts, in unequivo-
cal yet parabolic language, he was saying:

'I exhort you, brothers and sisters, to share in the re-
demptive action of personal sacrifices. I exhort you to expose

yourselves to the pyre of expiatory sacrifice. But take note: our faith requires a sacrifice without tragedy; a simple, silent sacrifice without preambles or rituals. It can be public, if you wish, but uncalculated, without one eye on sainthood, with no *mea culpa*, no pomp and no pride.'

He paused to swallow hard and no sooner had the silence absorbed the echoes of his last words and the faithful raised devout eyes to the pulpit, than his voice rang out again in such potent tones that all heads simultaneously bent again, eyes closed, as once more the preacher's voice engulfed the silence.

'I say unto you: Make haste! Plunge into the real swamps and find peace there, wrapped in the suffocating slime! What we need is a humble sacrifice, a sacrifice that will leave neither trace nor name. One that is entirely unlike Christ's sacrifice. To use a clear, precise image, it should be a subterranean sacrifice, a sacrifice made with downcast eyes. The cross is a sacrifice with its face to the skies, an elevated sacrifice in every sense of the word. It was a vertical sacrifice, worthy of the Son of Man. Was it not a mirror of every sacrifice, into which man looked and chose not to recognise himself? Now, I am not asking you to look in that mirror tarnished by the foul breath of sin. In this day and age of degenerate humanity, we need a sacrifice befitting the lower depths, because we are not worthy of Christ's example. Christ was the roof of humanity and we are merely the lower depths. Let our sacrifice then be worthy of us. Make haste, make haste! Seek out the caves . . .!'

He said all this with his arms raised, but no one could see his arms, for they were still sitting with bowed heads, paralysed by religious devotion. This time, the faithful knew that the preacher had come to the end of his Sunday sermon, but they did not stir, so touched were they by what they had just heard. Did they understand it? More than that. An overwhelming silence weighed upon the meditations of the faithful. Each body was questioning his or her soul about the correct meaning of that parable of the lower depths. A most unexpected sermon!

In the middle of the chapel, amongst all the bowed heads, one man suddenly rises to his feet. For a short time, he stands there, extraordinarily erect, powerful and hard, as firm as if he were nailed to the floor. Everyone is turned towards him, their heads looking up mechanically as if operated in unison by a spring.

The man leaves the row of benches. He heads for the door. As if borne along by an imperious impulse, he goes out of the building, leaving the doors half-open. The preacher emerges from his own meditations, hidden from the eyes of the faithful; he gets up from his seat and watches the solitary withdrawal of that one member of the congregation. At last, he descends from the pulpit, but no one takes any notice of him now. They have seen the man walk slowly to the door. They have seen him disappear. The whole congregation shudders. They saw him get to his feet and stand there motionless. They all stood up when the man opened the door to go out. Without leaving their places, they stare out of the door: the man, with deliberate step, is moving off into the distance. Can they still see him or not? He is heading towards the countryside.

Then, without warning, the faithful leave the rows of benches and follow the man. There he goes. They march silently along behind him. The preacher too. Where he goes, they follow a few steps behind. When the man stops, they stop. Whatever the man does, they do. The preacher too.

They go across country. They are all walking along now carrying picks and shovels, because the man took up a pick and a shovel. The march continues, silent, ecstatic. The man walks; that is all. He is followed by men and women and by the preacher.

When he reaches an open plain spreading out before them, the man stops walking. Behind him, the cortège stops too. Above their heads, vast space. Beneath their feet, flat, dry earth. The sky is cloudy, the sun cannot be seen. It is midday.

Still saying nothing, the man begins to dig with his pick and his shovel. The others dig alongside him with theirs, in the same piece of ground. The preacher does the same. For a brief time, picks and shovels work as if subordinate to the continual rise and fall of arms. When the hole is fairly deep and wide, the man sets down his tools and looks up at the sky. At that moment, everyone does the same; they put their tools down on the ground and look up at the sky. But the man has now lain down in the hole, which is longer than it is broad, made to fit his body. Lying horizontal and rigid on the dug earth, between his pick and his shovel, he has closed his eyes. He says nothing, he merely waits. Everyone gathers round the hole and takes up a shovel. Only one of those present is crying, unseen, some way from the group. It is the preacher.

All eyes are on the man, down below, apparently asleep. A woman sticks her shovel into the pile of earth and throws the first spadeful onto the man's face. Immediately, the others follow suit. It does not take them long to cover the man, lying there, horizontal, motionless, alive, in answer to that call for a sacrifice of the lower depths. He is no longer alive and the others stamp down the earth to leave it flat again.

The clouds have cleared now and the sun bathes the plain in light.

Further off, another hole is dug. This time it is that same woman who is buried alive. They move off and dig elsewhere. Another member of the faithful is laid to rest. Further off another hole is dug, and another and another and, over there, another. And fewer and fewer of the faithful remain. The sun is setting, appearing and disappearing between dense clouds. Before evening comes, a small group of the faithful are filling in a hole with the earth dug from it. The sky is the colour of lead and the violet horizon glows blood-red.

The sun is setting. Two men walk along carrying picks and shovels. They stop, stick their picks into the earth to loosen it, then use their shovels to dig. They have dug another hole like the others, with some difficulty this time, for they are tired. They watch the sun sinking down below the horizon, where there are now only thin ribbons of cloud. It is beginning to rain when the one remaining man has finished filling in the hole. He walks slowly away. He walks back in the encroaching gloom, a pick and a shovel on his shoulder. It is the preacher.

© Carlos Edmundo de Ory
Translated by Margaret Jull Costa

Carlos Edmundo de Ory (Cádiz, 1923) is the son of the modernist poet Eduardo de Ory and he grew up surrounded by writers and books. In 1942, he moved to Madrid where he was the co-founder of an Iberian branch of Dadaism, called Postism. The first and only number of a magazine they published was promptly banned, and a later manifesto met the same fate. In the end, he left Spain and settled in France, where he became the librarian of the Maison de la Culture in Amiens. He has always written both poetry and prose, but his work remained largely unpublished until the 1960s and 70s when collections of his short fictions came out: *Una exhibición peligrosa* (1964), *El alfabeto griego* (1970) and *Basuras* (1975), from which this story is taken. A selection of his poetry was published in 1970.

The Woman Who Came Back to Life

EMILIA PARDO BAZÁN

Four large candlesticks were burning, oozing large drops of wax. A bat had detached itself from the vaulted ceiling and was beginning to describe ragged circles in the air. A small, dark shape crossed the flagstones and sombrely, cautiously climbed one fold of the pall covering the tomb. At that precise moment, Dorotea de Guevara, lying inside the tomb, opened her eyes.

She knew perfectly well that she was not dead, but a leaden veil, a bronze padlock had prevented her from seeing and speaking. She could hear, though, and she had been aware, as if in a half-sleep, of what they did to her as they washed her and wrapped her in the shroud. She had heard her husband sobbing, felt her children's tears on her stiff, white cheeks, and now, in the solitude of the locked church, as she gradually regained consciousness, she was overwhelmed by horror. This was no nightmare, this was real. There was the coffin, there were the candles . . . and there she was wrapped in the white shroud and, on her breast, the scapular of Our Lady of Mercy.

Sitting up now, the joy of pure existence overcame all other feelings. She was alive; how good it was to live, to come alive again and not to fall into the dark grave. Instead of being borne down to the crypt at dawn on the shoulders of servants, she would return to her own dear home and hear the joyful clamour of those who loved her and were now weeping inconsolably. The delicious idea of the joy she was about to carry back to that house made her heart – weakened by the deep faint into which she had fallen – beat faster. She swung her legs over the side of the coffin and jumped down onto the floor; then, with the alacrity of thought common in moments of crisis, she drew up her plan of action. It was useless calling out or asking for help at that hour of the night, and yet she

235

could not bear to remain until dawn in the deserted church. She thought she could see the prying faces of ghosts amidst the shadows in the nave and hear the doleful cries of souls in torment. There was another option: she could leave via the Christ chapel.

It belonged to her; it had been endowed by her family. Dorotea always kept a flame burning, in an exquisite silver lamp, before the holy image of Christ on the cross. Beneath the chapel was the crypt, the burial place of the Guevara family. To her left, she could just make out the ornate railings decorated here and there in mellow, reddish gold. In her heart, Dorotea sent up a fervent prayer to Christ. Lord, let the keys be in the lock! She felt for them. All three were there, hanging in a bunch. The key to the chapel itself, the key to the crypt, reached by a winding staircase inside the wall, and the third key that opened a small concealed door in the carved retable and gave onto a narrow alleyway skirting the noble, lofty façade of the great house of the Guevaras flanked by towers. That was the door through which the Guevaras entered in order to hear mass in their chapel without having to cross the nave. Dorotea unlocked the door and pushed it open . . . She was outside the church, she was free.

Only ten steps and she was home . . . The house rose before her, silent, grave, enigmatic. Dorotea placed a trembling hand on the doorknocker, as if she were a beggarwoman come to ask for succour in her hour of need. 'This is my house, isn't it?' she thought, as she knocked again. At the third knock, she heard noises inside the mute, solemn house wrapped in its own thoughts as if in mourning weeds. And then she heard Pedralvar, the servant, grumbling:

'Who's there? Who's knocking at this hour of the morning? A curse on you whoever you are!'

'Open the door, Pedralvar, please. It's your mistress, Doña Dorotea de Guevara! Quick, open the door!'

'Go away, you drunkard! If I do come out there, I'll skewer you, I swear I will!'

'It's me, Doña Dorotea. Open the door. Don't you recognise my voice?'

236

Again there came a curse, this time hoarse with fear. Instead of opening the door, Pedralvar went back up the stairs. The woman knocked twice more. Life seemed to be returning to the austere house. The servant's terror ran through it like a shiver down a spine. She knocked again and in the hallway she heard footsteps, whispers, people scurrying about. At last, the two leaves of the heavy, studded door creaked open and the rosy mouth of the maid Lucigüela emitted a shrill scream. She dropped the silver candlestick she was carrying. She had come face to face with her mistress, her dead mistress, dragging her shroud behind her and looking her straight in the eye.

Some time later, Dorotea, clothed now in a dress of Genoese velvet with slashed sleeves, her hair threaded with pearls, was sitting ensconced amongst cushions in an armchair by the window and she remembered that even her husband, Enrique de Guevara, had screamed when he saw her; he had screamed and stepped back. It was not a cry of joy but of horror, yes, horror, there could be no doubt about it. And had not her children, Doña Clara, aged eleven, and Don Félix, aged nine, wept out of pure fright when they saw their mother returned from the tomb? They wept more grievously, more bitterly than they had when they had borne her there. And she had imagined that she would be greeted with exclamations of great happiness! It is true that a few days after her return, they held a solemn mass of thanksgiving; it is true that they gave a lavish party for relatives and friends; it is true, in short, that the Guevaras did all they could to show their contentment at the singular and unexpected event that had restored to them wife and mother. As she leant on the windowsill, though, resting her cheek on one hand, Doña Dorotea was thinking about other things.

Since her return to the house, however hard they tried to disguise the fact, everyone fled from her. It was as if the chill air of the grave, the icy breath of the crypt still clung to her body. While she was eating, she would catch the servants and her children casting oblique glances at her pale hands, and she noticed that the children shuddered when she raised her wineglass to her parched lips. Did they think it unnatural for people from the other world to eat and drink? For Doña Dorotea came from that mysterious country whose existence children suspect but of which they as yet know nothing. Whenever those pale, maternal hands reached out to tousle Don Félix's blond curls, he would pull away, his face as white as her hands, like someone avoiding a touch that curdles the blood. And if, at the fearful midnight hour, Dorotea happened to meet Doña Clara in the dining room next to the courtyard where the tall figures in the tapestries seem to stir into life, the terrified child would flee as if she had seen a ghastly apparition.

For his part, her husband, though he treated her with commendable respect and reverence, had not once put his strong arm about her waist. The woman come back from the dead rouged her cheeks, wove ribbons and pearls into her hair and doused her body in perfumes from the Orient, but all in vain. The waxen pallor of her skin shone through the rouge; her face still bore the marks of the funerary wimple they had placed upon her, and no perfumes could disguise the dank smell of the mausoleum. One day, Dorotea gave her husband a wifely caress; she wanted to know if he would reject her. Don Enrique passively allowed himself to be embraced, but his eyes were dark and dilated with the horror which, despite himself, peeped out of those windows of the soul. In those eyes, once gallant, bold and full of desire, Dorotea read the words buzzing in his brain on which madness was already beginning to encroach.

'People do not return from the place you have returned from . . .'

She took every precaution. Her plan must be carried out in such a way that no one would ever know anything: it would remain for ever a secret. She managed to get hold of the bunch of keys to the chapel and asked a young blacksmith, who was leaving for Flanders the next day with the infantry, to make her another set. One evening, with the keys to her tomb in her possession, Dorotea wrapped a cloak about her and left the house without being seen. She entered the church by the little door, hid in the Christ chapel and, when the sacristan had left the church locking the door behind him, Dorotea descended slowly into the crypt, lighting her way with a candle she had lit from the chapel lamp. She opened the rusty door, closed it from the inside and lay down, first snuffing out the candle with her foot . . .

Translated by Margaret Jull Costa

Emilia Pardo Bazán (La Coruña, 1852–Madrid, 1921) was a prolific writer of novels, short stories, essays, literary criticism, history and travel books. In Spain she knew all the famous writers of her time and even exchanged love letters with Pérez Galdós, the great nineteenth-century realist novelist. Her books deal unusually boldly with the position of women in Spain and with sexuality. Her most famous novels are *Los Pazos de Ulloa* (1886; *The House of Ulloa*, tr. P. O'Prey and L. Graves, Penguin, 1990) and *La Madre Naturaleza* (1890). She also wrote hundreds of short stories on all kinds of themes: tragic, fantastic, patriotic, historical, religious and allegorical, some of which are available in *The White Horse and other stories* (tr. R.M. Fedorchek, Bucknell University Press, 1993). This story is taken from the collection *Cuentos trágicos* (1912).

The Holocanth

JOAN PERUCHO

The holocanth is a tree that walks, a very dangerous tree with terrible, destructive instincts, for its favoured victim is man whom it attacks using a swift, retractable goad about three yards long. It was discovered by St Jerome one very hot day when he was doing penance in the desert, and then it seemed like a blessing from heaven to find a little cool, refreshing, rustling shade. Recently, the writer John Wyndham took advantage of the holocanth's hitherto unknown existence and appearance and, in his novel, *The Day of the Triffids*, created the fantastic, outlandish figure of the 'triffid', a plant which he humilatingly dubs 'industrial', but which, nonetheless, comes to dominate the world. We wish to reject this vulgar invention and re-establish the true origins of this great plant or tree whose historical name, as we have said, is the holocanth.

Very early Byzantine accounts state that Simon the Magus owned a holocanth for his private use and kept it tethered to a pole considerably longer than the botanical beast's stinger. According to these accounts, Simon the Magus had terrified the emperor Nero with it, indeed the first time Nero saw it, he was so frightened that he swallowed the stone of the cherry he was eating, and would have died a wretched death by choking had it not been for the Greek physician Philoctetes, who quickly and skilfully unblocked the royal throat. Nero, as you know, was not only refined, he was also sexually repressed – for this information I am grateful to Father Jordi Llimona – and he swore to avenge himself with extreme delicacy and elegance when the opportunity arose.

However, as I said at the beginning, it was St Jerome who, for the first time, came face to face with a holocanth wandering absentmindedly about the desert of Chalcis, where the saint was living as an anchorite. The surprise was mutual. The hideous plant, which walked on three roots-cum-feet in a to-and-fro motion, first forwards, then back, a truly abominable sight, stopped in its tracks and, presumably sensing something unusual about the saint, grovelled humbly at his feet. St Jerome held out a bowl of camel's milk which it ingested with precipitate delight. Then the holocanth disappeared rapidly over a hill, having first bowed politely three times. This strange apparition gave St Jerome much food for thought and the experience marked him for life, as one can see in his *Altercatio luciferiani et orthodoxi* and especially in his polemic with Rufinus about Origen, recounted in his *De principiis*, and in the famous letter of rebuttal that he sent to Rufinus, calling him a liar, a dissembler, a perjurer and even a heretic.

According to reports in our possession, the holocanth then proceeded to Antioch, where it was responsible for a horrific killing with its death-dealing stinger. Scholars maintain that this is the catastrophe referred to by the poet Pontius Meropius Paulinus, better known as Paulinus of Nola, when he writes:

Ecce repente mis estrepitum pro postibus audit et pulsas resonare fores, quo territus amens exclamat, rursum sibi fures adfore credens . . . ser nullo fine manebat liminibus sonitus . . .

It seems that many evil wizards have used the holocanth for abominable ends, for example, committing efficacious murders, sending people berserk, etc. One thing is sure, the holocanth appears only very occasionally, at most in groups of three, and in locations far distant from each other. We know almost nothing about their character, except that they like music and, in modern times, football, for in 1932, the top of a holocanth was seen rising above the stands at the San Siro stadium in Milan during the match between Arsenal and Inter. The police looked everywhere for it, but in vain, and the international press meted out harsh criticism to the fascist authorities, whose lack of foresight and diligence could easily have caused a disaster. No doubt the holocanth disguised itself in a garden or a public park, while the police patrols passed by, along with the firemen, the blackshirts and members of fascist youth groups lustily singing 'La giovinezza', until night fell and it could escape into the country.

In addition to certain historic sallies (the fall of the Western Roman Empire, the sack of Rome by Charles V, Napoleon's defeat at Waterloo, etc.), a few days ago, the holocanth's presence was felt again in Paris, following the strikes and demonstrations. It made its horrific appearance in the areas of Menilmontant and St Germain des Prés, doubtless prepared for anything. There were no casualties thanks to the joint action of students and police – a rare moment of collaboration – which put the murderous trees to flight. However, one holocanth, apparently of a sensitive, melancholy nature, was found in the foyer of the Boul'Miche cinema staring at the lewd stills from a sexy Japanese film. There was a great commotion during which the holocanth managed to escape disguised as a policeman. Some say it made off with a police van in which it drove through the barricades. If that is true, we have proof that the holocanth is not only dangerous, it is also a creature endowed with an alarming and superior intelligence.

© Joan Perucho 1998
Translated by Margaret Jull Costa

Joan Perucho (Barcelona, 1920) writes in both Catalan and Castilian and is one of the few Spanish writers to have written solely in the fantastic vein. His work is erudite, funny and highly imaginative. He has also written poetry, as well as books about art and gastronomy. He published his first book in 1947, but his best-known works are *Libro de caballerías* (1957), *Les histories naturals* (1960; *Natural History*, tr. David H. Rosenthal, Minerva, 1990), *Rosas, diablos y sonrisas* (1965), *Dietario apócrifo de Octavio de Romeu* (1985) and *Teoría de Cataluña* (1987). This story is taken from *Botánica oculta* (1969).

My Cristina

MERCÈ RODOREDA

All those years inside? . . . How on earth did you manage? they ask me. You'll have to sort out your papers. And they look at me and I see the ghost of a smile playing around their lips. Come back, they say, come back. But when I do come back, they get annoyed: call in tomorrow, we still don't know, call in the day after tomorrow. And one of them, the one with the moustache, holds out his hand with the first two fingers close together and makes a gesture as if to turn a key in a lock and he gives me a nasty look and says: If you don't come in to pick up the papers you know what will happen . . . He repeats the gesture . . . And I'm carrying around with me a sadness that is killing me, but nobody knows that. What happened, happened, and there were no witnesses. And I'm not complaining.

The sea was all groans and gusts and ragged waves and I was trapped and thrown, thrown and trapped, spat out and swallowed up and clinging to my plank. All was dark, the sea and the night, and the *Cristina* went down, and the cries of those dying in the water could no longer be heard, and all I could think was that there was only one person left alive, and that was me, because I was lucky enough to be just a rating and up on deck when it all started to go wrong. I saw dense clouds, though I had no wish to see them, then, stretched out on top of a furious wave, with all those clouds above, I felt myself sucked in, much further in than the other times. I went down, amidst whirlpools and frightened fish that brushed my cheeks, down and down, dragged by a great torrent of water within the water, down a great cliff, and when the water grew calm and gradually subsided, the tail of a fish larger than the rest hit my leg, and after that, I could not see the clouds, but a darkness deeper than any man born of woman has ever seen, and

245

the plank saved me, for without the plank I would probably have ended up in the same place as all the water that was swallowed. When I tried to stand up and walk on the ground I slipped and, though I thought I knew where I was, I preferred not to think, because I remembered what my mother told me as she lay dying. I was by her side, feeling terribly sad, and my mother, who was gasping for breath, found the strength to sit up, and with her arm, long and dry as a broom handle, she fetched me a tremendous clout and shouted in a voice that could barely be understood: Stop thinking! And with that she died.

I bent down to touch the ground with my fingers. It was slippery and as I touched it, I could hear very close by a sort of trumpeting groan which gradually became a roar. And between roars and groans, which were like the hoarse breath of old, tired lungs, the ground reared up, and I fell down, clinging to my plank. Half-stunned, not quite sure what was happening, all I knew was that I had to cling on for dear life to my plank, because wood is stronger than water. On rough water, a flat plank is stronger than anything else. I was curious to know where I was, exactly, and when one side of my brain began to hurt less I tried to go forward; everything was black as the ink from a frightened octopus, and the groans had stopped and all that could be heard was a glug-glug, glug-glug. The ground under my feet, for I was now standing up again, was of soft rubber, like the sap that flows gently from the tree trunk, rubber that is gathered, shaped and dried and then softened using heat, although in here it was cold and my teeth were chattering. Distracted, I found myself on the ground again gripping the plank between my legs. I stretched out an arm and touched the wall with the palm of my hand and the whole wall was moving like a never-ending wave, like an age-old disquiet. I picked up the plank from between my legs and slammed it into the moving wall, and both plank and I flew through the air and fell once more onto the muddy floor. That's it, I could use the plank! I stuck it in the ground and, when it was steady, I took a step forward, and in this fashion, struggling wearily onward, with many a fall on the way, I finally managed to reach a strange place: dark, and yet full of colours, which were not exactly colours, ghosts of colours, blue and yellow and red flashes that appeared and disappeared, that approached and retreated, colours that did not seem like colours, that were a fire yet not fire, which I can't explain, that were changing and elusive. There was a glimmer of thin, sickly light, and I went towards it and I saw the moon out there through a grille, made of bars, like railings. Clinging to my plank I let many hours pass. I think. Because who knows where time had got to. And when the moon went down the colours grew slightly iridescent, and it was then I realised that I wasn't breathing and that water was coming out of my ears, a little stream running down each side of my neck. And it was not water but blood, because my ears must have burst inside and, as I was running a fingertip over my neck, still warm with the blood, I felt a tremor coming from the depths of the place where I was and with that tremor came a surge of water that stank of half-digested fish. The water came up to my neck, and I was lucky that it stopped and gradually began to go down, but I was left stinking of fish. Blood was no longer running from my ears: air was going in them, for the path my air took had changed. I banged hard on the ground with my plank and nothing happened, not a groan, not a tremor. I walked on, clinging to my plank, amidst coloured lights, whether the same ones I had seen earlier, or different ones, I don't know, but they were slowly fading and between the bars on the grille came the light of the coming dawn and I felt the peace of the calm sea, something I can't explain, as if my world was about to vanish or something . . . I stopped and through the air that went in and out of my ears, I felt a mighty breathing amidst the lapping of the water. Then I seemed to be walking over stones, but it was the granules on a tongue, and then, suddenly, both plank and I went flying through the air again, and I felt myself captive in a giant embrace. One of those embraces that leave you breathless. I had nearly been expelled with a jet of water from the blowhole of a whale, and my plank had saved me from shooting out altogether, like a bullet. And I saw things I had seen many times before, but from such a different viewpoint! It was the largest whale on the seven seas, the glossiest, the most ancient. I had spent the whole night inside. Dawn was slowly breaking. I had my jaws trapped in the blowhole, and they were already beginning to ache, and I still hung on to my plank on the other side of the blowhole, my legs dingle-dangling, then I saw two rivers flowing into the sea, each very different from the other. The waters of these rivers were two different colours: the waters of one were crimson from red earth, the waters of the other were green with seaweed. And those two colours danced a slow dance of mingling and separation. Dancing, dancing, the dance of the two colours. I'm red, I'm all green. First, I'm putting in the red, now I'm rinsing out the green. The green penetrates below, then below that hides the red . . . And as I watched, the sun rose, the blowhole opened wide and I plummeted downwards like a stone. Then I could see what there was inside. At my feet, rocked by the water and the saliva, was a sailor. Lying on the tongue, not an arm's length from me, his tie knotted with a cord, the anchor on his sleeve, his trousers clinging to his legs, his face purple, his eyes open and empty. Three fish were nibbling at his hand. I shooed them away, and they left, but then obstinately came back. I was hungry myself, but I resolved to put up with it, and still clinging to my plank, I greeted the dead man and sang the national anthem. I spent three days chasing fish and running all over the place and, from time to time, a lash from the whale's tongue would slam me against her cheeks. Until . . . I hate to say it . . . I spent those three days trying to throw the sailor out. She clenched her baleens, and I clenched my teeth, and tightened my belt to increase my strength. The more I tightened my belt, the hungrier I grew, and I began to nibble bits of the sailor. He was hard and full of gristle. I was glad I was eating a sailor I didn't know, rather than having to eat one I did. Some big fish had emptied him of his insides while he was still floating in the water. He was all there, except for his eyes and his insides. That helped to preserve him, so I was able to make him last longer. I threw the little bones in amongst the ribs, but kept the bigger ones. The ribs on the right side were

248

scraped clean. Those on the left were a jumble of seaweed, seashells and molluscs. Rather than eat sailor all the time, I sometimes ate seafood. The worst thing was the thirst. But there's a solution to everything. One day, miraculously, a saucepan floated in. I immediately thought of rubber trees, and without a moment's hesitation I thrust the handle of the saucepan into the whale's cheek. The next day it was full of juice, and I could drink. Sea water, although salty, makes the flesh of fish sweet. I thrust the saucepan back in. I kept having to make new holes, because the wounds made by the saucepan closed up immediately. From time to time, if my concentration slipped, she would slam me against the roof of her mouth and keep me there for hours and hours. We sailed slowly on. By this time, I had cut seven marks on the ribs with the tip of my knife. Seven days. One morning, I charged the ribs to see if I could force a way through and everything started to whirl, and I was tossed all over the place, sometimes on top of the tongue, sometimes below, sometimes to one side, sometimes right up to the roof of the mouth, but up there I had the sense to shout: Stop, Cristina! I found myself sitting on the ground, with my plank across my chest. So it was then, without noticing it, that I christened her.

Peering out through the baleens I saw seas of every kind. All different kinds of blues, some the colour of wine, you name it, with golden waves and mountains of ice and mists at dawn. And me trembling and suffering. I used to tell myself: all the tears on earth flow down to the sea. And my clothes were falling to bits, rotting away. First of all, my trouser bottoms frayed, then my sailor's jacket fell to pieces, all my clothes just fell apart, I don't know how, and all I had left was my leather belt and my knife with its mother-of-pearl handle, thrust into the belt. Soon I had to make new holes in it. Sometimes, if I slept a little, I would dream that I was tightening my belt and inside the belt there was nothing left . . . A green coast! When I saw that coastline, I prayed. Again, I risked my life and battered the cheeks with my plank. Cristina dived. We stayed underwater for ages. When we emerged, my ears were popping like mad, but the baleens had opened like the doors of a

lock, and I floated off into the blessed sea, which now did not
seem to be made of tears, but of the laughter of all the fountains in the world. And my plank and I were sailing on the sea,
like this . . . rocked by the waves, towards the green land.
There were birds screeching by the shoreline and I thought
the breeze carried on it a scent of ears of wheat and pine trees.
But suddenly I heard her. Before I had time to turn round, her
shadow fell across me and she dragged me back inside her
again through the baleens. Then the bad times began. Six
months, every night spent hitting her from inside with the
plank, bashing her on the tongue with the thigh bone of that
sailor, God knows where he had got to. With my penknife I
cut crosses on the side of her palate and under her tongue. I
rammed the handle of the now rusty saucepan into her flesh
to start an infection, I pinched her with the buckle of my belt.
In the end, she stopped swimming; she just floated aimlessly
on the surface of the water, listing a little to one side. I made a
mark for every day by thrusting the blade of my knife into her
palate, which trembled like jelly, and white blood and red
blood gushed from the cuts. When one side of her palate was
ripped to pieces I started on the other. One day, I cut open
one of the granules on her tongue and I heard a groan like the
sound of the organ on the day of the dead. At night, she would
let out a scream from deep within her, as though all the bells
of all the belltowers in the sea were ringing at the same time,
drowned by the weight of the water and the salt. Cristina
rocked like a cradle, and she was rocking me to sleep, but I was
alert to that. I began to eat her. I would make a cross, then cut
out the meat below it and eat it, chewing it thoroughly, as I
had done with the sailor. One day, the groans sounded
human, and Cristina dived beneath the water and stayed
under for a long time. Although I breathed through my ears,
when we came back up to the surface, it was like returning
from a marine hell. I cut her tonsils, I propped my plank at the
entrance to her throat, and slashed crosses on her tongue.
Crosses and more crosses, for days and days. Sometimes I
would give her a clout with the plank on her palate, just
where it had least flesh. I never stopped. Her tongue was too

250

hard; I only ate the palate, and the flesh would grow in again, and I watched it grow like the grass in spring. When I thrust the thigh bone of the dead sailor under her tongue she would jump like a rabbit. But if ever I left her alone, she would sail on again, still listing a bit, and slow, as though the waters of the sea, tired of leaping and shouting, had grown thick and difficult. Time was passing, with its days, its months and its years, and still we carried on because, in the depths of a strange darkness, we felt that somewhere, in a place we never seemed to reach, we would perhaps find the last ray of light in the shadows, or that sliver of memory things leave behind when they vanish for ever. In the end, I grew weary. I sat huddled in a corner of her palate and she kept me there, protected by her tongue and I felt myself growing stiff, and it was her encrusting me with her saliva. And neither she nor I knew which seas we were sailing until one night, she ran aground on a rock and on that rock she died, her insides all covered with cuts. The beach was not far off, scarcely half an hour's row. I tried to open the baleens by hitting them with my plank, but it was no good because the plank was half rotted away at the ends and had got shorter and thinner. With enormous difficulty I scrambled out through the blowhole and when I was out, I slid down the huge curve of her back into the water, but I didn't feel anything because I must have entered a kind of limbo world. The sea cast me onto the sand and that's where they found me. When I woke up, I was in a hospital and a nun was feeding me milk fresh from the cow, and I couldn't swallow because my tongue and throat were like stone. And another nun, with a little wooden hammer, which she later told me they had had specially made, was tapping at my pearly crust, to free me from it. Initially, the crust began to break up under the hammer blows. Then, a few days later, it began to come away in bits, because the nun kept rinsing it with a bottle of specially prepared water. The nun was resigned to her task and she would say, 'Dear Lord, the skin under the crust looks like the skin of an earthworm.' And when she had got nearly all the crust off, and I only had a little left on my cheek and one side of my head, the nun gave me some linen trousers and said I had to go and see about my papers. And I went, and straight away they said all that about how had I managed for all those years, and did I imagine I could fool them ... And the wind and the rain, which sow and ripen, gradually began to give me back a smooth skin, and just as well that they did, for my whole body was stripped of flesh, like the roof of Cristina's mouth. When I had wandered long enough, I went back to the hospital and the nun asked if my skin hurt when I went out, being so thin, and I replied that my skin only hurt, and hurt badly, when she used to tap my crust with the hammer and pour over it that specially prepared water, which burned a bit on contact. Afterwards, I would get into bed, very carefully, and sleep only fitfully. One day, of course, they sent me away from the hospital, saying I was cured. Instead of milk from the cow, they gave me a nice big plate of hot soup and at the first spoonful, I started screaming and running, because my insides were like an open wound, rotted and eaten away because of all the putrid flesh I had taken from Cristina. I ran out into the street still screaming, just as the children were on their way to school, and a boy, half-terrified because I looked at him, pointed his finger and whispered to the others 'He's made of pearl'. My hands still sparkled with those little flecks that seashells have on their smooth side. And I could see the children's eyes, a flock of brown and blue eyes that followed me and never left me, that seemed to float in mid-air with nothing around them and were only interested in one thing. I stopped, with my cheek and half my head in their pearly crust, so tightly joined, so wedded to my flesh that the hammer had never been able to budge it. And I stood still until the children got tired of staring at me, and then I went right to the top of the cliffs, outside the town, high up, to the highest point of all, where the sea birds build their nests and where butterflies die in the autumn. And with my heart full of things that trembled like the stars in the night, I stood looking at the sea and at the darkness that was gradually covering it. Where the sun had gone down, a bit of light still lingered, then slowly faded, and when everything was dark, from out of the sea, emerged a calm, wide pathway of light and along that calm, wide pathway came my Cristina, spouting water, and me on her back with my plank, like before, singing the sailor's anthem. And from where I was standing, from the top of the cliffs, I could hear it plainly, down below, sung by me in the middle of that vast expanse of water, advancing along the pathway, with Cristina, who left a trail of blood in her wake. I stopped singing and Cristina stopped, and I could hardly breathe, as if all my strength had drained away with my staring, until gradually Cristina and I made our way, with me atop her, silent, but waving, to the place where the sea turns round and takes off into the distance . . . I sat on the ground with my knees drawn up and I slept with my arms on my knees and my head on my arms. And I must have been very tired, for I was woken by the morning light and the cries of the birds who don't know how to sing. They emerged in a flash of brilliant white from holes in the cliffs, great flocks of them, beating the air with their wings, and plunged headfirst into the sea, then rose again, screeching, with fish in their beaks which they fed to their young, and there were others, who, instead of fish, brought twigs and blades of grass, everything they needed to build their nests. I stood up, giddy from the sound, and the sea was as smooth as a roof, and I began to walk down to the town, and when I got to the first houses, a woman came out of a doorway, all dirty and dishevelled, and she hurled herself at me, and groaned and hammered on my chest with her fists and shouted, You're my husband, you're my husband and you ran away and left me . . . And I swear it wasn't true, because I had never been in that town, and if I had ever seen that woman I would have remembered, because her top teeth stuck out over her bottom lip. I brushed her aside and she fell to the ground, and with my foot I moved her carefully out of my way, because a child was watching us from a window. And I went back again to the place where they give you your papers. They were celebrating something, I don't know what. The point is, they were all drinking golden wine from small glasses. They were standing up and the one with the moustache saw me right away and came over with an expression that said he didn't want

253

any trouble and I saw another man, wearing cuff-protectors, and he was whispering to a third man who was as bald as a coot, and from his lip movements I could guess what he was saying: the pearl. And they all looked at me again and the one who had come over said to me once more: tomorrow; and he went with me to the door and practically threw me out into the street, repeating over and over like a song: tomorrow, tomorrow . . .

© l'Institut d'Estudis Catalans
Translated by Annella McDermott

Mercè Rodoreda (Barcelona, 1908–Girona, 1983) was one of Spain's principal women writers, and many of her poems, plays, stories and novels are specifically about the lives of women. Rodoreda lived in exile in Geneva for many years, and it was there that she wrote a number of her books, including her best-known novel, *La plaça del Diamant* (1962; *Time of the Doves*, tr. David Rosenthal, Graywolf Press, 1989). In 1980, she was awarded the Prize of Honour in Catalan Letters, and in 1981, the City of Barcelona Prize. 'My Cristina' is the title story from *La meva Cristina i altres contes* (1967; *My Christina and Other Stories*, tr. David Rosenthal, Graywolf Press, 1984).

From Exile

ALFONSO SASTRE

I had gone to that quiet little university town at the invitation
of a friend, who had been appointed to the Chair in
Philosophy there a year earlier. The University had set up a
little theatre and it was felt that I could usefully contribute a
lecture on my experiences. I was very happy to accept the
invitation. A play of mine had just opened to some acclaim –
it was my fourth piece, my career in the theatre having begun
with a play on an anti-war theme – and I was in the mood for
a few days' quiet and rest. Besides, there were other reasons
why I welcomed Dr. H.'s kind invitation: I had been stationed
in that same city during the war, twenty-two years earlier, and
had never gone back since, but, with the passing of time, what
was once a dreadful experience had become a nostalgic
memory. On the train, as we drew nearer to our destination, I
began to relive some old, forgotten sensations. The feel of the
rough khaki shirt on my skin: I was a bookish student. The
smell of baked-in grime that pervaded the barracks where I
spent the first three months of my life as an infantry officer. I
even seemed to hear, as we passed through a tunnel, the shots
from our pistols as we practised in the yard, against the wall. It
was raining. Out of the window I could see a damp green
landscape that also held a place in my memory: for the parks
of the town for which I was bound had been like that too,
green and damp, and probably still were. As night fell, these
feelings continued, to the extent that I completely forgot that
I had intended to sketch out a mental plan for my lecture in
the course of the journey. When it got dark, I had the impression that the young foreign woman sitting opposite me had
not closed her eyes, but was staring at me in the faint light that
came in from the corridor. Who had put the light out? I
hadn't noticed. Suddenly, the last night came flooding back to

me, I mean, the events of the night the bombs fell. I had drunk a few glasses of wine (too many, if the truth be told) with a fellow officer, in our usual tavern, opposite the barracks, and next to a dark, moss-covered square. When the sirens went, my friend and I left the tavern. It was night-time. The search-lights were sweeping the sky, and there was a wind on my face. For reasons I can't explain, I felt surprised when I looked at the flagpole on our barracks opposite. Stripped of the flag – which had been lowered – the flagpole gave me a feeling (how can I put it?) that there was something odd. People were not hurrying: they had got used to air-raid alarms.) A dispatch rider sped past on a motorbike, his siren wailing. My friend and I crossed the road and went into the barracks. We made our way across the barracks square, where the anti-aircraft guns had been hastily moved into position, and went into the officers' mess. It was deserted and half in darkness. We looked at each other, and it was then that I realised we had both drunk too much: my companion wore a look of foolish abstraction. I realised he had no idea what was going on, and when I heard the sound of the *Junkers* I began to tremble.

The barracks was hit by a bomb and the roof of the officers' mess collapsed in on us. Soon afterwards, in the hospital to which I was taken, I learned that my companion had been killed in the bombing. As for myself, when the region where the hospital was situated fell (it happened so suddenly there was no time for evacuation), I was taken prisoner. When I was freed, the war was over, and I was alone, with no money to finish my education. How I began to write for the theatre, and the circumstances by which I became a well-known playwright, have no relevance to these pages. In any case, that night in the train, my thoughts always came to a halt, over and over again, no matter how hard I tried to cross the barrier, at the night the bombs fell.

I arrived at my destination somewhat tired from the jour-ney. My good friend Dr. H. met me with a group of students. My friend and I embraced, and the young people greeted me warmly, to which I responded in kind. I realised at that point that my plays and critical essays were considered significant in that little world. I had noticed something similar on other occasions, on other journeys, when young people would gather round me, as though I had managed to express something they felt was important, and they wanted somehow to let me know.

And so there arose the usual situation, which in this case I would have liked to avoid: I was accompanied everywhere I went – first of all to my hotel, where they had reserved a magnificent room for me – and I was showered with attentions; there were constant questions, innumerable demonstrations of respect. I would have preferred to be alone for a few hours, to wander by myself round my old haunts and relive some of the feelings of that time when, amidst the horrors of war, we dreamed of a better world and mingled with so many people we would never see again. Yet how could I desert these young people, with whom it was, in any case, so pleasant to walk and talk? Eventually, in the late afternoon, I gave my lecture on the artistic and social function of university theatres, and after dinner, I said my farewells to everyone – I would be leaving early the next morning – and told Dr. H. that I felt like going for a stroll around the town on my own. He thanked me for coming and promised to be at the station the next morning to see me off.

So I walked off down the main street, where the darkened doorways, for some reason, gave me an unpleasant feeling. 'Terrifying places,' I said incoherently, as though remembering something. I was approaching familiar territory, the area surrounding my barracks. What would I find in its place? Had it been rebuilt? Beneath a street light that I thought I recognised was a street name I did not. Apart from that, everything else – the slope of the street, the coat of arms above the door of a large house, the clock tower – was exactly the same. 'Some things,' I thought superficially, 'never seem to change.' That thought consoled me a little for the melancholy I was beginning to feel, as I had on other occasions, about the passing of things we love, the death of cherished objects. This feeling has always made me fearful of returning to places I have been before, places where I've known people or loved someone. It began when I was a child and ever since then I have continued to experience in similar circumstances the same anguished emotion. On my way home from school as a boy, I was often afraid I would find the main door half-closed, and that would mean someone in my family had died. Once, when I was older, for I was in secondary school at the time, I did come home to discover the door half-closed: terrified, I rushed upstairs, to find everything as I had left it, and my mother smiling. I nearly burst into tears. And all through my life, as I say, I've had the same reaction. I tremble when I approach the scenes of my childhood. I rejoice in every tiny item that has not changed, it makes me feel relieved and hopeful, and I'm scared to go on looking, exploring more surfaces, because I know I'm going to find signs of deterioration and evidence of the ravages of time. I realise that everything tends to decay, and what I can't understand is how we manage to endure. Anything that is worn or dilapidated arouses this anguish in me; for example, wrinkles appearing on the faces of those I love. My heart turns over whenever I see someone I love falter on a staircase, or begin to breathe a little heavily after an exertion. 'Come on, chin up,' I think, nearly in tears; 'we mustn't give up just yet; hang on a bit longer, I need you and I wouldn't know what to do, where to look, if you weren't around. The fact of the matter is, when I think about death, my only consolation is that it will happen to me too. I couldn't bear to be the one left behind. If death has to come, let it take me too.'

What was I going to find that night? So many years had passed, I was surely going to find myself in another world. Everything I remembered – the tavern, the moss-covered square – would have gone; like so many things from that period, when I was still happy, because I had not yet learned to experience time as something that ravaged the soul. I was, I recalled, a sort of Epicurean in my modest way; I lived each moment and enjoyed or suffered every instant according to what chance brought my way; I was unaware of the past (I forgot it, let go of things as they faded and never thought of them again) and I felt no anxiety about the future; I could see nothing of what lay before me; I was blind to it and to every-thing else beyond the horizon of the immediate. What horrible destruction was I about to encounter? The passing of so many years is like a cataclysm. What would be left standing?

No, it was all just the same. When I reached the square, I was convinced that instead of the barracks, destroyed in the bombing, I would find a park or a tall building, or maybe another barracks built in a modern style. Or a convent. But no, the barracks had been rebuilt on the site, following the plan of the old one. The high tower . . . The sentry box, from which, no doubt, a pair of eyes was watching me now . . . the flagpole, with the flag at present lowered . . . I remembered my surprise on the earlier occasion, but I felt nothing special on seeing it now. I stood and gazed in delight at everything in the square. I felt the joy and relief that I mentioned earlier. I wanted to believe that, within existence, there are fragments that are incorruptible, and if we could somehow lodge in one of those we would be safe from destruction and decay. I was standing before one of those fragments now. Of everything present, only I had aged. How wonderful to see the green grass. I refused to contemplate how much of that lawn had died and been reborn in the intervening years. At eye-level, everything was exactly the same: the bronze statue, the bay windows on the houses, the bus stop, the door of the old tavern, on whose lintel one could read the notice, painted in ox-blood red: Wine Retailers.

Now for the difficult bit. I felt anxious just thinking about the interior of the tavern. Everything material might still be there, the stone, the metal, but what about the people? I thought of not going in, staying outside, and by not going in to find out, preserving the illusion that Señor P. would still be joking behind the bar. But what if it was true? What if Señor P., though now very old, was still there? It would be wonder-ful to see him, strong as the iron railings my tired gaze now rested upon. I went in. No, I did not notice any great change. The atmosphere was just the same as it had been in my time. It was as though I had only been away for a couple of hours in the middle of the day. There stood Señor P.'s daughter, apparently wearing the same apron she always did, and not looking noticeably different. 'So there are people, too,' I thought, 'who never change.' All the same, I was certain she would not recognise me. I looked her straight in the eye and ordered a glass of wine in the bantering manner we young officers had used. I meant it as a joke, to jog the girl's memory. To my surprise she carried on the joke with complete natural-ness: 'One glass of wine coming up, Lieutenant.' She had recognised me too. We both laughed then and I stared down at my wine, somewhat shyly. I was playing for time, turning it all over in my mind. I noticed that the girl was wearing black; probably for her father, though I seemed to recall that she had always dressed that way. So there was still room for hope. But how could I ask her? What if my question revived a dormant grief? I took a sip of wine and the taste had a magical effect, like one of Proust's *madeleines*, or the feeling Cocteau describes in his *Opium*. Revisiting the district where he lived as a child, as he ran his fingers over the walls of the houses, at the height a child's hand would reach, he heard the sound of memory playing in his head, like a gramophone record. The wine, of course, was the same wine as before. The local wine. There was nothing strange about the fact that it was the same, nor that the taste of it, associated with so many things from the past, should bring some ghosts to life. Helped by the atmos-phere of the place, with its echoes of military life: that officer sitting in front of a glass of beer writing a letter, whom, at first glance, in the dim light, I had taken for one of my former army comrades. The uniform, the way he sat! . . . nothing surprising about those, either. I ordered another glass of wine, then another; and it was only then that I realised how fond I had once been of wine. Yet this time, I felt it was doing me no good, indeed it was making me feel queasy. I now believe it was the wine that finally persuaded me to ask the girl, with feigned casualness: 'What about your father? Where is he?' 'He's inside, having a bite of dinner,' the girl answered. 'He'll be out in a minute.' This was great news, and it persuaded me to order another glass of wine and drink it exultantly, with a toast to those things that never die and a nod to good old

Parmenides, whose poem on the subject I tried in vain to recall.

So then I turned my attention again to the officer writing the letter and again I thought to myself, more forcibly this time, that he was very like my friend, Lieutenant R., the one who had died in the bombing raid and whose air of abstraction, in the empty officers' mess, I now recalled with a shudder. It was a searing vision. I stared fixedly at him and he seemed to feel my gaze on the back of his head. At any rate, he turned round, looking annoyed, but his face immediately cleared when he saw me, *and I realised that it really was him*. R. – for there was no doubt it was my friend – moved his lips and some words could be heard, in a tone I recognised, although I immediately noticed something odd: the movement of the lips did not initially correspond precisely to the words spoken, as though there were a slight fault in synchronisation, as sometimes happens with films; but on this occasion, the fault was quickly corrected and everything began to work smoothly. Lieutenant R. had greeted me by name and promised to finish his letter quickly and join me in a couple of glasses of wine and a chat. Though shaken, I agreed, so as to have time to think about what was going on; these strange events could hardly be blamed on the wine I had drunk.

The girl invited me, as usual, to have one on the house, and I was transfixed with fear on noticing my arm, resting on the counter; around it was the sleeve of a uniform on which I noticed the dull gleam of a lieutenant's stripes. So I did not initially register the fact that Sr. P. had come out into the bar, until I heard his voice commenting with his usual joviality on some aspect of the war, probably the scarcity and cost of everything. I raised my head slowly, hoping to see in his face something that would rescue me from this dreadful delusion into which I was sinking; but my shipwreck continued relentlessly. Señor P. was the same as ever, an elderly man smoking his famous pipe with youthful delight: 'So, Lieutenant,' he said to me, 'how goes the war? Will the front hold?' I tried to answer politely, but I could tell him nothing; perhaps because I was befuddled with wine, or perhaps because it had been a long time since the events he was asking about (if, indeed, I ever knew the answer). I stammered out a foolish reply and Señor P. must have realised how drunk I was, for he discreetly dropped the subject, puffing instead on his briar pipe and slowly exhaling the smoke.

When Lieutenant R. joined me and put a friendly arm round my shoulder, I offered him a drink without looking at him, nor did I look at him as he sat drinking it by my side. When the air-raid sirens finally began, I was incapable of running back to the barracks. R. told me later that I collapsed when I tried to stand up – a dispatch rider with a siren had driven noisily past the tavern – and that was what saved our lives. The next day, still suffering the effects of a massive hangover, I learned that the barracks had been destroyed in the bombing and that the wall of the officers' mess had collapsed, though no one could tell me if there had been anyone inside when disaster struck.

Our unit was transferred, and I was disciplined for not being in the barracks that night, when I should have been on call. When I tried to explain what had happened, it was useless: the year was 1938, and I couldn't be a post-war dramatist. R. died shortly after, fighting at the front, and I was sent to a psychiatric hospital in B . . ., by the sea. As the end of the war approached, I crossed over into France, where I suffered the rigours of a concentration camp guarded by Senegalese soldiers, until I managed to fix myself up with a labouring job in a small town in eastern France, near the German border. Having joined the French Resistance, I marched at the head of the troops that entered the town of T . . . the day France was liberated. I must have been drinking too much during all those years, for when I became aware of the danger it was already too late: I had become an alcoholic. I had a reputation as a heavy drinker who got into absurd scrapes. In this lamentable state, I enlisted in the Foreign Legion, at a time when there was a need for cannon fodder in Indochina.

As I write these lines, I am fighting in Indochina. For some time now, I've been drinking less and I'm even thinking vaguely of sorting out my life. I feel trapped in the military organisation to which I belong, yet I haven't the courage to desert. For the first time since the events of that night, I feel I'm progressing towards a certain serenity which allows me to ask myself certain questions without going mad. At first, I used to scream those questions aloud, and was carted off to hospital. Then I decided to take refuge in silence; but in spite of everything, I believe that my secret, however hard I try to conceal it, is obvious; although I must say that for some years now people have been fairly tolerant of my 'eccentricities'. I'm considered unsociable, that's all.

I've sometimes tried to recreate my plays from memory, and I put my failure down to the fact that my memory never was very good, except for remembering things whose loss brought me suffering: so the results have not been encouraging. I've only managed to write some vague approximations, a few crude, meaningless scenes. (As for thinking up new plays, I have never even contemplated it.) Some time ago, a Spaniard was attached to my company; when I asked about books of mine published in M . . . , he said he had never heard of them, nor, of course, of me. Incidentally, he was killed in the latest outbreak of fighting; a grenade shattered his skull. He's buried a few yards from where I'm sitting.

I'm writing this resting on a box of ammunition, by candle-light, during a lull in the fighting. My thoughts turn to Spain. I have no idea what's happening there. Drink, misfortune, prison, war and escape, these have been the building blocks of the barrier dividing me from my country, ever since I crossed the Pyrenees on that morning in March, amidst a climate of terror. No, I have no idea what has happened there since my departure, and I don't know what's happening now. If I think about it, I imagine that everything will be just as I knew it, except that I'm not there; everything is probably still as it was, but without me, and if I went back it would all be familiar.

Everything still the same, but without me! Or not? I mean, is someone perhaps taking my place, does he have the same friends as me, is he writing my plays? I ask that because, a while ago, I happened to hear that a young dramatist had written an anti-war play. Who is this young writer? What's his name? What's the title of his work? Mine was *The Squadron of the Dead,* but, as I mentioned earlier, I've been unable to reconstruct it. Anyway, is there someone doing in my place what I did, I mean (I'm finding it hard to put this into words) doing what I would have done? (In fact, I was right when I said 'what I did'. Often I can still hear the applause ringing in my ears.) If so, perhaps I am surplus to requirements there, just as I am here, caught up in a colonialist war which I detest; and yet . . .

And yet it would be nice to think I'm missed, that my absence is felt, that since I was mysteriously removed from that world, my absence has left a gap, at least in the affections of my friends. I think of Dr. H., for example. Is he still alive? Has he been given his Chair at the university in that town? And if that is the case, would he recognise me if I turned up now, but what do I mean when I say 'now'?

Am I truly missed in that world? Does anyone grieve for my absence? Do they say I 'mysteriously disappeared'? Will they have searched for my body? Will my obituary have appeared? Or was I never really there? Even for the friends I used to meet in the cafe? Are some of them feeling the same anguish as I do now (again it feels odd to say 'now'), exiled in other places? I pose all these questions with a serenity which, as I stated, I have only recently achieved. In any case, ever since the events that led to my stay in the psychiatric hospital, I've learned to be very careful about what I say to other people.

Well, my plan is to go back, if I get out of this alive. I can hear shots; maybe we're in for a hot time tonight. I'll land, if possible, somewhere near that quiet little university town, and I'll drive without looking to left or right straight to the tavern, because I know that for me there is no other way in, and that if I went anywhere else (the capital city where I enjoyed my modest successes, my home), it would be like a horrible wall bearing down on me, a wall composed of everything that is alien, strange and unknown. As I say, I'll go into the little tavern. Señor P. will be dead, and I'll be really pleased to hear that, and I'll drink to decay and to dear, gloomy old Heraclitus! And they will have renovated the place, and the

264

girl won't be young any more, she'll be a plump matron, who doesn't remember me at all; and, naturally, I won't try to jog her memory. Afterwards, I'll go back to the hotel (where I'm sure I have a room booked), to rest after my conversation with the young people and the slight effort my lecture represented (I should have planned it mentally on the train; I feel it was dull and repetitive because I didn't do that).

I hope that when I get to the station, early in the morning, my friend Dr H. will be there, waiting to see me off. And I'll go back, after this strange exile, to my life, my plays and all that is familiar.

© Alfonso Sastre
Translated by Annella McDermott

Alfonso Sastre (Madrid, 1926) is a politically committed playwright, who continued to live and write in Spain during the Franco period, when many other intellectuals from the left chose exile. His *Escuadra hacia la muerte* (1953) is an anti-war play, set during 'the next war' and was first performed by a University theatre group which Sastre himself had helped set up. The play was subsequently banned, and, in fact, although the texts were published, Sastre's plays were rarely performed in Franco's Spain. Sastre has also written critical articles and essays, and a book of short stories, *Las noches lúgubres* (1973), from which this story is taken.

Cervantes' Chickens

RAMÓN J. SENDER

Author's note

Someone had to write about Cervantes' wife's chickens and one of the avant-garde movements (surrealism) has provided me, normally so hostile to all such movements, with the *way* to do it.

Cervantes deserves recognition at least in the small things, since, as regards the large things, he was ignored during his lifetime and received recognition only after his death, when acclaim came from abroad and from foreign critics and philosophers.

An all too frequent occurrence in Spain.

I have always been troubled by Doña Catalina de Salazar's insistence on including her chickens in the marriage contract and I have taken it as clear evidence of the kind of ignominy to which any man of imagination in Spain has always been exposed, at least amongst certain sections of the so-called middle classes: for there was already a middle class in sixteenth-century Spain.

I have referred to surrealism as part of the avant-garde, but the truth is that it has been in existence from Apuleius' *The Golden Ass* to Dostoevski's 'The Crocodile'. The only addition made by the modern school is a slightly lyrical dimension created by an out-of-focus way of looking at real objects or by their deliberate distortion.

This lyrical dimension is absent from 'Cervantes' Chickens' for the simple reason that the incident is, by its nature, too sordid to require any distortion. Or perhaps the reason lies in my feelings of resentment, as a Cervantes enthusiast, which do not permit me to offer any poetic relief to the stupidity of that poor woman, Doña Catalina de Salazar.

The fact is that the chickens in the margin of the marriage contract have been crowing now for more than three centuries, crying out for a chronicler, as I said to Américo Castro when he mentioned to me how little had been written about Cervantes' private life. The only noteworthy, insightful comment that has been made, or which I recall, is that one of the dukes to whom Cervantes dedicated his finest work did not even bother to thank him, although the duke's assured place in history is due entirely to that dedication. Without it, he would long ago have been forgotten.

In Spain, more than in any other country, glory is *the sun of the dead*. That sun shines very rarely during the lifetimes of heroes, poets or saints, be they Hernán Cortés, Pizarro, Miguel Servet, Gracián or Cervantes. The envy of their contemporaries usually clouds the atmosphere.

Sometimes it becomes almost suffocating.

Especially the atmosphere breathed by Don Miguel de Cervantes Saavedra, who, after all his failures and disasters, was able to give us, in Don Quixote, a sublime self-caricature as the thwarted (but undefeated) gentleman.

He taught us too that not all those who play the fool in the name of God – humanitarian idealists – necessarily go to hell. Cervantes' heaven is vast, it surrounds the entire planet and is peopled by angels who repeat Don Quixote's words in every language in the world.

As a reward for his desire for symmetry – which exists in the moral world as it does in the physical world – Cervantes (who sought his Dulcinea in vain) was given, begging her pardon, the most stupid wife in all of La Mancha.

At first, what was happening to Cervantes' wife, Doña Catalina, seemed merely rather strange, then it became alarming and, ultimately, bizarre and incredible.

But it was true and can be confirmed by documents of the period.

For Doña Catalina de Salazar was turning into a chicken. Putting it bluntly like that may seem a little shocking, especially when one considers the chicken's rather libidinous reputation. The natural habits of chickens tend to be judged unfairly. I mean that Doña Catalina was a chaste and, above all, a faithful wife. I should have used the expression 'poultry bird' and avoided the word 'chicken' altogether, or used 'hen' instead, since that word has some attenuating grace. How to say these things, however, is the least of the problem.

With all these provisos and with all due respect, the fact is that Doña Catalina de Salazar *was* turning into a chicken, and if Cervantine scholars have not as yet come up with an explanation, one day they will with the help of the documents I have been able to gather together to the astonishment of laymen and to the satisfaction of scholars. The truth before all else.

Cervantes never spoke of this transformation, which began on the very day he read the marriage contract, where his brother-in-law, the cleric, had set down the bride's possessions, including five wool mattresses, six straw mattresses, a few reams of writing paper and two pigs that came and went in the yard.

On the day of the wedding, when the guests had all left, one person remained sitting in the corner of the room: an uncle of Doña Catalina called Don Alonso de Quesada y Quesada, whose family name suggests that his parents were first cousins, which may go a little way to explaining some of his eccentricities. He was a tall, thin, robust man with a noble, slightly crazed expression and he was dressed half as a military gentleman and half as a courtier.

Impressed by the man's decorative presence and by his

silence, Cervantes had initially regarded him with great respect.

But something unexpected happened. When they were about to sign the marriage contract, the bride paused with quill in mid-air when she heard her imposing uncle say the first and last words he would utter that day:

'Count the chickens and note them down too.'

Cervantes was confused for a moment when he saw the old serving woman approach the gentleman and whisper in his ear the number of fowl in the yard. Cervantes was deeply impressed by the secrecy surrounding the act. Don Alonso went over to the desk and, in the margin of the marriage contract, alongside the list of items in the dowry and the trousseau, he wrote: twenty-nine chickens. Half-recovered from his perplexity, Cervantes raised his eyebrows a little and, pointing to the contract, said:

'If you're putting down everything, Señor Don Alonso, you'd better include the cockerel as well.'

He said it with no ironic intention, but realised afterwards that it could have been taken that way. Don Alonso de Quesada nodded and added the cockerel to the list.

It seemed to Cervantes that this posturer, Don Alonso, was frighteningly, extraordinarily contradictory. His body was inhabited by two very different beings. That remark about the chickens was the last thing Cervantes would have expected Don Alonso to say; for he seemed to combine the appearance and the inner qualities of generosity and largesse of such heroes as Amadís de Gaula. Amongst the worthy people who have studied the matter, there are those who believe they can prove that the idea of noting down the number of chickens came from the bride's brother, the cleric. There are even those who say it was the bride's idea.

The truth is that it was Don Alonso, the uncle, who wrote it down.

For a moment, Cervantes thought that it would be good to separate the two people who seemed to inhabit Don Alonso's body, since together they created a monster. Doña Catalina laughed quietly, gleefully, and, seeing her husband still looking at Don Alonso rather oddly, said in a low voice:

'Don't pay any attention to my uncle, he's a bit reesty.'

Cervantes didn't know what Doña Catalina meant.

'Reesty?'

'He's always had my best interests at heart,' she added, still in a low voice, 'but he is a bit cockieleekie.'

That explanation wasn't particularly clear either, nor did it clarify her previous one.

Doña Catalina had run together those three words, 'a bit cockieleekie', and it seemed to Cervantes that, in the staccato way she said them, there was an allusion to the clucking of chickens.

From the day that Cervantes signed the marriage contract, he began to see in Doña Catalina's profile a vague similarity to that of a bird. One day, he discovered that she could look to the side with one eye, without turning her head, and that her eyes were becoming flatter, like the eyes in Egyptian paintings, and could move independently of each other.

This observation inclined him to presentiments which he himself dismissed at first, but to which he returned later as if, in them, lay the solution to a mystery. Despite these observations, Cervantes genuinely loved Doña Catalina, otherwise they would not have got married. That is one point on which everyone agrees.

In the birth of that love, various factors came together, as they usually do. Cervantes was not a man to fall in love at first sight; indeed he distrusted such things, although, naturally, the naked call to the senses played its part in the arousing of the attention that necessarily precedes love. Doña Catalina was very young, almost a child, yet she had been the one to initiate the relationship that so swiftly carried her to the altar. It is worth remembering precisely what happened because there was something odd about it, almost like something out of a novel.

Two years before, Doña Catalina and her brother had gone to Madrid and, contrary to her brother's wishes, she went to see a play by Lope de Vega at the Príncipe open air theatre. In the play, the title of which I cannot now recall, the heroine declared her love to the leading man and then placed him in various equivocal situations in order to win his heart and to put him in the dilemma of either marrying her or gaining the reputation of a cad. The young woman came and went dressed as a man and became embroiled in exploits as dangerous as any experienced by some of Calderón's heroines. All this struck Doña Catalina as unusual and daring, but perfectly possible since it happened in the theatre and was applauded by the audience.

Doña Catalina did not go quite that far with Cervantes. Nevertheless, emboldened by Lope's play, she wrote Cervantes a love letter. The letter, however, was anonymous and unsigned. Cervantes received the letter, for which he had to pay the postage – not the first time that this unlucky circumstance had obliged him to put his hand into his own pocket – read it with a smile and said to himself: 'It's a shame I don't know who this young woman is, nor where she lives, because she does seem to be truly innocent and truly in love.'

From the experience of many years, Cervantes knew that, generally speaking, he only attracted two sorts of women: the stupid and the mad. Sometimes he had wondered if the same thing happened to all men and that perhaps there were only two sorts of women in the world, whom only sweet maternity would one day redeem from their madness or stupidity. But he couldn't quite work out from Doña Catalina's letter which she was. She seemed neither stupid nor mad. She seemed merely rather outspoken and a little frightened by her own boldness. Twice in the letter she declared herself to be a maid.

Cervantes took a long time to realise that the letter had been written by Doña Catalina. In fact, he didn't find out until after they were married.

For her part, the young girl who had written the letter spent a year waiting for a reply. She couldn't understand why her beloved did not answer. She forgot that she hadn't signed the letter and that she hadn't given a return address. How could he respond? And the days and the nights passed without her receiving a reply, which made her feel humiliated and ashamed. Nevertheless, she found a way of meeting Cervantes and making advances that were half-coquettish, half-shy. Cervantes noticed and, like any other man, took the bait. His bride's embarrassment, or rather her feeling of frustration, lasted for some time, until Cervantes found out what had happened and said, laughing: 'How could I answer, if you didn't put your name at the bottom of the letter?' And he showed her the letter, which he had carefully preserved.

By then, Doña Catalina had already begun to cease being a woman. That is, while still continuing to be a woman, her transformation into a chicken had already started. And no one could do anything about it.

Some readers may find it odd that I should write these pages about Cervantes' wife, but I think the moment has come to tell the truth, the truth which was hidden in vain by Rodríguez Marín, Cejador and others who wished to preserve the decorum of the Cervantes family. There was always a mystery about Cervantes' conjugal relations, which no one denies. Why was his wife never seen living with him in Madrid or in Valladolid? It is as if he wanted to hide her away in the rustic gloom of the village. Why did he not take her with him? Some Cervantes scholars know why, but they still keep it a secret. I believe the moment has come to reveal that secret. It is because his sweet wife was turning into a chicken, although even she did not realise it, especially not at first.

Cervantes also took a while to accept the metamorphosis which was less a misfortune than what might be termed an unfortunate miracle. Cervantes did not know what to think. One night, she did seem to be aware of what was happening and she said, after looking at herself in the mirror:

'I look a bit of a birdbrain, don't you think?'

The writer smiled and laughingly called her his little chick; as everyone knows, lovers often give each other animal names and there are those who see in that tendency the satanic nature of sexual desire. Being a birdbrain was not so bad; that is, it was better than being a chicken. Cervantes began to observe her closely and noticed that her head was getting smaller and her legs thinner. Her chest and hips, on the other hand, seemed to be merging to form one large bulge.

One day he decided to go off to Madrid to try and sell a play, but Doña Catalina didn't want him to go and Cervantes postponed the journey twice. On another occasion, when he got a letter from an old comrade from the battle of Lepanto, who was writing to him from Bogotá – the city that was later to become the political centre of Gran Colombia – she said, stuttering a little:

'From Bogotá? A letter from Bobobogataaá?'

And it sounded as if she were clucking the way chickens do after laying an egg. A little girl, who was Doña Catalina's niece, thought that when they laid an egg, chickens were saying: 'putputputputputputput!', thus reminding people that they had a right to the corn that was given them. The little girl did a very good imitation of a chicken.

Cervantes was fond of the little girl. One winter's day, the writer carved her a dog out of the ice on the terrace. It had snowed, and the water dripping off a walnut tree had frozen, and Cervantes, occasionally blowing on his fingers, made a sculpture from it for the little girl. She, with her thick mittens on, played with the ice dog and even gave it a collar made out of pink ribbon. Then she left it on the floor of the terrace and later, when the sun came out, the ice dog melted. The little girl looked for it in vain and very sadly went to tell Cervantes:

'The little dog has peed himself to death.'

The stain left by the water stayed on the floor.

Time passed pleasantly. Cervantes laughed with the little girl and had affectionate talks with his wife, and when Don Alonso de Quesada made one of his rare visits, Cervantes did not argue with him when the good old man insisted that there was no heroism or merit in wounds caused by an arquebus, since the shot was fired from a distance, and that only wounds inflicted by the sword or the pike had any true merit. Don Alonso himself always dragged around with him a huge sword, which he wore on a goatskin baldric to save his bad back.

Cervantes, who had lost the use of his left hand after being

274

wounded by a shot from an arquebus and bore the scar of another on his chest, realised that Don Alonso wanted to belittle his glory as a soldier on land and sea. The old man had some very odd ideas. For example, he would not allow his name to be spoken at night because he saw in that fateful circumstance untold dangers that all had to do with Urganda, the unknown. He used to read books about chivalry and when, one day, Doña Catalina's brother, who was by nature impatient and a bit of a busybody, asked the gentleman what exactly he was doing in Esquivias, he smoothed his drooping moustaches and replied:

'I'm waiting, that's what I'm doing, waiting.'

'And what are you waiting for?'

'I am awaiting the ineluctable end.'

He sometimes spoke rather strangely.

Doña Catalina did not understand what Don Alonso meant. The priest understood very well and so did Cervantes. But Cervantes had lost any respect he had had for Don Alonso, with his illnesses and aches and pains and his haughty presence, and thought to himself that a man who could refer to his death as 'the ineluctable end' did not deserve much pity and that to speak in such rhetorical terms about death, with words lifted straight from some chivalresque novel, made him almost unworthy of it. Cervantes was unconsciously revenging himself for Don Alonso's views on arquebus wounds.

The discovery of the uncle's eccentricity, the cleric's meanness and, above all, the accelerating speed with which Doña Catalina was becoming a chicken made Cervantes think about one day leaving Esquivias.

He stayed there, though, for a while longer.

Life was pleasant there in the spring. The terrace looked out on the farmyard, and Cervantes, who remembered the marriage contract with its details of the dowry and the number of chickens, looked at the chickens sometimes and even passed the time counting them, half-amused, half-sad.

Sometimes he saw a sparrowhawk flying above and thought to himself that if that bird of prey swooped down and

275

took a chicken, there would only be twenty-eight chickens left, not twenty-nine, and he felt a little anticipatory shame thinking that he might be blamed for that diminution in the family assets. For he was sure the cleric occasionally counted the chickens, or that the maid did.

One evening, seeing that there were gypsies nearby, Cervantes went to bar the gate to the farmyard, just in case. He realised afterwards that taking that precaution was a debasement of his will, his consciousness and, above all, of his imagination.

But he stayed on for another month or so, watching what was happening to Doña Catalina. The girl's face was becoming more angular, her little snout sharper, more pronounced, her nose pointed, and her ears were growing smaller beneath her hair. One day as he was caressing her, Cervantes discovered two feathers; he tried to pull them out and Doña Catalina squealed. They were deeply embedded in her skin. Two long feathers like flight feathers or tail feathers.

There were other incidents too, one in particular which, though apparently trivial, was heavy with drama. Even years later, in his old age, Cervantes could never think of it without a shudder.

One day, Cervantes happened to be out walking with the barber and the village priest – another priest, not Doña Catalina's brother, who was priest in Seseña where he rode on an old nag – and they found amongst the rocks in a ravine a young falcon apparently fallen from its nest. It was not yet fully fledged and, like all young birds of prey, was ugly.

Cervantes picked it up with the excitement you feel whenever you take in your hands a small wild creature, a creature of God which, because injured, is entirely at your mercy. He looked at it and said to himself: 'Oh, king of the air with your terrifying, hooked beak, with your wings which, when outspread, are twice the length of your body, what are you doing down here? You could easily have been killed by a dog or by some innocently cruel child. But I will take care of you and feed you until you can fend for yourself and then you will fly to the heights which are your rightful kingdom.'

Naturally, Cervantes did not say this out loud nor did the falcon reply. Cervantes simply thought it. The others merely commented that the bird could be made into a good hunter and trained to hunt partridges or wood pigeons. Cervantes said that it would be unjust to make a slave of a bird whom God had made free, and when he went home, he fed it on small pieces of raw meat. He felt responsible for the young falcon's life.

The bird was allowed to live freely in the house. It hopped after Cervantes and would perch happily on his knees, enjoying the warmth of his body.

At first, Doña Catalina seemed quite fond of it, although she did complain about the mess it made everywhere. She watched warily when it was given meat to eat, but, as a friendly gesture, she put down some water for it in a bowl.

'Don't bother,' said Cervantes, 'falcons don't drink. They get enough water from the meat they eat and so they don't need to drink, at least not when they're chicks.'

When the cleric saw the falcon, he made a face and asked:

'Who brought that wild creature into the house?'

He said that such birds were not edible and there was therefore no point in taking them in. At the same time, Doña Catalina kept saying that the bird, which she called a vulture and not a falcon, was making a mess of the house.

When Cervantes went to Madrid to try and sell his play, he did not return to Esquivias for ten or twelve days, and when he did, he immediately asked about the bird.

'Oh,' said Doña Catalina, 'the wretched vulture tried to escape and it almost did too, because its wings have really grown quite a lot, but I managed to clip them and now it can't fly at all and it hops after me like a frog.'

Doña Catalina seemed to take a special pleasure in watching the falcon trying vainly to climb the three steps in the kitchen, hopping up and falling back again. Cervantes swallowed his anger and said in a loud voice, once again, that it was not a vulture, but a falcon.

Cervantes thought that the clipped feathers were the creature's final feathers and he watched the bird in silence, filled by a deep, dark anxiety. The bird fluttered its wings, trying to fly, but, each time, was bitterly disappointed. Doña Catalina had turned it into a frog.

That night, Cervantes was thinking about the falcon and feeling guilty.

Seeing the falcon, that lord of the air, walking behind him and trying vainly to go up the steps in the kitchen, with one wing folded and the other dragging, Cervantes thought:

'Why did my wife Doña Catalina do something so cruel?'

Then it occurred to him that the progressive chickenization of Doña Catalina was perhaps at a critical stage and that her decision to clip the falcon's wings represented the more or less conscious intention of a vengeful chicken. For falcons are the age-old enemies of chickens.

Cervantes thought that, whether knowingly or not, Doña Catalina was trying to avenge her sisters, the chickens. And he lay awake all night thinking about it. His wife was in amorous mood, but Cervantes was not interested. The falcon had trusted him, it had come to love him and to follow him, it came up to him opening its wings and flapping them as if to say: 'Soon I'll be able to fly.'

But Doña Catalina had clipped its wings. The poor falcon fluttered them in vain. Without its flight feathers it would never be able to soar. It seemed such a terrible misfortune that Cervantes even considered it might be better to kill the falcon than condemn it to an earthbound existence. He felt desolate every time he saw the bird trying to clamber up the kitchen steps and fall back again with one wing open and the other folded, but both equally useless.

The falcon had been given a life of twenty-five or thirty years amongst the clouds, lording it over the north winds and the mountains with their glaciers and green woods. But there it was, unable to climb even two steps.

There were other reasons for Cervantes' melancholy. He had not managed to sell his play to anyone in Madrid, and the failure worried him. He did not know what to do with himself that day, so he went out onto the terrace. He stood there counting the chickens. They were all there. The falcon was perched on his shoulder. The bird sometimes whooped and chirped, and the chickens, recognising the cries of a carnivorous bird, grew frightened. They all remained absolutely motionless for a moment and stared up at the falcon.

When Cervantes saw that there were still twenty-nine chickens, he remembered that they did occasionally eat a chicken, thus upsetting the number, and yet there were always twenty-nine, and one day he noticed that, whenever a chicken was killed, his brother-in-law, the cleric, had them buy another one so that the total number in the chicken run was complete according to the marriage contract.

It was a courtesy that made Cervantes laugh, but his laughter did not stop him worrying about the twenty-nine chickens. The fact that he had to be grateful for that courtesy left him feeling fatigued and perplexed.

Meanwhile, Doña Catalina continued her transformation from woman to domestic fowl. The worst thing was that, as his wife was gradually turning into a chicken, Cervantes did not know what to think of her or of his brother-in-law or of old Don Alonso who came on Sunday evenings to play cards with the cleric and the priest from Esquivias. Sometimes he didn't even know what to think about himself; was it possible that he was married to a chicken? It must be, there was no possible room for doubt.

Doña Catalina was not getting any smaller. If she did turn entirely into a chicken, she would be an enormous one, with a vast beak and comb and wings. And Cervantes watched her, although not too closely. Some changes were more revealing than others.

Doña Catalina's way of talking remained the clearest indication. That is, not her way of thinking or of communicating her ideas, but the tone and timbre of her voice. There is a considerable difference between the voice of a human being and that of a chicken. There are birds like the parrot, the crow and the magpie that can imitate our voice, since the size of their tongue and the concave lower part of their beak allows this. But chickens usually only squawk or cackle with a tone of voice completely *sui generis* and quite unmistakable.

One day, sitting at the table, she said to Cervantes, without turning her head:

'Any more correspondence from the captain in Caracas?'

In that repetition of the syllables 'co' and 'ca', in different, slightly fractured tones, he again heard the voice of the chicken: 'Any more correspondence from the captain in Caracas.' But the letter had come from Bogotá not Caracas and Doña Catalina, perhaps guided by her chicken instinct, had made a mistake and chosen Caracas because it best suited her cackle.

Cervantes told her that it wasn't Caracas, it was Sante Fe de Bogotá and she, raising her elbows and moving them up and down like someone trying to fly, laughed at her own mistake, and her laughter was frankly and unequivocally the cackle of a broody hen. She said: 'From Bobobobobogotáaaa.' And she said it so loudly that the whole house shook.

Cervantes wondered what would happen if she became pregnant; when her time came, would she give birth as a woman or as a chicken?

On another occasion, Cervantes heard his wife talking to her niece. They didn't know that Cervantes was listening and Doña Catalina was saying something slightly indelicate:

'I don't pee any more, you know. I never pee like you and like other people. Now I only pooh.'

The niece went to tell Cervantes, who was sitting on the terrace reading his own book *Galatea* and wondering sadly whether or not the Inquisition would intervene should his wife's metamorphosis continue.

With the clip-winged falcon on his shoulder, Cervantes was looking out over the yard. The chickens came and went. Again he counted them and there were twenty-nine plus the cockerel.

'My wife and my brother-in-law,' he thought, 'take great care keeping count of the chickens. They obviously don't want to cause me any worry.'

The strange thing is that Doña Catalina knew all the birds in the farmyard. That very afternoon she came out and started talking to her husband about the chickens, giving each one a different name. Cervantes listened to her in sorrow and amazement.

'That one,' said Doña Catalina, 'is Broody, the one with a ribbon tied round its leg, and the one scratching under its wing with its beak is Chick, the sister of Chickadee, next to her, who was born from the same clutch of eggs. You see that one having a little drink and lifting its head so that the water goes down into its crop? That's Dapple, who lays eggs with little green and yellow freckles on them, like a partridge egg. Then there's Pouter, she's standing next to Pigeon and the one we call the little Widow Lady.'

'Who calls her that?' Cervantes ventured, slightly timidly.

'Why, everyone in the house. Even Don Alonso.'

Cervantes didn't dare to respond and Doña Catalina went on:

'That one's called Cockette, because sometimes, even though she's a hen, the silly creature tries to get on top of another hen to cover her, and over there is Craw, the one who sleeps to the right of the cockerel. To the left sleeps Bib who, along with Craw, is the plumpest. Until recently Pigeon was. The chickens that sleep beside the cockerel are always the fattest in the chicken run and are heavier than the other birds, even if only by half an ounce. Then there's that naughty one we call the Parson, because its parson's nose is almost bald and set unusually high. Do you see?'

'Do you know them all?'

'Well, I've been here so long, with nothing else to do but say the rosary on Saturdays – but here comes Scrabble, always dancing back and forth, and then Leghorn, who's a different breed altogether, my grandfather had nearly six hundred of them when I was a little girl and he sold them all for breeding to various buyers from Valdemoro.'

Doña Catalina was clearly pleased by that sale of six hundred Leghorns and the memory was a source of family pride.

'And there in a circle are China, Egg and Patch, the one without many feathers on her chest. There's another one we call Paunch, but you mustn't get them muddled up, because although they're both very plump-breasted, Patch's breast is almost bald. Caper is behind her, the one that looks as if she's wearing one of those shiny cloaks women in Galicia wear, and there's Panache, who's clucking because she's just laid an egg, the beauty. She's next to Clutch, who's the best mother of them all, always looking for eggs to hatch, her own or another's. Behind her is Pip, who was ill a little while ago, and the one hopping out of the wicker basket is Coop, who takes care of the chickens, once they've had their second moult, until we chop their heads off. She's a very good friend of Draggle, who feels the cold and is always drawing one foot up into her stomach feathers. She's related to Thistle, who also feels the cold, and then there's Dewlap (before eating a worm, she always swallows and regurgitates it two or three times), Bounce, who can walk both backwards and forwards, especially when the cockerel's looking at her, Crest, Socks and Rochet. And that's the lot, may God preserve and increase them. Ah yes, I forgot about that one, Dumpy, who looks as if, like me, she's wearing petticoat, underskirt, slip and chemise.'

Cervantes listened to all this with amazement and compassion, and Doña Catalina mistook his amazement for admiration. She took the same pride in her Sunday best as some birds do in their feathers, for she was still lovely in her youthfulness even though the metamorphosis was now far advanced.

That evening, the two priests and the barber were playing cards with Don Alonso. Cervantes' wife had given them a jug of wine and some peppers on a plate, to quench their thirst. Cervantes did not want to play because, apart from the fact that the group of four was complete, he preferred to amuse himself with the falcon on the terrace. Watching it vainly fluttering its wings, he believed himself responsible for the bird's misfortune. Now fully-fledged and, by its very nature, free, the falcon would sometimes look up at the sky and it must have felt bemused by its inability to follow its instincts as a high-soaring bird.

Cervantes loved the bird and stroked the crop feathers beneath its beak with his finger. Sometimes the falcon would give Cervantes' finger a playful nip, entirely without malice, and Cervantes would laugh. The bird seemed to laugh too, but it was more like a shrill whoop, a shriek. When the chickens heard it, they stopped eating and looked round, alert.

On some afternoons, as the sun was setting and it was nearly night, a falcon or gyrfalcon flew high above the village, emitting a sharp cry, as if of lamentation. A cry of pain, though not necessarily physical pain. Hearing it, Cervantes would wonder if perhaps it was not the falcon's father or mother. And he felt sad for himself, for the falcon and for the bird that flew by overhead, keening. On those occasions, he looked at Doña Catalina in a cold, distant manner, yet still without rancour.

He could feel no enmity for that woman, despite everything, as he watched the mournful bird fly across the skies. And he thought: 'I too would weep sometimes if I were not afraid of seeming ridiculous.'

That same day, when Doña Catalina came out onto the terrace, they were talking about their usual things. For example, Cervantes mentioned that they had eaten two chickens and yet there were still twenty-nine of them in the yard. She hastened to remind him of her brother's respect for the matrimonial agreement which was, after all, part of the sacrament. But Cervantes wasn't listening, intent on the cry of the sparrowhawk flying by overhead.

Meanwhile, the chickens were going inside to roost. The last rays of light glinted on the broken glass set into the dry adobe on the top of the walls, defending the chickens from possible attackers, for there was an encampment of gypsies nearby.

Seeing the chickens going in for the night, Doña Catalina said:

'You see. Not one of them dies a natural death. It's off with their heads and into the pot.'

'And isn't that a natural death?' said Cervantes humorously.

And he laughed, but stopped when he noticed a look of displeasure on her face. It was as if Doña Catalina found such humour dangerous, although no one would have dreamed of chopping her head off.

Then pointing to the falcon, his wife said again:

'He does nothing and yet he eats his own weight in raw meat.'

'How do you know?'

'Someone told me.'

'Who?'

She hesitated for a moment. She herself did not know who had told her, but she clung to the idea. Cervantes thought: 'Perhaps she knows it by instinct.' That is, by her gallinaceous instinct of defence and survival.

At that time, Doña Catalina's arms were becoming shorter and the skin on them granular like chicken skin; sometimes she would shake them as if they were wings.

Cervantes was growing more and more worried about it all.

When they went into the house, the two priests, the barber and Don Alonso were still playing cards. Don Alonso lifted his nose, grave and aloof. Doña Catalina's brother, with a piece of paper and a pen by his side, was greedily noting down each hand as if, by that means, he could find out what cards the others had. And the four of them sat in silence.

Don Alonso put a three of spades down on the table and said:

'Draw.'

By that he meant that he was forcing the others to put down all their trump cards. This annoyed the barber and he replied angrily with words worthy of some loutish gambler:

'Curse the man's arse.'

Cervantes laughed to himself again and thought: 'The barber is merely talking like the man he is, but will Don Alonso tolerate such language?'

While they were playing, they often said strange things in a rather mechanical manner, and the barber was really put out at having to lose a trump card. He threw it down in the middle of the table and said:

'Cuckolds have all the luck.'

Fortunately, Don Alonso was a bachelor and the other two were priests. They were, therefore, invulnerable to such insults.

Cervantes could still not understand how Don Alonso's noble, decorative appearance fitted with the barber's vulgarities, although ever since he had heard Don Alonso himself say that they should note down the number of chickens, he really had no right to be amazed at anything. Observing his wife's continued transformation, he said to himself: 'Nothing that happens around me seems in the least bit reasonable.'

Reasonable or not, that same week he noticed that his wife's petticoat was sticking out a little at the back. This was because her tail feathers were growing. At the same time, her legs were getting thinner and appeared to be covered with dry, scaly skin.

Doña Catalina's front now formed a single rounded mass with her shoulders and her almost atrophied breasts. Her neck was becoming scrawnier and her light, inquisitive head looked warily from side to side. One afternoon, with a sideways glance at the falcon, she said:

'That curved beak is meant for tearing flesh.'

Doña Catalina rarely spoke now, but she looked at the falcon again and said, as if afraid:

'I certainly wouldn't carry him on my shoulder, the way you do.'

She said this several times. The sense was the same, but the words were always different, because they began taking on the cacophonous tones of a poultry fowl. So, what she said the last time was:

'I couldn't carry that cockatoo, he could kill you that cockatoo could.'

'Why, are you afraid he'll go for you?'

When she said words that resembled a cackle – could-carry-cockatoo-kill – her voice faltered. The illusion that she was actually cackling was so precise that the players looked up from their cards just as the chickens did when they heard the falcon, although this time for quite the opposite reason. It wasn't a falcon, but a chicken.

Nevertheless, only the niece dared to express her surprise. It happened in a very roundabout way. Cervantes and the little girl were up on the terrace, when she said: 'My aunt says that I take after her and that I'm already a little chick.' But the little girl had spent the week pestering the adults about something else which no one seemed to understand. She was going to a school run by nuns and, in the morning, an old nun taught them arithmetic and she would write the usual numbers on the blackboard, from one to nine. She called them figures.

In the afternoon, another nun took the class and she also called numbers figures, but she wrote the seven with a cross through the downward stroke, like a belt or a tail. And the little girl kept asking her great uncle what she'd asked everyone else:

'Why does the seven have a little tail on it in the afternoon but not in the morning?'

No one paid her any attention. Her great uncle, Don Alonso, said to her one day:

'What little tail is that?'

'The seven grows a tail in the afternoon.'

When Doña Catalina saw how insistent the girl was, she even feared that she might not be quite right in the head. Doña Catalina had recently discovered that numbers were of Arabic origin and had taken against them. They were Moorish and therefore things of the Devil.

Cervantes also heard the little girl asking the question and he was the only one who took any notice and tried to clear up the mystery. When he realised what it was all about, he laughed and even wrote something down on a piece of paper and put it in his pocket. Then he said:

'Ask your teacher in the afternoon. What's her name?'

'Sister Circumcision of the Baby Jesus.'

Cervantes laughed even more and thought that perhaps Sister Circumcision would circumcise the seven and then the little girl's worries would be resolved.

But Cervantes did not often laugh. He would look at Doña Catalina and say to himself: 'She doesn't realise. She probably never will.' Perhaps out of a sense of family propriety, her brother the cleric said nothing and the others kept quiet too. But the whole thing was beginning to seem like a terrible outrage on the part of Fate.

However, Cervantes doubted that the barber and Don Alonso had actually noticed. Doña Catalina continued to dress like a woman and her clothes covered most of her body and concealed the strange metamorphosis. When she noticed these peculiar things happening to her body, she said to herself sometimes:

'I wonder if I'm pregnant.'

When she said the same to her husband, he stood there breathless for a moment thinking that it wasn't pregnancy but chickenization or gallinification. Even Cervantes, who was usually so concerned with words, did not know the correct term for it.

Doña Catalina no longer left the house. She wasn't really aware of her true state, but her brother and the maid would sense when she wanted to go out and stop her doing so. To prevent her going to mass at the church, her brother would celebrate it alone in the house where they had consecrated an altar.

The day that they celebrated the first mass at home, Cervantes, deeply shocked by his wife's transformation, decided to leave Esquivias. He did not dare to say so openly because he feared that they would hurl themselves upon him and accuse him of having brought witchcraft to the village from Salamanca, where he had been a student, or even from Algeria, the land of the Devil.

One day after supper, the cleric said:

'Strange things are beginning to happen in this house.'

For the moment, he said nothing more, but then he exorcised the corridors and sprinkled them with holy water.

Cervantes was frightened, thinking: 'Will he dare to speak openly?' If he did, what would Doña Catalina's reaction be, for, up until then, she had not admitted to herself what was happening. What the cleric said that day was quite different. He merely regretted the lacunae he had noticed in his good sister's memory.

Cervantes said nothing, but he remembered a corporal he had met in Algeria and how the poor man used to say the same thing. Exept that the corporal would say: 'There are lagoons in my memory and there comes a point when they all join up and there's just one big lagoon whose waters overflow and flood everything. I don't know what to do. Perhaps there's nothing I can do.'

Cervantes was worried because he believed that an obsession with gradually merging lagoons in the memory was or could become a real obsession, that is, a fixed idea instigated from outside by the Devil. When those ideas were instigated from inside, it was not called obsession but possession. He knew his demonology as did everyone else in those days.

Don Alonso came to the house less and less often. It seems that the transformation of his niece Doña Catalina produced in him a great silent unease. On the other hand, he would never have dared to stop visiting her altogether.

Cervantes tried to forget about it, but, as you can imagine, he couldn't. One afternoon, he was leafing through *Galatea* and thinking about writing the second part, when Catalina drew him from his thoughts with a question:

'How much did you get for that book? I mean how much did the bookseller pay you in total.'

'I can't remember exactly. I think it was eight hundred reals.'

Doña Catalina, who had never shown any interest in reading the book, uttered a kind of throaty tremolo, a flutter of sound produced by alternating depressions and dilations of her windpipe; then she said:

'My grandfather got far more than that for the six hundred chickens he sold to the breeders in Valdemoro.'

And she went to the kitchen, unwittingly displaying, beneath her skirts, her ever more prominent parson's nose, and she did so now with a certain family pride.

At the time, Cervantes was thinking of writing the second part of *Galatea*, in which the heroine, after escaping into the countryside with the fortunate shepherd with whom she had fallen in love, was sculpted by Pygmalion and left in marble form in the marketplace, revealing to the public all the secret and more or less tragic weaknesses of its maker, I mean of the artist who sculpted it.

But Cervantes did not know whether to write that second part or not. If he did, he would have to put himself in Pygmalion's place and offer up to the public his soul's most delicate innermost feelings, expressed through the statue of *Galatea*. Cervantes had his modesty and he hesitated. Besides, in order to write it, he would have to make use of the reams of paper in the house, which also appeared in the marriage contract. He did not dare to do so.

Meanwhile, he saw Don Alonso coming along the road; he was taller than the farmyard wall and his soldierly hat appeared above it, betraying his presence from afar.

The falcon's wing feathers had regrown, to the great and secret delight of Cervantes, who watched it day by day.

'He's growing fast,' he said with satisfaction.

Doña Catalina, looking askance at the falcon, took some while to reply and at last did so in the most surly fashion.

'It's a parasite, that's what it is.'

As on other occasions, this got mixed up with other sounds and she stuttered a little. A papapaparasite, she said. Cervantes was watching her. When she tried to correct her stutter, she merely stuttered more and took even longer to finish the word. Cervantes said:

'It's just a young animal. Children are incapable of earning their own living and therefore depend on their elders. So it's not a parasite. When it can fly . . .'

'It will never be able to fly because I clipped its wings.'

'In a week's time it will be able to fly as high as its parents.'

She knew that, with its wings spread, the falcon could now get up the three kitchen steps in one jump. Cervantes thought he saw a look of disappointment on Doña Catalina's face when she realised this. That made him wary. The idea that the bird might escape provoked in his wife something akin to the panic shown by the chickens in the yard, and her reaction was one of strange, contained aggression.

Cervantes saw that he would have to protect the falcon and

that the best thing would be to allow him to live outside the house. Above the terrace, there was an opening between the flat roof and the attic with its wooden beams. This place was separate from the inside of the house. Cervantes put a few handfuls of straw up there in order to make the place more comfortable and to protect the falcon somewhat against the cold – although its feathers were now a good defence – and he took him there at night.

He was right to do so, since Doña Catalina could not sleep, or so she said, for thinking about the falcon's sharp, curved beak.

A few days later, something alarming happened. Doña Catalina was now undeniably a fully-fledged chicken. Cervantes had withdrawn some time ago to sleep in a separate room in order to avoid any intimate contact and, since he did so during Lent, both she and his brother-in-law thought it was a question of abstinence, especially praiseworthy during periods of official devotion.

But one night, Doña Catalina went into Cervantes' room intending to sleep there, although not in the bed like a person, but perched on the bedhead like a bird. Like an ordinary, common-or-garden chicken. Cervantes couldn't sleep. On her perch, Doña Catalina took little sideways steps, to the right or the left according to Cervantes' movements in the bed as he tried to avoid her. She, on the other hand, sought him out.

Cervantes was afraid that the chicken, once it had dropped asleep, would fall on top of him, since it could not in such a short time have become completely accustomed to the habits of birds.

All the following day, he felt troubled and upset. Inside his head was a tune that he had heard being played on a flute in the street and he couldn't get it out of his mind; the melody repeated itself again and again. He had a slight tremor in his crippled hand.

For three further nights, Doña Catalina continued going to Cervantes' room to sleep and she installed herself there as she had on the first night. When she took off her dress, she was naked, that is, dressed in her feathers. She would cover her head with a cap or a ruffled shawl, thus hiding the lower part of her face as far as her nose, that is, as far as her beak, because her nose had hardened first into cartilage and then into two separate bony parts. Her mouth disappeared. Although Doña Catalina seemed quite normal and in a way indifferent to the change, there was something in her that stopped her making any wifely advances.

And as she perched on his bedhead, the night became one long nightmare for Cervantes.

During the day, the priest would look at his sister, but say nothing. For when Doña Catalina was dressed and wearing a shawl over her head, she hid her condition fairly well. The worst thing was when she had to talk, for she almost always got lost in a tangle of sounds, unable to articulate more than the occasional isolated word and never managing to say anything concrete. She could communicate her state of mind, for example, happiness, sadness, love or hatred, more by tone of voice than through words. (Although, as regards hatred, she had no call to hate anyone.)

Cervantes wondered if he should consult the priest in the village – he didn't dare talk to his brother-in-law – but he was still suspicious and he felt uneasy whenever he thought about the Inquisition. The problem, therefore, grew worse and on some days it was particularly oppressive.

Luckily, the falcon escaped and Cervantes never saw it again. It must have found its parents because the bird of prey that used to pass at night shrieking, weeping, never came again. And Cervantes thought: 'At least the falcon is safe, thank God.'

When Doña Catalina knew that the falcon had flown, she stayed in her room for two whole days cackling and repeating garbled sentences. Her voice, however, was no louder than that of the other chickens even though she had a far greater thoracic capacity than they. And Cervantes still could not sleep. He had not slept for seven nights and he remembered that only with great difficulty can a human being survive more than ten nights without sleep. After that period of resistance, a person's health declines rapidly; he felt genuinely alarmed. During the day, he came and went, but he was unsteady on his feet.

Doña Catalina, on the other hand, installed once more on the bedhead, slept very well. It must be said in her favour that she did not carry with her the smell of the chicken coop and that she never did her business anywhere except in the toilet. Of course – and I hope the reader will forgive these sordid details – she no longer peed, as she had remarked to her niece one day, some time before.

There was another grave setback. The cook announced that she wanted to leave. Cervantes was afraid she would broadcast the news to the world, but the priest, perhaps harbouring the same fear, convinced her that she should become a nun in a closed order; that was a happy solution to the problem and avoided the need for any talk of chickens.

Things were becoming difficult for Cervantes and not only because of Doña Catalina's metamorphosis. Some were beginning to think that Cervantes did nothing inside or outside the house. It's true that he was still in that honeymoon period when life outside comes more or less to a full stop, but both the cleric and Doña Catalina took every opportunity to speak in glowing terms of other relatives who made good money. After talking about one of them and describing their many abilities, Doña Catalina always said the same thing:

'He's worth a fortune that one.'

She said it with great conviction and in an emphatic tone that rather wounded Cervantes. On that occasion, she was talking about a relative who was a collector of taxes and, as if that weren't enough, the cleric added:

'*He* doesn't spend his time writing plays.'

And Doña Catalina said what she always said:

'He's worth a fortune that tax collector.'

But Cervantes felt that in order to do such a job he would need money and guarantees.

One morning, very early, there was a great racket in the farmyard and Cervantes went out and saw a huge cat running away, one of those old cats, well-fed and adventure-loving, who patrol other people's farmyards. The cat shot off as if the Devil himself were after it, but it took no prey with it. However, it had apparently wounded a chicken and its victim was squawking and dragging one bloodied wing.

'It was the vulture,' said Doña Catalina.

Cervantes hated the falcon being called a vulture. He said that he had seen a very large cat running off, as big as a small tiger, and that the falcon was not to blame at all.

Then Doña Catalina said lightly to her brother that Cervantes had seen a tiger in the farmyard and the cleric exclaimed:

'Good heavens, there have never been any tigers in this part of the world.'

She insisted that her husband had seen a tiger.

For the moment, things remained as they were, but on Sunday, Don Alonso turned up again to play cards and, shortly afterwards, he was joined by the barber and the priest. They all discussed whether or not there were tigers in Spain. A majority were against the idea. Cervantes tried to say that tigers lived in Asia and that there were none in Africa either, as he well knew because he had spent six years in Algeria. But whenever he started to speak of far-off lands, they looked at him suspiciously as if they were thinking: 'Does he think he's better than us because he's been in Africa, in Cyprus and in Italy?' The barber, meanwhile, was thinking something else entirely. He was thinking that, despite having travelled in far-off lands, Cervantes clearly hadn't made any money.

That evening, Cervantes tried to draw out Don Alonso. The cleric defended Don Alonso's silence, although Cervantes had merely asked him how he spent his considerable spare time during the week. When the cleric said that, in his day, Don Alonso had traded with certain chicken-breeders in Valdemoro, who had stalls in the market at Medina del Campo, Doña Catalina intervened on her uncle's behalf, but her gallinaceous pronunciation meant that she could not be understood.

Don Alonso, in his role as constable of Castile, had once been a good agent, buying eggs and other poultry supplies for

Doña Catalina's grandfather. Once, when he found out that a muleteer was going to Pinto with a wagon and that he was bearing a letter from his brother, the priest, to a man who bred chickens, Don Alonso asked the cleric to give him the sealed letter and he wrote on the back: 'I'll be on the Valdemoro road on the fifteenth. If you've got any grit, come out and meet me on the road.' And he signed it.

He meant that he wanted him to come out and sell him some grit for the chickens, but the man misunderstood and instead came out and gave Don Alonso a good beating. That unfortunate incident, told in good faith by Doña Catalina, made Cervantes laugh. His laughter proved infectious, and his wife, with her lace cap on and her shawl covering half her beak, cackled loudly, to the amazement of the two priests.

But Don Alonso, concentrating on his cards, said:

'It was a misunderstanding, that business of the grit.'

Cervantes was seriously considering leaving Esquivias as soon as possible. When he managed to stop laughing, he asked:

'What happened then, Don Alonso?'

The village priest, arranging his cards in his hand, replied on Don Alonso's behalf:

'He retired.'

Seeing again that dual quality of grandeur and misery in the old man, Cervantes didn't know quite what to think.

They talked again about the disturbance in the farmyard and, since there were no tigers and because it seemed odd that an ordinary cat would be so bold, there was a tendency to hold the falcon responsible. Cervantes' opinion, even though he had seen what had happened, was not taken seriously. 'They know,' he thought, 'that I'm an interested party and that I would defend the falcon even if it were to blame.'

The others' obsession troubled him a little, though. And the tremor increased in his atrophied hand.

On another day, from his usual position on the terrace, where he was sitting with the niece, he saw all the chickens crowding round to peck at the bird that had been wounded by the cat. The victim was still on its feet, but it was having a hard time fleeing its colleagues who, as they usually do in such circumstances, had decided to kill it. Doña Catalina announced from the window:

'Before they kill it, we'd better cut off its head and take it to the kitchen.'

The little girl said sadly: 'Those chickens are awful, they're just a lot of tittle-tattlers and nosy parkers.' Cervantes liked the way the girl spoke. He took the same interest in words as children did in sweets or gamblers did in cards.

Cervantes looked at his hand, destroyed by the wounds of war, and remembered the wound in his chest. He thought he found some similarity in the attitude of the people there towards him. He too had wounds that rendered him vulnerable.

His wife, when she got undressed to go to sleep – and she still insisted on doing so in Cervantes' room – would stand there naked, covered in feathers, as much a chicken as any other chicken, but so huge it was almost frightening. As I said before, she always kept her cap and shawl on, though quite why one doesn't know. Cervantes didn't dare to ask her, but he imagined that she did so in order to disguise the change, at least as regards her face. A woman's vanity.

And, as usual, she leapt onto the bedhead and immediately fell asleep, only to wake towards midnight, when the cockerel began to crow. Since she weighed as much as a normal adult, any movement on her perch, however slight, shook the whole bed, and Cervantes, who was asleep, would wake up startled and turn onto his other side only to have the same thing happen again shortly afterwards.

Sometimes the bed vibrated with Doña Catalina's heart-beats. Finally, out of sheer exhaustion, Cervantes learned to sleep despite everything.

During the day, he continued pondering what had happened in the farmyard with the wounded chicken. It did not take much thought to realise that in the house, and possibly in life as well, the same thing was happening with him. Because he lacked a hand, they perhaps wanted to make him aware of his vulnerability.

It was not long before they learned that Cervantes

sometimes avoided eating pork, though not all pork. For example, he liked a bit of well-cured *serrano* ham when there was a leg of it hanging in the larder; on winter evenings, a slice of ham with a little preserved tomato, a piece of bread and half a glass of wine was a pleasant, cheering snack. Afterwards, sitting by the fire for an hour, not doing anything, just dreaming and dozing, was a real delight.

His wife, in her chicken state, watched him. His brother-in-law did too. On Sundays, Don Alonso and the priest from Esquivias would also spend an unusual amount of time studying Cervantes, albeit less intently and, out of politeness, more surreptitiously. Cervantes would then withdraw to his room to write. The fact that he left the room in order to write did not, however, seem to them to justify his existence. One day, when Cervantes said he was going to his room 'to work' rather than saying he was going 'to write', there were sideways glances and ironic remarks.

That evening, the cleric said to Don Alonso: 'My brother-in-law Don Miguel de Cervantes comes from a family of converted Jews.' Cervantes was fair-haired, with a broad brow and an open expression. It's true that he had a sharp, hooked nose and full, prominent lips, although his mouth itself was small. In any case, Cervantes' rather solitary, evasive nature was very different from that of other writers who were not descended from converted Jews, for example, Lope de Vega. Nor did Lope de Vega have an aquiline nose or prominent lips, that same Lope whom Doñ Catalina had applauded in a play at the Príncipe theatre.

It seems that Lope was jolly, sociable, carefree, with something of the deceptive spontaneity of all good actors and aristocrats. When you looked closely at Cervantes, there was something peculiar about him.

The Sunday cardplayers began to look at Cervantes in the same way that the chickens looked at the hen that had been attacked by the giant cat. Cervantes didn't know whether it was because he came from a family of converted Jews or simply because he had an injured hand and a wound in his chest. These doubts troubled him.

Cervantes remained uneasy, for he was extremely sensitive and could read people's secret thoughts, especially when he perceived in them some hostile intent.

That unease was still not serious as yet. Cervantes was not a man to be easily alarmed; indeed, as he had shown on more than one occasion, he was, by nature, steadfast and calm. But he felt uncomfortable when he sensed that the ground beneath him was becoming slippery. This was what was beginning to happen in that house. On the other hand, it seemed that Don Alonso also came from a family of converted Jews, although he was perhaps more distantly related.

In the farmyard, the wounded chicken was close to death. The others spent the whole day tormenting it, and when Cervantes saw it resting on its breast on the floor, with one leg stretched out behind and its head swaying from side to side like a pendulum, he said to himself that it must have only a few hours to live. Doña Catalina, who was watching as well, seemed to hesitate for a moment; then she gave a sudden, discordant cry, went into the kitchen, emerged with an axe and, going over to the chicken, she carried it to the wooden sink in the shed and cut off its head with one blow.

The oddest thing was yet to come. Doña Catalina left the axe impaled in the basin; she tried and failed to get into the chicken house and, when she realised that the door was not wide enough for her, she gave up, squatted down in a corner of the shed and laid an egg – an egg that was neither larger nor smaller than those laid by the other chickens.

When she had done so, she clucked a bit, albeit rather quietly and modestly, as if aware that what she had done was not quite nice in a lady.

Cervantes felt distraught.

Before getting married, he had tried to find out about his fiancée's family and he learned that her grandparents came from Toboso. Like any fiancé in his position, he was inclined to dreaming. As with the names of many other Spanish cities and villages, Toboso was a name made up of two Hebrew words: *Tob* meaning good and *oss* meaning secret. Thus, in

Hebrew, Toboso meant 'the good secret' or 'the hidden good'. Cervantes remembered that, before getting married, he had given Doña Catalina a name which seemed to him both poetic and precise. Cervantes was a great admirer of the *Celestina* and when he gave his fiancée this ideal name, it occurred to him to do so in imitation of the names of Melibea and Melisendra, the wife of the Infante Gaiferos. If they were sweet as honey, then Doña Catalina must be sweet too. Thus he called her Dulcinea and, in an allusion to her lineage, del Toboso. Altogether, the name meant 'Sweetness of the secret good' – half-Spanish and half-Hebrew. No one knew that Cervantes could read Hebrew. He couldn't speak it or write it, but he had felt curious about the semitic languages and had learned a little of them during his long stay in Algeria.

Cervantes was also so familiar with the Old Testament that, when he saw Don Alonso, the first thing he thought of was the prophet Ezekiel. He didn't know why, but he couldn't help it. Ezekiel lived after the great mass exodus of the Jews.

The names of that old gentleman – Alonso and Quesada – seemed particularly suggestive to Cervantes. But Quesada could equally well have been Quijano or Quijada, and it occurred to him that by adding the pejorative suffix 'ote', the name was even more evocative. In Hebrew the name would be Quichot, or *quechote*, which meant certainty, truth, foundation, and is a word that is always cropping up in the Jewish scriptures.

Quesada was a name full of allusions to human grandeur, and adding the suffix 'ote' made it grotesque, but, although it was both grandiose and grotesque, it was, above all, the truth. A great Hebraic truth. Like Ezekiel and even more like David, Don Alonso seemed at once mad, wise, grave and grotesque, and Cervantes watched him from a distance and reflected. That old man aroused in him feelings of admiration, respect and amusement.

This was all very interesting, but it was nothing beside the culminating event of those days: the metamorphosis of Doña Catalina. When Cervantes saw her carry the dead chicken and hand it to the cook, he wondered how she had managed to pick the chicken up, for her hands were no longer visible at the end of her arms. Then he saw that at one end of the wings, peeping out from her sleeve beneath the larger feathers, she still had four small, almost atrophied fingers – the thumb had already disappeared – with the same prehensile capabilities they had had before.

Doña Catalina turned and was explaining something to Cervantes about the dead chicken, but Cervantes was only half-listening, concentrating as he was on discovering, amongst the feathers at the end of her sleeves, her prehensile fingers. With the dissonant, up-and-down intonation of a chicken, she was saying:

'Dead yicken wa Pigeon.'

She said it once more in confused, laboured words. She repeated her ideas again and again, forgetting that she had already said them, and Cervantes was thinking: 'She saved the chicken to give it to us for supper. But by killing it with one blow of the axe in the basin, Doña Catalina has done in a moment what the other chickens have been trying to do for the last few weeks.'

She was still talking about Pigeon.

'Gotta sprise to take tothe vetswife whos justada baby.'

'You mustn't do that yourself,' said Cervantes, 'that wouldn't be right in someone of your station.'

Cervantes wanted to avoid her going out into the street and attracting attention. She was now a huge chicken. Her tail stuck out beneath her petticoat and they'd had to sew an extra hem on her dress to hide her thin chicken legs. She still wore shoes into which she managed to cram her five gnarled toes, but she walked very unsteadily and so, whenever she could, she went barefoot. She walked better then, although she did so with her legs apart, swaying her hips. Her almost floor-length skirts discreetly covered her feet.

Doña Catalina was talking about Pigeon again, as if the poor bird were a human being and Cervantes could not help hearing in her words an allusion to his own one-handed condition.

The truth is that all those who entered the house, that is,

the two priests, the barber and Don Alonso, seemed to have silently agreed to guard Doña Catalina's secret out of a kind of discreet shame. They never talked about what was happening, although they thought of nothing else. As for the maid, she would soon be leaving for the closed order, but first, the priest would warn the prioress that the woman was rather eccentric and was apt to say rather strange things. Thus, if the cook referred to Doña Catalina's transformation, no one would be surprised at the convent and none of the nuns would feel obliged to believe her.

As one can imagine, Cervantes was the person most bewildered by all this, but also the person who best concealed it. He had not had intimate relations with Doña Catalina for some time and she seemed not to miss it. She wanted only a little tenderness, which seems natural enough, although there is no evidence that chickens have any great need for affection. Cervantes would occasionally say some kind, albeit rather forced, words to his wife. He wanted to leave Esquivias as soon as possible, but he didn't know how.

He had promised to make some financial contribution to the family expenses and he had not yet managed to do so. He didn't know where to get the money from. Cervantes was quick to sign up for and to contract obligations that seemed to befit his rank, but often he did not know how to meet them.

It was not easy talking to Doña Catalina because her speech was becoming less exact and more nonsensical with each passing day. Besides, Doña Catalina couldn't remember what she had said from one moment to the next and so spoke in a tangential fashion.

One day, Cervantes realised that Doña Catalina's transformation was less shocking to his friends than the growing suspicion that there was Jewish blood in his family. Cervantes wasn't Jewish, but he did come from a family of converted Jews. It was of no real importance. We are all blood relatives. All those who live on this planet. If we picked up a pencil and started calculating the number of our grandparents, generation by generation, we would soon reach a time, still within the Christian era, when the number of our blood relatives was ten times greater than that of the population of the entire planet. This, like all numerical matters, is perfectly clear and can be proven on paper.

Therefore, we all come from Jews, Moors and Aryans, from Laplanders at the North Pole and from Egyptians. And we all have amongst our ancestors saints and blasphemers, virgins and whores, princes and hanged men – sometimes both in one person. We all have emperors and beggars in the family.

Cervantes was extremely prudent. He never spoke ill of anyone. If someone mistreated him, he might remark on it, saddened, but his sadness was not irreversible. He appeared to be burdened by a sense of guilt.

He was a good man, secretly good, and worthier than anyone of Dulcinea del Toboso, that is of 'the sweet woman of the secret good'.

Before leaving Esquivias, he first asked his wife if he could sell the young vines in Seseña or offer them as a guarantee so that he could set himself up as a tax collector. Doña Catalina did not say no. She even promised to talk to her brother. But did Doña Catalina's opinion carry any weight?

Cervantes had also thought seriously about leaving for the Indies, a common refuge for the unfortunate. However, to get authorisation he would need a certificate of purity of blood because there was a great deal of fear and ill-feeling regarding those suspected of Judaism and even those who had recently converted. This was a new law.

Cervantes had asked for that authorisation, but the response was a long time coming, and he was not very hopeful, because withholding an answer is usually a king's way of saying no.

On the day that Cervantes spoke to his wife about the vines in Seseña, she started, with her usual volubility, to talk about something else – having first said that, yes, she would talk to her brother. She started discussing chickens. The world of chickens seemed to interest Doña Catalina more and more each day, which is hardly surprising, considering what was happening to her.

That day was a Sunday and his brother-in-law, the cleric, had ridden back from Seseña on his old nag. It was a rainy morning and the cleric was preparing to celebrate another mass in his house. Cervantes used to help him, taking a certain pride in the careful pronunciation of the Latin phrases in the Gloria.

But the cleric, who was carrying his umbrella furled because it had stopped raining, went up to the terrace and opened the umbrella so that it would dry. As the ribs expanded and the cloth stretched, the nearest chickens bolted; but most frightened of all was Doña Catalina herself, who, without realising it, spread her arms wide and took an enormous jump backwards.

The cleric apologised in pained tones – it saddened him greatly – and left the umbrella open on the terrace. Doña Catalina approached Cervantes again, speaking in a sorrowful, chicken-like warble in a minor key, and when she saw that the cleric had gone into the house, she started talking again about Pigeon. Cervantes listened and then, rather impatiently, said to her:

'Doña Catalina, can't you talk about something else?'

Then she changed the subject, remembering that Pigeon had been eaten and she would not be taking her 'sprise' to the vet's wife who had just had a baby.

When she changed the subject, however, Doña Catalina started talking about another chicken, the one called Draggle, who seemed always to be cold and to be shrugging her shoulders and fluffing up her feathers. She spoke about the chickens as if they were people. According to Doña Catalina, Draggle was from the same clutch of eggs as the late lamented Pigeon, but from a different father, and she behaved quite differently. She was timid and stubborn, yet she was always first on the scene when the cockerel called them over when he had unearthed a worm.

You might easily think that the cockerel preferred her, because, sometimes, when he had the worm in his beak and even if three or four other chickens came up to him, he would only ever give it to Draggle. It's true that, recently, the chicken had been sleeping on the cockerel's right-hand side, which meant that she enjoyed his favour, and it was true that she had grown fatter and weighed a few ounces more than the others.

Doña Catalina said all this as if she were recounting news from the court about the royal family. Then she started talking about the cockerel, in a barely comprehensible manner:

'No one like Caracalla frscratching the earth and finding, finding, finding . . . A great one for finding is Caracalla.'

Bored, Cervantes asked:

'So the cockerel has a name?'

Cervantes thought that Caracalla seemed a more suitable name for a chicken than a cockerel. At the same time, he remembered that he had been in Rome at the famous Caracalla hot springs that were still used and to which all kinds of people went, including some rather dubious types.

Lately, the sounds Doña Catalina made were increasingly difficult to understand.

That morning, for example, she said:

'Don Caracallasalwiz pestring me, but sDraggle getsthworm.'

Before, she used to use the names of saints and of God himself in her exclamations, but she no longer did so.

All the time she was talking, she kept looking at the open umbrella with a respect bordering on awe. Later, when her brother the priest went to collect it, seeing that it was dry – he used it in both sun and rain – he took it down and left it lying loosely furled on the ground. Taking a step back, she said:

'Careful whatchyoudo, brother, the dead brolly looks like a dead chicken now and Señor Caracaracaracalla will go all shy.'

Hearing this, Cervantes said to himself: 'There's Señor Caracalla watching over his farmyard, lord and master of his chickens, simultaneously arbitrary, despotic and generous.' And seeing that Doña Catalina spoke of the cockerel with respect, he added to himself: 'I would like to be a Macrinus to that Caracalla.' Macrinus was the man who assassinated the Emperor Caracalla in the third century. Cervantes knew a little Arabic and rather more Hebrew, although he was not fluent in either language. He could read some passages from

Ezekiel in the original, but that was not a virtue he could boast about. And Macrinus meant butcher.

He would have had to be a Quevedo with relatives in the royal palace and wearing the habit of Santiago before he could declare in public that he could read Hebrew. There were allusions to the oriental world in that murderer's name. Macrinus was a Phoenician name, like the Macrina in Seville, which was the mosque where the Arabs who prepared meat for the market used to pray. Later, the mosque became the sanctuary of Macrina or Macarena, and the Macarena Virgin was believed to help bullfighters. History tends to repeat itself one way or another.

Doña Catalina was still talking and when she was in that loquacious, gallinesque mood, Cervantes wanted only one thing. He wanted to leave that village. To go as far away as possible. For the present, they wouldn't let him go to the Indies, but he would have liked at least to go to Andalusia or even to Old Castile, to Valladolid, where the court was.

The cleric started to look askance at Cervantes for one of the following reasons. Because he had found out that Cervantes had an illegitimate daughter by the actress Ana Franca with whom he had had an affair: a daughter whom Cervantes loved and who was called Isabel de Saavedra. Or because he himself regretted having married his youngest sister to a converted Jew or to the son or the grandson of converted Jews, a man twenty years her senior and with only one good hand. Or because he had found out that, before Cervantes went to Italy, he had killed a man in a duel, for which reason he was condemned to ten years in exile and the amputation of his right hand, a sentence that, fortunately, was never carried out. Or simply because he was suspicious of the interest Cervantes had frequently shown in those young vines in Seseña.

At any rate, the cleric behaved in an honest manner – so said Doña Catalina – for when Pigeon died, he immediately amended the marriage contract. No other part of the assets listed in the contract had been altered or touched by Cervantes, not even the reams of paper that had tempted him several times when he was considering writing the second part of *Galatea*.

The other priest, the one from Esquivias, was a devout, silent man and rather greedy too, but only as regards canonical matters. He never let a peasant off paying his tithes nor would he miss an opportunity of getting something out of his richer parishioners. At first, he had had high hopes of Cervantes, but when he saw that Cervantes wrote poetry, he raised his eyes to the roof beams in his abbey and made a chewing motion, four or five times, with his mouth empty. It was a gesture he made in moments of great discomfiture. He chewed the way goats chew, with nothing in his mouth.

The priest from Esquivias wanted to feel good about himself, just like anyone else. The ecclesiastical profession brought with it honours and certain privileges. One evening, after a few glasses of wine – Doña Catalina was drinking mead – he wanted to know what right Cervantes had to be addressed as Don Miguel. When he found out that Cervantes' mother had been of noble blood and Cervantes himself a soldier of rank, he said to himself that Cervantes was merely an impoverished gentleman and therefore worth less than a farmer with sixty-four hectares of land. He expunged him from any hopes he might have harboured.

One day, the priest made an allusion which rather alarmed Cervantes. He was talking about those who preferred to use oil rather than pork fat when frying eggs. Then he asked Cervantes if Ana was a Jewish name and what it meant. Cervantes knew that Ana meant 'here', 'present', 'now', but he merely said that he was not as well versed in the humanities as Don Francisco de Quevedo and that in Salamanca he had studied only canon law and grammar. Besides, Ana was the name of the actress by whom he had had his daughter Isabel.

Cervantes kept silent, but he felt rather uneasy thinking about Doña Catalina's metamorphosis. Whenever the priest visited the house after the 'Ana' incident, he behaved as if Cervantes wasn't there, and the barber did the same, although he did so with a rather more rustic, vulgar lack of consideration.

The only person who never bothered Cervantes was his brother-in-law, but his scrupulousness over the details in the marriage contract – adding and subtracting chickens – was somehow slightly offensive.

The moment came when Cervantes would willingly have left the house and Esquivias empty-handed just to feel free again. Lying in bed at night, with his wife now entirely a chicken, an enormous chicken, perched on the bedhead, he was tormented by the idea that Doña Catalina might have spoken to her brother about the vines in Seseña.

He could no longer talk to her, that is, he could only understand her very approximately and with great difficulty.

Nevertheless, Cervantes wanted to know once and for all whether or not he could dispose of the vineyards, and that day, on the terrace, he asked her:

'Have you spoken to your brother about what I asked you, about the vineyards?' She gave a kind of half-answer:

'Don Caracalla and the papaparish pppriest and my brother are cococonsidering it and frmnowuntilthenovthear . . . frmnowyuntil the end ovtheyear . . . frmnow . . .'

She did not complete the sentence because Caracalla, who was scratching at the ground and taking two steps forward and one step back as if engaged in dancing a minuet, discovered the inevitable worm and called to the chickens with his *gorgogoriaerr* . . . And Doña Catalina herself leapt over the handrail and ran to him. But she was too late because Draggle had got there ahead of her. Then Doña Catalina returned to the terrace and said by way of an excuse:

'She's incococobating.'

It wasn't just that she was imitating the chickens, she was forgetting her own language. She had said 'frmnowuntilthenovthear' instead of saying 'from now until the end of the year': and 'incococobating' instead of 'incubating'. Everything in her was retreating, just as her skirts were retreating above her parson's nose.

Cervantes drew one hand across his forehead, sighed sadly and went into the house. At that moment, he met Don Alonso who had just arrived, even though it wasn't a Sunday. He was carrying a book in his hand, a small book by Luis de Ávila entitled *Spiritual Garden*, a paraphrase of Sem Tob's *Zohar* – Sem Tob means Good Man. Cervantes was greatly surprised. At the time, apart from the Talmud, the *Zohar* was the most important book in Jewish religious writing, the crème de la crème of Hebraic thought in which it was said that David had been a kind of jester to God. David who had danced naked for his servants and who was not afraid to appear absurd or grotesque because he knew that the invulnerable and inviolable divinity was far above even man's most shameless clowning, far above the sublimely ridiculous and the pettily grandiose. Far above the gentleman who had advised them to write down the number of chickens and had got beaten up on a road, far above even the wife turned chicken.

Cervantes felt that he understood Don Alonso with all his contradictions, even his noble silences and his laughable pronouncements. And Cervantes left Esquivias that same day and never went back. He left without the vineyards. He went to Andalusia to gather supplies for the expedition on the *Invincible*, which was defeated shortly afterwards. Everyone knows the sonnet he composed later on, mocking the Duke of Medinasidonia and the sonnet that he dedicated to Philip II. Cervantes was justifiably proud of those two sonnets, he who put so much effort into writing poetry.

As for Doña Catalina, we have been unable to find out anything further about the life she lived after the transformation we have described. A pity.

Translated by Margaret Jull Costa

Ramón J. Sender (Chalamera [Huesca]1901- San Diego, USA, 1982) left home when he was seventeen and went to live in Madrid where he worked as a journalist until he was sent to Morocco for his military service. He based his first book *Imán* (1930) on his experiences there. He was imprisoned for his anarchist views and fought for the Republicans in the Civil War. When his wife was killed, he went into exile with his two children, finally settling in the United States, where he taught Spanish literature at the University of Southern California. He wrote over forty novels, as well as essays, newspaper articles, biographies and eight collections of short stories. His best-known works are: *Mr Witt en el Cantón* (1935), *El verdugo afable* (1952), *Réquiem por un campesino español* (1953) and his fictionalised autobiography *Crónica del alba* (1942–66). This story is taken from *Novelas de otro jueves* (1969).

The Condemned Man

JOSÉ ÁNGEL VALENTE

The man looked at death and swore gruffly. His hands were tied tightly behind him. His body still smelled of the wild, and there were bits of plant-life caught in his tangled, almost virgin hair. The hunt had been a long one. So he looked at death and spat. Behind him was a low wall across which darted swift, electric lizards that grew suddenly still in the sun. And the sun was that outrageous explosion of light that blinds or that dissolves the visible world. The sun was like hard metal cutting the eyes, slicing through the very root of one's gaze. The man was standing in front of the low wall against which the hard, useless bullets would ricochet, the bullets that he would not retain inside his trapped animal body, which was all there was to destroy.

So, he said to himself, this is the moment. He peered at the soldiers in the firing squad where they stood against the sun, at the officer who had beaten him until he bled and who was now conducting the great concert. So, this is the moment. He realised that the plot had run its course and that he was nothing but a taut thread stretching from the overheated barrels of the rifles to his own heart. And his heart was beating like a many-winged creature. A taut thread, he said. If only someone could cut it!

Suddenly, he noticed that beneath the bonds bruising his flesh his whole being was becoming unexpectedly flexible. Slowly, carefully, he began to wriggle himself loose, as if disguising the movement beneath his apparent rigidity. A command rang out and the firing squad mechanically took up its foolish stance ready for the grand finale. But the man felt as if he could now slip free not only from the grip of the ropes, but also from his own skin, his broken bones, the rags sticky with blood clinging to the sweat-matted hair on his chest. He made one last effort. He felt a different blood flowing through him, subject to a different thread, and he saw before him his own feet, his battered boots, gutted, vanquished, and next to his boots, before his own rigid, erect body was himself, like a large green lizard and, he realised, another thread now bound him to the everlasting centre of the earth. Then came the obscene sound of shots fired. The lizard ran, magnetic, invincible, over the broken wall and saw his human body standing, rigid, not fallen, but victorious, like a statue, in defiance of the grand finale, while the firing squad fell back uttering an opaque cry, like a second volley of shots, a cry of terror.

© José Ángel Valente
Translated by Margaret Jull Costa

José Ángel Valente (Orense, 1929) studied Romance languages at the Universities of Santiago de Compostela and Madrid, and later taught at Oxford for three years. From 1958 to 1980 he lived in Geneva and now divides his time between Almería, Geneva and Paris. He is known mainly as a poet and has won the Spanish Critics' Prize twice, in 1961 and 1980, the 1988 Príncipe de Asturias Prize for Literature and the 1993 Spanish National Poetry Prize. He has also translated the poetry of Gerard Manley Hopkins and Kavafis into Spanish. The book from which this story was taken, *El fin de la edad de plata* was first published in 1973, and reprinted in 1995 following the publication to great acclaim of a French translation in 1992.

My Sister Antonia

RAMÓN DEL VALLE-INCLÁN

I – Santiago in Galicia has long been one of the world's shrines, and there people still wait and watch intently for a miracle . . .

II – One evening, my sister Antonia led me by the hand to the cathedral. Antonia was much older than I. She was tall and pale with dark eyes and a rather sad smile. She died when I was still a child. But how well I remember her voice and her smile and the ice of her hand when she used to take me to the cathedral in the evening! . . . Above all, I remember her eyes and the luminous, tragic flame that burned in them when she looked at a certain student walking in the atrium, wrapped in a blue cloak. I was frightened of him. He was tall and slim and had the face of a dead man and the eyes of a tiger, terrible eyes set beneath hard, slender brows. His resemblance to the dead was further increased by the way his knees creaked as he walked. My mother hated him and, in order not to see him, she kept the windows of our house that looked out on the Atrio de las Platerías firmly closed. On that evening, as on every evening, he was walking along, wrapped in his blue cloak. He caught up with us at the door to the cathedral and, drawing a skeletal hand from beneath his cloak, dipped it in the holy water and held it out to my sister, who was trembling. Antonia looked at him pleadingly, and he murmured, smiling:
  'I'm desperate!'

III – We went into one of the chapels, where a few old ladies were following the Stations of the Cross. It is a large, dark chapel with an echoing wooden floor beneath the Romanesque vault. When I was a child, the chapel seemed to me imbued with a rural peace. It gave me the same cool pleasure as the shade of an old chestnut tree, as the vines that grow over certain doorways, or as a hermit's cave in the mountains. In the evenings, there was always a circle of old ladies praying. Their voices, fused into a fervent murmur, bloomed beneath the vaulted ceiling and seemed to illumine like the setting sun the roses in the stained glass windows. You could hear a glorious, nasal flutter of prayers, the dull sound of dragging feet, and a small silver bell rung by the altar boy, while he raised his lit candle above the shoulder of the priest spelling out the Passion in his breviary. Oh, when will this soul of mine, so old and so weary, immerse itself once more in the soothing shadows of the Corticela Chapel?

IV – It was drizzling and night had fallen when we crossed the atrium of the cathedral to go home. In the large, dark vestibule, my sister seemed afraid, for she ran up the stairs, still without letting go of my hand. When we got home, we saw my mother crossing the anteroom and disappearing through a door. Without knowing why, I was filled with mingled curiosity and fear; I looked up at my sister and she, without a word, stooped and kissed me. Despite my great ignorance of life, I guessed my sister Antonia's secret. I felt it weigh on me like a mortal sin as I crossed the anteroom which was full of smoke from an oil lamp with a broken jet. The flame in the lamp formed two horns and reminded me of the Devil. At night, lying in the dark, that resemblance grew inside me and would not let me sleep and it returned to trouble me on many other nights.

V – A few rainy evenings followed. The student strolled in the atrium of the cathedral in the occasional dry intervals, but my sister did not go to the chapel to pray. Sometimes, while I was doing my homework in the living room filled with the perfume of faded roses, I would open the window to see him. He was always alone, always with the same tense smile on his face, and, as night fell, such was his deathly appearance that it struck fear into the heart. I would withdraw from the window, trembling, but I could still see him before me and was unable to

312

concentrate on my studies. From the large, closed, cavernous room, I could hear him walking about, his shinbones and kneecaps creaking . . . The cat miaowed outside the door and seemed to me to be saying the student's name:

'Máximo Bretal!'

VI – Bretal is a hamlet in the mountains, near Santiago. The old men there wear pointed caps and serge smocks, the old women do their spinning in the stables because it's warmer there than in the houses, and the sacristan runs a school in the atrium of the church. With him keeping time with a baton, the children learn to speak the ornate language of mayors and scribes, chanting the charter of rights of an ancient family long since ruined. Máximo Bretal belonged to that family. He came to Santiago to study Theology and, to begin with, an old lady from the village who sold honey would come every week to bring him maize bread and bacon. He lived with some other poor theology students in an inn where one paid only for the bed. Máximo Bretal had already taken minor orders when he came to our house as my Latin grammar tutor. The priest at Bretal had commended this action to my mother as a charitable deed. She was visited by an old lady wearing a lace cap who came to thank her and brought her a basket of pippins as a gift. Later, it was said that the spell that bewitched my sister Antonia must have been contained in one of those apples.

VII – Our mother was very devout and did not believe in omens or witchcraft, but occasionally she resorted to them as explanations for the passion consuming her daughter. By then, Antonia was beginning to acquire the same deathly air as the student from Bretal. I remember seeing her working on her embroidery at the far end of the living room, blurred, as if I were seeing her in the depths of a mirror, her slow movements apparently responding to the rhythm of another life, her voice dull, her smile somehow removed from us. She looked very white and sad, adrift in a mysterious twilight, so pale that she seemed to have a ring around her, like the moon. And my mother, drawing aside the curtain at the door, would look at her and then noiselessly depart.

VIII – The sunny evenings returned with their tenuous golds, and my sister, as before, took me to pray with the old ladies in the Corticela Chapel. I would tremble, fearful that the student would reappear and hold out to us his ghostly hand dripping with holy water. The fear made me look up at my sister, and I would notice that her lips were quivering. As we approached, Máximo Bretal, who was in the atrium every evening, would keep disappearing and then, as we crossed the cathedral nave, he would reappear in the shadow of the arches. We would go into the chapel and he would kneel on the steps leading down to it and kiss the stones on which my sister Antonia had placed her feet. He would remain kneeling there, his body like a tomb, his cloak over his shoulders and his hands clasped. One evening, when we were leaving, I saw his shadowy arm reach out in front of me and pinch between his fingers one corner of my sister's skirt:

'I'm desperate! You must listen me, you must know how I suffer . . . Don't you even want to look at me now? . . .'

White as a flower, Antonia murmured:

'Leave me alone, Don Máximo!'

'No, I won't. You are mine, your soul is mine . . . It isn't your body I want, for death will come for that sooner or later. Look at me, let your eyes confess themselves to mine. Look at me!'

And the waxen hand tugged so hard at my sister's skirt that it tore it. But her innocent eyes confessed themselves to those other pale and terrible eyes. That night in the darkness, I wept to think of it as if my sister had actually fled the house.

IX – I continued studying my Latin homework in the room filled with the perfume of faded roses. On some evenings, my mother would enter like a shadow and silently sink down on the great crimson damask sofa. I would hear her sighing and catch the murmur of her voice as she said the rosary. My mother was very beautiful, white-skinned and blonde, and always wore silk; she had two fingers missing on one hand and on that hand she always wore a black glove; the other was like a camellia and covered in rings. This was always the hand we kissed and the hand she used when she gave us a caress. The other hand, the one in the black glove, she would conceal in her lace handkerchief, and only when she crossed herself did she reveal it entirely, so sad and so sombre against the paleness of her brow, against the rose of her mouth, against her Madonna-like breast. My mother was praying as she sat on the sofa, and I, to take advantage of the ray of light coming in through the half-open balcony windows, was studying my Latin grammar at the other end, my book open on one of those pedestal tables used for playing draughts on. One could barely see in that large, closed, cavernous room set aside for best. Occasionally, my mother, emerging from her prayers, would tell me to open the balcony windows wider. I would obey in silence and make the most of that opportunity to look out onto the atrium, where the student would still be pacing up and down, amongst the twilight mists. Suddenly, that evening, while I was watching him, he disappeared. I went back to chanting my Latin verbs and then someone knocked at the door of the room. It was a Franciscan friar recently returned from the Holy Land.

X – Father Bernardo had once been my mother's confessor and, returning from his pilgrimage, had thought to bring her a rosary made of olive stones from the Mount of Olives. He was an old man, small, but with a large, bald head; he reminded me of the Romanesque saints round the cathedral portico. That evening was the second time he had visited our house since he had returned to his monastery in Santiago. When I saw him come in, I left my grammar and ran to kiss his hand. I remained kneeling, looking up at him, awaiting his blessing, and it seemed to me that he was making the sign of the horns with his fingers. I closed my eyes, terrified by that work of the Devil! With a shudder, I realised that it was a trap he had laid, like the ones that figured in the stories of saints that I was beginning to read out loud to my mother and to Antonia. It was a trap to lead me into sin, similar to one described in the life of St Anthony of Padua. Father Bernardo, who, according to my grandmother, was a living saint, was too busy greeting the older member of his flock, my mother, and forgot to utter his blessing over my sad, shorn head with its ears wideset as if ready to take wing. The head of a child on whom weigh the sombre chains of childhood: the day's Latin and the fear of the dead and of the night. The friar spoke in a low voice to my mother and she raised her gloved hand:

'Leave the room, child!'

XI – Basilisa la Galinda, an old woman who had been my mother's nursemaid, was crouching behind the door. I saw her and she grabbed my clothes and put her wrinkled palm over my mouth:

'Don't call out, my dear.'

I stared at her because I found in her face a strange resemblance to the cathedral gargoyles. After a moment, she gave me a gentle shove:

'Off you go, child.'

I shrugged my shoulders to free myself from her hand, which had soot-black wrinkles on it, and I stayed by her side. I heard the voice of the friar say:

'It's a question of saving a soul . . .'

Basilisa gave me another shove.

'Go away, you're not supposed to hear . . .'

Hunched by the door, she pressed her eye to the crack. I crouched down near her. Now all she said was:

'Just forget everything you hear.'

I started laughing. She really did look like a gargoyle. I wasn't sure whether she looked like a dog or a cat or a wolf. But she bore a strange resemblance to those stone figures reclining or leaning out above the atrium on the cathedral cornice.

XII – You could hear them talking in the room, though the friar's voice dominated:

'This morning, a young man who had been tempted by the

Devil came to our monastery. He told me that he had had the misfortune to fall in love and that, in despair, he had sought access to infernal knowledge . . . At midnight, he had invoked the power of the Devil. The evil angel appeared to him on a vast ash-strewn beach full of great rushing winds that made his bat's wings tremble beneath the stars.'

I heard my mother utter a sigh:

'Dear God!'

The friar went on:

'Satan told him that if he signed a pact he would bring him good fortune in love. The young man hesitated, because he has received the baptismal water that made him a Christian, and fended the Devil off with a cross. This morning, as dawn was breaking, he arrived at our monastery and in the secrecy of the confessional he made his confession to me. I told him that he must renounce his diabolical practices and he refused. My advice was not enough to persuade him. His is a soul on its way to damnation! . . .'

Again my mother moaned:

'I'd rather my daughter were dead!'

And in a voice full of a terrifying mystery, the friar went on:

'If she were dead, he might triumph over Hell. If she remains alive, perhaps both will be lost . . . The power of a poor woman like yourself is not enough to combat infernal knowledge . . .'

My mother sobbed:

'What about the grace of God?'

There was a long silence. The friar must have been immersed in prayer, considering his response. Basilisa la Galinda had me clutched to her bosom. We heard the friar's sandals approaching, and the old woman loosened her grip on me slightly in order to prepare for flight. But she stayed where she was, held by the voice that said:

'The grace of God is not always with us, my daughter. Like a spring it flows forth and like a spring it can run dry. There are people who think only of their own salvation and never feel love for other creatures. They are the dry fountains. Tell me, what did your heart feel when I told you that we were in danger of losing a Christian? What are you doing to help avert this black accord with the infernal powers? Do you deny him your daughter so that he may have her from Satan?'

My mother cried out:

'Holy Jesus is more powerful than that.'

And the friar replied in vengeful tones:

'Love should be given equally to all creatures. Loving a father, a son or a husband is like loving figures of clay. Albeit unwittingly, you too, with your black hand, are raining blows down on Jesus on the cross just as the student from Bretal did.'

He must have been holding out his arms to my mother. Then we heard a noise as if he were leaving. Basilisa and I moved away from the door and we saw a black cat slip past us. No one saw Father Bernardo leave. That evening, Basilisa went to the monastery and came back saying that Father Bernardo was leading a retreat, many leagues from there.

XIII – How the rain beat against the window panes and how sad the evening light was in every room!

Antonia was sitting near the balcony embroidering, and our mother, reclining on the couch, was staring at her hard, with the hypnotic gaze of glass-eyed statues. A great silence hung about our souls; all one could hear was the pendulum clock. Antonia paused once, lost in thought, her needle poised in the air. Our mother sighed on the sofa, and my sister blinked rapidly as if waking from a sleep. Then the bells of many churches began to ring. Basilisa brought in the lamps, looked behind all the doors and barred the windows. Antonia went back to daydreaming over her embroidery. My mother beckoned me to her and kept me by her side. Basilisa brought in her distaff and sat down on the floor near the couch. I could hear my mother's teeth making a noise like castanets. Basilisa fell to her knees, looking at her, and my mother moaned:

'Get rid of the cat that's scratching beneath the couch.'

Basilisa bent down:

'What cat? I can't see one.'

'Can't you hear it either?'

Striking the floor with her distaff, the old woman replied:

'No, I can't hear it either.'
My mother shouted:
'Antonia, Antonia!'
'Yes, mother.'
'What are you thinking about?'
'Nothing, mother.'
'Can you hear the cat scratching?'
Antonia listened for a moment:
'Not any more.'
My mother shuddered:
'It's scratching right by my feet, but I can't see it.'
Her fingers dug into my shoulders. Basilisa wanted to bring a lamp closer, but it was blown out by a gust of wind that rattled all the doors. Then, while our mother shouted, holding my sister by the hair, the old woman used an olive branch to sprinkle holy water in every corner of the room.

XIV – My mother withdrew to her bedroom, the bell rang and Basilisa ran in to her. Then, Antonia opened the balcony windows and looked out at the square with somnambular eyes. She moved away, walking backwards, then fled. I remained alone, my forehead resting against the panes of glass, where the evening light was dying. I seemed to hear shouts from inside the house, and did not dare to move, under the vague impression that the shouts were something I should ignore because I was a child. I did not move from my place by the balcony windows, going over and over my fearful, childish thoughts, all tangled up with the nebulous memory of being told off sharply and shut up in a dark room. It was like a casing about my soul, the painful memory, shared by precocious children, of listening, with wide eyes, to the conversations of old women, of leaving my games to listen. Gradually the shouts subsided and, when the house was once again in silence, I fled the room. As I went through a door, I found Basilisa.

'Don't make a sound, young master!'

I stopped on tiptoe outside my mother's bedroom. The door was ajar and from within came a sorrowful murmur and a strong smell of vinegar. I slipped in through the crack, without moving the door or making a sound. My mother was lying down and had a great many cloths soaked in vinegar wrapped about her head. Her black–gloved hand stood out against the whiteness of the sheet. Her eyes were open and, as I went in, she turned them to the door, without moving her head:

'My child, shoo away that cat at my feet!'

I went over to the bed and a black cat jumped to the floor and ran away. Basilisa la Galinda, who was standing at the door, saw it too and said that the reason I had been able to frighten it away was because I was an innocent.

XV – And I remember my mother one very long day, in the sad light of a sunless room with its windows slightly open. She was motionless in her armchair, her hands folded on her breast, still with a lot of cloths wrapped about her head, and her face white. She didn't speak and, when others spoke, she turned her gaze on them, imposing silence. That was a day without hours, immersed in a kind of early evening gloom. And that day ended suddenly, because servants rushed into the bedroom carrying lamps. My mother was screaming:

'The cat! The cat! Get it off me, it's clinging to my back!'

Basilisa came over to me and, with a great show of mystery, propelled me towards my mother. She crouched down and whispered in my ear, her chin trembling, the hairs on the moles on her face brushing my cheek.

'Make a cross with your hands!'

I did so and Basilisa placed them on my mother's back. Then she said in an urgent voice:

'What do you feel, child?'

Frightened, I replied in the same tone of voice:

'Nothing, I don't feel anything, Basilisa.'

'Can't you feel her burning?'

'I can't feel anything, Basilisa.'

'Not even the cat's fur?'

'Nothing!'

And I burst into tears, frightened by my mother's shouting. Basilisa lifted me up and put me out in the corridor.

'You naughty boy, you must have committed some sin, that's why the evil one isn't frightened of you!'

She went back into the bedroom. I remained in the corridor, full of fear and anxiety, pondering my childish sins. The shouting continued in the bedroom and servants came and went through the house carrying candles.

XVI – That long, long day was followed by an equally long night, with candles burning before all the holy images and muttered conversations being held outside doors that creaked as they opened. I sat down in the corridor, near a table on which stood a candlestick with two candles, and I started thinking about the story of Goliath. Antonia, who came by with a scarf pulled low over her eyes, said to me in a shadowy voice:

'What are you doing here?'

'Nothing.'

'Why aren't you studying?'

I looked at her, astonished that she should ask why I wasn't studying when our mother was ill. Antonia disappeared down the corridor and I returned to the story of that gigantic pagan whom a mere stone could kill. At that time, more than anything else, I admired the boy David's skill with the slingshot. I intended to practise next time I went for a walk by the river. I had a vague, fantastical idea that I would aim my shots at the pale brow of the student from Bretal. And Antonia came by again carrying a small brazier in which she was burning lavender.

'Why don't you go to bed, child?'

And again she ran off down the corridor. I did not go to bed, but I fell asleep with my head resting on the table.

XVII – I don't know if it was one night or many, because the house was always dark and candles were always burning before the images. I remember hearing in my sleep my mother's shouts, the maids' mysterious conversations, the creaking of doors and a small bell being rung out in the street. Basilisa la Galinda came for the candlestick, took it away for a moment and brought it back with two new candles in it that barely gave out any light. On one of those occasions, as I raised my head from the table, I saw a man in shirtsleeves sitting opposite me, sewing. He was very small, with a bald head and a scarlet waistcoat. He greeted me with a smile:

'So the scholar fell asleep, did he?'

Basilisa trimmed the candle wicks.

'You remember my brother, don't you, my dear?'

Though dragged from the mists of sleep, I did remember Señor Juan de Alberte. I had seen him on certain afternoons when Basilisa took me to visit the cathedral towers. Her brother would be sitting beneath the vaulted ceiling, darning cassocks. Basilisa sighed.

'He's here so that he can go and call for the holy oils from the Corticela Chapel if they're needed.'

I started to cry and they told me not to make a noise. I could hear my mother's voice:

'Shoo the cat away! Shoo it away!'

Basilisa la Galinda went into the bedroom which was at the foot of the stairs leading up to the attic, and emerged bearing a cross made of black wood. She murmured a few obscure words and made the sign of the cross on my chest, on my back and on my sides. Then, she handed me the cross and took her brother's scissors from him, large, rusty tailor's scissors that made a metallic sound when you opened them.

'We must do as she asks and set her free . . .'

She led me by the hand into my mother's bedroom; she was still shouting:

'Shoo the cat away! Shoo it away!'

As we went in, Basilisa said in a low voice:

'Go over to her very slowly and put the cross on the pillow. I'll stay here by the door.'

I went into the bedroom. My mother was sitting up, her hair dishevelled, her hands extended and her fingers clenched like claws. One hand was black and the other was white. Antonia was looking at her, pale and imploring. I walked

322

round her and looked into my sister's eyes – they were dark, deep and dry of tears. I climbed noiselessly onto the bed, and placed the cross on the pillows. Basilisa stood hunched in the doorway. I only saw her for a moment, while I was climbing onto the bed, because, as soon as I placed the cross on the pillows, my mother began to writhe about, and a black cat slipped out from under the blankets and escaped towards the door. I closed my eyes and heard the snip of Basilisa's scissors. Then she came over to the bed on which my mother still lay writhing and carried me out of the room. In the corridor, near the table behind which lay the tailor's dwarfish shadow, by the light of the candles, they showed me two black strips of material that stained his hands with blood and which he said were the cat's ears. And the old man put on his cloak and went off to call for the holy oils.

XVIII – The house filled with the smell of wax and the confused murmur of people praying . . . A vestmented cleric rushed in, his fingers to his lips as if commanding silence. Juan de Alberte guided him through the various doors. The tailor's stiff, dwarfish figure ran ahead of him, looking back over his shoulder, his cloak dragging on the ground, his cap held between two fingers the way artisans do in processions. Behind them came a dark, slow-moving group of people, praying in low voices. They walked through the centre of the rooms from door to door, keeping strictly to that path. Various shapes could be seen kneeling in the corridor, and their heads began to appear one by one. They formed a queue that stretched as far as the open doors of my mother's bedroom. Inside, knelt Antonia and Basilisa, wearing mantillas and each carrying a candle. A few hands appeared from beneath the dark cloaks and pushed me forwards before returning swiftly to the crosses on their rosaries. They were the gnarled hands of the old women who were lined up along the wall, praying in the corridor, their slender shadows cleaving to their bodies. In my mother's bedroom, a weeping woman, clutching a per- fumed handkerchief, and who looked to me as purple as a dahlia in her Nazarene habit, took me by the hand and knelt down with me, helping me to light a candle. The priest walked around the bed, mumbling in Latin, reading from his book . . .

Then they lifted the covers and revealed my mother's feet, stiff and yellow. I realised she was dead and stood there terrified and silent in the warm arms of the beautiful woman, all white and purple. I felt like crying out in terror, but I felt too an icy prudence, a subtle tedium, a perverse modesty as I was held between the arms and bosom of that lady all in white and purple, who bent her face to my cheek and helped me hold the funerary candle.

XIX – Basilisa came to take me from the lady's arms and led me to the edge of the bed where my mother lay stiff and yellow, her hands tangled in the folds of the sheet. Basilisa lifted me up so that I could see the waxen face more clearly.

'Say goodbye, my child. Say: Goodbye, mama, I'll never see you again.'

She put me down, because she was tired, and then, after taking a breath, lifted me up again, placing her gnarled hands beneath my arms.

'Take a good look. Keep the memory for when you're older. Now, my child, kiss her.'

And she held me over the dead woman's face. I almost touched those still eyelids and I started screaming and struggling in Basilisa's arms. Antonia suddenly appeared on the other side of the bed, her hair wild. She snatched me from the old servant's arms and held me to her, sobbing and choking. Confronted by my sister's desperate kisses, by the gaze of her reddened eyes, I had a sense of great desolation . . . Antonia's body felt oddly rigid and there was a strange, stubborn look of pain on her face. Later, in another room, sitting in a low chair, she held me on her knee, stroked me, kissed me again, still sobbing, and then, squeezing my hand, she laughed and laughed and laughed . . . A lady fanned her with her handkerchief; another, with frightened eyes, opened a bottle of perfume; another entered carrying a glass of water trembling on a metal tray.

XX – I was sitting in a corner, plunged in a state of confused sadness that made my head ache as if I were about to be sick. Sometimes I cried and sometimes I distracted myself listening to others crying. It must have been nearly midnight when the door was flung open and there, at the far end of the room, flickered the flames of four candles. My mother lay in her shroud in a black coffin. I went noiselessly into the bedroom and sat down on the window seat. Three women and Basilisa's brother were keeping vigil round the coffin. From time to time, the tailor would get up and spit on his fingers to trim the wick on the candles. There was a kind of clownish skill in the way that dwarfish, elegant tailor in this scarlet waistcoat nipped the wick and puffed out his cheeks to blow on his fingers.

I listened to the women's stories and gradually my crying stopped. They were telling tales of ghosts and people who had been buried alive.

XXI – As day was breaking, a very tall woman, with dark eyes and white hair, came into the bedroom. She kissed my mother's barely closed lids, unafraid of the cold of death and hardly shedding a tear. Then she knelt down between two candles and dipped an olive branch in holy water and sprinkled it over the corpse. Basilisa came in looking for me and beckoned me to her:

'Look, it's your grandmother!'

My grandmother! She had come by mule from her house in the hills, seven leagues from Santiago. At that moment, I heard the sound of hooves striking the stones in the courtyard where the mule had been tethered. The sound seemed to resonate in the emptiness of that house full of weeping. My sister Antonia called to me from the door.

'Come here, child!'

Basilisa released me and very slowly I left the room. Antonia took me by the hand and drew me into a corner.

'That lady is your grandmother. From now on, we're going to live with her.'

I sighed:

'Why doesn't she give me a kiss?'

Antonia thought for a moment, while she dried her eyes.

'Don't be silly. First, she has to pray for Mama.'

She prayed for a long time. At last, she got up and asked for us, and Antonia led me over to her. My grandmother was now wearing a black shawl over her curly, silver hair that seemed to emphasise the dark fire of her eyes. Her fingers lightly brushed my cheek and I still remember the impression it made on me, that rough, peasant hand, entirely bereft of tenderness. She spoke to us in dialect:

'Your mother is dead and now I will be your mother. You have nowhere else in the world to go . . . I will take you with me because this house is to be shut up. We will set off tomorrow, after mass has been said.'

XXII – The following day, my grandmother closed up the house, and we set off to San Clemente de Brandeso. I was already outside, mounted on a mule belonging to a peasant who had sat me in front of him on the saddle, when we heard the sound of slamming doors and people calling for my sister Antonia. They did not find her and, their faces contorted with fear, they came out onto the balconies, then went back in again and ran, calling for my sister, through the empty rooms, where the wind rattled the doors. From the cathedral door, a woman spotted her on the roof, lying in a faint. We called to her and she opened her eyes to the morning sun, as frightened as if she had just woken from a bad dream. A sacristan in cassock and shirtsleeves had to use a long ladder to get her down. And as we were leaving, the student from Bretal appeared in the atrium, his cloak buffeted by the wind. He had a black bandage round his head and, beneath it, I thought I could see the bloody wounds left by two lopped-off ears.

XXIII – In Santiago in Galicia, which has long been one of the world's shrines, people still watch intently for a miracle.

© Dr Carlos del Valle-Inclán
Translated by Margaret Jull Costa

Ramón del Valle-Inclán (Villanueva de Arosa [Pontevedra], 1866-Santiago de Compostela, 1936) was a novelist, playwright and poet and one of the great literary figures of his day. Apart from brief excursions to Mexico and Argentina, he spent most of his adult life in Madrid writing newspaper articles, short stories, novels and plays and participating vociferously in the literary circles that met in many of the cafés. He wrote novels on a variety of subjects – the Carlist wars, an imaginary Latin American dictator, the corrupt court of Isabel II – but is perhaps best known for the *Sonatas* (1902–1905; *Spring and Summer Sonatas* and *Autumn and Winter Sonatas*, tr. Margaret Jull Costa, Dedalus, 1997 and 1998) and for his remarkable plays, particularly, *Divinas Palabras* and *Luces de Bohemia* (both 1920; *Lights of Bohemia*, tr. John Lyon, Aris & Phillips, 1993; *Divine Words/Bohemian Lights/Silver Face*, tr. M. Delgado, Methuen, 1993). This story is taken from *Jardín umbrío* (1903), a collection of ghostly tales set in Galicia.

In Search of the Electrifying Double Act

ENRIQUE VILA-MATAS

I know not all that may be coming, but be it what it will, I'll go to it laughing.

Stubb, in *Moby Dick*

One April afternoon a few years ago, when my name was still Mempo Lesmes and I was very young and a starving, unknown actor, I got lost in the labyrinthine outskirts of San Anfiero de Granzara and I came across a large mansion surrounded by an overgrown garden, the Villa Nemo. I had no problem getting into the house, there was no lock, no knocker on the door, it was an abandoned house, abandoned, it seemed to me, in the fullest sense of the word, for I found signs that, as well as being abandoned by its owners, it was a house that had also somehow abandoned itself. I was fascinated by the whole idea and I walked in the garden for a long time imagining the house abandoning itself to its own fate in the darkness of the night. In a state of great excitement, walking along one of the galleries open to the winds, I told myself that if, one day, I succeeded as an actor, the first thing I would do would be to buy that house and make of it my residence of choice.

Some years passed and I became a successful movie actor. A minor (but very meaty) role in *The Trunk of Fools* shot me straight to stardom. People found the way I gnawed on a toothpick a revelation. My agent was thoughtful and astute enough to change my name to Brandy Mostaza and from then on it was plain sailing. I was signed to star in *The Loves of Mustafa*, the comedy which, by opening to me all the doors of popularity, wrought a spectacular overnight change in my life. I achieved my greatest success with *The Many Moods of Young Brandy*, the television series that shone so brightly in the sixties and which now, like everything else I

329

did, has been relegated to the most complete and humiliating oblivion.

What contributed to my irresistible rise was the extreme, comic thinness of my body (people laughed because when I walked, I looked like a leaf being blown along by the wind), but that same physical quirk was soon to tell tragically against me. I bought Villa Nemo, put the garden in order and restored the house, I built a large swimming pool, I began throwing extravagant parties every Friday night, and the labyrinthine outskirts of San Anfiero de Granzara filled with men and girls who came and went like moths among the whisperings and the champagne and the stars. Every Friday, crates of oranges and lemons for the cocktails arrived from a fruiterer in San Anfiero, and every Saturday these same lemons and oranges left Villa Nemo by the back door in a pyramid of pulpless halves. I had lots of girlfriends, I danced boleros, I began many beguines, I sang songs to love. But misfortune was lurking in the most brightly lit corner of my festive garden, and, without realising it, I began to let myself go, to abandon myself. As if there were some secret link between the house and obesity, I gradually began to put on weight, and when I realised what was happening, no diet could stop the irreversible process, the tragic transformation. And so I reached the last Friday of the seventies, all dressed up and with not a girlfriend in sight, transformed into a Brandy Mostaza who was unrecognisable, a monstrous fatso who had lost his comic spark.

'For some time now, you haven't been able to see the wood for the fat,' my agent warned me that day.

'What wood?' I asked, pretending that I didn't know what he was talking about.

'Oh, come on! Just tell me one thing: how long is it since anyone offered you a contract?'

Since I had earned a lot of money, the fact that people had stopped giving me contracts didn't particularly bother me. I was much more worried, for example, by the sudden, alarming absence of girlfriends and the steadily declining numbers of guests at my parties. I was incapable of seeing that everything, absolutely everything, was indissolubly linked.

'And tell me,' said my agent, 'why do you think no one offers you movies any more, or, if they do, why they only want you for awful minor roles?'

'Well,' I said, 'I suppose it must have something to do with my putting on a few pounds.'

'You suppose!'

Baron Mulder, who was quite blatantly and openly eavesdropping on us, joined in the conversation.

'My friend Brandy's fatness,' he said, toying with his monocle, 'is a splendid monument to the flesh, to excess and to human kindness.'

You might think that he was saying all this because he was even fatter than I was, but I had an inkling too that, for some hidden reason which I could not pin down, he was trying to flatter me in order to gain my sympathy as a preliminary to getting something out of me.

My suspicions were soon confirmed when, an hour later, I bumped into him again in the garden and he started talking to me about his ancestors, the Mulders and the Roigers, revealing to me that both branches of the family had lived in Villa Nemo at one time and that they had suffered all kinds of misfortunes there. He was a bit drunk and very garrulous, and a shameless doom merchant. From all that he told me (he even had the impertinence to ask if his ancestors' ghosts were quite happy haunting my house) I drew one clear conclusion: Villa Nemo had a baleful influence on all its owners. That was why I was surprised when, as he said goodbye to me that night, he asked how much I wanted for the house.

'My friend,' he said, 'I'll be honest with you. As a fat man, your future in show business looks pretty bleak. Let's not fool ourselves. The public preferred you thin. I know that before too long you'll be having money troubles and I'd like to help you out. Sell me Villa Nemo, submarine included, and then go off on a trip, a trip round the world.'

I was just about to ask him about the submarine when his monocle fell out. I stooped to pick it up for him, but he ground it angrily into the earth. Then, he did a few eccentric tap dance steps and fell flat on his face on the grass. Something strange happened to me then, for when I saw him fall onto the grass, I felt an enigmatic impulse rise up inside me, an unstoppable desire to turn a somersault in the air and to perform a circus number with the baron at the end of a party which, it must be said, had turned out to be positively soporific.

'Take my advice, as a friend,' said the baron as he got to his feet, 'and sell me your house.'

And then he clapped me hard on the back and disappeared into the night. My agent was at my side and could not believe what he had seen.

'Brilliant, absolutely brilliant,' he said. 'Did you see the wit and elegance with which he crushed his monocle? Underneath, the baron is a high-voltage comedian. If you could go back to being as thin as you used to be, though alas, I fear you never will, you could be one of the most successful double acts the cinema has ever seen.'

'You're not saying . . .'

'Why not? I'm talking about those odd pairings of actors who only gave of their best because, how can I put it, because there was something odd in each of them that triggered the growth or the emergence into the light of the hidden electricity lurking deep inside the other. An electrifying double act.'

'I see,' I said, coolly saying goodbye to two former lovers who had become firm friends, 'do you mean like Laurel and Hardy?'

'Exactly, and Abbot and Costello too. Your thinness and the baron's extravagant fatness could have made you into a very successful double act. Unfortunately, the partner you need now would have to look very different from the baron. That was what I wanted to talk to you about.'

He led me to a bench in one corner of the garden, near the swimming pool. And there, while I watched the painful parade of ex-girlfriends bidding me farewell with the most wounding and taunting of smiles, he showed me an album full of photographs of thin actors who might be able to save my career if I joined forces with them to form a double act.

'Wouldn't a better solution be to ask the baron to slim

down until he's reed-thin?' I said, joking, depressed by the parade of mocking girlfriends and by the fatigue brought on by the lateness of the hour.

'Well, it's your funeral,' he said threateningly, saying good-bye with a look that told me he would take no further interest in my career.

But the following morning, apparently recovered and as if wanting to give me one last chance, he turned up again at Villa Nemo with his album of photos of thin actors.

'Look at this one,' he would say, pointing to one.

'And look at that one,' I would reply, taking it all as a joke. But the joke did not last long. In the days that followed, I ended up doing try-outs with many of those thin actors, try-outs that always ended in utter disaster. Seeing that there was not a single actor in the whole country with whom I could form an electrifying double act, we put advertisements in the papers. But that didn't work either. Then my agent suggested that perhaps the actor I was looking for lived abroad and that perhaps (and here began my downfall) he wasn't an actor at all, in which case, I would have to seek him in the street, or rather, in the streets of the world.

'You must exhaust every possibility,' he said. And that reasoning carried me far off, it even took me to the streets of Hong Kong, in pursuit of a thin man who turned out to be a complete non-starter. Just when I was despairing of ever finding a partner and was already in deep financial trouble, my mother, may she rest in peace, came to my aid:

'In Calle Rendel,' she said, 'in the bookshop with the same name as the street, there's a skeletal assistant with a most unpleasant face and a name that would be more at home in a cakeshop. He's called Juan Lionesa and he might just be the man you're looking for.'

Some hours later, Juan Lionesa stood before me – his dark hair, cut pudding-basin fashion, framing ruddy cheeks and an expression of mingled tedium and mystery. I had just asked him for a copy of *The Divine Comedy* and I found myself studying him from head to toe. He, instead of looking for the book, did exactly the same, that is, he subjected me to a close visual inspection that verged on the embarrassing, then he said:

'Didn't you used to be Brandy Mostaza?'

That 'used to be' rather shook me.

'And you,' I replied, 'never used to be anyone, which is much worse.'

'Oh, come on! You're not going to tell me my little observation offended you?'

I hate the word 'observation' and that pedantic, impertinent bookseller's ugly face. I gave him a rather angry look and silently, roundly cursed him, but he barely batted an eyelid. Suddenly, something extraordinary happened. When he did finally get round to attempting to locate a copy of *The Divine Comedy*, he glanced over at a (rather empty) shelf and stood for a moment in profile to me. I saw then, that in that position, Lionesa's features, his left profile, were curiously like mine in the days when I was thin and successful. His left profile, reminiscent of a heron on heat, was enough to make the most serious-minded of mortals laugh. Unwittingly, Lionesa possessed the essence of the comic quality that I had lost, the secret of my former success, a real gold mine. My mother had been absolutely right.

'Listen,' I said in a very confidential tone of voice, 'I need to talk to you alone, outside the bookshop, do you understand? It's about a matter that might interest you. And since you obviously don't have a copy of *The Divine Comedy*, give me something else, something by Jules Verne, for example.'

He arched his eyebrows and the expression on his face changed radically, as if the reference to Jules Verne contained some transcendental message. And then, slowly and very respectfully, he said in a low voice:

'The cake will travel by balloon.'

I could merely have assumed that he was mad or that he was simply making fun of me, but for some reason I had a sudden hunch that those words might be a form of password (and they were, but not the kind I imagined). At first, I thought that Lionesa had sensed in me a being who, in many respects, complemented him and, because of that, he had invented a secret language just for the two of us, words that allowed us to understand each other, but prevented anyone else from understanding what we were talking about.

'The cake will travel by balloon,' I said, thinking that by my reply I was doing no more than recognise the strange electrical current that seemed to unite us, thinking too that with those words I was acknowledging the status of the secret language that had just sprung into being between us.

'The cake will travel by balloon, and I'll be at Jacob's Bar at half past eight,' he said. Shortly afterwards, I left the bookshop with a copy of *Five Weeks in a Balloon* under my arm. I read the first few chapters while I was waiting at Jacob's Bar for Lionesa, who arrived punctually. He was wearing dark glasses and had his coat collar slightly turned up. He greeted me from a distance, with a lift of his eyebrows, but when he came over to me, he acted as if he didn't know me. He sat down on my left, at the bar, presenting me with his anodyne right profile. He ordered a beer and just when I was thinking he was about to ask me about the matter that had brought him there, he acted as if he expected nothing at all from me, except the cake that was supposed to be travelling by balloon.

'OK,' he said, still not looking at me, addressing me as 'tú' and keeping his head absolutely still, 'when I finish my beer, pass me the cake, and good luck, comrade. Ah, one piece of advice. Next time, try to be a bit cleverer and more discreet and make sure you get the password right.'

So it *was* a password, but not the kind of password I had expected. I had stepped right into the eye of a hurricane, doubtless a plot or some sort of espionage ring. I cursed myself for not having simply disappeared before, when I left the bookshop. I was angry with myself for not guessing that Lionesa was a conspirator awaiting some secret message about Jules Verne or about a balloon.

While he was slowly drinking his beer, which I would have to pay for, I was weighing up how best to extricate myself from that particular mess and I finally decided that I would simply say that, for reasons beyond everyone's control, the cake would be delayed for twenty-four hours. And, bold as you like, I told him; no one has ever looked at me like that, with a look, first, of utter astonishment, immediately superseded by one of terror.

'There's no need to look at me like that, just because there won't be any cake until tomorrow,' I said loudly, out of sheer nervousness.

That was how I talked when I found myself in difficulties. I would either go off at a tangent or race madly ahead. Lionesa, however, seemed unable to believe what was happening, while everyone else in the bar was under the impression that drink had just brought about the birth of a friendship between two complete strangers; one drunk even rewarded us with a smile and a burst of loud applause. It was obvious to me that the marked difference in our physical appearance made us an attractive pair. Lionesa was clearly not of the same opinion, indeed everything seemed to indicate that he saw in me someone who, for whatever reason, had just set him a deadly trap.

The strange electricity between us meant that suddenly, like someone throwing out the main ballast from a balloon, I lost all my nervousness and transferred it to him. I felt very calm then – I would go so far as to say that I have never felt more serene – and I decided that there was no reason to get alarmed and that the most practical thing would be to put the record straight and tell Lionesa the whole truth. I explained that I had gone to the bookshop because I was looking for a thin man to work with me in films which were guaranteed to be a great success if only I could find the ideal partner.

'And that ideal partner is me, is that what you're trying to say?' he asked with such a degree of aggression and distrust that I thought he might kill me.

'Yes, of course. Please, you must believe me. I've got no interest in politics whatsoever. There's been a misunderstanding, that's all. I came into the bookshop because my mother told me that the man I was looking for worked there. I've been all the way to Hong Kong in search of the man who could help save my career. And now all I've got is my house,

Villa Nemo, because I've lost everything else trying to relaunch my career. I need you to join forces with me, to be my artistic partner. Otherwise, I'll have to sell Villa Nemo and I'll be out in the street. Help me, please.'

'Take a good look at me,' he said and in his coat pocket there appeared what might well have been a gun. 'I'm pointing a gun at you, so cut the crap, pay for the beers and just walk out of here ahead of me, and no funny business.'

It was like a nightmare. I paid for the beers and we went out into the street. Lionesa hailed a taxi and, as he did so, we were walking so close to each other, that our legs and overcoats became entangled and we both tripped and fell to the ground. I managed to trap Lionesa's tie beneath my great bulk, but he sprang up, slightly flustered, and again pointed his gun at me. Everyone in the street was laughing and enjoying the spectacle, which confirmed me in my view that I had found my ideal partner and that, if only politics and that wretched gun had not got in the way of our rise to stardom, we could have been an electrifying double act.

When I got into the taxi, I realised how difficult it would be to escape once the taxi was moving, since I could barely get my body through the door and Lionesa himself had to heave me into the cramped interior. As we were driving through the city, past the area around Parque Rendel, I was filled by a feeling of profound melancholy. I looked sadly out of the window wondering if I would ever again see those trees I had so often felt drawn to. And I wondered too if I should bid farewell to life. Even in the most desperate situations, I have never lost my sense of humour. I'm one of those people who believes that life is utterly laughable and that life itself is made up of pure laughter and that, although we may have no idea what awaits us at the end, the best strategy is to go to it laughing, with a tragic lack of seriousness. Perhaps that was why I was able to look at Lionesa in a relaxed manner and say with a broad smile:

'May one know where you are planning to kill me?'

I saw the taxi-driver trying not to laugh. It was clear, or so I thought, that from the very first, he had found us irresistibly funny, well, not everyone hails a taxi in a twosome, rolling around on the ground. To conceal how much he had enjoyed our circus act and how much we had made him laugh, or perhaps simply in order to participate in what must have seemed to him a great festival of humour, the taxi driver cleared his throat and said to Lionesa:

'Excuse me, it was the corner of Juárez and Verlás you wanted, wasn't it?'

'No, it was the corner of Verlás and Juárez,' replied an angry Lionesa, who did not seem entirely himself. His uncertainty and the half-hearted laughter that had taken hold of me (I kept thinking that I was about to die and I found the idea highly amusing) encouraged me to move closer to him as soon as we stopped at a traffic lights. I was, and still am, a great actor. I leaned forward in a strange manner, thrusting my chin forward and showing my teeth. I reckoned that Lionesa would not be prepared for that. My face, normally soft and bland, hardened into something resembling a stone mask, deathly white to start with, but deepening to a dark red that spread out from my cheekbones, and finally became black, as if I were about to choke. I thought Lionesa would be unable to bear it and would faint, but he didn't, he simply sat there looking at me strangely.

'Such a pity, we would have made a mint,' I said and head-butted him hard. I came down on top of him with my whole weight, stone mask included. He lost consciousness. After some strenuous bodily manoeuvrings, I managed to get out of the taxi and take refuge amongst the people thronging the entrance to the metro. I glanced back and, seeing no one following me, I gave a sigh of relief. I got into a carriage on line 5 in the belief that I was travelling towards freedom. Poor fool, I didn't know what still awaited me. That same night, minutes after talking to my agent, who did not believe a single word I said, the phone rang in Villa Nemo and a criminal voice informed me that they had kidnapped my mother. If I went to the police to tell them about either the kidnapping or the plot, they would kill first my mother and then me. If I did not pay them a million dollars in ransom money, I would

338

never see my mother alive again. When I had paid them and they had set her free, little would have changed, except that my mother could be with me once more, although if I subsequently went to the police with the story, I could not be with my mother, since, as well as being a million dollars poorer, I would also be dead, and dead men don't live with their mothers.

I had no option but to sell Villa Nemo to Baron de Mulder. I told him that I needed the money in order to go on a long trip.

'I always knew,' he said, 'that sooner or later you would get rid of Villa Nemo, which is a house intended for a large family like mine, not for a confirmed bachelor like yourself. You would be better off travelling and having a purely functional apartment where, instead of throwing parties for multitudes, you could have intimate suppers for two,' and he winked lewdly, 'don't you agree, my friend?'

'I haven't thrown a party for ages,' I said. 'Not since I got back from Hong Kong.'

With the money the baron gave me for the house, I paid off the ransom and they returned my mother to me, but she was a changed woman. Since I was now ruined, I had to go and live with her, and she spent all day every day blaming me for the kidnapping.

'You got into bad company,' she would say. 'You can't fool me. You got yourself into some mess or other, and I was the one who had to pay. The proof is that you won't go to the police.'

It was useless explaining to her that I suspected it was a band of thugs of the kind who enjoy killing for killing's sake. Going to the police would only provide them with the opportunity for a cruel reprisal. My mother didn't believe me. Besides, however much I declared my innocence, events conspired against me. My mother and I began getting visits from members of the revived cult of British wizards demanding information about unguents that would help them to fly and so forth. In the end, my mother lost all patience and disinherited me. Tormented by remorse, she began to age rapidly and, though she no longer spent her days reproaching me, she wouldn't talk to me either, but passed her time writing down in a red notebook the salient details of all the funerals that passed by beneath her window. When she had noted down thirty-three interments and some eighty or ninety different details, she herself died. She may well have died of grief for having so unjustly disinherited me, for she knew that she was leaving me destitute. It could not be said that life was exactly smiling on me, but, nevertheless, I remained true to my principles and I smiled back at life.

Moreover, I got a taste for the streets, and I became an interesting vagabond, simulating madness, which proved most profitable, because people took pity on me and gave me money. My madness consisted in walking all over the city carrying a pair of drumsticks and with them beating out on the pavement a rhythm as emphatic as it was meaningless, leaning clumsily forwards as I advanced along the street, drumming hell out of the cement. My new life, including nights spent in the metro, became a source of great satisfaction to me. It was marvellous not having to read newspapers or receive visits from British wizards, to pass the Rendel book-shop occasionally and make a V-sign at them through the window, as an anonymous tramp. It was wonderful being able to earn a living doing street theatre, a daily rendition of the most refined madness an obese actor could manage.

Since I read no newspapers and had only transient contacts with other wretched tramps, I did not find out for a long time that Villa Nemo had been destroyed by a fire in which the baron and all his family had perished. On the cold winter's day when I learned this news, I thought to myself that the fire, which the police had written off as an accident, might well have been caused by the British wizards. It occurred to me that they might have thought the baron was me. Unable to do anything more for him, I said a prayer in the company of another tramp and, shortly afterwards, dying of curiosity, I went to see Villa Nemo, where I savoured the morbid pleasure of strolling about, bearded and ragged, amongst the ruins of what had once been my dazzling mansion. Only four walls remained standing and the house was very much like the house I had discovered one April evening years before, the house that had so fascinated me. The garden was beginning to grow wild again, there was no lock or knocker on the door. It had returned to being the same abandoned house I had seen that first time, a house so adept at self-abandon.

I thought about Villa Nemo in the days that followed and an irresistible electric force urged me to return, to return and live there again. And last night I came back to stay. Very excited, standing on one of the galleries open to the winds, gleefully looking out on the now totally wild garden, I decided to come and live in the house, or rather, in what remained of the house. I told myself that, after all, not only was it the ideal dwelling for a vagabond like myself, it was also the most familiar, comfortable place I knew and doubtless ideal for parties for one, for the intimate parties that would be held each night after my exhausting travails as a mad beater of pavements.

That is what I thought last night, when I returned to live in what had once been my luxurious bedroom. And perhaps because I could not stop thinking about all that or perhaps because of the cold (which my one blanket could do nothing to disguise), I took a long time to go to sleep. Around midnight, I was again woken by the cold. I began considering making a fire out of what remained of a wardrobe that had partially survived the blaze and which I knew very well, for it had once belonged to me. While I was weighing up that possibility and as if the wardrobe had realised my intentions, I seemed to hear the sound of creaking and moaning emerging from its depths. I thought it must be my imagination, but the creaking came again, and then the sound of chains, and finally, a heartrending cry.

'Who's there?' I said, lighting a match and still not entirely losing my calm.

No one answered. By the light of that slender match, the wardrobe seemed different from the one I had known. It looked like an upended submarine. It was an art deco design, which I had never noticed before either. I remembered the words of the baron when he had suggested I sell him Villa Nemo with the submarine included. And I remembered too when he had asked me if his ancestors' ghosts were quite happy haunting the house. The match burned out, and for a few seconds, plunged into darkness, I felt a certain respect for the shadows, which I soon put paid to by lighting another match.

'Who's there?' I said again, trying to keep my voice firm and steady. I received no reply that time either, but just as I was preparing to go back to sleep, the creaking resumed. I realised that I must confront the situation whatever the consequences, and then, commending myself to all the saints in the world, I wrenched open the wardrobe door.

Nothing. There was nothing and no one inside. I went back to my bed, wrapped myself in the blanket, and tried to get to sleep. I was once more considering turning the submarine into a good blazing fire when the creaking recommenced, this time accompanied by an unmistakable lament.

'Don't burn me,' I heard a voice saying. 'If you do, I will offer no resistance, but I fear that, in the attempt, you will lose all your strength. I am a spirit.'

'Who's there,' I said again, feeling alarmed this time.

'It's your friend, Baron de Mulder. My ruin in this world was forged in this very room, in this house I lost all my family, in this wardrobe I kept my finest clothes. This house is mine: let me have it.'

I didn't dare light another match, afraid that he might think I was about to set fire to the wardrobe.

'I would never have recognised your voice, Baron,' I said, trying to recover my presence of mind.

'If you could see me, you would appreciate the great physical change I have undergone too. The fire transformed me into a pale, emaciated figure who spends each night standing in this wardrobe. It's a pity you can't see me and have a good laugh. It's a pity you still belong to the land of the living and cannot appreciate the truly comic nature of my slender, supernatural appearance.'

I tried to explain to him that it did not seem logical to me that, given that he was a ghost and had the chance to visit all the most beautiful places on earth (for I presumed that distance now meant nothing to him), he should choose to return to the one place where he had suffered most.

'I know I'm foolish,' he said, 'but I enjoy it, just as I love being thin and miserable. Because, my dear friend, I have great natural reserves of laughter, and I laugh all the time and, the more miserable I am, the more I laugh.'

And he laughed. And had he not already been dead, he would have died laughing right there and then.

'You laugh in a terribly serious way,' I said. 'I don't know that you could really call it laughter as such. Listen to mine, for example.'

I demonstrated to him how to laugh in a cheerful, carefree manner and, as I did so, I felt the gentle but powerful connection between his laughter and mine. There was a current of mutual sympathy between us, the stimulating solidarity of the wretched. And there was something very strange in both of us that triggered the growth or the emergence into the light of a hidden electricity lurking deep inside the other.

I remarked on this, but he did not reply. Then I thought that perhaps it was because what I had said had made him anxious. After all, what I had said was all very well, but the fact was we could never be a truly electrifying double act if I did not take a fundamental step (which only I could take) that would place me, like the baron, outside my dirty, crumpled clothes, outside my beard, this room, the submarine, outside this life.

That is why now I am waiting for night to fall and for the baron to return to his wardrobe. I have everything ready, the strychnine with which I will take that last fundamental step and which will allow me at last to form an electrifying artistic double act, an act that will soon be going on tour, a triumphant tour of outer space.

© Enrique Vila-Matas
Translated by Margaret Jull Costa

Enrique Vila-Matas (Barcelona, 1948) has published both novels and short stories: *Impostura* (1984), *Historia abreviada de la literatura portátil* (1985), *Una casa para siempre* (1988), *Hijos sin hijos* (1993), *Lejos de Veracruz* (1995) and *Extraña forma de vida* (1997). He has also published two compilations of essays and articles: *El viajero más lento* (1992) and *El traje de los domingos* (1995), and is a regular contributor to the Spanish daily newspaper *El País*. 'In Search of the Electrifying Double Act' was originally published in a collection of stories about imaginary suicides – *Suicidios ejemplares* (Anagrama, 1991) – which, like much of his work, is a disconcerting mixture of comedy and tragedy.

A Poor Man

ALONSO ZAMORA VICENTE

It is very likely that, amongst these people thronging the station to greet the trains as they come in, I will find the man I am looking for. It is likely too that, when I kill him, I will be doing him a favour. From the barrier, in the passageway leading out of the station, I have often observed the faces of travellers. Tired, tetchy people with hesitant eyes. Destroyed by some family tragedy, a bereavement, a financial disaster, perhaps an adulterous relationship. Others, with the wide, vacant, gentle eyes of those who have just been told by a doctor that there is no hope. Yes, in that mass of lives arriving on the nine o'clock train, amongst those who are off to the station cinema to pass the time as they wait, I am bound to find the man I have to kill. For I have to kill a man. I can't leave it until tomorrow. Everyone at home is away and I can do what I like. It will be a most valuable experience. A man without a name, without an address, perhaps someone who has already considered suicide. A man who will bear in the lines in the palm of his hand the astonishing warning that today, Saturday, he will meet me.

It wasn't hard to find him. There are many people who think about death, who call to it, who dream of it as they lie resting. As usual, I was leaning on the railings that separate the passageway from Customs. Even if there had been another ten thousand people, I would have spotted him at once. Each time he bent his knees as he walked, he was swathed in burgeoning light, in an irrepressible lassitude. There he is. He threw his suitcases down on the customs officers' bench like someone sloughing off . . . I don't quite know what. His shoulders are too hunched, the line of his lips too anxious for so impersonal an act as opening up his suitcases for a border guard. I think that was when he saw me for the first time. I won't be so

345

foolish as to say that he smiled at me. He could no longer smile by then. But perhaps his eyes . . . He must have been asking himself, like so many other people in Customs, where should I look? All smugglers ask themselves that question; I have sometimes asked myself the same thing. But that wasn't why he was doing it. It was because *I* didn't know where to look. That is why he noticed me.

Perhaps that is why he said nothing when, with much arm-waving, they relieved him of a pearl necklace, a film projector, a few packets of American cigarettes and a bundle of German marks. By then, he could only speak to me; his life belonged to me, but I could not enter the Customs area. When the formalities were over, I approached him; he was crumpling up the receipt for the confiscated items and putting it in the pocket of that large camel hair overcoat that attracted the attention of the station employees and the police. Even the soldiers on station detail turned to look at him. I will have to get rid of that overcoat. When I thought that, I went cold.

We sat down for a while in the station café. He confessed that he had eaten nothing all day. We barely spoke. It was as if everything had already been said, and we had set off into new territory. It was pleasant looking out through the windows at the bustle in the station, barrows piled with luggage, groups of hikers returning home with their rucksacks fuller than when they had arrived and carrying small pots as souvenirs. People, passport in hand, queuing up at the various offices, for the police, the bureau de change, the Department of Health. A couple are desperately kissing, the young man is a soldier; my companion looks at them, unsmiling, and says: Bah! People go up and down the steps to the lavatories. A blind man, selling lottery tickets, taps insistently on the wall with his stick. The woman at the stall selling postcards and newspapers hands over the accounts to a short, hunchbacked man who has arrived for the night shift. The lights of six different trains have come on simultaneously above the announcement board. Six times there is the same crush of people, the same weariness at the station exit and the same cries of 'Taxi! Taxi!' and 'Do you need a hotel?' 'Looking for a cheap place to stay?' That is when I invited my guest to come home with me. We will be alone, you can rest. I don't know what he said in reply, because, as I was talking, the loudspeaker from the station cinema blared out its latest programme, including news of the floods in Bavaria, and I couldn't hear what he said. I noticed, though, when I looked at him, trying to guess at his response, that his deep-set eyes were pale, in contrast to his thick, black beard. I was afraid that he might die before I could . . . I don't know what his answer was, but he came with me.

My house is not far from the station, but we took a long time to get there. I've walked that same route several times a day for years. It was the first time I'd counted the clocks as I passed: five, excluding the station clock. The clock on the tower of the Trinitarian convent, with its light still bearing traces of the dark blue paint required by the civil defence, the clock on the central lamp post at the Navas de Tolosa roundabout, where the traffic policeman has his little hut, then the one at Winter's the clockmakers, on the corner, with words instead of numbers on the face, the really ugly clock in the square and the one outside Omega. Perhaps it only took the usual fifteen minutes, but it seemed longer. He kept walking more and more slowly, whilst I was walking faster and faster. I almost had to drag him across the final junctions. We both knew perfectly well what was going to happen. My anger was growing from my elbows down, and a distant, desolate night was sprouting on his shoulders. Crossing the square – it was a quarter past ten (he said twenty-two fifteen, which made me think that he must speak a different language) – you could hear the powerful thrum of the river. A group of students emerged from a café along with a gust of cigarette smoke and the voice of a female singer: 'I go in search of death . . .' It frightened me and, deep down, I cursed her. He continued walking, his shoulders hunched, no longer daring to ask after his suitcases, which we had placed in the left luggage office.

He was panting as we went up the stairs. The shadow of the bannister imprisoned his breathing, a coming and going, an

347

escaping and a sighing. I felt all my irritation crumble when I turned and saw a confident sadness bloom on his lips. It seemed to me that he was counting the steps. I was tempted to encourage him, to offer him my arm, to say a few words of consolation, We're nearly there, or It's the next floor, or You'll be able to rest soon. I did not do so. It occurred to me that any criminal would do his best to say nothing, to avoid meeting one of the neighbours on the stairs, no . . . no . . . When I turned the key for the second time, I still thought I could see the ruin of a smile on his face, perhaps it was the light, or the hot breath of the heating.

On other occasions, when my family went off to stay in the country, I would take advantage of being alone at home to get together with friends until late at night, or to arrange a romantic assignation. Tonight was different. I wanted to kill a man. He was there already, sitting in the hall, asking me where the bathroom was, with exasperating docility. I was just beginning to think that it was all going to be too easy when, suddenly, I felt afraid. The furniture blared, the curtains filled up with grubby white shadows, a deceptive clamour rippled in my ears. I made my way quickly to my bedroom. He was in the bathroom and stayed there for some time. I put on all the lights. How would I do it, who was he, and what would happen afterwards. He's coming out, I heard the sound of water, the bolt, footsteps, he's coming down the corridor, he sneezed, he must have stopped to look at a painting and wipe his nose, he's coming now, he appears in the doorway, his coat over his arm and his trousers undone. He lets himself fall onto the bed without saying a word. If only he had said something.

There's no point strangling him. He stretched out comfortably on the hard mattress of my unmade bed, cleared his throat twice, rubbed his shoulders as if settling down to sleep, and then he died. I didn't need to kill him. Having nothing else to hand, I covered him with the mattress from the other bed, where my brother sleeps. The sadness that oozed out from him when we were coming up the stairs was now penetrating the room, filling it with an all-pervading chill. I was just about to sit down and think about him properly for the first time when the telephone rang, Chonita was inviting me to an improvised cold supper; then she could drive me out into the country to join my family. I rushed out, forgetting completely that it was Saturday and that I was alone in the house, forgetting that I had gone to the station and that in my bedroom a man had, well, died, I didn't kill him, though I had wanted to.

I don't understand this feeling of anxiety. My arm hurts, both arms do, I feel an enormous weight on one side, I'm gasping for air and my breath is sour. I have woken in the middle of a nightmare. Someone, in my apartment in the city, was going through my papers, trying on my clothes, signing my name, using my pen, addressing obscene remarks to Chonita's photo and smashing the frame containing my school leaver's certificate. I woke up feeling ice cold and crying out because I saw that he was about to turn over the mattress on my bed, because then . . . My God, what have I done. Three months have gone by now, and I haven't given that man a single thought. Whether I killed him. Or didn't kill him. I'm on the verge of tears trying to work out whether I did this thing that so shames and horrifies me, or if, on the contrary, it was a dream, an hallucination that comes and goes, a painful, crazed toing and froing, piercing my temples and my throat. I should leave, I will. I look at the clock: it's stopped. I peer out of the window: I cannot tell the time by the stars, which I can barely identify, and, besides, sleep overwhelms me. I go back to bed and . . . Yes, there's no doubt about it: I can almost hear his voice ('I haven't felt like eating all day'), his breathless gait ('do you think the suitcases . . .' 'do you think they'll give me back the necklace'?) I don't want to remember any more. He'll be there. Perhaps his body began to stink as it decomposed and someone has noticed it. The woman upstairs has a dog and they say that dogs can sense when someone has died. It's probably been scratching at the door, and . . . Another possibility is that my mother had someone go in and do the cleaning one day and they will have found him there and removed him. Or the police will have, because he was a foreigner, that is, he came into the country with a passport. He said twenty-two fifteen, rather than a quarter past ten and . . . Three months have gone by. I don't know if I killed him or not. But I know that I took him home intending to kill him.

During the journey, I tried several times to start up conversations about a corpse being found in . . . a foreigner who . . . Nothing. No one took any notice. Either no one knew anything about it, or else it was a frequent occurrence. When silence falls, I smother my disquiet by reciting verses to myself. 'With ten cannon on either side, with a following wind and sails unfurled . . .' or 'Remember the sleeping soul . . .'. I also count the beating of the wheels on the tracks, tata-tracata, tata-tracata, ten, eleven, twelve . . . eighty, eighty-one . . . or I watch the telegraph wires, in stiff parallel lines, rising and falling. I vomited out of the window just thinking of the smell in my room when I go in there.

I left the station hurriedly. I kept expecting someone to call out to me, the police most likely. I didn't dare glance over at the café. At the newspaper stand, the little hunchback was putting on an overall and opening up the kiosk.

No one saw me come in. The concierge's room was closed. I couldn't get the key in the lock because, in my haste, my pulse was racing, a terrifying, disorderly tumult in my wrists. I put all the lights on. Nothing has changed. No one has yet been into my room. The two mattresses, one on top of the other. I boldly removed the top one. And underneath, on the hard mattress, the one on my bed, could be seen the hollow left by a crudely human figure, blurred and imprecise around the torso and the legs, precisely delineated around the impression left by head and ears. Filling this hollow is a glittering, pearly dust. It looks like mica. A dazzling, exfoliated mica which, in the light, casts pink shadows. That was all that remained. I carefully gathered up this sediment in order to dispose of it. I brushed out the hollow left in the mattress. At least it didn't smell. When my family arrive on the next train, they won't notice a thing. Everything has gone better than I expected. I have four hours to check the house and do any tidying up that may be necessary.

I have decided not to bother with supper. I need to remove all traces from the house. I sat down to think what I should do with this packet of human dust. Throwing it into the rubbish could prove compromising. The rag and bone men poke around in the rubbish with a stick, with a wire, and God knows what else. They spend hours and hours in the warm sun in the outlying areas, near where the main roads leave the city, selecting and classifying the things they carry about on their carts from day to day, a heavy, malodorous, dusty sadness. I will not throw my package into the rubbish. I fear the erudition of rag and bone men. I will not burn it either. I don't even know if it would burn. It's likely that heat would get rid of it. But that would involve going down to the cellar, to the boilers, and finding some excuse with which to deceive the boilerman. It would be foolish to arouse suspicion unnecessarily. I could go out and, like someone aimlessly, distractedly wandering the streets, throw it over the fence surrounding a building site, to join stones, lost rubber balls, rusty tins, dented basins, and cartons, lots of cartons, perhaps even the odd dead animal. Or else scatter it in the area that's been cleared around the new mental hospital. But that would be risky. I don't know how *it* might evolve and probably . . . I could sit down now and study those fat tomes on Pathology, Economics, Biology, and find out what, over time, happens to human remains. But I don't much feel like it. I did leaf through one once, but I didn't understand a word: too many formulae. I haven't got time to mug up on it all now. And I have to finish this business by midnight. I have to sleep and rest, in order to be refreshed and cheerful in the morning, with all my muscles in their proper places, like new. As if nothing had happened and as if I hadn't gone to the station one Saturday as night was falling and invited a traveller to come to my house. I must be confident and calm about it: that's most important.

It would be best to go out to the New Bridge or to the Roman bridge if there are fewer people there, and throw the

351

package into the water. I can foresee many dangers, but for the moment it's all I can come up with. Now, sitting in the parlour, opposite a statue of Our Lady of Sorrows with real hair and genuine silver brooches, sitting underneath the enlargement of a photo of my sister Lolita's wedding, trying so hard to look genteel, the poor thing, leaning dreamily on her husband's shoulder. I can't come up with a better idea: so off to the river and be done with it. I looked at my father's graduation photograph, fifty-five lawyers from Madrid University, all with beards, and it seemed to me that all fifty-five of them were shouting to me, urging me on, almost proud of my resolution: to the river, to the river.

Of course there are many occasions when one does not feel comfortable at home. Today is one of them. I have secured my package, painstakingly tying it up. Then I wrapped it again in an old special edition of *La Voz de la Región*. It's a very neat package. On the top there's the Queen of England at the celebrations held when she crossed the equator and a spine-chilling report of a plane crash. On the bottom there's the society column. I remember now, as I pass the mezzanine and glance through the weddings, that I forgot to get a present . . . The package, the wretched package, weighs a ton . . .

In the street. There are still a lot of people about. That's because it's the start of the fine weather and everyone is out walking, trying to make the evening last as long as possible. Everything is alight, contented, a sudden, frank outpouring. I plunge down the pavements, gladly drinking in their healthy vitality, shopwindows full of light, my package weighing heavy in my arms, clothes shops, piles of socks, jackets, rain-coats, end of season sale, a large U Certificate on the hoarding outside the Odeon cinema, depicting an allegory of the Wild West, the sheriff's star dangling drunkenly from one corner, and Pedrell the florist's, a mean little place selling clay flower-pots from Catalonia and scrawny carnations kept deceitfully erect with wire. Soil and seeds for sale. The miracle of Casa Simón's radiant shopfront: bottles of liqueur, cognac, wine, bottles of every size and shape, and the photographs by Lumière; I always stop to look in the window and try to decide who's pretty and who's ugly in the photos, I've seen him somewhere or other, she's the woman I saw that day on the stairs, pulling up her stockings, and from this angle he looks just like . . . I hold the package more tightly under my arm. What did he look like? He could be any of them. The same surprised, shackled look, an identical degree of resignation. The jeweller's, a dazzling flight of lights, the shop selling leather and sports goods, skates, skis, rifles, nets, thermos flasks, sets of folding cutlery, plastic cups, picnic baskets, shoes for hiking and cycling, tennis balls: Sensible. Economical. Use a Remington electric shaver, suitable for all voltages. Shoeshops, pharmacies, hardware stores, the package still weighing heavy in my arms; another cakeshop, over the door, the name Suchard flashing on and off, a clock above it. A café full of young people, the windows open, cigarette smoke gusting forth, laughter and jokes from the table by the window, occupied by students and vulgar women plastered in makeup. I can't go in, even though someone calls to me, because of this package. The river is still a long way off and the package is very heavy and, from time to time, I have to stop. That man over there, I can see him raising his hand to his hat, I sense that he's going to ask me about my father, the usual tiresome vacuities: When did you get back? What a surprise! How did you enjoy the last three months? And I can't say that I've spent the last three months like this, shut up at home, remembering nothing. The bookshop. I linger for a moment at the window, novels by Pierre Loti, José María de Pereda, Padre Coloma, something by Shakespeare, the collection of Araluce Classics. The usual rubbish. The Winkler Encyclopaedia. All the Science and Art of the World for just a few reasonable instalments. Learn about electricity. Surgical pathology, First Year, by the professor who teaches the subject. My package. (Good evening, how are you, All the best, Nice to see you, Give my regards to your family.) There are too many people. A bar: someone emerges drunk, cursing, and starts throwing up just by the door. The policemen on duty continue walking along on the opposite pavement, completely unmoved, then surreptitiously duck down the next street. The silence of a steep street with no shops in it. The woman selling newspapers by the railings round the monument to Columbus: *La Noche*! All the football pool results! A convent bell; a pallid, distant grief drops asleep above the flowering acacia trees. Children playing in a circle. The bell. A strident, speeding car. Ring-a-ring o' roses. Another car. The bell. A pocket full of posies. The light on a balcony goes on in a dark façade and someone yells: Conchita! Paquito! Time for bed, you've been playing out there long enough. The damp neglect of the now black street that leads to the bridge. Tourist posters hiding in the darkness. Cold. My package, I'm going to throw the package in the water. At the last roundabout, by the entrance to Las Rondas, the arrows on the road mark vague distances heading off into the night. To the frontier, 6 kilometres. Cars: queue to the right.

I put the package down on the ground for a moment, to rest. By the light of a tram, it looked enormous, pulsating. I tried to hum a little tune, but I couldn't. The river is close now. Onward.

I've walked along this avenue leading to the New Bridge so often. Whenever I have, the palms of my hands always tingle with a secret happiness. The rows of trees, the lights of the petrol station, the white arrows on the asphalt indicating the directions, the notices stating how much weight the bridge can take . . . All so familiar, so mine. And now I read everything, lingering over every letter; I look at it all as if bidding it a final, abandoned farewell, my teeth wet with sad saliva. My package. It's so heavy. I'm going to throw a . . . I should say 'man' into the river. And nothing changes. The clumps of rhododendrons are the same as last year and the lights on the jetty blink amongst the blaring music from the gramophone. All the same. Only I am more . . . I don't know what. I've killed a man. Now I am sure that I killed him. The trees tell me so with a bow that only I understand; I know it from the way the lovers fall suddenly silent as they huddle together on the benches as I pass.

354

Surrounded by silence, for the first time since I set foot in the street, when I left the house with . . . And now I realise that perhaps I have been too hasty. I should have found out more about the dust I swept up from the mattress . . . Even by just looking in the encyclopaedia, under Decomposition. There was bound to be something about it there. I should have read the article on the Soul too, just in case. It was thoughtless of me, but what's done is done. I can feel the cool air from the river. My skin prickles and I stop on the edge of the pavement: I didn't check all the rooms in the house. And what if . . .? Oh, honestly, a dead body can't move, and, besides, it was still on my bed. Where I found it. No, no, I mustn't go back now. The river is so close And in a few moments . . .

In a few moments. And that's the worst thing about this ridiculous stubbornness of mine. In a few moments it will be worse than now. Much worse. I am going to throw a man, or what remains of him, into the river. A man, with his hands, his sorrows, his problems, his prejudices. I don't know how to swim, my friends look at me contemptuously when they find out, and I'm going to throw a man into the water. Perhaps he doesn't know how to swim either. I'm going to plunge him in, wrapped in newspaper, with all the news of the day, political parties, crimes, United Nations fiascos, sixteen dead on the Israeli frontier, the meat prices for the whole week and Gina Lollobrigida's latest film. Into the water. He'll soon rot. I don't know, I haven't been able to ask anyone, if that dust resembling mica will float, dissolve, precipitate, submerge, form compounds, encourage algae, or . . . Who knows. The only certainty is that I don't know how to swim, maybe he didn't either. But his hands would have been accustomed to waving hello or goodbye, to winding up children's clockwork toys, to peeling mandarins. The fish will eat those hands. The light is on in the customs shed. The customs men are playing cards on a rickety table, and a few glasses of wine leave large rings on the surface. One of the men calls trumps and the other, pushing back his cap, unleashes a curse. A few runny-nosed gypsy children are watching, enthralled, as the cards are placed on the table, jacks, threes, aces, the occasional queen, the four kings with their crowns firmly on their heads. A car races by, overtaking me. A brief, neutral good evening directed at me; they go on playing. He too would have said Good evening and he would have doubtless enjoyed counting the circles left by the strong wine on the table and comparing them and, evoking some outdoor bar, when he was a student, when he saw similar circles one evening, now yellow with memories, perhaps with a pretty, willing young girl. I'm drowning. Now I can clearly hear the hum of the sluices and the obstinate knocking of the water against the sides of the Sunday boats. On some afternoon, somewhere, he would have gone down to a river and heard that persistent gurgle, violins, damp, a few towers looming on the shore, lights on the bridge, a woman gesturing obscenely to him from the balustrade. He probably wouldn't have gone with her, he seemed such a pathetic chap. He had pale eyes. I don't know how to swim, yet I'm going to throw him into the water. That man, as innocent as me; that man, who, doubtless, one dull Sunday, after dozing for a while in an armchair, drank a glass of cognac to set himself up, to keep him going, on to the next thing and let's see what happens, and he would have gone slowly out into the streets to see faces and shopwindows, and towers and advertisements, and the promising farther ends of the long streets, when the chill five o'clock air bursts upon the paving stones and doorways, and hearing the song of a young single woman behind a window or in a courtyard, and watching the little boys leaving the children's session at the cinema and peeing by the side of the road, seeing who can pee furthest, to the horror of the little girls, and then he would have knocked at a door, I can almost see it now, it could be my front door, but I can't see who opens it . . . No, I can't possibly have killed a man like that, who used to say Good evening, and Always and Never and Later, or simply Oh well!, perhaps he was a fan of costume dramas, he probably smoked black tobacco and drank rum, or was interested in the history of Latin America. Because I killed him, I did: he died of my wanting so much to kill him . . . But the package drops into the water, it fell quickly, confirming the second law of motion governing acceleration and the principle of When an object is totally or partially immersed in a fluid, it experiences an upthrust equal to . . . circular waves, getting gradually lighter, dragged along by the current, and a fleeting struggle to relive innumerable remembered returns, the night at the station, the five clocks on the way home, the journey, many other journeys, the sleepy clarity experienced that time with my first girlfriend, endless exams, the broken nose I got when I fought Pedro Juárez for the photograph of Jeannette Macdonald, and the foolish, white joy of my first communion, and more things and people that he had never recalled, now present, pointlessly and randomly restored to him, the waves on the river superimposed on those of a far distant beach, all blue, the little bucket leaving the sand in ordered geometric patterns, the water that goes and never comes back, cold, damp, everything black now, becoming lost in the depths of the river, a deep sigh, a star smooth again on the calm surface, a compact, gradually hardening solitude closing in above the hum of the sluices.

I hurried back home. It must be ages since I left. I don't know where the time has gone. I have a vague feeling that there is some difficult matter I must resolve, that there is something I have forgotten. Perhaps I should set off early tomorrow on a journey. The men in the booth were still playing and I thought I saw a couple of women with them. They'll make the most of their night there alone. No one greets me. The few people I meet pretend not to know me. Just as well, that makes everything easier. It's awful walking through a city where everyone knows everyone else, or thinks they do. I'm fed up with all the Good luck, See you later, All the best, I'll bring it round later. Bah! The street door was open. The concierge was standing outside on the pavement talking to a group of women. She just looked at me and said nothing. Poor woman. I raced upstairs and, unthinkingly, rang the bell. Out of habit, I leaned over the stairwell and saw the concierge looking fearfully up at me. A question was forming inside me, did she not recognise me. As soon as the maid opened the

357

door, they're obviously back, I pushed straight past her. The maid, who's easily frightened, gave a cry. I go straight to my bedroom, I'm tired and want to lie down. I lie down on the still unmade bed without bothering to take off my clothes. I hear noises in the corridor, alarmed voices. It's not possible, You don't know what you're saying. I almost recognise the inflections of those voices, although every time I hear Who is he, they sound farther off, stranger and more desperate. Someone knocks at the door. I don't want to be bothered. When I don't answer, the door opens cautiously and through the narrow crack I see my mother, my sister, the two maids, my little cousin Chucho who they must have brought back with them from the country and who is a terrible little whinger, I see how frightened they all are, they're trembling. I start to feel uncomfortable. I get up to tell them to let me sleep, that I've already had supper and that I won't be going to university tomorrow, and I find my father, visibly shaken, doing his best to speak calmly. I don't really understand what's wrong with him. He began by saying, and I can't reproduce his cold tones, that I must have got the wrong apartment. That room belonged to his son (yes, I know, but, in that case, why mention it!) and that there had obviously been some mistake (how could I mistake the room and the hollow in the mattress?) and Be so good as to leave, sir, otherwise I shall be obliged to . . . I suddenly saw their serious, hostile faces. They didn't love me any more. I wondered darkly if they had discovered something. But it's odd, this unanimously scornful look of suppressed fury. 'This is my son's room, You must have made a mistake,' my father was saying again, calmer now. I didn't say anything. I realised that when they rapped at the door it was not in order to offer me some supper or to ask Where have you been? How was the journey? nor to let me know they were back. It was in order to throw me out, to inform me that the room was no longer mine. I sensed that it would be useless telling them that I had slept for some months on that mattress and that it was almost mine, that . . . There was no point. Who was I. Where can I go now, where can I stretch out my weary bones tonight. I put on my overcoat, which was draped over

358

the back of a chair, and I left. My father no longer looked like my father when I said Goodnight, the expression on his face had grown so hard. As for the others . . . They, who are usually so easily reduced to tears, didn't shed a single one. Six heads, far up on the first landing.

I buttoned up my trousers as I was going slowly down the stairs. It had grown cooler outside in the street. I turned up my coat collar and set off in no particular direction, feeling faintly desolate. I would like to say something out loud, but I'm afraid I might not recognise my voice. I say nothing. At least tomorrow I can collect my German marks from the Customs and leave, and perhaps begin to live. It's twenty-three twenty and I'm hungry. I haven't eaten anything all day and now . . . But where am I going to sleep. Who can I explain my sadness to. I'll take good care of the tickets from Customs and Left Luggage and tomorrow I'll decide what to do. Now I'm going to go for a stroll about the city, although with my unshaven face . . . I do wish people wouldn't keep staring at my overcoat . . .

Translated by Margaret Jull Costa

Alonso Zamora Vicente (Madrid, 1916) is a renowned literary critic and linguist, author of the standard work on Spanish dialectology. He was a professor at Madrid University and at the Instituto de Filología in Buenos Aires. Throughout his life, he has also been, in his own words, a Sunday writer of short stories. His books include: *La voz de la tierra* (1958), *Primeras hojas* (1959) and *Vegas bajas* (1987). He won the 1980 Spanish National Prize for Literature for *Mesa, sobremesa*. 'A Poor Man' is taken from *Smith y Ramírez* (1957) a collection of seven stories about the anxieties of life in the city.